SEAN RUSSELL

THE INITIATE BROTHER
GATHERER OF CLOUDS

Moontide and Magic Rise:
WORLD WITHOUT END
SEA WITHOUT A SHORE

The River into Darkness:
BENEATH THE VAULTED HILLS
THE COMPASS OF THE SOUL

THE
COMPASS
OF THE
SOUL

BOOK TWO OF
The River into Darkness

SEAN RUSSELL

DAW BOOKS, INC.
DONALD A. WOLLHEIM, FOUNDER
375 Hudson Street, New York, NY 10014

ELIZABETH R. WOLLHEIM
SHEILA E. GILBERT
PUBLISHERS

First Printing, August 1998
1 2 3 4 5 6 7 8 9

DAW TRADEMARK REGISTERED
U.S. PAT. OFF. AND FOREIGN COUNTRIES
—MARCA REGISTRADA
HECHO EN U.S.A.

PRINTED IN THE U.S.A.

For Peter Stampfel for rescuing my first book from the slush pile, and Besty Wollheim for patience and insight.

A man may move either westward through life, following the light, or eastward toward the gathering darkness. It is a kind of orientation of temperament that is set in our earliest years; an emotional compass. One either pursues one's dreams or one's memories, and it is an exceptional man who, once his compass has been set, can alter it even a point or two.

HALDEN: ESSAYS

Chapter One

S HE was reborn from the earth, emerging from a dark womb of stone into the ancient light of a new morning. A shaft of diffuse light lanced through the trees to caress her skin. Warmth . . .

Let it sink into my very bones, Anna thought, almost certain she would be cold to her center for the rest of her days.

A bird lighted on a branch not a yard away, regarding her with a darkly glittering eye. *"Chuff,"* it said, the single syllable floating up like a bubble of sound.

"Shoo," she responded. There was something about its bill— blood-red and decurving, like a scimitar.

"Chuff," it said again, though less surely this time, and took two steps closer, shuffling its red legs along the branch.

"I am not food for you yet," she whispered, and managed to wave a hand, driving the bird from its perch. It settled a few yards away, staring back at her with its head cocked, an eerily intelligent look in its glittering eye. And then it fell to flight and sped off into the heart of the forest.

Anna closed her eyes. Sleep. She must sleep. Sleep for years, she was sure. And thinking that she drifted into a nightmare: swept

helplessly along the course of an underground river, fighting for air
. . . struggling to live.

Something bounced off her temple, and Anna opened her eyes
to find the sun higher, providing a coverlet of delicious warmth. She
had stopped shivering.

"*Chuff. . . .*"

The bird perched above her. "Whose pet are you?" she asked,
then realized an acorn lay but an inch away. Had it dropped that
for her?

She turned her gaze back to the bird, and then sat up, suddenly
filled with wonder. "But you are no one's pet, are you?" she whispered. "*Flames!*" She patted a pocket in her waistcoat and removed
a square of wet linen, then glanced back at the bird.

"Farrelle's ghost, but it must have begun already." Tentatively
she reached out a hand to the dark-feathered bird—crowlike with a
red bill and legs of the same hue. But the bird hopped away, only a
foot; and there it stayed.

"*Chuff,*" it said again.

Anna laughed. " 'Chuff' yourself." Gingerly, she unfolded the
linen and spread it out on the ground in the sun. She separated
each precious seed, blowing on them gently. The seed had been her
salvation; without it she would never have found the resources to
survive the trip out of the cavern, even though eating it raw produced only a fraction of its power.

The bird began to hop about excitedly, and she turned a warning
gaze upon it. "This is not for you," she said.

Overwhelmed by sudden weariness, she leaned back against the
bole of a tree, but kept her eyes open, afraid the bird might make
free with her seed. Where were the others? Certainly they must be
some hours ahead. She had waited as long as she possibly could
before following them out.

Anna had arrived at the pool and collapsed, too exhausted to
start back up the tunnel in search of another passage. There her
candles had burned to darkness. Not knowing what to do when she
heard the others approaching, she had crawled into a crevice and
lay still, sure anyone could hear the pounding of her heart. By the
poor candle light, Erasmus and the others had not seen her nor had
they the energy or inclination to search. She had watched them go

into the watery passage. Heard them shouting back and forth between the chambers. And when she thought she could wait no longer and still have strength, she had followed.

The thought of that water-filled passage caused her to pull her limbs close. She trembled.

"Do not think of it," she warned. "Do not."

She had survived! And here she was . . . on the surface of the world once more. Reborn to the light. Reborn—for certainly she had been in the netherworld these last days. Days! Could it have been only days?

"But what to do?" she whispered. Deacon Rose had been with the others, and she knew that he would soon be hunting her. Hunting her even now, perhaps. Did he think she had escaped ahead of them?

"What to do?" she whispered again, feeling her eyes ease closed. She forced them open. Up. She must press on. As soon as the seeds were dry, for she could not let mold touch them. They were more precious than diamonds. Almost more precious than life.

Had Halsey escaped, she wondered? Did Eldrich think they had all died in the cavern? Difficult to answer. She no longer presumed to have even the slightest knowledge of the mage's mind. He had deceived them—trapped them with disturbing ease—and only she had escaped, and that only by a near-miracle.

The Entonne border was nearby, and Anna could almost feel it offering haven. If only her resources were not so depleted! Food and rest were utterly imperative, for she had endured beyond her limits. Food and rest and clothing. And money. Anna had not a coin in her possession. But where? Where could she go that Eldrich would not suspect?

Perhaps Halsey had escaped unnoticed. He was wary and meticulous in his precautions. Eldrich might well have missed him. Flames, if she had only paid heed!

No use flogging herself with this. Survive. That was her task now. Her obligation.

Carefully she rolled the seed around on the linen, which lured the bird nearer, extending its neck to watch.

"What bird are you?" she asked. "Not a rook, I think, but some distant cousin. Cousin to the carrion crow. Dark-eyed and cunning.

Cold-hearted, too, I'll wager. Perhaps you are the perfect familiar for me, then. For all those who were close to my heart are gone, and they will never be replaced. Not if I am to succeed in what I must do." Saying this she wrapped the seed up again and buttoned it carefully into her pocket before rising stiffly.

Her mind was made up. It might be dangerous, but she could not proceed without knowing what had befallen Halsey. If he had fled, he would leave signs. Things so subtle that even a mage might miss them. And if he had been discovered . . . Well, if he'd been able, he would have left signs of that, too.

A waning moon sailed west until cast up on a shoal of cloud: stuck fast in the heavens.

Anna crouched in the midst of a stand of shrubs, watching. The house that Halsey had leased was just visible through the branches. At intervals she could see the old man pass before the window, pacing, his stooped carriage unmistakable. It was his habit to pace when problems beset him. Perhaps the pain clarified his mind somehow, or maybe it was penance.

But still she watched, and had been doing so for several hours. He was alone, she was sure of that. Some time earlier, a local woman had arrived with his dinner, stayed to clean the rooms a little, and then departed, carrying away the tray of dishes she'd brought. No others had come or gone, or even strayed nearby. Still she waited. Impatience had been her undoing once. Their undoing.

When Halsey began to blow out the lamps, she moved from her place, still stiff and weakened by her ordeal. A woodsman had fed her the previous night; fed her and set her on the path to Castlebough. She had made a slow journey through the woods, accompanied by her chough, for that is what the woodsman called the bird—the obvious appellation.

She had hidden herself here earlier in the day, and had she the resources, would have watched another day yet, but her exhaustion was too complete. Knowing that warmth, food, and company in her sorrow lay so near weakened her resolve.

Before the last lamp was doused she tapped on the window. Silence from within. She tapped again.

"*Chuff,*" said her familiar, somewhere in the darkness.

Halsey appeared, standing well back from the glass, looking very unsure.

"Halsey . . . 'Tis I. Anna. Can you not let me in?"

She saw him reach out to support himself, and then he hurried toward the door. A moment later she was inside where the old man took both her hands in his own and kissed them, as though she were a daughter returned from the dead.

"My dear girl. My dear Anna . . ." He looked at her, words clearly failing him. "What of the others?" he said, his voice almost disappearing.

She began to speak, but her own voice failed, and she merely shook her head and looked down, expecting tears to come—but they didn't. She was too exhausted to mourn. Farrelle's oath, but she felt empty.

He kissed her hands again. "Come inside, child. You look like you have survived the ordeal of Helspereth. Come in and I will bank the fire."

She left Halsey bending awkwardly before the hearth while she found clean clothing. Returning a few moments later, she wrapped herself in a thick blanket and curled into a chair before the flames.

"I am warming some soup," he said solicitously, "and there is bread and cheese. Not much, I'm afraid."

"Anything will be welcome. Only two days past I thought I should starve to death. . . . A crust would have seemed a cake then."

A blackened pot was suspended over the flames, and a board of cheese and bread produced. Again, Anna was surprised at how quickly her appetite was slaked. For a few moments they sat, saying nothing. Each time she looked up, Halsey was staring at her, the unspoken questions held in check only by compassion and concern for her.

She took a long draught of wine, and then resettled herself in the chair. "It was a long journey . . ." she swallowed the last word, and continued in a near-whisper, "down into the cavern." For a moment she closed her eyes, thinking of Banks drowned and the others buried alive. But she forced herself to go on. Forced some substance into her voice. "Long, arduous, and filled with wonders, though we had little time to stop and marvel. As we traveled, I sensed a vision, and despite our haste, we stopped so that I might search for it. None of us believed what I saw. Not even me. . . ."

The story took some long time to tell, and Halsey nodded in wonder again and again. When she spoke of the collapse of the cave and the murder of their companions, he rose from his chair and paced off across the room, shaking his head and raising his hand to stop her when she started to admit that he had been right. And then he came and settled painfully back into his chair and motioned for her to continue.

When the tale was finally told, they sat watching the flames inexorably consume the logs, turning them first to glowing coals and then to ash.

"He is a monster," Halsey said at last. "He . . ." but the old man did not finish.

"So he is," Anna whispered.

"Have you the seed still? Did you preserve it?"

She produced the small bundle, unwrapping it with extreme care, and held it out to him. In all the years that she had known Halsey, Anna had never seen him react so. His always stiff, unreadable countenance seemed to dissolve, and his eyes glistened suddenly. For a moment he sat unmoving, not even breathing, she thought, and then he reached out slowly. But just as his hand was about to close over the seed, he drew it back, and placed it tight to his heart.

"No. You keep it," he said. "You risked everything to possess it. And the others . . . they made the sacrifice so that you might have it. No, it is meant to be yours."

"But you have talent, as well. Talent and far more knowledge. Certainly we should cultivate it and both attempt the transformation."

He shook his head. "No. I am too old. Too old and no longer strong. It falls to you, Anna. That is clear to me now."

She sat quietly, trying to absorb what he was saying. Certainly this is why she had taken the risk of coming here. To find an ally, and to have his council.

"There is something more," she said. She went to the window and threw it open. Making the noise one might make to attract a pet, she leaned out, searching the shadows. "There! Do you see?"

Halsey came and stood beside her. "I can't make it out. What is it?"

"A chough, I was told. Much like a rook or a crow. It greeted me as I left the cave and has accompanied me ever since."

Halsey stared out into the darkness. *"A familiar,"* he said. "Teller be praised. Such a thing has not happened since the days of Alan Dubry." He looked at her, his eyes shining. "Perhaps your vision was not wrong. Skye opened a door, and see what we have found?" He shook his head. "Who among us would not accept the greatest sacrifice to make a mage? A mage at this point in history."

She turned away from the window. "Don't say such a thing. Everyone, even Banks . . . No, I could not live with such a thought. That I had sacrificed them all to my vision. . . ."

He put a hand on her shoulder. "But you did no such thing, Anna. You could not have known. But even so, no one would have hesitated. A *mage*. A mage who will live beyond Eldrich. It is the dream we hardly dared to dream. You, Anna, will preserve the arts. You will rediscover what has been lost."

She moved away, perhaps unable to accept the responsibility.

"The cost was too great," she whispered.

"It was great, yes, but all the more reason to seize this opportunity. Let no one's sacrifice be in vain."

She nodded. There was wisdom in this, she was sure. Such a cost. Something must come of it. "Then what are we to do?" she said softly. "How must we proceed?"

He turned back to the fire, but his eye lit upon the seed and lingered. "We must vanish again. Perform the rites that will hide our escape from anyone using the arts to seek us. We must begin tonight."

"But I am so tired—" Anna began to protest, and Halsey turned on her.

"Tonight!" he said firmly. "Eldrich is near. Already he has almost destroyed us. I fear that it is this seed he seeks. Perhaps it has been this seed all along, for let me tell you something, Anna; this seed must be Landor's own. Do you understand? Not seed that was cultivated in this world, but came from beyond. We have long known that the seed lost its power from one planting to the next—

but this . . ." He gestured to the precious bundle. "Use it sparingly. And it must be cultivated—as soon as you can manage."

Saying nothing, Halsey disappeared, returning a moment later with a book. This he passed to her. "Here are some few things I've set down these past years. Knowledge that you do not have. It is in Darian, so there was little chance that it would have been understood if it had fallen into the hands of another."

"But why give me this now?"

"We cannot know what might happen. Now come quickly. We will perform the ritual and leave no trace of our flight for the mage or his servants. No one will be aware of us again until it is too late."

Quickly, they prepared the few things they would need to travel at speed. Horses were saddled, burdened with baggage, and led away from the house lest they sense the arts and bolt.

Halsey began to light candles. Seven tapers were arranged in a pattern on the floor, and then he took a scented oil and marked the walls with Darian characters. Using the same oil he began a pattern on the floor, chanting as he did so.

"You will perform the enchantment," he said as he completed the pattern.

"But . . ." she began to protest, and then realized that he was right. She was the mage emerging: the spell would facilitate the process, and certainly now her powers outstripped Halsey's own.

She took up ashes from the fire and sprinkled the still warm powder evenly over the pattern. When she was finished, she made seven marks upon her face with the ash and then moved to the pattern's center.

"*Curre d' Efeu,*" she began. "Heart of flame. . . ." The enchantment was not long but it was rather intricate and required precise motion and control. Once Halsey prompted her, for her mind still suffered from fatigue, but she carried on, knowing the importance of what she did.

Fire erupted in the hearth again, and when she placed a hand near the floor and spoke, she drew a line of flame out from the logs. It spread around the pattern.

She was into the spell, to the point where it would be dangerous to stop, when a fierce tapping drew her attention. The chough was at the window, frantically beating its wings and beak against the glass.

Anna blocked out the sounds, the questions.

Halsey spoke unexpectedly, his deep, gravelly tones forming Darian with an authority that none of the others had ever mastered. But what was he doing?

The room seemed so far away, the world so remote, so dream-like. Halsey sprinkled something over the pattern, holding an object in his hand—an object of dread.

And then the realization gripped her, dragging her back to the world, to the present.

"Halsey!" she called out, but he raised the hand that held the dagger and continued in his efforts—sprinkling blood from the wound at his wrist along the pattern.

"What are you doing?"

"Do not stop," he said, not looking up from his task. "Go on, child. You will ruin us both."

And so she continued, chanting a long string of words, drawing up the candle flames.

Halsey stopped, suddenly, just as she reached the spell's end. "Eldrich found me," he said, his face contorting in pain and guilt, "I was to wait here to be sure that none of our people emerged from the cave—a simple task, for Eldrich was all but sure no one had survived. For this small service I would be rewarded—something greater than I would have expected." He shook his head, a tear streaking his cheek. "But when I saw you . . . alive." He met her eye for a second, begging something. "Eldrich has put his mark upon me, Anna. I can never escape him." He began to speak Darian, a spell she did not know. The fire in the pattern rose up suddenly, and the characters on the walls burst into flame. He called out, and before Anna realized what he would do, the old man plunged the knife into his own breast.

He turned toward her as his knees buckled. *"You are free,"* he whispered, and toppled into the rising flames.

For a moment Anna stood transfixed. Unable to believe what she saw. Unwilling to believe the horror of it. All of them gone. Every one.

Alone. She was utterly alone.

And then a crashing against the window drew her, and she saw a tiny dark eye beyond the glass, and realized that the spell no longer offered protection. With one final look back at Halsey, enveloped in flame, she swept up her skirts and fled.

Chapter Two

WITHOUT a sign from anyone, the mage's procession of two carriages had rolled to a sudden stop, leaving the countess wondering what apparition they had encountered now.

Eldrich stepped down to the gravel and disappeared soundlessly into the wood.

The countess watched him go. *As silent as a shadow*, she thought, and shivered.

For the first time she saw all of her traveling companions: Walky, of course; a darkly handsome man of perhaps thirty; the drivers; and four other servants. The mage's entire entourage.

The drivers saw to their teams, and the others stood about in isolated silence, as though casual speech were forbidden to the followers of a mage.

Silence, the countess thought. *He lives in the silences.*

Under the pretense of finding the least obstructed view of the stars, she edged closer to Walky, finally catching his eye.

"What goes on, Mr. Walky?" she whispered.

The little man shrugged, put a finger to his lips, and slipped away before she might speak again. Thus chastened, she found an outcropping of stone at the roadside and made it her seat, vowing that she would never become as servile as these others.

Why have I agreed to this? she wondered again, though not yet sure what she had involved herself in. The ancient woman at the roadside—herself: the Countess of Chilton—the mere thought of this apparition quelled all of her doubts for a moment. She closed her eyes, trying to drive out the image—a woman pathetic in age and loss of mental faculties.

Better any fate than that, a voice inside her warned.

But there was more. A certain feeling of inevitability, a crumbling of resistance—the feeling of giving one's self up to a seduction, to another. And to desire.

Desire.

But was it real, or was she merely under some form of enchantment?

A shadow flowed out of the wood and onto the road: Eldrich's wolf.

She heard her breath catch and she froze in place, as though it were a wild beast and she its prey. For a moment it paused in the starlight, slowly turning its head as though searching, and then it darted into the wood again.

The countess let out a long breath. What did he want of her?

The moon sailed among the stars, illuminating the solitary clouds that passed before it. From deep within the wood a nightingale burbled its liquid song. The countess tried to silence her inner voice. To be aware of the night. Traveling with a mage would require that she learn patience and attentiveness. And silence.

She did not know how long she listened to the winds' whispered conversation, observed the heavens, before Eldrich reappeared—two hours, perhaps three.

The stooped silhouette crossed to Walky and the handsome man. She could hear them speaking; words like stones dropped into a brook and just as comprehensible. The three conferred briefly, and then Eldrich went directly into his coach.

Walky came to her.

"What is it?" she asked. "What has happened?"

"The unforeseen," Walky said hoarsely. "Come. I will ride with Lord Eldrich and the countess, if you will allow it."

She nodded, smiling at this odd gesture of consideration. As he took her arm and led her toward the carriage, the countess could see the others releasing the team from the second coach, which they began to turn around in the narrow road.

They are going back, she realized, as she stepped up into Eldrich's carriage.

They moved off as she settled herself.

At last, she could bear this dismissive silence no longer. Her anger boiled up, and she drew a long breath. "What has happened?" she asked, feeling her heart beating—like a child asking forbidden questions.

Dark silence was her answer, and she felt her anger boil over. Did he treat everyone with such disregard?

"There is a hunting lodge," the mage announced, his musical voice betraying no trace of emotion. "Not distant. We will stop there."

It was a concession, she knew, though hardly informative. Only where and what, not why.

The countess should not have been surprised to find that mages cared little for the niceties of property rights. Walky and the servants quickly had the building open and began setting it to rights, as though it were their own. Lamps were lit, fires built in the hearths, sleeping chambers aired and beds prepared.

And where am I expected to sleep? the countess wondered. She stood before one of the hearths, warming her back, her arms crossed stiffly before her. *I feel as uncertain as a young girl*, she thought. *But there is not a petal of romance in the air.*

Will he want me? That was the question. The desire was there; palpably so, but would Eldrich give in to it?

With other men she would know. Their intentions were easily divined, but the mage was not like other men.

Walky appeared from a dark hall. It seemed that Eldrich and his servants had no need of light—a strange thought. No need of light.

"A chamber has been readied for you, Lady Chilton," he said, taking up a candle.

She remained by the fire a moment more, suddenly reluctant to leave its warmth.

"Where is Lord Eldrich?" she asked, her voice oddly hollow in the massive room.

"Engaged," Walky replied.

Still the countess did not move.

"The mage is involved in matters of great import, m'lady," he said. "Matters that are little understood by others."

"So you do not know what goes on?" the countess asked.

Walky nodded. "I know very little, I'm afraid. Best Lord Eldrich answer your questions."

"He does not seem much inclined to answering questions."

"All in good time, m'lady," he said. "All in good time. One cannot rush a river, but wait and the stream will carry you where you wish."

"Rivers flow in only one direction, Mr. Walky," she said, not heartened by his choice of metaphor. "And I fear I have the patience of a mortal: I like my answers immediately."

"It is something you will adjust to, m'lady," he said softly and gestured for her to follow.

"Perhaps," she whispered to herself. Eldrich's words came back to her. *I am one hundred and thirty-three; all other estimates you have heard are wrong.*

The countess was but five and twenty.

She sat in a window seat before the open casement, her knees drawn up and clasped by woven fingers. A nightingale trilled its melodious song, and unknown insects added strange counterpoint.

The hour was unknown to her. Late, no doubt, but still she did not proceed to bed. She perched in the window listening to a nightingale offer enticements to a mate.

At least he sings, she thought. *A shred of gallantry.*

The bed, with its curtains and coverlets folded back, took up a much greater place in her consciousness than in the room itself. And it offended her somehow, like a statement of presumption.

"What does he want of me?" she asked the night, and leaned her head back against the cool wood. She closed her eyes and felt such sweet relief. The air seemed seasoned with such a complex fragrance. She drank it in deeply, as though hungry for it. Late. So late. And she was but five and twenty.

She awoke to a touch on her cheek. A kiss? Opening her eyes, she found Eldrich standing between herself and the bed. Oddly, this did not startle her at all. Indeed, she did not feel quite herself—as though she floated in time, somehow.

"Do I dream?"

"There are those who claim that life is nothing else," he answered, the music of his voice touching her, stripping away the last cords of gravity binding her to the world.

"The nightingale . . . he has stopped."

"Yes." His eye did not waver, but remained fixed on her—not unkindly, but not kind either.

"What will you do with me?"

A smile, like the shadow of a winging bird. "What would you have me do?"

Yes, what? "I cannot bear to be left wondering. I cannot. . . ."

His gaze did not waver. "No," he said quietly, a voice like a soft wind, "it is a terrible thing."

Chapter Three

K ENT walked his lame gelding along the black river of road, and contemplated his own recklessness. One did not canter by night along a road known for its potholes and washouts. Not with the moon hidden by overcast, stars visible only through tears in the cloud.

He patted his mount's nose, trying to calculate the distance to the next travelers' inn. Not far in miles, though several hours at this pace. Some knight off to save the fair lady he had turned out to be.

Kent crept along the road in the faint starlight, aware of the precipice to one side. The sound of flowing water floated up to him and increased the illusion that he walked along the dark surface of a river.

He stepped, mid-calf, into water, and brought his lame mount up short. Cursing, he peered into darkness, trying to gauge the width of the washout. To his right, the river of road seemed to have overflowed its bank and the substance of night whirled there in a slow eddy.

It was a spring, he realized. In that backwater of darkness would lie a drinking trough and a fount where humans might slake their thirst and take their rest upon stone benches.

"I think this will be our inn this night," he explained to his gelding, as he led it into the liquid shadow of the trees. Here both horse and man drank.

Kent tethered his mount where it could reach the grasses growing at the margins of the wood, and sank down onto a stone bench, pulling up his collar against the small wind. Daylight was some hours off, but Kent could not sleep. Thoughts of the countess haunted him. An image of a large carriage charging through the hills, drawing farther and farther away from him.

It even occurred to him that his horse's lameness might not be entirely natural. He snorted. No. Certainly that had been the result of his own imprudence, not the arts of the mage.

He shifted, seeking greater comfort, but the stone refused to yield.

Is the countess Eldrich's lover? he wondered again. Willingly his lover? He did not think so. Certainly she had been horrified when told she had been in the company of a mage. That had not been an act.

He stared up at the stars, picking out the constellations and trying to see new shapes in them, then giving them appropriate names. The Dragon became a woman weaving: the Weaver. The Twins, with some stretch of the imagination, became a carriage. And the Hunter could be nothing but a Mage.

Does he know I pursue him? Kent wondered. *Is it possible?*

Just then, the gelding whickered. He could feel its excitement in the dark. His first thought was wolves, yet then he realized the gelding's reaction was not fear but anticipation.

Someone approached.

Kent went out onto the shadowy road, gazing into the darkness and listening. Was that the sound of a horse? He stood, staring down, concentrating his senses and finally was sure he heard the sounds of horses—several of them, to the east.

He stared off into the night, relief washing through him. If luck was with him, he would be in Castlebough this night, and on the road again before midday.

Around the shoulder of the hillside a dark shadow appeared against the low stars, the sound suddenly clear: a large carriage drawn by a team, Kent was almost certain. And how quickly they came.

Then he realized that he had seen no coach lamps. He froze in place, confused, and then he rushed back into the shadow. Tearing the horse's reins free, he began dragging his mount up into the trees. It stumbled and tried to pull away, but Kent resisted, coaxing it along, blind in the dark. Up they went, diagonally now, on some kind of foot track—likely a path to a lookout point. He could not see the track but felt it underfoot, and the horse came along more easily.

When his breath failed him, Kent stopped and bent double—not enough wind left to even curse. The sound of horses pounding along the road came up, slightly muffled, through the trees.

And then it died.

Kent did curse then, in a whisper.

Do they know I'm here, or do they stop only to water their team?

He stroked his mount, jiggling its bit as a distraction. *Make no sound,* he willed it. *Make no sound.*

And then the horses moved again, the sound of hooves, slow, like tumbling rock. Kent realized they had delayed only to negotiate the washout.

"Flames," he swore. It must be Eldrich. Who else could see such a thing in the dark? But why was the mage returning to Castlebough? Racing back to the city he'd just vacated? There was no explaining the doings of a mage.

Was the countess with him? That was Kent's only question. Certainly she must be. There might be a chance that he could rescue her yet.

"What is it?" came a half-familiar voice, muffled by its journey through the trees.

"The road is washed away," came another voice.

"Shall I climb down?" The first voice drifted up to him again, teasing him with tones he thought he should know.

It couldn't be Eldrich, could it? The ramifications of this stopped him cold.

"It might be best, if you don't mind, sir."

Kent heard the click of a carriage door, and then the complaining of springs as the horses edged forward. A pause, then a surge as the carriage rolled up out of the trench.

"That will do, Mr. Bryce."

Again the door sound, and then the carriage set off, far too quickly on this dark night.

Bryce? The man who had accompanied Sir John? He felt a wave of relief. The man was clearly an agent of the mage. But why was he returning to the town his master had so recently abandoned? Kent could not imagine, but clearly Eldrich and the countess still traveled on.

Kent edged back down the trail, hoping his mount did not stumble and crush him. At the spring he let the gelding drink once more, and then set out, lame mount and all, along the dark river that bore the countess away.

Chapter Four

THE ruin was still smoldering when Bryce arrived, the stone hot to the touch. Out of the coals, cranial walls rose up, window openings gaping, glass melted into frozen pools, dripping from the sills. Bryce could sense the death here—the death of the house. Perhaps more.

The roof had collapsed, leaving only a few beams, blackened and burned to half-thickness, which angled down from the stone walls like the tines of a rusted rake. He turned over a roof tile with his foot and a gasp of caustic smoke escaped, stinging his eyes.

In what he guessed to be the center of the room, he probed into the ashes with a stick, dredging up a heavy object blackened by the fire but unmistakable. A dagger.

"He will not be pleased," Bryce said to himself. "Not in the least pleased."

There was other evidence of the arts as well, not all of it perceptible by the usual means. But beyond the house there was nothing.

"Flames, it was a powerful drawing," he said. He turned over more tiles with his branch, and was rewarded with more smoke, which seared his nostrils and lungs.

Crouching at arm's length, he plumbed the ashes and turned

up something else. A charred object that stopped him. *"Blood and flames. . . ."* The bone slipped back into the ash, like a corpse into a pallid sea.

Bryce stood suddenly, looking around at the ruined house, horrified by what had been done. "The mage must know. Immediately he must know! He sacrificed himself—and there can be only one reason for that."

Chapter Five

THE five who escaped the cave had been transported to the sanitarium and put under the care of the physician and his staff. Not that they were badly injured—exhaustion and need of nourishment being the most dire of their physical hurts. Even Clarendon's damaged knee did not appear so serious in the light of day.

Erasmus stood before the mirror staring at the gaunt figure who looked back apparently distressed by what he saw. The figure in the glass had somewhat sunken eyes and a slight hollow to the cheeks that even the freshly trimmed beard did not hide. But what struck him most was the cast of his face—a man who had learned a terrible truth.

"There are truths men never recover from," Beaumont had once said.

A mage tried to murder me, Erasmus thought, and turned away, unable to bear the stranger's look.

Erasmus lay down on his bed, thinking that he might just let sleep take him once more—if only he could dream something sweet. Instead, each time he slept, he tumbled back into the nightmare of the cave: hopelessly lost; starving; cold to the soul; water rising relentlessly.

But the weariness was greater than his fear of nightmares, and his eyelids fluttered closed.

"Erasmus?"

Erasmus opened his eyes to the muted light of late evening. For a moment he wondered what chamber this was, and then realized he was not in the cave at all.

"Erasmus?"

A man sat on a chair in the center of the room.

Erasmus propped himself up on an elbow, squinting at this apparition in the shadows. "Who is that?"

His eyes adjusted to the light, revealing a precise, dark-eyed gentleman. A stranger, yet there was something vaguely familiar. . . .

"Do I know you, sir?" Erasmus asked, dropping his feet to the floor and perching on the bed's edge, his head swimming.

The man still said nothing, but stared at him for a moment.

"You don't remember?"

The voice: bitter . . . older. Erasmus found himself standing, as though drawn up by a will other than his own.

"Percy? Flames! Is it you? Percy . . . ?"

The man's gaze faltered, blinking.

"But I thought . . ." Erasmus stumbled to silence, his throat constricted. The room spun and he fell back to the bed.

"You thought I had burned?" the other said softly.

Erasmus could not bear the man's gaze, and looked down. "Yes," he whispered. "I thought you dead."

Erasmus stared at his unmoving shadow and heard every accusation contained in that silence.

He looked up suddenly. "All these years I thought you dead. I thought . . . I cannot tell you what joy it gives me to see you alive. Alive and whole."

Percy did not answer, but stared at Erasmus as though he had been paid the gravest insult.

Erasmus nodded. "Yes," he almost whispered. "I know what you must think. But I was only a child. How could I have known what would result?"

"So, unsure of the dangers, you pushed me forward to perform the ritual, not daring it yourself."

Erasmus looked back to his dark outline on the floor. "It was an act of cowardice. Yes. But the act of a child, all the same. I am sorry for your sufferings, Percy. No day goes by without my thinking of it—regretting it." He looked up. "But you are whole, thank all gods. Eldrich made you whole again."

Percy's face hardened, masklike, eyes narrowing. "Whole? No, I am not whole. And I am tied to the mage. Tied to him until the end, while you have walked free, inconvenienced only by your paltry guilt. But I am his servant, Erasmus. Healed, to all appearances, but his servant still. You cannot know what that means. You can't begin to know."

Erasmus stared at the man, and felt the rage and contempt hurled at him. All he could say in defense was that he had been a child, a mere boy—but that would not gain him pardon here. Not before the sufferings of this man, whose judgment had been passed long ago, and likely renewed every day for all these many years. No, Erasmus had been condemned in absentia, and there was nothing for it but to hear the sentence.

"It is long done, Percy, and my regrets cannot undo it. So what is it you will have of me now? My continued suffering, heightened by your lack of forgiveness? Or is there some act of contrition? Is that what you have come to ask?"

The man who had been his dearest friend and ally in childhood laughed bitterly. "Forgiveness? I have been tutored by a mage, Erasmus. It is a word without meaning to me, a human weakness which was burned away long ago. No, there is nothing you can do for me. The mage, however, is not done with you yet, Erasmus Flattery." For a second the mask became almost human as he said this, and the voice was tinged with a certain pleasure.

He lifted a foot and set the ankle on his knee. "Begin with the story of how you came to be here in Castlebough. Leave nothing out. You know how exacting the mage can be."

Erasmus shook his spinning head, hoping that he dreamed, but something told him he did not. This was Percy, returned after all these years. Returned with the accusations Erasmus had hurled at himself this same span of time. Justice; very rare in the world of the mage.

Realizing that there was nothing else to be done, Erasmus told his tale, beginning with meeting Hayes in the brothel, and the bizarre story he'd told of Skye, the Stranger, and a mage.

During the entire explanation Percy's countenance did not alter. Even the failing light could not soften the bitterness and disdain.

What has he suffered? Erasmus wondered. *Did not the mage heal him? Look! Is there the slightest scar or burn? No, he is a handsome man, of great bearing and presence. Yet he hates me still.*

The light in the room faded as the story was told—faded like hope—and when he came to the end, his inquisitor was nothing but an indistinguishable shadow in the room's center.

For a long moment Percy was quiet, and Erasmus could not see his face to judge the impact of his tale. "One would think, by your story, that you'd given up the ways of a coward," he said coldly. "What of this girl? You saw no sign of her after the drowned man?"

"None. But unless she could swim, it seems very likely she, too, was drowned and carried away by the stream."

Percy shook his head. "She did not drown. No, she is living yet. And Eldrich will not be pleased to hear of your part in this."

"Me? What have I to do with it?"

"Was it not you who managed the escape from the chamber? You were never meant to escape, Erasmus. You cannot begin to realize the harm you've done."

Erasmus could hardly credit what he'd heard. "Did Eldrich expect us to sit meekly in the cave and starve?" he said incredulously. "Even a mage must know more of human nature than that!"

Percy rose from his chair and went to the window where he looked out into the twilit valley. Erasmus could barely make him out—Percy's inhuman precision blurred to indistinct silhouette.

"What is it you want of me?" Erasmus asked again, guilt no longer bridling his impatience.

No answer. A silhouette as still as sculpture.

"Find this girl, and Eldrich will lift the sentence that has been passed against you."

"What? What sentence?"

"You trespassed in a sacred place, Erasmus. For that you were to have paid with your lives. And then you aided the girl's escape. All of you have earned Eldrich's displeasure."

Erasmus had turned on the bed so that he could watch his dark friend, and now he almost writhed where he sat. "What is it you're saying? Was I not to tempt the Tellerites out into the open? Was it not intended that I lead them down into the cave so that Eldrich could destroy them? Was this not my purpose all along? And yet, for doing Eldrich's unspoken bidding, my life is forfeit for violating the chamber? And then I am also charged with managing our escape?"

"When you stand before a mage, Erasmus, an appeal to logic is futile. They do not care much for the niceties of human regulation. You violated the chamber. There can be no 'mitigating circumstances.' You aided the escape of Eldrich's enemy. One should never interfere in the affairs of a mage, especially not one bent on revenge. If you and your companions can find the girl, you will escape Eldrich's judgment against you. Tell that to your friends."

"The priest as well?"

"The priest especially. The church . . . Eldrich will deal with the church." A protracted pause. "This girl took king's blood from the chamber. It must be surrendered to Lord Eldrich. Do not even touch it—especially you, Erasmus."

Percy turned toward Erasmus, but he was still only a dark mass before the window. "Find her," Percy said softly. He tossed a roll of paper on the bed. "And when you have her, this will allow you to alert the mage."

He swept out of the room, and Erasmus realized he no longer saw the erect, forceful man, but someone bent and broken. Someone scarred by fire and loathing.

For some time he sat, unmoving, then he went to the open window and looked out over the valley. The lake glittered in starlight.

So his nightmare had come true. Percy had returned from the grave to confront him, to accuse him. And what a terrible husk of a man he was. Burned hollow, no matter what Eldrich had done to heal him. Poor child. Erasmus could not help but remember the boy—innocent as rain, as trusting as a young bird.

What a monster Eldrich was. What a terrible monster. And all over this young woman—who, despite her duplicity, hardly seemed evil to Erasmus. No, she seemed far less malevolent than the mage. And now he must find her and offer her up to Lord Eldrich.

Remembering what Percy had said, Erasmus lit a lamp and unrolled the curling papers. Immediately he felt the room grow chill. The writing was Darian.

An enchantment.

He was halfway through before he realized it was familiar—*the spell innocent boys had used to summon fire.* The spell that had immolated Percy Bryce, burning away the germ of his humanity.

Chapter Six

THE bruised joy of survivors was all but absent among those who had escaped the cave. They still wore the haunted look of men just awakened from nightmare. Erasmus thought they had been through quite enough.

Unfortunately, he could see no way to spare them. Their deliverance had been illusory. Erasmus regarded each of the silent faces in turn, and almost to a man their gazes slipped away. Only Rose was bearing up.

"I had a visitor this evening," Erasmus began, his voice uncertain. "Not a welcome one." He could see them all stiffen, as though about to receive a blow. "A servant of Eldrich."

All eyes snapped up briefly, alert now, like the eyes of animals surprised by the hunter.

"I'd hoped we had escaped. That our ordeal was over, but instead Eldrich has found us." His mouth was suddenly sticky-dry, the flesh like a sponge.

Only Deacon Rose did not appear frightened. Indeed, his eyes shone with interest. "I don't know where to begin. Eldrich claims that we have committed a great offense against . . . his kind." He was almost whispering now. "That is the crux of it. But all is not

28

dark, for he has offered us clemency if we will but perform a single task for him."

"*Clemency!?*" Clarendon exclaimed, drawing himself up in resentment, one sign of life at least. "For what crime?"

"I'm afraid the Deacon was right, Randall. We trespassed in a place the mages hold . . . sacrosanct. For this alone our lives should be forfeit. We then added to this crime by aiding the escape of Eldrich's enemy, damning us doubly in his eyes."

Kehler began to protest, but Erasmus held up his hand.

"There is no court of appeals when dealing with a mage, Mr. Kehler. I know what you will say: 'Was it not Eldrich's design that we lead the Tellerites into the cave, to their ruin?' Yes, and yes again to any arguments of logic and justice, but the justice of men has no bearing in the affairs of the mages. Only their own mysterious code, and according to the strictures of that code our lives should be forfeit for what we have done. Unless we are able to accomplish this task."

The survivors looked at each other, all of them still, almost hunched, like the hunted. How battered they all looked, how haunted by their brush with death.

They were nearly buried alive, Erasmus thought.

Poor Kehler looked almost as aged as Clarendon, with his hair going gray too early, his posture stooped by fatigue. Even the bright curiosity of his eyes had disappeared.

Hayes looked only slightly better. His light hair and the blue of his eyes saved him from the dark look of his friend, but he no longer looked boyish, not even when he smiled.

Only Deacon Rose appeared unchanged by their ordeal. His vitality remained. Even his complexion still bore the mark of the sun, not the pale scar of their escape from the darkness. Deacon Rose retained his ability to appear at peace, his practiced charm. The eyes could still smile beneath the cap of gray hair.

Deacon Rose shifted in his chair. "We are to find the girl and her remaining colleagues," he said, not showing the least surprise.

Erasmus nodded. "Yes, but there are no others, only Anna."

"How do we know she is even alive?" Hayes asked.

"She is alive," Rose said, "or the mage would not seek her."

"But, Erasmus," Hayes protested, "certainly Eldrich can find her more easily than we. After all, we are not masters of the arts."

Rose interrupted, for he seemed suddenly rejuvenated. "But the Tellerites have ways of hiding themselves from practitioners of the arts. That is the reason for Eldrich's elaborate ruse to draw them out into the open—to force them to reveal themselves—and Anna will not make that mistake again. No, she must be hunted down by natural means, like any criminal."

Hayes sat up abruptly, his upper body swaying in a small circle as though he had been set off balance. "But what has Anna done to me? Nothing for which I would see her murdered, and that is certainly what Eldrich intends if she is found. Am I to participate in this crime to save my own precious skin?" He shook his head, pushing out his lower lip. "I will not be party to such a thing, no matter what the cost. It is not just Eldrich who has a code."

Both Kehler and Clarendon nodded, the little man muttering, "Hear, hear," under his breath. Then he looked up at Erasmus. "What of you, Erasmus? Will you carry out this errand of cruelty for Eldrich?"

Erasmus felt himself mired in some sort of mental ooze, as though still not quite awake—not quite back into this world from the murky world of cave and nightmare. Would he do this? What justification could there be other than self-preservation—and he knew what it was like to live with that.

He shook his head. "Let me tell you this, if any of us refuse Eldrich's mercy, it will not be a simple matter of paying with our lives. Mages are more vengeful than you know. Men have suffered a lifetime of unspeakable torture for angering a mage. You should think hard on that before you make any decisions."

Rose stood suddenly. "Listen to me. It is more than fear of torture that should be taken into account here. Eldrich has not set out to destroy the followers of Teller for petty vengeance—as notorious as his kind might be for such acts. I have read the confessions of the Tellerites, the heretics who hid within the church. The intentions of their conspiracy were not so innocent as one would expect from meeting young Anna and Banks."

Clarendon stood, red-faced, and Erasmus thought he would

storm from the room, but Hayes put a hand gently on his arm. "It will cost us nothing to hear him out, Randall."

Rose paused to look at the small man, and then continued. "There has been much speculation about the disappearance of the mages. We don't know why only Eldrich remains, but from the confessions of the heretics I learned this: Augury was at the heart of the mages' decision." He began to pace stiffly across the floor between Erasmus and the others, looking at no one, as though he rehearsed a speech. "What, precisely, the vision revealed I cannot tell you, but it was frightening and apocalyptic—frightening even to the mages. It would seem that they were divided in their interpretation of the vision. How consensus was reached is unknown, but somehow it was eventually accepted that the catastrophe would result from the arts or their practice. How else could they have arrived at the decision to erase the arts from this world? To hide their last vestiges for the good of the earth, perhaps for the good of mankind?"

The priest stopped his pacing and met the eyes of his audience, all attentive now, even Clarendon captive.

"The Tellerites will keep the arts alive at all costs, that is their avowed purpose. They either do not believe in the augury of the mages, or do not care, I don't know which, but they are willing to take all risks to see their purpose accomplished. Do you see? Anna and Banks might have seemed innocent—and perhaps in some ways they were, but even so they are willing to risk the apocalypse to possess the arts. An apocalypse even the mages feared."

Rose stood in the center of the floor, looking around at the others, his fists clenched tightly at his sides.

"What do you say to this, Mr. Flattery?" Clarendon asked softly, like a man too tired to argue. "Is there any truth in the priest's ravings or is this another in his long string of deceptions?"

Erasmus shook his head. "I don't know, Randall. I don't know. Eldrich did not confide in me, nor did I learn much of the mages' history—a secret they guard assiduously. I wish I could say more, but . . . It is certain that Eldrich is determined to see the end of the arts in his lifetime, there can be little doubt of that. Is Eldrich driven by revenge to destroy the Tellerites? I think it would be naive to deny the truth of that, but given the circumstances it seems to be more than just revenge. The Tellerites clearly want to keep the arts alive—Deacon Rose is right in this—and it would seem that Eldrich is equally determined that this will not come to be."

"But the priest has lied repeatedly," Clarendon began, but Kehler interrupted.

"Be at peace, Randall, there is some greater evidence that the Deacon tells the truth, this time. I saw references to the Tellerites— the men the church calls Teller's bastards—in my researches at Wooton. Whether their confessions were true, I cannot say, but they were not just a convenient invention of Deacon Rose. According to the Tellerites, the mages did have a catastrophic vision. Teller's bastards were aware of some part of it, perhaps from their own augury, but they believed it did not apply to them, but only to the mages. I did not connect it to this—the disappearance of the mages. Only now have I heard that suggested."

Kehler bounced to his feet, animated, unable to remain still. He stole the floor from Rose with his outrage and frustration. "But what are we to do? If we were to choose the path of honor, we would refuse to involve ourselves in this conflict of the mages, this struggle in which we cannot even begin to gauge right from wrong. Yet Erasmus has put such a fear into us—into me at least—that it would appear our only course of action is to obey Eldrich or self-murder to avoid a lifetime of unimaginable horror." He threw up his arms and then let them fall limply at his sides. Suddenly he was very still. "Or do we accept that Eldrich has some reason other than revenge for his pursuit of the Tellerites, as the Deacon suggests? That there is some justification for what he does? Some justification that even we would accept?" He shook his head, touching a hand to his brow. "I cannot know the answer. It is not as though Eldrich will show leniency toward Anna if she is found—of that I'm certain. There will be no charity, no application of reason to turn her away from her purpose. No, if we deliver Anna to Eldrich we will be party to murder, in one form or another." He stood like a scarecrow, his arms rising as though waving ineffectually at crows.

"But, Mr. Kehler," Rose said, his voice calm and reasonable— the tone Erasmus had come to identify with his most egregious lies. "Many criminals do not comprehend the harm that they do, yet they go to the gallows for their crimes, all the same. We make no

allowance for this other than madness. If we are to be utterly generous, we might say that it is not so different with Anna. She does
not know what will come of her actions, nor, perhaps, does she
want to know. But whether her intentions are good or evil, I am
convinced that great harm will result all the same. An apocalypse,
Mr. Kehler. An event so frightening that the mages would renounce
the arts to avoid it. *Renounce the arts!*

"I think we can hardly imagine such a catastrophe, for surely it
is more terrible by far than any war contrived by man. A war to
wound the very earth itself. Who would not give his own life to
prevent such a thing? I would, certainly. Better we live with the guilt
of our actions than allow the apocalypse. Moral cowardice comes in
many forms, Mr. Kehler, and all shades—not simply black and
white. The life of one for the lives of many, and perhaps more besides." He turned in a slow circle, like a clockwork-toy, regarding
each of them in turn.

Clarendon looked through him, addressing Erasmus. "What say
you, Mr. Flattery? This priest could justify any atrocity, I think, if it
would benefit mother church, but I distrust his ever-so-reasonable
rationalizations. 'A tongue so sweet it should be cut out and fed to
dogs,' were the words of Beaumont, and I feel they apply doubly
here."

Erasmus rubbed his palms into his eyes, feeling the burn. "I fear
we are too depleted by our ordeal to make wise decisions. One
can always rationalize when one's life is threatened. This must be
guarded against. Let us weigh all that has been said on the scales of
our conscience, try to sleep, and decide in the morning."

The others nodded at this, perhaps happy to put off passing such
a verdict.

"But I have already made my decision," Deacon Rose said, rising
to his feet, almost lightly.

"Do not be hasty, Deacon Rose," Erasmus said. "Eldrich's servant intimated that his master would deal with you. It was ominously said. Best take this night and look into your soul. Sleep the
sleep of the innocent, gentlemen." Erasmus turned and left the
room.

E rasmus stood upon his balcony and stared up at the wandering star that had trailed across the heavens these past weeks. "A wondering star," he said aloud, for so he had misunderstood the term as a child. A star that wondered—as did he. What could such a star think about? The question of a wondering child, riding through the heavens on the back of this miraculous planet.

The ancients believed such natural phenomenon to be signs, portents—of evil, almost invariably, but sometimes of favorable events as well.

"And which do you presage?" he asked, the wondering child not quite absorbed into the knowing adult.

"Mr. Flattery?"

Erasmus started, unsure of the voice's source.

"Sir?"

One of the attendants stood, poised in the door.

"Excuse me, Mr. Flattery. I knocked but had no answer. I wouldn't normally intrude, sir, but you have a visitor. . . ." The man's eyebrows raised. "It is the Earl of Skye, Mr. Flattery."

"Skye?" Erasmus must not have looked pleased, for the attendant blanched.

"Is it too late, sir? I would have asked him to return tomorrow, but he seemed so anxious to see you, and . . . well, he is the Earl of Skye."

"No, that's quite all right. Can you show him up?"

A moment later the silver-maned Skye appeared, even his movements, strong and graceful, almost feline: the lion of empiricism.

"It is a great honor," Erasmus began, but Skye waved a hand to cut him short.

"Hardly. I must begin by apologizing for intruding like this and at such an hour. You're unharmed by your adventure, I take it?"

"Largely, yes."

The two men settled themselves in wicker chairs. Despite his obvious need to see Erasmus, Skye appeared curiously reluctant to speak. He kept shifting in his chair, looking as though he were about to begin—but then demurring.

Erasmus did not know what he could say that would allow the man to overcome his reticence.

"Mr. Flattery, I . . . Oh, where to begin?" the empiricist muttered.

"I know the Peliers Lady Chilton showed me belonged to you," Erasmus prompted.

Skye looked at him obliquely.

"Yes? Well, you also went down into the cave in the company of Kehler and Hayes. I don't know what they might have told you."

Erasmus nodded. He had assured Hayes he would keep his confidence.

"We were trapped in the cave for several days—a section of the roof fell in, you see. For most of that time we were convinced we would die there—taking anything said to the grave. I don't think they would have broken their word otherwise."

Skye nodded. "Indeed. Under the circumstances I cannot hold them responsible. I'm only glad they survived, for it was partly due to me that they came to be in that cave in the first place. Perhaps they told you this? Flames, but it is a long story."

"I have learned of a number of things: the story of Compton Heath and the Stranger; Baumgere's discovery of the crypt and his search of the caves; the Peliers, of course."

"And what did you find in the cavern?" He leaned forward, his gaze fixed on Erasmus in anticipation. "What was it Baumgere sought?"

Erasmus sat back in his chair. "We found nothing but a section of a cave never before explored. We almost found our deaths. As to Baumgere—I had hoped you might tell me. What was he looking for?"

Skye nodded, sucking air through his teeth. "Exactly. What?" He shifted in his chair again. "I believe he was searching for the way to the land of the Strangers. He wanted to know from where they had come, for the Stranger of Compton Heath was but one. There were almost certainly others.

"You saw the painting of the man crossing the bridge? Yes? It depicts the Compton Heath Stranger, I'm certain. He passes over a bridge from one world to another, and what awaits him? A dark carriage, just as the carriage came for the real Stranger." He looked steadily at Erasmus. "Was it Eldrich? Is that what you think?"

"I don't know for certain, but it seems very likely."

"Then mages were interested in these things. It is not surprising; but why, do you think?"

Erasmus shrugged. "The affairs of mages are a mystery to men, Lord Skye. If these Strangers came from somewhere else— Well, the mages were almost all possessed of an enlarged curiosity, something that I'm sure you understand."

"Of course, but from where did they come? That is the question." He rose out of his chair, agitated, and went to look out the window, hands on his hips, his frock coat thrown back. "Baumgere seemed to think that the entire myth of Faery resulted from the visits of Strangers. Do you realize what such a thing would mean to our concept of the cosmos?"

"May I ask you a question?" Erasmus ventured.

Skye faced him. "By all means."

"There is a group interested in such things. I have only met two of them. A man named Banks and a young woman who goes by the name Anna Fielding. She is unique looking, hair a faded red . . . I can't think how to describe her."

"Looks as though she has had part of her life drained away? Part of her very being?"

"Yes, that's her. She's in her early twenties, mid-twenties at the latest, though she does look drained. I have never seen anyone like her."

Skye returned to his chair. He appeared still, now, and lost in thought.

"Obviously, you've met her."

"Yes," Skye said softly, "or at least I assume it was she." He rubbed his hand over the chair's wicker arm. "It was an odd thing. I went to visit a friend at her home. . . ." He proceeded to tell Erasmus the story of meeting Anna, though it clearly unsettled him. When he finished, he sat brooding as though he had forgotten the purpose of his visit.

"It was an even stranger meeting than you realize," Erasmus said. "I think Eldrich arranged it."

"She was his agent?"

"No. She was the precise opposite. She is his enemy, or at least that is Eldrich's belief. Centuries ago a renegade apprentice of a mage—a near-mage—made off with some texts that had belonged to his master. It was during the war with the church so the attention of the mages was focused elsewhere. This man created a secret society, the purpose of which was to learn the arts of the mages. To eventually rival them. Anna was a member of that society."

"What? Are you saying that centuries later these people persist?"

"Not the same people, obviously, but others. Their descendants in purpose if not in blood. You were put into danger—from Moncrief—so that Anna and her colleagues would save you, thereby revealing themselves."

"That is preposterous!"

"So it would seem, but the mage uses people without them ever realizing. You see, the followers of Teller—that is how these renegades are known—practice augury. They had a vision of you, Lord Skye. In it you opened a gate for them, and beyond stood a man who held a book of lore . . . and other talismans of power. They had to keep you safe, you see. You were to open a gate to knowledge and power. That is how they revealed themselves to Eldrich, who sought them out to destroy them."

"You're seriously suggesting that I was a dupe in Eldrich's plot. That he would use me so? A man in my position! I can't accept that." The man placed both feet firmly on the floor and leaned forward, elbows on knees, hands about his face.

"Nevertheless, it is true. Eldrich cares nothing for rank, nor even genius. He would toss away a man's life for his own purpose without qualms. Indeed, he would deal with the King this same way, should it suit him. Mages are above the laws and morality of men, or so they believe. You were used, Lord Skye, as was I."

Skye stared at him now, his eyes wide, lip almost trembling with rage. "I appeared somehow in the augury of these people? Is that what you're saying?"

"Precisely. They catch glimpses of events that might come to be, but these are filtered, somehow, filtered through the recesses of the mind so that they emerge in symbols—visions. You have the Peliers. What did Pelier do but somehow catch glimpses through time?"

Skye said nothing for a moment, suddenly calm. But it was more than calm—he was shocked into silence.

"Lord Skye? Are you well, sir?"

Skye nodded, still saying nothing, then he rose slowly and went to stand before the window again, his shoulders drooping a little. He took several deep breaths of the cool air. "Have you seen the wandering star?" he asked, his voice both soft and weary.

"Yes."

Skye nodded. "Do you know my history, Mr. Flattery?"

"I'm sure everyone in Farrland knows something of your story."

"I find that surpassingly strange, but nonetheless let me acquaint you with it again. There are some few things of which most are unaware.

"I was an orphan, taken in by a kind family. At fourteen I fell from a horse and apparently lay near to death for several days, and though I recovered, the memory of my life before that time was lost. The physicians said that in time I might recover some of what was lost, though it was far from a sure thing." He rubbed his fingers over the palm of his other hand as though trying to erase the lines. "And memories do come to me at odd times. Occasionally in dreams, but often waking. I cannot explain these for they seem to be brought on by certain emotions, as though my feelings at a particular moment are so like those of a past time that some shard of memory catches in them. More often it is just the emotion—or a memory of emotion—and the incident from my past remains just out of grasp." He shook his head, lifting a hand to his brow. "However, odd fragments of memory come to me, and they are truly strange. They are of my younger years, but not of my adopted parents' home. Most often I have visions of a strange city that I cannot identify. Or I have what seem to be memories of ideas—as though they are not truly mine. The laws of motion came to me thus, and many other things as well. And in my dreams I sometimes fly through the air. . . ." He fell briefly silent, oddly distressed by this confession.

"I have had dreams of soaring like a bird," Erasmus said, feeling he must reassure the man somehow. "And certainly, when inspired, many have said it seemed knowledge they had always known."

"Yes, but these dreams and waking memories are so consistent, as though I spent my youth in another land. Much has been made of my manner of speech—it almost seems to be slightly accented.

A result of my accident, everyone assumes. . . ." He looked at Erasmus over his shoulder, the starlight turning his mane of hair to silver, his face pale as snow. "Words come to me. Words no one has ever heard. They have no meaning, yet they are words nonetheless. I can feel that they roll of my tongue with great ease. And there is more. I remember characters—written characters—that I have never before seen."

"Like those in Pelier's painting?" Erasmus asked.

Skye looked back to the window, shaking his head. "No; unlike them. But neither are they like any script I know."

Erasmus struggled to make sense of Skye's words, to understand what disturbed the great man so. "Do you think you're having visions like Pelier? Is that it?"

Skye shook his head, pressing fingers to his eye's inner corner. "Perhaps. . . ." He paused, taking a long ragged breath. "But I fear it is madness," he whispered.

Erasmus was stunned by this sudden admission. "You have the most celebrated mind of our time, Lord Skye. Certainly your thoughts seem lucid, utterly logical. And if you are having visions . . . celebrated men and women have experienced the same. The mages practiced augury. Pelier was not entirely alone."

"Pelier went mad, you know—self-murdered." The great empiricist raised a hand, touching fingers to the glass. He pulled his hand away suddenly, animating his slumping frame. "Do pardon me. It was not my intention to burden you with . . . this."

Erasmus did not feel it a burden, though he didn't understand why Skye had chosen to confide in him. Did it explain the earl's interest in Pelier? Or was there something more?

"You cannot know what it is like to lose part of your life—your childhood. Years gone, and these fragments of memory—memories or dreams—floating up. They are like ghosts, but ghosts within. All so very strange.

"Do you know there are no records of my birth? I was a foundling, or so it is said. Though I have tried, I cannot find who my true parents were." He hesitated. "I am a mystery to myself. A stranger, in my own way." He fell silent again, moving his fingers over the glass, over the reflection of his face, Erasmus realized.

"Your parents have passed through?"

"Long ago."

"Had they no friends? Someone must remember your arrival at your parents' home. They had servants, a nanny?"

Skye continued to move his fingers, almost tenderly across the cold pane.

"None I can find. The servants I remember had not been with the family long—my parents were not easy on their domestic staff." Erasmus could feel the man's burden of suffering in the silence. As distressing as Erasmus' own.

"I—I'm not sure why you have told me this."

"Nor am I."

Silence again. Skye dropped his hand, but continued to gaze at the glass, at his reflection and the darkness beyond. He turned toward Erasmus, not meeting his eye. "I've taken enough of your time, Mr. Flattery. Excuse my ramblings. You and the others are safe—that's the important thing. Pleasures of the evening to you."

Erasmus barely made the door to let the man out, and once Skye had gone, he found himself staring at the same window as though something would be revealed to him there, or he would see what Skye saw. "How very odd," he whispered. "What had he meant to tell me?"

Certainly Skye had been wrong about one thing. Erasmus knew precisely what it was like to lose his childhood. But what had Skye said? *"I am a stranger—in my own way."*

Erasmus raised his hand to the glass to smear the slick of condensation and watched his reflection distort. And what was that he saw? A faint light? A wondering star?

Chapter Seven

THE brook they camped beside chattered incessantly, the clatter of rocks rolling in the streambed. Aromatic pines scented the breeze and rippled in the gusts along the hillsides.

The beauty of the surroundings went unnoticed by Anna. She stared at the roughly drawn map again, considering. Could she make her way from here?

Her guide assured her that it was simple, the landmarks unmistakable, but still, she was born and bred to cities and tame countryside, not mountains and wilderness. She gazed over at her sleeping guide, the wind tugging at his hair, sun burnishing his young face.

"The sleep of grace," she whispered.

He had been the woodsman she'd met upon escaping the cave. After Halsey's sacrifice, she had returned to him, remembering his boast that he knew the hills better than most men knew their gardens. If he'd only realized where his immodesty would lead.

Anna folded the map with tenderness, as though it were the last letter of a beloved.

"Give me strength," she whispered to no deity in particular. "If I am to survive, this is who I must be."

In her years with Halsey and the others, she had been spared so much—so many burdens the others had shouldered.

"If I am to survive," she whispered.

She looked again at the young man, his face softened by sleep. So content and trusting.

They had lain together the three nights since she had found him again. Anna had not protested. It felt good to be held, to have a few moments of oblivion, escape from her sorrow. There had been some guilt in her surrender as well, knowing what the future might bring.

I cannot tarry, she told herself. *I am hunted.*

She drew a long breath and forced herself to cross to her companion, sinking down by his head. Gently she smoothed his brow. Gently.

"You will always have your hills," she whispered, but he did not stir.

Whispering phrases in Darian, she produced a small, silver blade. A tear fell onto the young man's cheek, running off as though it were his own. In a quick motion she cut the carotid artery, pulling her hand away from the blood, watching it spread out onto the ground.

The brook sang its hollow song. Rocks clattering over rocks.

She put a hand to her face for a moment, horrified by what she'd brought herself to do. The knowledge that she was left no choice did not comfort her. A flutter, and her chough landed on a saddle, watching the proceedings with keen interest.

Dipping her fingers in the warm lake of blood, she made marks upon the man's face, upon his chest. She spoke words in Darian and chanted mournfully, tears still falling onto his cheeks and mixing with the blood.

The rite lasted the morning. Time she did not have, but she was not yet as callow as a mage—as callow as she would have to become. Fire consumed the body, and smoke drifted up into the hills, releasing the woodsman to his mountains and the unfettered wind.

"Your spirit will always watch over this glen," she said to the flames, the twisting pillar of smoke.

The ash she gave to the brook, to the river it would become, the distant lake, and then, one day, the sea.

"You will return as rain," she said, as the brook turned the gray-white of spawn. "Or lie upon the hills as snow."

The chough bounced from rock to rock in the racing brook, intent on what she did, inquisitive, its intelligent eye aglitter.

"Yes, I have become a monster, too," she said to her familiar. "As cold of heart as the carrion crow, swooping down upon the innocent to pluck out their eyes."

"Chuff," the bird said, releasing the single syllable with such conviction that one would think it an entire sentence, the articulation of avian thought.

"This man would have been my betrayer," she said to the bird, her voice a bit plaintive. "If I had let him go, the followers of Eldrich would certainly have found me." She paused, the chough's cold eye meeting hers. "But why do I tell you? You don't care what atrocities I commit—do you—cousin to the carrion crow?"

The bird tilted its head, staring at her one-eyed, as though struggling with the language of humans, then suddenly, dipped its blood-red bill into the murky water.

For a moment she stood appalled, then she thrust her hand into the milky waters and drank, tasting the salt of blood, the bitterness of ashes.

Chapter Eight

As the morning sun lifted, a line of shadow and light descended the hillside, illuminating each tree like a green flame.

Erasmus had wakened in darkness, too troubled to sleep, and at the first sign of gray, had stepped out into the sanitarium's sprawling garden.

"I have become a troubled man," he told himself.

He was troubled that morning by more than just the visit of Percy Bryce. His thoughts had turned to the countess, as though her company were a haven from the madness in which he found himself.

As soon as he had been able, he had sent a note to her, but no reply had come, and the silence was beginning to magnify his growing feelings of isolation. Certainly, she did not hurry to visit him or bring him comfort, and Erasmus was beginning to accept that it was but a night's indiscretion, soon forgotten—by the countess, at least.

" 'The dove-gray wing of morning.' "

Erasmus, seated on a bench, turned to find Clarendon looking down from nearby steps, his wolfhound, Dusk by his side.

"Ah, Randall! Is it Faldor? 'Awash in dew drop stars,' or some such thing. Is that the line?"

"Very nearly. You slept no better than I, I take it?" Clarendon put a hand on the great dog's shoulder as if to reassure him that Erasmus was a friend.

"I managed a few hours, but then woke and could not stop my fevered mind. And I fear I have little to show for so many hours of concentration."

Clarendon came down the stairs, favoring his injured knee a little. He lowered himself to one of the benches, Dusk sitting close by. The dog had found his master somehow, or perhaps having heard of Clarendon's escape from the cave, some kind soul had brought the dog up to the sanitarium—either way, the beast had barely left his master's side since the two had been reunited. "I have seldom experienced such indecision myself. We are being asked to take so much on faith. Could Eldrich not have provided even the slimmest of explanations? If the mage has perfectly good reasons for pursuing the followers of Teller, could he not at least have said so? Given us some justification? Farrelle's ghost, but I am not one to be bullied, I will tell you that. It is not my nature to make decisions out of fear—or ignorance. One would think a mage would be wiser in the ways of men."

Erasmus nodded. So one would think. "The mages have long used fear, or promise of reward, to motivate those who did their bidding. It would appear they think us little more sensate than beasts. They only seem to exhibit subtlety when manipulating those who are unaware. As though there is challenge enough, then. I'm afraid, Randall, that we'll get no more explanation than we have. Whether we accept the priest's reasoning, that the followers of Teller are a great danger to us all, is the question."

Clarendon nodded, reaching down to gently massage his knee. "Yes. If Kehler had not corroborated some of what the priest said, I would reject his explanation outright. The man is the greatest blackguard I have ever met—and he has his own reasons for wanting to destroy Anna. I think him as capable of vengeance as any mage!" He paused, obviously tired yet, searching for his train of thought. "Kehler, however, has forced me to have second thoughts. And there is this entire matter of the disappearance of the mages. The only explanation I have heard that makes sense is that they are erasing magic for fear of the harm it will do sometime hence. Even

Kehler had read about their augury—a cataclysm." He met Erasmus' gaze. "Do we accept the truth of this and go seeking Anna's destruction, or are we merely grasping at any explanation that will allow us to survive? Are we motivated by cowardice?"

"I can't imagine that you have ever been motivated by cowardice, Randall. Whatever your decision, it will reflect your integrity and courage. I confess, I trust your judgment in this more than my own."

Clarendon looked at Erasmus for a moment, lost in contemplation. "Mr. Flattery, I journeyed with you down into the cave and saw you prove your courage repeatedly. Beyond all doubt. Who among us swam the Mirror Lake? Led the traverse above the falls? And went into the water-filled passage in the end? No, your courage is not in question. One act in childhood, Mr. Flattery does not make the pattern of a life. Every man among us, I'm sure, has some act that they regret—that they feel was not an act of bravery. The rest of us were fortunate that our small acts of timidity resulted in no serious injury to those we thrust forward. No, you will not choose out of cowardice. I worry more that you might choose unwisely for fear of being timorous. That is a real danger and you must guard against it, Mr. Flattery."

Erasmus was surprised at how grateful he was for this vote of confidence.

"Tell me, Mr. Flattery," Clarendon began, his voice dropping, "what do you think we found down there? Oh, I know, it was the burial chamber of Landor, but was it somehow a passage? The gate to Faery, that Baumgere sought?"

"I believe Anna suggested as much, though why we should accept anything she said as truth I don't know. But certainly it seems likely. It marked the place where the first mages emerged into our own world. Emerged like the Stranger of Compton Heath; if you believe in the Stranger. . . ."

Clarendon nodded. "What choice have I but to believe?" he said softly.

At that moment a tall woman appeared below them, walking along the edge of the man-made lake. She appeared to be seeking others, looking in at every bower, at each bench. Erasmus could almost sense a desperation in the way she moved.

Erasmus found himself rising from the bench to watch her. This movement caught her eye and she stopped, staring up at Erasmus and Clarendon. Quickly she began to toil up the small rise, and a moment later she appeared at the stairhead.

There she paused, as though suddenly shy or unsure of herself. Erasmus thought her a most interesting woman; tall and well formed, yet her hair was cut like a boy's, her dress plain. In fact, now that he could see her well, he thought her a mass of contradictions: boyish; womanly; wearing a badly fitting dress of cheap materials, but over that a knitted shawl of fine silk in subtle color and design. This could be no one but the countess' friend, Marianne Edden.

Erasmus felt the smile appear on his lips. The countess must be here as well, searching for him inside, perhaps.

"Mr. Flattery, I hope?" she said.

"Erasmus Flattery," he replied, making a leg. "And you are Miss Marianne Edden, I take it? This is my friend, Randall Spencer Emanual Clarendon."

She smiled at Randall, who made a low bow.

"It is an honor, Miss Edden," Clarendon said, "for surely I have read all your books, some of them twice, and I will tell you, they are all improved by a second reading."

Marianne nodded at this, hardly seeming to register the compliment.

"Is Lady Chilton here, as well?" Erasmus asked, both relieved and entirely flattered that the countess would come to visit him.

"No, Mr. Flattery. That's just it. The countess is gone. Run off. And I am worried beyond the ability of words to describe . . ." She hesitated, glancing at Erasmus' companion.

"Shall I leave you?" Clarendon asked softly.

"If you don't mind?" Erasmus asked, and with a gracious bow the small man brought his dog to heel and was off.

Erasmus felt the sudden need to sit, dreading what Marianne might say next.

Marianne came and sat on the adjoining bench. "It is strange beyond all measure," she began. "The countess went off in a carriage at a moment's notice and left not a word of explanation. This is utterly unlike her, I will tell you. And this just a day or two after Averil Kent came by late at night with the strangest story."

"Kent? What has he to do with this?"

"Well, it is not a short story, but I will try to explain. You see, Kent had apparently seen the countess entering a carriage outside our door late in the night. And she was dressed for the bed. He thought her manner so strange that he made shift to follow her." She went on to tell of Kent finding the countess returned to the house, but appearing to sleep sitting up, and then all that had happened since.

Erasmus only shook his head, feeling so utterly without resources, without hope in this matter. He had been barely a pawn of the mage—someone whose life could be tossed away without the slightest concern. What did this woman expect him to do?

Marianne had finished telling her story, and stared at him. "Has this been too much in your reduced state, Mr. Flattery?"

"No, it is nothing to do with that. Were I at the peak of my powers, I would feel just as I do now." But he did feel suddenly ill, and weak beyond measure. He felt his limbs tremble from just the effort of sitting upright. "I will tell you in all honesty, Miss Edden, that there is absolutely nothing that can be done—and no one regrets this more than I. Eldrich . . ." He groped for words. "The mage is a force of nature, Miss Edden. Completely remorseless, and without regard for our laws or principles. Eldrich cares no more for people than a lightning bolt cares for its victims.

"Whatever Eldrich wants from the countess, he will have. Flames, he can make a woman burn with desire for him if that is his whim. There is nothing to be done, Miss Edden, but pray. Pray—if you are able."

Marianne put her hands to her face, her eyes glistening. "Mr. Flattery . . ." she said. "Mr. Flattery . . ." but no more.

"I hope Kent does not catch up to them. I wish I had been here to stop the man." He hung his head at the thought of the painter encountering Eldrich. "But it is unlikely that Kent will overtake them. Mages can travel unnaturally fast when they so desire, and never change a team to do it." He shook his head. "No, Kent is likely safe."

Erasmus' head spun, and he broke a cold sweat. His thoughts

seemed to scatter, like a flight of doves released—a mad flutter in all directions. At least Kent had shown courage—born of ignorance, unquestionably, but courage all the same.

And what of Erasmus? Erasmus who had experienced the countess' favors.

He shut his eyes for a moment, trying to stop the spinning. There was nothing to be done. One did not sneak into the house of a mage and steal away the fair damsel. Not in this world.

He thought of the countess lying close to him, the scent of her hair, her perfect lips tugged into an involuntary smile of pleasure and happiness. To think that Eldrich had simply stolen her away— against her will!

Marianne put a hand on his arm. "Can Eldrich simply abduct one of Farrland's most noted citizens with impunity? There is nothing anyone can do? Martyr's blood, is it the tenth century? Do mages rule the land again?"

"They have never abandoned their rule," Erasmus said, "except to appearances. No, others have been spirited away by a mage and— But excuse me, I frighten you. Perhaps we are entirely wrong in our thinking. The mage is very likely treating the countess with all respect. It is not impossible that she went with him of her own accord. Mages can be very persuasive, even without employing the arts."

The clearing of a throat drew their attention.

Erasmus turned to find Hayes standing at the stairhead.

"Your pardon," he said. "We have convened in your room, Erasmus."

"A moment," Erasmus said, nodding.

He stood, too quickly, and the world wavered.

"You are in the same lodgings?" he said to Marianne. "I will come later if I can, or send word. Let me think on this, Miss Edden. I . . . Let me think."

They appeared almost to huddle close in the room, as though they were back in the cave clinging together for warmth and support. Only Rose sat apart.

"What choice have we been left?" Hayes asked, the bitterness not masked by the quietness of his voice.

"Very little," Clarendon said. "I, for one, would not be ready to accept the justifications of this priest—who would stop at nothing to see Anna dead—but for the word of Mr. Kehler." He looked over at Kehler, as though asking for further confirmation.

Kehler nodded. "I can only repeat my words of last night. There was some cataclysm feared by the mages, and, yes, I do believe that is why the mages have trained no apprentices. I think it is very likely that Anna represents a danger, and not just to the designs of Eldrich. But I am loath to turn her over to Eldrich's justice." He looked at Erasmus now. "What if we were to find her and then deal with Eldrich? Could we not ask leniency for Anna in exchange for giving her up to Eldrich?"

Erasmus felt his head shake. "It might be very unwise, Kehler. Angering the mage is likely to make things worse for all concerned."

"But if Eldrich had no choice but to negotiate?"

"And how would you hold him to his word?" Erasmus asked. "Let me assure you, Eldrich would not feel bound by any agreement we reached. He will do as he pleases."

"There are ways to hold even a mage to his word," Rose said.

The others looked at the priest in surprise.

"The church made pacts with the mages in which both sides were bound to fulfill their part. It can be done."

"If we could find her, it would be worth attempting," Hayes said quickly. "What say you, Erasmus?"

If we find her, Erasmus thought, *I shall alert Eldrich by immolating myself—a living beacon. Yet if I refuse to search for her, I will face the justice of Eldrich.*

"Even if we agree to try to treat with Eldrich," Clarendon said, "there is no way we can trust this priest to keep to his word. He has proven that repeatedly."

"I seek only to protect my church, Mr. Clarendon, and despite what you think, I would derive no satisfaction from Anna's suffering or death. I believe she does not understand the consequences of what she does. No, I do not wish her harm. Let us find her and then treat with Eldrich. I think Mr. Kehler is right. Even a mage must make bargains out of necessity."

Chapter Nine

A prism of sunlight angled beneath the eaves, delineated in
dust motes and by a luminous rectangle on the polished
floor. Particles moved within the geometry, their motion too languid
to be real.

The awareness that this was no dream formed very slowly, and
then crystallized suddenly. The countess pushed herself up on her
elbows, realizing that she was in the offending bed and wore not a
stitch of clothing.

"Farrelle preserve us. What has been done to me?"

For a second she shut her eyes, searching her memories. She
had been sitting in the window, afraid to proceed to bed, and had
fallen asleep. A nightingale had been singing. And then Eldrich had
appeared. . . . But had he really? It seemed almost a dream now.

But how had she come to bed? Try as she might, she could not
remember. The countess clutched the covers to her.

Why did I agree to this? The open window drew her eye. Could
she slip away? Escape? Surely she had not made the decision to
come here of her own free will. She must have been bespelled.

A memory surfaced of the woman at the roadside, and the
countess collapsed back into the bed, covering her eyes.

"I am a vain, despicable creature," she sighed. But she knew it was not so simple—there was a fascination as well. She was in the company of a mage. *A mage.* A man whose powers and myth were beyond understanding. A legend. And the last of his kind as well.

"Some women are only besotted with rogues," she said. And though she had always thought them fools, she was suddenly a bit more sympathetic. "Is it the danger, then?"

She did not know. It was a mysterious attraction, like a spell perhaps, but often such things were. Or a kind of madness. All she knew was that she had not the mental discipline to turn her thoughts from Eldrich for long. And her thoughts of him were almost all encompassed by questions. Who was he behind his distant manner? What was it that drove him? How did he manage the feats that he performed?

"And what does he want of me?" she whispered. "Or has he had it already?"

A tap sounded at the door, and then it opened a crack.

"Lady Chilton?"

"Is that you, Mr. Walky?"

"Yes, Lady Chilton; Walky. We are to make a beginning this day. Will you break your fast in your room, or will you come down?"

"In my room, I think. We are to make a beginning . . . ? Of what?"

"Your part in the bargain, Lady Chilton. There is little time and much to do. I will return immediately after your meal, if you will allow it."

The false deference grated on her. She thought it highly unlikely that a refusal would be allowed.

"Until then, Mr. Walky." Now what was this? Somehow she had not thought her part of "the bargain" would be carried out with Walky.

Breakfast was simple but adequate. The countess found herself suffering a little disappointment. Couldn't mages eat exotic fruit out of season, famous and long-ago wines with dinner? Could there not be some sign of these legendary powers? Or was the use of the arts for mere indulgence beneath Eldrich?

The countess held back her sleeve and refilled her glass cup with coffee. Lifting it, she remembered the sunlight pouring into the room when she woke. How like liquid within glass it had appeared, dust motes moving slowly, aimlessly through the liquid light. Touching each other only by chance.

Like humans, she imagined. *Floating through life with little thought or purpose, but see how the light illuminates them for an instant here and there.*

She glanced over at a mirror and, given the circumstances, thought she looked remarkably herself. Not tired or frightened. In fact her color was a bit heightened, as though she were in a blush of pleasure, like a woman newly in love. This caused her to color even more. Her dark tresses fell in lustrous curls, and her eyes, set too wide apart, appeared gray this morning, for they changed with her mood and the color of her surroundings. Men wrote poems praising her eyes—and her mouth, which was full and sensuous. She shook her head. What a terrible vice vanity was. A foolish weakness, and the countess knew that, in all the ways that mattered, she was no fool.

A familiar tap on the door drew her attention.

"Mr. Walky? Do come in."

The rotund little man appeared, and she found herself smiling. How like a caricature he was—or like a character in a children's book. A bit distracted, disheveled, but there was something more there. . . . Had Erasmus suggested the man's memory was not quite sound? The countess thought it unlikely. He would not still serve the mage if that were the case. Eldrich would not be one to put up with incompetence. No, Erasmus must have been wrong—but then he had been only a child.

Walky hovered by the door.

'I'm quite finished—well, except for my coffee. Would you care to join me, Mr. Walky? They have provided another cup."

"Kind of you," Walky mumbled as he took the second chair. The countess filled his cup, which seemed to fluster him a little. He was the servant, after all.

It was only then that she realized Walky had set a book on the table—a book with an ancient leather binding, its title faded to unintelligible hints of gold.

"So, Mr. Walky, what is it we shall do?" the countess asked as casually as she was able.

Walky tilted his head to one side and looked at her quizzically. "You do not know?"

She tried to hide her embarrassment by sipping her coffee. "Lord Eldrich has told me nothing."

"Nothing? Even yet? But you agreed. . . ."

She nodded, not sure what to say. *Yes, an intelligent woman can make a foolish bargain. Do not look so disappointed.*

Walky's eyebrows lifted, and then settled as his brow knit in concentration—as though he had little time to spare for contemplating the folly of others. He placed a callused hand on the book, gently. "We are to begin your studies, Lady Chilton, and here is our reader. The primer, or more properly, *Alendrore Primia*—the first book of Landor."

The countess had begun to lift her cup, but put it ungently down, staring at the book. "Erasmus told me that, while in the house of Eldrich as a boy, you left a book in the schoolroom. A book written in a strange language and filled with odd diagrams and drawings. He said that when it was discovered that he'd had the book, he was punished."

Walky did not look at her but nodded slowly, gazing at his hand on the book. "Punished? You need not worry, Lady Chilton. It is the mage's will that you begin your studies with me."

"To what end?"

"Best you ask that of Lord Eldrich, Lady Chilton."

She nodded at the book. "You are not really so forgetful, are you, Mr. Walky? And books of the arts are not left lying about for schoolboys to discover."

Walky did not answer, but continued to stare though his focus was inward now.

The countess reached out and placed a hand softly on Walky's arm. "Tell me honestly, Mr. Walky, will Eldrich use me so heedlessly? For surely Erasmus was supposed to discover the book—to suffer some terrible regret all these years, though what purpose this served I cannot imagine."

Walky had become utterly still. She could feel the muscles of his arm tensed beneath her fingers, yet he did not move his arm away.

He has not known a tender touch in who knows how long, the countess realized. *How old is this man and how long has he been living a monk's life in the service of Eldrich?*

She felt his muscles relax suddenly, and his eyes pressed closed. He sagged a little, as though something at his center collapsed.

"Please, Lady Chilton," he said, the constriction of his chest squeezing the words flat.

The countess gazed at the man, who seemed suddenly to be suffering, pressed his arm gently, then let it go.

Mr. Walky removed his hand from the book and sat back in his chair a moment, careful to keep his gaze cast down.

"The primer," he began softly, still not meeting her gaze, "is the first book in the study of the arts."

For a long moment the countess heard no more. *The study of the arts.*

Chapter Ten

THE baggage made a pyramid of battered leather in the corner of Sir John's room: a monument to his resolve, for he was in no hurry to return to Avonel. Having been abandoned here by Bryce, Sir John had been tempted to prolong his visit. Even a few days without worries of Bryce appearing at his door would be a great gift. Shirking duty was not, however, in Sir John's nature.

Bryce. . . . And to think he had asked Sennet to find out what he could about the man! Sir John was certain Sennet had not uncovered the truth, or anything like it. Bryce served the mage, and so, indirectly, did Sir John. A thought that invariably caused him such anxiety that his hands shook and blood drained from his face, leaving him sweating and slightly disoriented.

"Dinner," he said aloud, intentionally turning his mind to matters more appealing. It was unfortunate that Kent had run off on his fool's errand, it would be good to have company this evening. But Kent had his obsession with the countess driving him—driving him to ruin, Sir John was certain. Poor fool. These artistic types, they were so . . . *capricious*. Kent would come to regret it.

Sir John pulled on a frock coat of royal blue and regarded himself in the mirror. Still a passable-looking man, younger in appearance than most his age. A woman could do worse, he was sure.

A banging on the lower door interrupted his self-appraisal, and he watched his face sag as the confidence drained away.

"It is only the landlord, come to be sure I need no help."

Sir John took a lamp and descended the stairs, unbolting the door.

"I am hardly a ghost, Sir John," Bryce said. "You need not look so. Will you not invite me in?"

Sir John tried to regain his composure. "Certainly, certainly. I am surprised, as you see, as you had left so abruptly. . . ."

Bryce pressed past him, pounding up the stairs with his customary energy. Sir John struggled to keep pace, the light swaying around them in the narrow stairwell.

Bryce eyed the small mountain of baggage. "Just in time, I see. But what have you done? Purchased another wardrobe? You had less than half this when we came."

"It belongs to a friend, I'm carrying it back to Avonel with me."

"What friend is this?" Bryce asked.

Sir John hesitated, almost certain this inhumanly precise man would catch him in a lie. "Kent. Averil Kent. He's run off somewhere in his pursuit of beauty." Sir John shrugged. "Artists . . ."

"Ah." Bryce turned a chair slightly and took a seat, Sir John's deception apparently unnoticed. "Matters have changed, Sir John, and we have need of your services again." Bryce spread his hands and touched the tips of the fingers together. "There is a woman we must find. Find at all costs. She goes by the name of Anna Fielding, though she will not likely be using that name now. Fortunately she is uncommon looking: about twenty-three or -four, above average height for a woman. Her hair is straight and long—past the shoulder—and the oddest shade of red-blonde; as though it had been drained of color, or faded from too much time in the sun. 'Washed out,' is how one described it. But it does not stop there: her entire appearance is the same, as though she has had some of her life drained away, yet her manner belies this, for she is as vital as any her age."

"Is this not the young woman said to have gone down into the cavern after Erasmus Flattery and the others?" Sir John thought to cover his discomfiture with a question.

"The very one."

"But none of her party emerged. I have heard that Flattery and his friends said they all perished."

"She did not," Bryce said firmly.

Sir John shifted his weight to his other foot. "What am I to do?"

"You are to go to the Admiralty, to all of your most influential friends. This woman must be found and, above all, must not escape by sea. The ports have to be watched, watched as never before."

Sir John stared at Bryce. "And how am I to accomplish this? Am I to tell the Sea Lord that an unknown gentleman must have this girl for unknown reasons? Flames, Bryce, I cannot perform miracles!"

"Tell them whatever you must. That she is a criminal. That she has stolen something from one of Farrland's most influential citizens—which she has."

Bryce shook his head. He was tired of it. Utterly exhausted by the lie. "Why do I not simply tell them the truth?" he said, suddenly a bit breathless. "That Lord Eldrich wants this woman for his own reasons."

It was the only time Sir John had ever seen Bryce taken by surprise. No matter what happened now, he had that satisfaction, at least.

Bryce touched the corners of his mouth with finger tips, then he almost smiled—an act Sir John had thought unnatural for him. "Sir John, Sir John. Curiosity can be the greatest curse of man." Bryce rose from his chair, pacing across the room, the soft touch of his boots on carpet, then the brittle sound as they struck wood.

Bryce turned suddenly on Sir John. "You were better off not knowing, you realize?"

"So parents tell their children, but ignorance is a curse, I believe."

Bryce fixed him with his unreadable look. "Eldrich wants this woman found," he said firmly. "It would be very unwise of you to try to back out of our arrangement now."

"You need not threaten me, Mr. Bryce. I understand my position. But you ask a miracle of me. I am not the King's Man, after all."

Bryce gazed at him intently for a moment and then moved to the writing desk, uncorking the ink bottle and taking up a pen. After a moment he motioned for Sir John, and removing a small box and a thick sheaf of papers from his coat, placed them with the newly written letter into the knight's hands. "Take these," he said. "You will deliver them to a lodge on the road from Castlebough. You see, I have drawn a map." He went over the directions so that Sir John could not mistake them.

Sir John looked at this, and the folded letter in his hand, "I have sealing wax," he said.

This appeared to amuse Bryce. "Read it, if you like."

Sir John hesitated a moment, not sure why, then he unfolded the paper. But it was no script he knew. He heard his breath catch and he looked quickly up at Bryce.

"He will want to speak with you, Sir John. You may not think ignorance such a curse, then."

Chapter Eleven

WHEN she watched his hands, she thought of a dancer. The movements were so fluid, the long, elegant fingers so sure. Even performing simple acts, like unstopping the bottle, they seemed to perform a dance. And everything he touched, he touched so lightly, as though the force commonly used by men was never required of a mage.

Eldrich tipped the bottle into the mortar and out tumbled small seeds, like peppercorns. He took up a pestle and began to crush them, releasing a pungent fragrance into the air.

"The seed was carried here by the first mages and has been cultivated by my kind ever since. It is the most precious commodity in the known world, for without it there are no arts, no 'magic.' One may study the arts for a lifetime and have talent in abundance, but without the seed to release that talent—" He continued to move the pestle, crushing the seed to powder, his beautiful hand moving in slow rhythm. "The elixir is simplicity itself to make, that is why we guard the seed above all else. It is death to touch this seed without the express permission of a mage. In my household only Walky may handle it. Teller stole seed, for which his life was to be forfeit, but he escaped us." He continued grinding the seed to a fine powder.

The countess began to feel distinctly uncomfortable, though she was not sure why. As though she were afraid her hand might slip, and she would touch the seed and pay the arbitrary price.

"When the seed is first taken, waking dreams often occur. Some of these are 'visions,' though that depends upon the nature of one's talent. One will often begin to dream vividly when asleep, as well. It is good to note such dreams down when waking, for one can never be sure of their significance and they are soon forgotten." He stopped and stared down into the mortar. Satisfied, he lifted the steaming kettle off its hook over the fire and poured water into cups. Taking up the mortar and a dagger, he apportioned the powder into the cups, stirring them with the blade. The countess watched it glint in the candlelight, a little mesmerized by the movement.

"A transformation is initiated by the seed, for the path from man to mage is not merely through learning. It is more profound than that—profound and irreversible." He lifted one of the cups and, leaning forward, set it before her. The second cup he raised, his dark gaze upon her.

"Me?!" she said, finally realizing that this was not to be a mere demonstration. "But I am no mage's apprentice!"

He continued to regard her. "No, but in this world you are the closest thing. Do not drink it all in one rush, but sip it slowly your first time. You might find the experience a bit overwhelming other-wise."

The countess drew her hands back off the table. Transformation? What in this round world was he talking about. "I did not agree to this."

"Indeed, you did. You simply did not ask what our bargain entailed." He held out his cup as though about to offer a toast. "Raise it," he said, the music in his voice suddenly very cold.

She found this command so chilling, so utterly disturbing that she moved her hands so they all but touched the cup.

"It is also the seed which lengthens one's years and preserves the vigor and appearance of youth—like the apples of immortality."

"But there was a cost to obtaining those apples," she said softly.

"There is always a cost. The seed is habituating. You will require it. There are other effects as well, but these can be mitigated. Think of it, Lady Chilton. You have but to drink, and you will avoid the fate you saw at the roadside. The fate of all those who do not die young. The ruin of age, the loss of physical powers, of one's mental acuity, of memory, of one's past. It is a loss of dignity, Lady Chilton, the likes of which most cannot imagine . . . until it is upon them. But not for you. Youth. Imagine it. I am a century and a third old. A century and a third. Fifty years ago I looked no more than thirty." He raised the cup to his lips, his eyes still on her, and then they closed—in pleasure, she thought.

She touched the cup, felt the warmth through its ancient glaze, for the cups themselves seemed very old. For a moment she stared down into the rising vapor, as though trying to see her future. The realization that this was a decisive moment, perhaps *the* decisive moment, of her life settled into her like glacial waters.

There is no road back, she told herself, numbness flooding through her being.

She raised the cup with two hands, for it had no handle, and inhaled the vapor. Her hands trembled as the rim touched her lip, and a drop spilled upon her dress. Closing her eyes, she tasted the liquid. It had no flavor she could name, though it was pungent and spicy.

She swallowed. And again. The liquid seemed to flow warmly throughout her body, as though it ran into the veins, driving out the numbness.

And then the dim room grew suddenly dark. She walked among the walls of a ruin, a castle or some great edifice. A moon rose above a toppled tower, and a hawk flitted from ledge to lintel overhead. Columns rose up or lay shattered on the ground. As the moon rose, it reflected on a pattern set in silver into the stone floor.

The beauty of the pattern struck her—intricate scrollwork winding among the precise lines of a geometric pattern. A silent wind rustled her dress. It was only then that she noticed the quiet of the place. Even her own footfall made not a sound.

Skirting the pattern she went on, deeper into the ruin. At a balustrade looking out over a moonlit valley she found a man, a small falcon perched upon his wrist.

For a moment she stood, afraid to approach. But then he turned slightly, and she saw that it was Kent, an aged and wrinkled Kent. For a moment he gazed directly at her, but registered nothing. Even so, she could see the sadness and loss in his eyes—as though she looked through them into the desolate valley beyond.

"Where am I, Kent?" she asked, but he turned back to the valley, the bird fluttering up from his outstretched arm.

A shadow moved among the columns, someone tall and stooped. "Lord Eldrich?" she tried to call, though her voice emerged thin and weak. The figure blended into the shadow of a column, leaving her unsure of what she had seen.

I am alone. Alone but for a silent, aged Kent who cannot hear when I speak.

For a moment she collapsed on a fallen column, overwhelmed by sadness. Tears appeared, running down her cheeks, but when she went to rub them away, she found tiny, pear-shaped diamonds in her hand. They glittered in moonlight and shrank away, dissolving on her palm, leaving her skin cold where they had lain.

"Flames," she heard herself whisper.

Surprisingly, she felt no fear, only a vague disquiet and uncertainty.

This is a vision, she told herself. *You have taken king's blood and walk within a waking dream. No harm can befall you.*

She entered a round courtyard, though perhaps it had once been a chamber, its roof worn away long ago. In the center stood a fountain, empty of water and filled with spiderwebs, the strands silvered by moonlight. A sculpture of pale stone rose out of the web—a woman bent back beneath her lover, her face half-formed but lost to passion. Her lover bent over her with both tenderness and passion though she could not understand how both these states had been conveyed.

"It is not me," the countess said, her voice trembling. She pressed a hand to her heart and felt it beating wildly. "It is not Eldrich." But the man's face was obscured, and she could not say.

The bird that had perched upon Kent's wrist alighted on the edge of the fount and regarded her with its unsettling gaze.

She skirted the sculpture, averting her eyes, but it drew her, and she glanced that way again. It had moved, she was sure, as though animated by the slow passion of stone. She fled through the first opening that offered itself.

Here she came upon a second balcony, and looked out over the moonlit valley. A lake shimmered in the distance, but the valley was in shadow. Trees, she thought she saw, perhaps hedgerows, and here and there regular shapes that could be houses or the structures of men.

For the first time she heard sounds, a low dirge, like monks chanting. The sound seemed to float up to her from a great distance, and then she saw the singers—men bearing a litter up a blue-shadowed stair. They passed through a shaft of moonlight, and she could see it was a bier they carried, and the singing was indeed a dirge—a lament of great power and sorrow.

"What king is this?" she whispered, for somehow she was sure that such music could only befit a king.

A breeze moved her hair and seemed to whisper next to her ear. . . . *auralelauralelaural* . . . She looked up at the sky, filled with stars, their light diffused into soft haloes. The heavens seemed to be spinning slowly, and she turned to follow. Faster it went, and the world tilted beneath her. She fell.

". . . *lauralelauralelauralelaura* . . ."

A hand rested lightly on the countess' shoulder; she could feel the warmth of it through the fabric of her dress.

He is touching me, she thought. Every finger was distinct, and her breath caught. The hand was so still. Only a mage could remain so motionless.

She opened her eyes and found she lay upon a divan in the great room, a single candle trembling on a table. Eldrich sat near her head, one hand resting on her shoulder. He was awake, she was certain by the sound of his breathing. But she was so tired. . . . Her eyes shut of their own accord.

"What do you want of me?" she whispered.

"What did you dream?" he asked, ignoring her question.

"I saw Kent standing on a balcony beneath a moon, looking out over a shadowed valley. A hawk rested upon his wrist. A pattern of moonlight was woven into the stone floor. . . ." She struggled to remember, to remain conscious. "And a dry fountain filled with spiderwebs held a sculpture of a woman . . . and a man."

"You knew them?"

"No," she said quickly, then remembered to whom she spoke. "The woman might have been me. The hawk lighted upon the fount as though it required something of me and I fled. Out onto a second balcony. Below me men chanted, a sad lament, and bore a body upon a bier. Only a king deserved such music, I thought. Only a king, yet there was no great train, no procession. Only a handful of men, as though this king died in exile. And then the stars began to spin, and I fell."

Eldrich said nothing, and she felt herself falling away.

"If it was a vision, does that mean I foresaw a death?" she managed.

"Perhaps," Eldrich said softly.

"But whose?"

"Sleep," Eldrich said. "Sleep in peace, and let dreams trouble you not."

Chapter Twelve

K ENT walked through the night, through the moonlight that passed over the land like a searching owl. His increasingly lame mount slowed him, as did the shadows of hills which flowed across the road in black pools.

And then the darkness began to pale, giving way to a still dawn, filled with the silence of calling birds—a world contained within a pearl.

The stableman looked askance at this city dweller who brought his horse in so injured, riding foolishly by night. Kent hardly cared what anyone thought, only let him sit and eat some food, then he would have energy to feel abashed.

He took a table in the near-empty common room, and leaned his head back against the wall, closing his burning eyes.

Food and coffee arrived after a moment. Guests came down to break their fasts, the men stepping out to check on the readiness of carriages. The travelers were bound for Castlebough or another scenic town, some few going to the border beyond and down into Entonne. They had that air of anticipation and release that people on journeys so often displayed. A great contrast to his own state.

The painter leaned his head on his hand as he ate, slumping in his chair.

I must look in a sorry state, he thought, and though his appearance was usually important to him, at that moment he did not care. How far ahead was Eldrich? Too far to ever be caught by natural means? The entire endeavor seemed even more foolish by the fresh light of morning than it had in the darkest hour of the previous night.

Kent rides off to slay a mage and win the hand of fair lady. Flames, but he was likely making a perfect ass of himself. Luckily there was no one there to see.

"Kent?"

The painter looked up.

"Sir John!"

"Kent, this is as far as you've traveled?"

Kent nodded sheepishly as Sir John took a seat at his table. "Have you been watching Eldrich?"

Kent shook his head. "No, they must be in the lowlands by now."

Sir John fell quiet, breaking eye contact abruptly. "Ah . . ."

"And what of you, Sir John? What's led you to be traveling by night?"

"I was called away suddenly," Sir John said.

Kent eyed him. "A servant of the mage passed me as I traveled—I heard him speaking to his driver. It occurred to me later that this might be the man with whom you had dealings. Is it business of the mage that you are on?"

"No, just . . . business." But the words had little strength in them.

"Well, at least I shall have a traveling companion until our ways part."

"But, Kent." Sir John stared down at his hands folded on the table, hanging his head like a man suddenly ill. "Kent, I don't go to Avonel." He took a long, uneven breath. "Do not ask me more."

Kent sat back against the wall, gazing at the suddenly wretched man. *What does he do for the mage?*

"Will you want your carriage back?" Sir John asked, forcing his gaze up, shaking off his mood.

"No. I should travel faster by horse. You managed through the night with those wretched lamps?"

"Yes, well enough."

A servant came, and Sir John asked for a meal. The meal was interrupted only by small talk, neither man speaking his real concerns. Finally, as Sir John was about to rise, Kent put a hand on his arm. "Is there nothing you can tell me? Do you know where the mage has gone? Where he has taken her?"

Sir John tugged his arm gently free. "Kent, there is nothing you can do. Nothing anyone can do." He leaned closer so that no one else might hear. "I have been forced to dissemble once to keep you from harm. I shall not get away with it twice. Kent . . . I implore you, give this up." Sir John swept from the room, the eyes of everyone on him, wondering what disagreement beset these two gentlemen.

The road wound its way along the bottom of a high valley awash in the translucent green of spring. The breeze fluttered leaves and the sunlight caught them like sparkles on the sea. Kent sat his horse at the valley's head, watching. His trap, which bore Sir John, appeared in a gap in the trees, then disappeared beneath a wave of phosphorescent green.

"Have you been watching Eldrich?" Sir John had asked.

The mage was nearby—it could mean nothing else. The countess was here, somewhere.

Sir John must know I follow, Kent thought. *But is he going to meet the mage?* Certainly Sir John had never encountered Eldrich before; his fear the night they had seen the mage proved that. There had always been an intermediary. . . . But at the recent inn, Sir John had looked almost as frightened as he had the night above Baumgere's home, though this fear was overlain by resignation.

What, other than a mage, could inspire such terror?

Kent nudged his horse forward, out of the shadow of the trees. He felt like a knight riding into hopeless battle. It was one thing to pursue a mage with little chance of ever catching him, and quite another to think that he might actually come face-to-face with this terror. Whenever these fears appeared, he would think of the gratitude of the countess, and this would drive him on, even if it did not drive the fear away.

The shadows of the hills sundialed across the valleys, and the sky tones softened to near-pastels. Darkness was not far off, and yet Sir John hardly slackened his pace. Kent would catch glimpses of him between the green seas of hills.

The painter began to wonder if he had misread Sir John altogether. Perhaps he was not going to meet the mage. Kent wasn't sure if he felt dismay or relief at this, for his own courage ebbed and flowed by the hour.

Occasionally his mind would stray to what Eldrich might be doing with the countess, and the pictures that appeared in his mind caused him such anguish that the resultant anger would solidify into resolve. For an hour he would not care what Eldrich might do to him.

The limb of the sun bobbed on the crest of a western mountain and shadows stirred in the depths of the forest—restless for release.

Kent pushed his mount forward now, wanting to close the gap between himself and Sir John. Would the man travel in darkness? Kent still wondered how he had managed the previous night.

"The mage and his servants have no need of lanterns," he said aloud. A sign, surely, that Sir John's situation had changed.

Kent topped a rise which provided a long view of the road ahead, but there was no sign of Sir John.

"Martyr's blood!" Kent swore, and set his tired horse to race the gathering darkness.

Sir John brought his trap to a stop before the lane Bryce had marked on his map. Stepping down to the grass he paced quickly forward, looking into the deepening green of the wood. The lane wound into the trees, revealing no sign of men or habitation.

"Farrelle preserve me," he whispered. Sir John had never dueled, but he was certain approaching a duel would be no worse than this.

He thought seriously of climbing back into his carriage and hur-

rying on, down into the lowlands. On the coast he could take ship
for some foreign port—escape. Escape Eldrich.

But some part of him knew this was impossible. One did not
escape a mage.

He found his breath coming in short gasps, and his hands shook
a little. His horse snorted, and Sir John jumped, whirling around.

"Take hold of yourself, man," he muttered, trying to calm his
heart.

With utter resignation he climbed back into the trap and set off
down the lane, into the heart of the wood.

It was only a short distance to the lodge, which stood in the
midst of a lawn and a seemingly abandoned garden. The last light of
the day found its way here, creating long shadows, like incursions
into the world of light.

The lodge was stone and dark wood, and Sir John was certain
that if it had been inhabited by anyone else, it would not have had
such a threatening air.

Sir John could not imagine what would befall him here, but in
his heart he knew that his life would never be the same after this
night—as though he were about to make a pact with a devil.
Flames, but he wished he had never met Bryce. Better ruin, both
social and financial, than this. He was about to become the servant
of a mage!

But you have been one for some time, he reminded himself, a
thought that brought no comfort.

He stopped the trap before the main entrance. As he stepped
down, the door creaked open and a mild looking, silver-haired servant appeared.

"Who are you, sir, and, pray, what is your business?" the man
asked.

"Sir John Dalrymple. Mr. Bryce has sent me to deliver a letter."

The man nodded, and disappeared inside. The ordinariness of
the servant's appearance and manner made the situation somehow
more macabre.

Although it was only a moment before the servant returned,
twilight rose from the trees, shadows bleeding out across the lawn,
enveloping everything in their path.

The servant held aloft a lamp. "Come in, Sir John," the man said as though it were not an invitation to give up one's soul.

The lodge was not well lit inside, and though it was a common structure for its service, it took on a more ominous appearance for its darkness.

The servant led him quickly on, saying nothing. They saw no one else, as though the place were empty but for the mage and this one aging manservant.

Sir John forced himself to go forward, his nerve very near to breaking, but he had passed a threshold and there would be no turning back now.

As they came to a hall below a heavily built stair, the servant bid him wait and disappeared down a hallway, leaving Sir John with only the light of the faintly flickering hearth.

He sat on a hard, wooden bench, and without warning, bile burned up his throat as though his rising fear had spilled over. *Farrelle's flames, man*, he chided himself. *Eldrich isn't going to murder you.*

The hollow echo of footsteps sounded somewhere above him, falling lightly, then descending.

Could this be the mage? Sir John wondered, and though he wanted to rise, to greet his fate standing, he shrank back into the shadow, fighting to catch his breath.

A faint glow tripped lightly down the stairs to his right, touching each step in turn before it spilled onto the polished floor. The footsteps followed, hardly more substantial—as light as a girl's, but even and purposeful.

The lamp appeared, and then its bearer—a woman darkly dressed, long tresses swept back from her beautiful face by silver combs.

She passed the cowering figure of Sir John without the slightest notice, and carried on down the hall, like an apparition.

The Countess of Chilton, Sir John realized, and he hadn't the wit to speak, to ask after her, as any gentleman should. Again he choked on his own bile.

You are still of use, he told himself. *Bryce came to you with instructions. They're not done with you yet, so you are safe from harm.*

The flames in the hearth flickered and pulsed, like a tiring heart. Sir John felt his slim hopes fade with the dying light.

A door opened, and a lamp appeared in the hallway the servant had taken. Footsteps reached him, loud in the silence—two sets this time. As the servant neared, Sir John could see that another followed behind, just on the edge of the light.

This time he forced himself to his feet, standing bent, his knees none too steady. The servant stopped before him, and the second man came into the light—a small round man of almost comical aspect.

Was *this* the great Eldrich?

"I am Walky," the little man said. "You have a letter from Mr. Bryce?"

Sir John nodded, speech having abandoned him, and reached into his coat for the missive which he proffered in a trembling hand.

Walky took it, paused as though contemplating Sir John, said softly, "A moment," and then followed the servant up the stair. The lamplight retreated after them, flowing up the treads like a bride's train.

Sir John collapsed back onto his bench, staring at the embers glowing in the hearth, a lone flame that whisped up, wavered, and was inhaled into the glow. He waited in the dark, watching for the return of lamplight, listening for footsteps. For some moments he sat, his growling bowel the only sound.

"Have you never heard that a mage walks in perfect silence?" came a musical voice, and involuntarily Sir John threw himself hard against the wall. A shadow on the last stair might have been a man.

The hearth erupted into flame, but the shadow on the stair remained untouched by the light.

"Have you any idea what Bryce wrote?" the shadow asked.

Sir John could not speak but only shook his head.

Silence, as though a great beast contemplated him—wondering if he would be worth eating.

"He believes that you cannot gain the support I require from the powers in Avonel—at least not of your own influence. . . ."

Sir John was not sure if it was a question and remained frightened into silence. *Had his use ended? Was that why he was sent to Eldrich?*

"I'm waiting . . ." came the musical voice, perhaps touched by amusement.

"I would not gainsay," he gasped involuntarily, "Mr. Bryce."

"That is your answer?"

Sir John nodded.

The shadow stepped to the floor, and though it crossed before the fire Sir John saw nothing but a gathering darkness which passed silently down one of the unlit hallways. The flames in the fire died away, returning Sir John to the dark.

He moves without sound, Sir John thought. *Could be standing beside me at this moment.* He pressed himself back into the wall, half-raising his hands as if he would ward off a blow.

Footsteps sounded again, lamplight lilting down the stairs.

The servant and the small man appeared.

"We have prepared a room," the small man said, his voice not unkind.

Sir John nodded, but he found he could not rise.

"Sit a moment," the man called Walky said. "Many find their first meeting with the mage . . . strangely overwhelming."

The two men waited in utter silence, as though there were nothing odd at all in the situation.

Finally Sir John pushed himself up and, though not perfectly steady, thought he could go on.

He followed the others up the stair, terrified at the thought that he was expected to spend the night here—in the house of the mage. But to what purpose? Had he proven himself unworthy with his admission? What would be done with him?

He clutched the rail as they went, up to a landing and open hallway. A door stood ajar emitting a soft light. Here they stood aside and let Sir John enter. A lamp and fire burned within.

"The fire will take the dampness from the room," Walky said. "You will find everything you need here. Sir John," he said, making sure of the other's attention. *"Do not leave your room*, and I say this for your own safety. If you need anything at all, ring the bell. Do you wish food?"

Sir John shook his head.

"Then I bid you sleep well." He turned to go.

"But," Sir John hesitated, "what will be done with me?"

Walky shrugged. "Only the mage knows," he said, and the two men went out, closing the door firmly behind them.

T he wandering star appeared, a tiny flame in a mother-of-pearl sky. Slowly the opaque dome dissolved to the infinite depths of night, and stars flickered into focus. Kent stood, immersed to the shoulder in the edge of the wood, his field glass trained on the lodge.

He'd found the lane, open gate, and the signs of Sir John's passing. Having hidden his mount he made his way through the twilit wood.

His trap stood before an outbuilding, proving him right—Sir John was inside. But was this where the mage dwelt and, more importantly, was the countess here? Kent hoped with all his heart to find her in an open window and whisk her away before even the mage realized what had been done. But most of the windows were dark, and those that displayed feeble light never framed a silhouette, let alone one so fair as the countess.

Kent stepped out onto the lawn, for moving through the wood made far too much noise, and slipped quietly along the edge of the trees. At the back of the house he scrutinized each window, with the same result. One would almost have thought the inhabitants asleep—perhaps like the old tale, asleep for a hundred years.

He passed behind the stable and paddock, arriving at the lodge's far side. The windows here provided no more information than the others. From far off a howl floated through the trees—not an uncommon sound in the hills at night, but with Eldrich at hand it sent a chill through Kent. For a long moment he froze in the shadow, listening like a frightened beast.

" A small bird," the countess said, "like a hawk, though more colorful. It hovered before my window."

"A kestrel," Eldrich said. "It is a small falcon. I saw one at the edge of the wood today—and did one not appear in your vision?"

He nodded, as though giving his approval, though his gaze was far away.

"What will happen now?" the countess asked. "Will it . . . come to me?"

"A familiar is not a pet," Eldrich said, shaking himself from his reverie. "You might lose sight of it for days at a time—but if you are agitated, angry, frightened, it will appear. Not just then, of course, for it performs a duty. In times of danger you will see it, and you will know. The familiar has been called a reflection of the soul—but I think it is more like a shadow. Imagine if you stood with your back to the sun and looked down at the earth—and you saw the shadow of a hawk . . . or a wolf."

Eldrich began to eat again—something that he did with little sign of pleasure. Wine he appeared to enjoy—but food seemed a mere necessity. The silence returned, the silence in which he seemed barely aware of her. She watched his hands as he manipulated his utensils, the long fingers curling around the bowl of his wineglass, white against red.

The countess thought he had the most elegant hands she had ever seen, almost articulate in their movements. The fingers were long and fine, certainly the hands of an artist. A shiver coursed through her at the thought of his touch. She had begun to dream of his hands, hands reaching out of shadow and caressing her.

She glanced up at his face; his large eyes appeared to be focused on something unseen. His presence disturbed her, especially in the silences, and this often forced her to make conversation.

"I have noticed something else; my throat . . . It seems tight, somehow. I feel it when I speak—though not all the time."

Eldrich barely nodded. "Yes, it is the king's blood," he said, his voice reaching out and brushing her intimately. "It will give you a voice like . . . there is no description, for it is hardly human. But we will keep your voice as youthful and mellifluous as it is now. I will speak to Walky."

The countess nodded. She had barely seen Eldrich since their arrival here, and now she found him strangely subdued. Oh, he was as remote as ever—that had not changed—but the arrogance that so offended her was largely absent. He seemed like a man in mourning—as though he had lost someone close to him.

This impression was only offset by the two occasions during the meal when she had found him staring at her. The intensity of his gaze had unsettled her completely. She had known such looks too often to wonder what they meant.

He desires me, she thought. *Despite all of his feigned indifference, he desires me.* She felt a wave of warmth sweep through her core and her face and neck colored. If she had been standing she would have wavered.

"*What is it he wants of me,*" she had asked Walky, naively.

"*He will tell you in his own good time, Lady Chilton,*" Walky had said, but she had an answer, here. He wanted this, and something more. The something more was what frightened her.

He desires me, yet steels his will to resist. She felt her head shake, overwhelmed by confusion of thought and feeling.

Eldrich reached out and drew a sheaf of paper toward him, holding his hand upon it as though contemplating the content.

"From Mr. Bryce," he said suddenly, pushing the papers toward her.

He did not say if she was to read it or not—for all she knew it might have been an explanation for his state of distraction—but she took it up and began to read.

It was a long letter running to several pages, precise in the extreme, from the hand through the observations, which were few but stated with a vivid clarity. The letter retold the tale of Erasmus and the others who had gone down into the cave and dealt at length with a chamber they had discovered—Landor's chamber, they called it—and the escape of a woman named Anna with the seed of the king's blood.

A few days earlier the countess would not have understood, but now, as a somewhat-unwilling initiate in the seed, she realized this was a cause of the greatest concern.

Eldrich lifted his wineglass while she read, abandoning all pretense of eating. Walky came in and stood by silently, as though sensing his master's need.

"What does it mean?" the countess asked at last, mystified by what she had read. "Who was Landor, and why did he leave seed buried far beneath the surface?"

Eldrich looked like a man so overwhelmed that he was about to take refuge in wine. She could not imagine the mage acting in this manner. The mage!

"Landor . . ." Eldrich said, staring out into the descending darkness. "Landor was among the first—he *was* the first. First and most skilled of the mages who journeyed to Farrland from beyond. Why did he leave seed? For those who wished to make the journey back from whence they came. I can think of no other reason. But it is difficult to say what Landor might have planned, for he lived so long ago that he has become a myth. Yet it was Landor who found the way—the way by darkness. Landor who led the others, and laid the foundations for the arts in these lands." Eldrich paused, lost for a moment attempting to see into the past. "All of this is of little more than scholarly interest now. This woman, Anna, has the seed— Landor's seed. . . ." He rocked forward in his chair and stared down at the table, unsettling her with the strangeness of his manner. "It is a disaster beyond any I had contemplated," he whispered. "More than a disaster." He shook his head, beginning to raise his hands to his face as though in horror, but he caught himself and stopped.

"Have I been so unworthy, Walky, that I should be punished so?" he asked, not even glancing at his servant.

Walky shifted from one foot to the other, his wrinkled face etched with concern. "It is not a matter of worth, as you well know," Walky said. "It is the seed, sir, it is the arts themselves, struggling to live. They are like a man being suffocated; he will find his greatest strength just before the end." The little man shook his head. "The arts will not pass away without a struggle, sir. We have long known it."

Eldrich said nothing for a moment, then nodded agreement. "No, they will not." It was almost a whisper.

A sudden ferocious howling brought Eldrich half out of his chair—not startled, but alert.

A moment later a servant appeared. He said nothing at all, but Eldrich dropped his napkin on the table and he and Walky quickly followed the man out.

The countess found she could not continue with her meal and went to the double doors that looked out onto the lawn, hoping to see what all the commotion was about. Although she could hear voices, there was not a lantern or light to be seen.

"What has happened now?" she wondered aloud.

The voices faded away and she heard only footsteps crossing the lawn—the servants, not Eldrich, she knew.

Will I walk so silently one day?

Voices rumbled down the hall and into the room, no words discernable. She found herself gravitating toward the door, desperate for some clue as to what went on in this house. Some indication of what might be expected of her.

Quietly, she opened the door a little wider, leaning close, listening. She even dared to peek for a second but could see nothing at the hallway's end. Then, very distinctly, she heard her name; and from a familiar voice, too.

"My word," she whispered, but before she could pull open the door to go out, footsteps sounded, and grew louder. The countess retreated into the room, taking up her wineglass.

Whose voice had she heard? Not Skye's. Erasmus? That seemed most likely.

A moment later the door swung open and Eldrich came in—followed by Kent, of all people. Kent who had warned her to flee.

She knew immediately why the poor man was here: on her behalf. Now what would be done to him?

Eldrich paused, glancing back at the painter, who looked frightened near to collapsing. "Do you know this man?" he said, with more than a little accusation in his voice.

She nodded. "Yes. . . . But Kent, what are you doing here?"

"He is rescuing you, I take it," Eldrich answered. "Somehow he is under the impression that you are not here of your own choosing."

The countess felt near to tears, both from frustration with Kent and fear of what Eldrich might do. Some part of her was touched as well. What a noble fool the painter was, setting off to confront a mage.

Kent looked even more like a boy than usual—a truant, standing before his school master. His fair hair was in disarray, the skin around his eyes tight with fear, eyes bright with hope. Standing near to Eldrich he seemed small, almost fragile. She feared he did not understand the gravity of his situation at all.

"Kent," she said as softly as she could, "your journey has been in vain."

Kent did not respond, but only stared at her, deeply suspicious, blinking back tears, she was sure.

She turned immediately to Eldrich. "What will you do with him?"

Eldrich shrugged, taking up his seat at the table again.

She thought desperately for something to say, something that would save the poor man. "Averil Kent is an artist of surpassing abilities, Lord Eldrich. Can you not release him? He'll promise to interfere no more. Won't you, Kent?" she said looking at the painter, imploring him with her eyes to agree.

As she went to speak to Eldrich again, he looked away, and she stopped on the first syllable.

Finally Eldrich looked over at Kent. "Do you paint?" he asked, taking the countess completely off guard.

Kent nodded.

"Paint portraits of Lady Chilton and myself, and if I judge them worthy, I will release you." He nodded to Walky, who came forward to lead Kent away.

"But he is not a portraitist," she said, "and does he even have his painting box with him?" She looked back at Kent who shook his head.

"Everything he needs can be found here. Apparently much of the 'art' that graces these walls was painted by some talentless member of the family." He turned to his servant. "Walky," he said, needing to give no more instruction than that.

And Kent was led out, looking like a child-criminal leaving the court—and not to freedom.

The countess turned back to Eldrich, but he was no longer in his chair. She caught a glimpse of his shadow as it slipped silently out onto the dark lawn—the shadow of a wolf.

Despite the hour, Walky arrived soon after the countess' summons. He looked a bit concerned as he came through the door.

"Is something wrong, m'lady?" he asked, persisting in his use of the ancient form of address.

"No, nothing, but I wish to speak to Kent. Is that possible?"

"It would not be wise, m'lady," he said shaking his head.

"I see. But would it be forbidden?"

"Only Lord Eldrich could say, m'lady."

The countess glowered at him for a second, but could not keep it up. The little man looked so genuinely sorry that he couldn't give her the answer she desired.

"Will he be all right?" she asked very quietly.

"All right, m'lady?"

"Yes, will Eldrich . . . harm him? Kent did not mean to interfere. It was only concern for my welfare that brought him here. Eldrich can hardly blame him for that."

Walky knit his brows together and looked at her, tilting his head a little. "But he is the painter, Lady Chilton. The first good sign we have had in days. I hardly think he will be harmed. No, my master will reward him—or so I should think."

The countess hardly knew what to say. " 'He is the painter'? Whatever do you mean?"

Walky shrugged. "Lord Eldrich has been awaiting the painter—and he has finally appeared. Do not be afraid for Mr. Kent. No, there are other matters far more worthy of our concern." And with that he bowed and let himself out.

Chapter Thirteen

I T was absurd to even contemplate sleep, so Sir John sat at his
window, open to the night, and stared out at the shadowed
wood, and beyond it the hills silhouetted against the stars.

Insects and frogs filled the night with their peculiar love songs,
and a nightingale held forth periodically, the sound like bells tumbling
down a distant waterfall.

A family of deer came out onto the lawn to crop the soft grasses,
and a pair of fawns gamboled awkwardly about the doe.

"What will he do with me?" Sir John wondered. He pushed the
window wide, a breath of soft air cooling his face. When imagining
the course of his life, the young John Dalrymple had never contemplated an occurrence such as this—held captive by a mage.

"Perhaps you are merely a guest," he suggested, as though he
spoke to another—a guest who could not leave, however; not even
his room.

Would he see the countess again? The thought of an ally in this
place was very appealing. If he could speak with her, he could find
out if Kent's fears were true, that she was here against her will—
assuming she knew her own heart in this matter. But it would be

good to know so that he might communicate this to Kent if he met the man again—which seemed very likely given recent history.

Suddenly the deer started on the lawn, held utterly still, then bounded off into the wood, passing quickly into silence. Kent wondered what could have caused this action, but then he saw—a wolf padded quickly across the grass, head down, neck extended. Sir John felt his pulse quicken at the sight.

What a ferocious beast, he thought.

And then there was a sudden crashing in the underbrush, and the branches of a tree began to sway. The wolf released a terrible howl, and leaped at the trunk, twisting as it returned to the earth where it stared up into the branches, howling pitilessly.

Sir John almost reached to stop up his ears when a door banged open and men erupted onto the lawn. They kept their distance from the wolf, speaking in hushed tones, and then fell silent. Even the wolf ceased its howling, though it held its position, trembling with anticipation.

A shadow appeared among the servants, and Eldrich spoke to the beast, though Sir John did not know the words. The wolf suddenly slunk away growling and muttering, casting glances back over its shoulder at whatever had been treed.

Eldrich spoke again, this time in Farr, adding a string of foreign syllables. The branches of the tree began to shake and sway. A moment later a figure appeared in the poor light of the lawn, and even though it was barely more than a shadow, Sir John knew immediately who it must be—poor, foolish Kent.

Sir John did not know how much time had passed since Eldrich had discovered Kent, but certainly time enough for any kind of revenge, and Sir John had imagined several varieties, all of them unspeakable. Twice he had gone to the door, even placed his fingers upon the handle, but the futility of it coupled with Walky's warning kept him in his room. The thought of that wolf skulking the halls was enough to suppress any noble act Sir John might contemplate.

He returned to his view of the starlit garden, where he could discern very little but could imagine a great deal. What would the mage do to Kent? At least it gave him something else to consider while he waited, though the question had not changed but for the name.

What would he do to Sir John?

All the while his eyes played tricks on him. He thought he saw the wolf again, and then the deer, but could be sure of neither. Was that the countess crossing through the shadow of the trees? He listened, trying to parse the sounds of the night, searching for those that were human. A pale edge of light appeared, like the glitter of moonlight on a railing. This line extended and bent suddenly, tracing thirty degrees of arc, then bent in and crossed itself. This went on for some minutes until a figure of some complexity glowed on the lawn.

Moonlight on silver, or low flames of mercury. A shadow could be discerned now, moving slowly around the pattern. A shadow Sir John had encountered before. *Eldrich.*

Sir John had crouched down below his windows so that he could just see over the sill, wondering if Eldrich knew he watched. The arts were forbidden to men, after all.

Perhaps he does not care what I see because my use is done, Sir John thought.

A second shadow appeared, not so dark as the first. *Kent*, Sir John wondered, but then the person stepped into the pattern of silver light and shed her shadow like a robe. A raven-haired woman, as pale as the moon, for she wore not a stitch of clothing.

Sir John heard his breath indrawn. The Countess of Chilton; it could be no other. Despite his fear he felt a surge of sudden desire.

The musical voice of Eldrich began to chant, and silver characters appeared in the air briefly only to flare into nonexistence. The pattern grew in brightness, rising up until the countess appeared to stand in the center of an intricate silver cage. The musical chanting continued. It echoed in Sir John's mind, as disturbing as the event he witnessed, yet he could not tear his eyes away.

Suddenly the silver cage shattered, a sound like breaking crystal, and though not loud, painful to the ears. A shadow lay on the lawn, whimpering, Sir John was sure. The darker shadow of Eldrich bent down to bear the countess up, carrying her toward the house.

Sir John continued to stare at the dark lawn, the pattern burned into his brain. What had he seen, and why had it left him with such a feeling of horror—and why did this night linger so?

Servants arrived an hour after dawn, bearing hot water and the other articles for Sir John's toilet. He had barely finished dressing when a knock sounded on the door.

"Yes?"

The door opened a crack, and the small man of the previous night looked in.

"Ah, Walky, is it?"

"Yes, Walky. Lord Eldrich will see you now."

Sir John froze for a second, then nodded. He thought a condemned man might be allowed a final meal, but apparently such traditions meant little to a mage.

He followed Walky down the stairs, slightly bolstered by the morning light streaming in the windows, but only slightly. Fear was still tangible. He felt himself sweating, though it was not overly warm, and that sweat seemed to have an odd, sickly-sweet odor.

They came to a set of doors which Walky opened just enough to allow a man to pass, and nodded Sir John through, his countenance maddeningly neutral.

Inside he found a large, bright room, but Sir John noticed nothing more, for his gaze fell immediately upon Lord Eldrich, who sat at a table bent over a sheaf of papers, sipping coffee.

Sir John stood utterly still, trying to catch his breath, wondering if he could hide any of his fear at all. Eldrich languidly turned a page, and continued as though Sir John were not there. The small box that Bryce had him deliver sat upon the table, closed, its contents still a secret. Despite the fact that it bore no lock, Sir John had not dared to open it.

"Few have set eyes upon a living mage," Eldrich said without looking up, the musicality of his voice strangely repellent now.

What was he to answer? That he was honored?

Eldrich continued reading. "And fewer still remember it after the fact."

The mage looked up suddenly and set his cup down, patting his mouth with a square of yellow linen. "I have need of the cooperation of the Farr government—meaning this man Moncrief, I assume."

Sir John nodded.

"Bryce explained what is to be done?" He raised an eyebrow, not without humor.

"Yes. This young woman who goes by the name of Anna Fielding must be found."

Eldrich nodded. "Though surely she will be using some other name now. To aid in this endeavor Bryce will send you an officer who actually met her, though he did not recall it immediately. No matter. She can be identified by him. I am most concerned that she not take ship for the island of Farrow. Is that clear. . . ? Good." He reached forward and picked up something from the table. "You will deliver this to Moncrief and await his response—which, unless the man is a complete fool, will be immediate and favorable. He is not a complete fool, is he?"

"By no means."

Eldrich sat back in his chair, clasped his hands, and eyed Sir John. "Bryce tells me you are a particularly valuable and astute servant, Sir John, and Bryce is sparing with his praise. It occasionally serves me to have gentlemen in places in society who are aware of whom they serve and might even have some small knowledge of my larger purpose. You are such a man, Sir John."

Sir John bowed his head, partly to hide his own shock. "I—I am honored."

"No, you are dismayed, but that is no matter. I trust you will serve me with utter commitment and unwavering loyalty. Do you know what that means, Sir John?"

"I think I do."

"I am not talking about the mere definition of the terms, you realize."

Sir John nodded, confused.

Eldrich stared at him a moment, letting the silence extend until it seemed it must fail. "Loyalty unto death, Sir John."

Chapter Fourteen

"I didn't like the sound of it. I said, 'Any man who wants to avoid the road returning to the lowlands is hardly to be trusted.' ' 'Tis not a man,' my brother said, 'but a woman, and a pretty one, too.' " The guide patted the neck of his sturdy mount, blinking rapidly.

"Did he tell you her name or describe her?" Erasmus asked.

"He said only that it was a woman and that she would pay him handsomely."

Erasmus glanced at Clarendon who nodded.

"Do you know the way they traveled?" Erasmus asked.

The man nodded.

"Can you take us?"

"I was going to set out in three days anyway. I thought Garrick to be back yesterday. He hadn't intended to take her all the way, but only through the most difficult sections." He shrugged. "It is likely that he's taken her farther than he first agreed. The paths through the hills aren't so clear as a lowlander might wish."

"We need to find this woman—immediately. Can we engage you to take us?" Clarendon looked very intent. "But we need to leave today."

"That'd be hard, sir," the youth said. He could not have been more than sixteen.

"Hardship is to be expected," Clarendon said quickly, reaching into his pocket and finding three gold coins. "Would this hasten matters?"

The boy's mouth dropped open briefly. "Aye. But even so, it will be late in the afternoon."

"There will be five of us," Clarendon said. "I have my own horses and outfit."

"Five!" The lad was dismayed.

"Don't despair," Clarendon said, taking the boy by the arm. "We will all pitch in, as will my staff. Come along. We'll begin by seeing Mr. Tanner about horses. . . ."

They went single file through the highlands, along the narrow paths and hidden ways known only to huntsmen and the falconers who sought nests to rob in the high cliffs. Following the roll of the hills they passed through various bands of vegetation: On the ridges wind-sculpted pines, stunted and sparse, grew out of rock painted with orange-and-green lichen; in the valleys they found spring flowers and lush, deciduous trees. Along certain streams grew a golden-leafed willow found only in the hills—there could not have been a thousand of them in all the world.

Pryor, their guide, stopped to survey the path again, as he had been doing off and on all day. Erasmus was surprised to find that paths in the hills were not as rare as he'd imagined. They had even passed through two small settlements—large family holdings, he'd gathered, but still unexpected. No one had seen Anna or Pryor's brother, which was not surprising. Anna had a lifetime's experience hiding herself—if it was Anna they were following.

But who else could it be? A woman returning to the lowlands secretly. Rose had argued that only two should follow their guide into the hills, the others staying behind to search elsewhere. But it soon became clear that Rose was determined to take this route, which made the others suspicious. Clearly the priest was convinced this was Anna, though no one could guess why he was so certain.

Kehler worried that they were following a false trail—after all, the guide, Garrick, had conveniently told his brother where he was going. But then, the meeting with his brother had been acciden-tal—if one believed in accidents.

Pryor searched among the bushes beside the trail, bending low to the ground, examining the branches. From among the foliage he lifted his hand, teasing out something invisible—then a glint of red-gold twined in his fingers and trailed in the breeze.

Erasmus dropped to the ground and took the strand of hair, holding it up to the light.

He showed it to the others who all nodded—not even Rose showing any elation.

"Well, we know we're not being misled," Kehler said. "Or, at least, it's very unlikely."

Pryor took the reins of his horse and led them on, eyes scanning the ground. When he was certain which path had been taken, he mounted again, and they traveled more swiftly along the valley floor, the new leaves fluttering nervously in the breeze.

Anna stared at the hand-drawn map again, looked up at the peaks around her, then back to the map. Nothing was where it should have been. She was lost. From her breeches she produced a pocket chronometer and used it, with the position of the sun, to determine south. Unquestionably this valley was running the wrong way. She had mistaken the pass, and now wasn't sure what to do. Retrace her steps and hope to find the right way, or carry on and see where this led? Her map didn't extend far enough to tell her what lay ahead. The chances of becoming even more disoriented were great.

"Chuff?" her familiar said, the syllable sounding distinctly inter-rogative.

"Back," she decided. "We must go back."

She checked her string of horses, mounted, and crossed over the small creek three times, muttering an enchantment as she went. On her first crossing she tossed the wing bone of a hawk into the stream; on the second, a coal black stone; on the third she let a feather fall. A feather from her familiar. It sailed off on the current, fluttering on the ripples, glinting in the sunlight.

At least she would lay down a false trail and confuse anyone who tried to follow, especially by unnatural means. Halsey had always said that apparent lost efforts must be put to use whenever possible.

Thoughts of the others caused her to bend over in her saddle, as though she were in actual pain. Grief had its grip on her, she knew. She caught Chuff looking at her oddly at times—that intelligent glittering eye. For a beast with a vocabulary of a single word it managed astonishing shadings in its speech, and one of those was concern. She was hearing this tone too often, now.

One could hardly be cheerful after what I've been through, she thought. But still, it was a danger. Grief led to brooding, and brooding took her focus away from the matter at hand: survival.

Eldrich would be looking for her, and for the first time a mage had a starting point; he knew where she had come from. She was in more danger now than she had ever been—even escaping the cave.

He will learn that I have seed.

Did the mage know what lay in the cavern? Somehow she suspected he did not. He would never have sealed the chamber off if he'd known what lay within. But once he learned, Eldrich would be desperate to find her. More than desperate.

"But where would he think I have gone?" she asked aloud, for that was the game. Each trying to outguess the other. Does he know that I am alone? Did Halsey tell him there were no others?

She traveled, lost in both thought and place, until she passed a small pool. Here she stopped for a moment, tethering her horses so they could not sully the pool. It was near to sunset. This would be her camp tonight.

She gathered a handful of tiny white blossoms, and then firewood. For a long time she sat by the edge of the pool, thinking, *I am stronger now, my talent deeper. There might be something to see.* Not merely darkness as there had been that night in the house where Halsey died.

The last light in the sky seemed to coalesce into stars on a black field. Anna took a long breath and began the ritual, careful in its preparation. The marks on the ground, the figure that burned in her mind. An eerie ringing—the songs of stars. She stared down into the pool, at the points of light which floated there, and then closed her mind, holding what she had seen.

Pain! Searing pain, as though white-hot iron had been thrust into her brain. She wavered but held her concentration. For an instant she opened her mind, reeling toward the void, then cast the flowers onto the water. She felt herself collapse at the water's edge, like a great bird too exhausted to land softly. She heard herself crying. Nearby Chuff spoke his single word of fear, over and over.

Chapter Fifteen

THE brushes were inferior and the easel not to his liking, but under the circumstances such matters were trivial.

You are painting to save your life, Kent reminded himself.

He looked at the portrait he had begun of Eldrich, feeling more than a little satisfied. He had been allowed to make only one brief sketch of the mage, but the image was unusually distinct in his mind, even for Kent whose visual recall was particularly good. He suspected the arts at work in this were not entirely his own.

He had caught something of the mage's presence, Kent flattered himself to think, for Eldrich seemed to have a still center of power—the calm eye of the storm. The darkly brooding visage had not been so difficult—much could be done with shadow—but even so the eyes were not quite as they should be. How did one portray a gaze that penetrated even the walls of time? The thick black hair and dark brows could not have been more in character for a mage—as though an actor had chosen them.

"Yes," Kent said softly, "you may have imprisoned me, Lord Eldrich, but I have captured something of you as well."

He turned away from the portrait, back to the blank canvas sitting on the easel, and felt the jangle of nervous expectation. The countess was to sit for him, and should arrive at any moment. Of course it was utterly unnecessary that she model, but he did not tell Eldrich that. Kent could recall the countess as clearly as . . . well, there was nothing he could recall as clearly. Closing his eyes, her image came vividly to mind in a hundred poses and varying moods. No, Kent did not require that she sit for him at all. But to see her and speak with her again!

The door clicked and swung open, revealing the countess. She stopped as she closed the door, looking intently at Kent, her manner anything but happy.

"Oh, Kent. Why were you so foolish?"

Kent felt himself look down, his cheeks burning. "I thought . . . I thought the countess had been abducted."

She continued to stare at him unhappily, and then nodded twice. "But as you see, I am here of my own choosing, and you have endangered yourself for naught."

"I didn't know," he said softly and looked up. "But how can you be sure that you have chosen to be here? How do you know that Eldrich has not used his arts to influence you?"

"Because I know, Kent. Trust that this is so." She came across the floor to the chair that had been set out for her, then hesitated as she arranged her skirts to sit. "But should this not be a divan? Yellow with new-world foliage and warblers, wasn't it?"

Kent felt the blood rise into his face, but he nodded, looking down.

"It was a lovely portrait, Kent. Better than I deserved," she said, almost tenderly. "Thank you."

Kent picked up a brush and palette, words suddenly seeming utterly inadequate. He began to paint before looking at his subject.

Every time he did look that way, the countess' soft eyes were upon him. He could not believe what hope he felt each time their eyes met, but there was no joy or pleasure in the countess' look, only anxiety and sadness. Nothing to cause him hope at all.

"What did you think to accomplish, Kent?" the countess asked suddenly.

What indeed? Kent wondered. But he knew the answer—he was not that unaware of his inner workings. He hoped to prove the depth and truth of his feelings. He hoped to prove himself worthy. Even though Eldrich might strike him dead, she would know.

He shook his head. One could not admit something so adolescent. "I hoped to learn the truth of your disappearance—whether you had gone of your own volition or no. Beyond that . . ." He shrugged.

This partial lie was followed by total silence. She did not believe him, he knew.

"You followed Sir John?" she asked, giving up the censorious silence.

"He is unharmed, I hope?" The truth was that Kent had hardly thought of the man since the wolf had treed him.

"To the best of my knowledge, yes."

It was hardly reassurance. How much did the countess know of what went on in this strange household?

"This little man, Walky. Is he the man I saw handing you down from the carriage in Castlebough?"

"I assume so. He is the mage's servant; not a house servant, but servant in the arts."

Kent did not understand what this meant, but he continued to work. The light streaming in the windows illuminated the countess in a way he found particularly maddening. It was almost unfair that beauty should be concentrated to such a degree in one woman. Unfair and baffling. Even as he studied her for the portrait, the truth of her attraction eluded him. What was its source? Could he ever hope to capture it as it had captured him?

"Kent, do you know what has befallen Erasmus?"

"I . . ." The phrasing of the question was distinctly odd. "He had not returned from the cave when I left Castlebough."

She looked down at her hands twisting the corner of her shawl.

"Is there some reason for concern?" Kent asked casually, the memory of the countess and Erasmus coming back—causing anguish and taking his breath away at the same time, as it always did.

"Something the mage said. Perhaps it meant nothing." She realized she had started referring to Eldrich as Walky did—the mage. *One can't help but acknowledge his difference*, she thought.

"What will happen . . . when I finish the portraits?" Kent had begun to ask what would become of her, but felt he had no right to pose such a question.

"I don't know, Kent. I hope Lord Eldrich," she made herself use the title, "will keep his word and release you."

"You say that as if there were some doubt?"

She stared at him intently. "I don't mean to frighten you, Kent, but he is a mage."

Kent nodded. And as such not bound by the mores of men. Unless certain rituals were performed, or so the old tales said. A mage could be bound to his word by the arts, though, if it were true, likely no one alive today would know how it was accomplished.

Rays of sun created a slanting backdrop of pure light to the countess' black curls, and Kent began to paint the sunlight using brighter colors than he would have expected—yellows and near-white. As though he were trying to heighten the contrast between the mood of the countess and the brightness of the spring day—almost a contrast of seasons. It was one of those unforeseen occurrences that invariably filled Kent with delight—a decision made on some other level, surprising for its rightness.

He glanced up and found the countess hanging her head, as though absorbed in some private pain.

"Lady Chilton? Should we pursue this at some other time?"

She straightened up immediately. "No. The mage wants our portraits done with all speed." She tried to smile. "Have I changed my position altogether?"

Kent considered, shook his head, continued to gaze at her a moment more, and then returned to his canvas. It might be true that the countess was here of her own choosing, but he had seen it—profound doubt at this decision. Profound doubt and near-despair.

Chapter Sixteen

"T HE ulna," the mage said softly. "One of the bones of the forearm." Eldrich turned the charred fragment over gently. He had contemplated it for a day, consulting certain texts frequently. "Halsey was more resourceful than I realized," he said to Walky. "Men are so easily underestimated. It is a lesson mages have never learned. And if I do not learn it. . . ?"

The house creaked around them, in the grip of the storm. A wind dropped down the chimney, setting the fire in the hearth fluttering. Eldrich continued to stare at the bone Bryce had sent. It lay in a dusting of black ash upon a square of linen, so fragile that, left to the elements, it would be worn away in hours. Halsey's last remains would vanish on the wind, as Teller's followers had always done.

"Resourceful," Eldrich said, picking up the train of his thought, though not really speaking to the ever-attentive Walky, "but in the end he didn't quite know what he was doing. His knowledge was not complete—fortunately." The mage sat back in his chair, looking up at Walky. "Bring me seed."

The mage ground the seed to powder, breathing in the aroma released when the husks cracked. From a hook above the fire he took

a kettle and poured, steaming water hissing into the ancient cup.
Eldrich felt his nostrils flare—even after all these years—his eyes
closing with pleasure, anticipation.

He watched the slow swirl of liquid as he stirred, the steam
coiling up in the firelight. Into the cup he spilled black cinder scraped
from the bone, watched it float, spinning on the surface, then slowly
soak through, turn slick, and founder. He stirred again, muttering a
line of Darian, and raised the cup to his lips.

"I will know you now."

Dipping a finger into the cup he bent to the floor and outlined his
shadow, whispering the lines of an enchantment, and felt himself
begin to float. He drained the cup and stood, the storm breaking
around him in foam and spray. Yet for all its fury the wind barely
rustled his coat. Eldrich walked across the rolling seas as though
upon a dark, writhing landscape. Pale crests rose up, then toppled,
tumbling to ruin. Far off, bright wires of light shot from cloud to
cloud or flashed deep within the storm. Eldrich turned slowly, surveying the world, feeling the turmoil—his turmoil. From long experience he knew one must accept the reality—not argue it.

All around him was the rumble and hiss of seas as they raced
and plunged to chaos and rose again. A whale's back glided by,
glistening, spume blown off on the wind. A storm petrel skittered
across the surface, a prisoner of the wind.

"Where are you?" Eldrich whispered.

Beneath his feet a knot of kelp slowly rolled to reveal a face;
bone-white blossoms for eyes.

No one he knew, Eldrich thought at first, but then . . . "Halsey?
Have I found you despite all?"

A wave crest tumbled to foam, tearing away strands of the kelp,
bits of the lips and jaw.

The mouth moved. "I have found you," it said.

Eldrich felt himself lift on a crest, foam breaking around his
knees.

"He's come for you, Lord Eldrich. Even now he is near. Nearer
than you know." The face grimaced, the blossoms that were its
eyes fluttering in the gusts.

"Who?"

But another wave fell upon the decaying face, tearing it apart and leaving nothing but a carpet of pulp and detritus spread upon the sea.

"Who has come?" Eldrich said again.

He went on, not really walking but somehow floating above the seas that crumbled and lifted beneath him. The taste of salt and king's blood, the bitter ash of Halsey's death, fresh in his mouth— like blood and iron.

Something dark before him. An enormous leviathan, he thought at first, but a flash of lightning revealed a ship, thrown on its beam ends, foundering in the crashing seas, its crew washed away.

Eldrich stood upon the seas, and watched the great vessel heave up one final time, then in a rush of water and escaping air, it rolled and slipped beneath the surface, into the lightless world below.

For a moment Eldrich remained, his emotions as confused as the sea—horror, and wonder, and fear. There was nothing but visions of death.

Then he realized the top of a mast bobbed in the water, almost vertical, a pennant or scrap of sail fluttering from its tip. He went closer, drawn to see the flag, but a few feet away it became a coat worn by a sailor clinging to the last fragment of ship. A dark, little creature, shadow-eyed and light-limbed, not quite human. It eyed the mage warily, curling back its lips and hissing as Eldrich approached.

The mage hesitated.

A wave swept over the small man, burying him in pale foam— liquid starlight.

The mast top swayed and bobbed as the wave passed, the creature still clinging desperately, its coat torn away. In the eerie light its feet and legs appeared to have fused in shadow.

He bared his teeth at Eldrich again, though no noise was heard. Then, to the mage's amazement, the creature uttered a curse of demons in Darian—the mage tongue.

"What are you?" Eldrich asked.

It only cursed him again, making a quick sign with a hand which was swiftly returned to the moving mast. A third wave broke over the creature, and for a moment Eldrich thought this one would do for it. But again it was there, the mast spinning slowly, gyrating like a top about to topple. And there it clung, its clothing torn away to reveal a dark, glistening skin, like a whale back—an odd shape to its hips and legs, more fish than man.

Suddenly the water erupted all around, wingless birds rolling into the air, only to slip back into the chaotic seas. *Dolphins*, Eldrich realized.

They curled out of the sea at every side, describing their perfect arcs, as numerous as raindrops. The creature on the mast was suddenly alert, chattering in Darian.

Yet another crest broke nearby and swept toward them, dolphins capering in the foam. And in the bright sea foam Eldrich thought he saw a shape—a woman borne by the wave.

The creature cried out as the wave overwhelmed him. Casting free his grip, he leaped into the sea, in among the dolphins and the sprite, if that's what it was.

Once its head broke the surface, searching out Eldrich, and it bared its teeth again, in triumph now. It called out once more in Darian and was lost in the storm—a last slap of its tail upon the broken surface.

She comes not for you, it had called.

A glow, bone-white, broke through the cloud and spread over the shattered sea, chasing wave crests like streaming veils. Eldrich turned to see a bubble moon float up, casting his shadow on the water like a stain upon the spinning world.

Chapter Seventeen

A N unsettling wind, disturbed in its patterns, invaded the Caledon Hills. It swept down slopes, moving the branches of trees like an army of advancing giants.

Horses became skittish, dancing away from the madly swaying branches and forcing their riders to struggle for control. Erasmus felt his own nerves begin to fray, and was surprised to hear Clarendon upbraid Kehler when the younger man's horse shied in front of him.

"There is no profit in this," Clarendon said suddenly, embarrassed by his outburst. "Let us find some shelter from this cursed wind and make a camp."

There were no dissenters to this plan.

As they searched along the valley bottom, lightning splayed toward the eastern horizon—a jagged tear in the dark cloud. A moment later they felt the drumbeat of distant thunder. The initial flash seemed to be a sign, and the sky was shattered over and over.

Their guide, Pryor, in better control of his mount, had ranged ahead and appeared now and then among the trees, searching for a suitable site to make camp. Finally they caught up with him, off his horse, staring at something on the ground.

Erasmus and Clarendon came up next, and saw the dark stain of ashes, the charred remains of logs sticking out like blackened bones.

"Quite a cooking fire," Erasmus said immediately, noting the size.

Pryor nodded, his eyes still fixed on the ashes.

Clarendon dismounted. "This is as likely a spot as any. There is water and we might find some shelter from the wind in that stand of trees. We shall have rain soon enough, and I fear we will have to manage as the beasts do and simply endure it."

The others began dismounting, relieved to be off their nervous mounts. Hayes and Kehler took charge of the horses, glancing over at their guide, who had not moved from the fire pit.

"Pryor. . . ?" Kehler prompted.

The lad stirred, looked up, clearly not sure why he had been disturbed, then realized he shirked his duties and roused himself to help.

Erasmus began to collect firewood, which was in short supply in the immediate vicinity. Returning with a small armload a short time later, Erasmus found Rose crouched down and stirring the caked ashes with a stick, watching a stream of gray carried away on the wind.

A scorched fragment surfaced, like something dredged from the seabed. The priest remained immobile for a second, realization sinking in.

Bone . . .

"Why?" Erasmus whispered.

"To leave no one to tell where she had gone."

"But can a mage not take away a man's memories?"

"Yes, but she is not a mage. Who knows what she can do and cannot do?"

Erasmus' coat billowed around him, fluttering like a sail.

Rose shook his head, dropping his stick and sitting back on his haunches. "It is said an enchantment can be strengthened by blood."

"Not human blood," Erasmus said quickly.

"Yes, human blood, too, though even the mages had strictures against such evil." He nodded at the fire. "If she believed he had to die—"

Erasmus let his armful of wood fall in a clatter about his feet—sticks bleached and bone dry.

Hayes and Kehler finished dragging their tack in under the low sweeping branches of a fir, and left the horses to Pryor. The boy was a willing worker and took seriously his responsibilities as guide, making his earlier lapse seem oddly out of character.

Kehler was about to make his way back to the fire pit, but Hayes motioned for his friend to walk with him. They set off up the draw, the wind suddenly pushing against them with such energy that they leaned their entire weight into it—like soaring birds.

Finding a flat stone in the lee of an outcropping they sat themselves down, and there, beneath the wind, what seemed like quiet descended. Now that he had his friend alone, Hayes didn't know how to begin. Kehler waited, appearing to listen to the wind, to gauge the growing darkness. In the distance the lightning continued unabated, branching like veins of pure, instantaneous light—then gone.

"You don't need to say it, Hayes," Kehler said softly, his words all but buried beneath a roll of thunder. "If I thought for a moment that all our endeavours would lead to—" His voice caught and in the gathering dark Hayes could see him shake his head sadly. "I only thought we would make a great discovery. That we would write a book that everyone would want to read and that we should make a tremendous success of it all." He turned to Hayes, his voice very low. "And I thought you would escape your poverty, Hayes. That is what I hoped. Never for a moment did I think it would come to this, and that in the end we would have nothing to show for it." He hung his head. "If only our notes had not been ruined. . . ."

Hayes was a little taken aback. He had not for a moment intended to accuse his friend of . . . of anything. "No sense regretting that," Hayes said as warmly as he could. "Eldrich would never allow us to publish our story anyway. It was a great adventure, Kehler, but no one beyond our small band will likely ever know of it. Mages have ways of insuring silence. Poor Doctor Ripke proved that."

"Not quite. In the end he spoke to me. Remember? But I know what you're saying." A peal of thunder silenced them a moment. "I fear that, rather than improving your circumstances, I have made them appreciably worse, Hayes."

"Worse?" Hayes regarded his dejected friend. Poor Kehler was not doing well. "They could hardly have been worse. But no, Kehler, rather than making matters worse, all that we have seen and done has made them better. You see, I feel . . . I don't quite know how to explain . . . I feel more whole, somehow. I don't know what it is. . . . Perhaps seeing the wonders we have seen has altered my perspective on the world. The concerns of the educated classes seem suddenly terribly foolish and petty, and as a result my fall in society seems rather insignificant." He smiled, though not with joy. "In some way, I am the better for what has happened. Do you see? My circumstances are not improved, but *I* am. If we survive, I shall thank you for it, Kehler. I shall thank you, despite all."

Kehler gazed at his friend through the murk, as though wondering if he jested or perhaps had lost his reason altogether.

Hayes thought poor Kehler did not look bettered by their adventure. The young scholar seemed reduced somehow. It was not just that he had lost weight and his bones and joints had grown more prominent—but he seemed smaller, shrunken. Shrunken, the way old men appeared shrunken. The skin on Kehler's face had lost its youthful luster, and the area around his eyes darkened as though he'd been bruised. If Hayes had not known better, he would have guessed his friend to be seriously ill. Fortunately Kehler's energies had not failed, and he remained almost as wiry and nimble as ever.

"You did not bring me out here to blame me for our ruin?" Kehler said, somewhat surprised. "To excoriate me for leading you into this. . . ."

"No, anything but. In fact, riding through these hills in silence has brought a kind of clarity to my mind. I've been mulling over everything that's happened these past months—the recent weeks most prominently. When you look at all the events clearly, you realize how truly odd some of the coincidences were. The fact that the family of Erasmus Flattery, the man who served Eldrich, were my neighbors, and that I should have found him at the brothel—where I was taken by sheer chance, or so one would assume."

Hayes could barely make out his friend in the growing darkness, except when lightning flashed and illuminated his face in a shockingly unnatural blue-white.

"Yes, it is very odd," Kehler said, sounding both relieved and tired, "but we have said as much before. Even Erasmus has mentioned it. Clarendon has said several times that he does not believe in coincidence, and I am coming to agree with him."

Hayes nodded. "Yes, Clarendon." He took a long breath and plunged on. "I have been mulling over the events that led us to this pass and have begun to realize that I know why *we* are here; Skye set us off on this quest which eventually led down into the cave where we hoped to make our names, to say nothing of monetary considerations. Erasmus is here because he has always been involved—as the child who lived in the house of Eldrich and the man the mage hoped might draw out the Tellerites. Rose is here because of his church and their determination that no one gain the arts now that the time of mages wanes. And that leaves Clarendon. Curiosity is his avowed reason. He led Erasmus down into the cave hoping to learn what Baumgere sought."

"Yes, but he is here now because Eldrich has commanded it," Kehler said, involving himself readily in the dialogue which seemed a confirmation of their friendship, somehow—the cause in which they both believed.

Hayes nodded his agreement. "So it would appear, but he displays a determination that no one but Rose seems able to conjure up. I have begun to think that Clarendon's purpose is something else, certainly something more than he claims. We both know how difficult it was to journey down into the cave, how frightening it was at times, how dangerous. Curiosity, even strong curiosity, would hardly be enough to make a man take such risks."

"Well, I don't know about that, Hayes. We were largely driven by curiosity."

"And the desire to make our names and perhaps a tidy profit." Hayes smiled. "We also have, according to Erasmus, 'the impetuosity of youth,' which Randall cannot claim. But look at how Clarendon proceeds now. He is a man with purpose. I don't quite know what the purpose is, but he does not seem to have the ambivalence toward this task that we feel. He may have begun by protesting and proclaiming his principles and opposition to Eldrich, yet I see little evidence of this now."

Kehler tilted his head to one side, thinking. "It seems to me to be rather a thin argument, Hayes. What is it you think he seeks?"

Yes, what?

"I confess, I don't know. But consider our first evening at Clarendon's house. Do you remember? He told us his personal history almost immediately, as though he could not wait. Is that not odd for a gentleman? We were only acquaintances of a few hours, after all. It was as though he had to tell the story quickly, as if by doing so he might forestall any questions. As though he did not want us to start wondering. Clarendon is so genuine and has led such a difficult life, or so he tells it, that who would question him?"

"I was rather touched by the trust he exhibited, telling his history to strangers," Kehler protested.

"As was I, but think of it. We have hardly thought to question his motives since. However, Teller left more than one band of followers behind, each unaware of the other."

"Now, Hayes," his friend protested, "this is not mental clarity but overactive imagination!"

Hayes felt blood rise in his face, partly from embarrassment. Was he grasping at straws? "Really? The man has a beast that will hardly leave his side—a wolfhound, yet. And what is the familiar of our last living mage but a wolf? It is an odd coincidence, and Clarendon does not believe in coincidence, I might remind you."

Kehler shook his head, almost smiling, but a flash revealed that the smile would not hold and dissolved into troubled shadows. "Do you really think he is a follower of Teller?" he asked, lowering his voice.

"Well, I don't know. It isn't very likely, I suppose. I only meant to point out that I don't believe we know why Clarendon is here. There is more to his story than he has told, or so I believe. He is a mystery masquerading as a tale of hardship and betrayal—an excellent ploy to gain our sympathy and trust—but there is a mystery there, all the same."

Kehler looked up at his friend, the doubt almost visible through the darkness. "If what you say is true, is he a danger to us, do you think?"

"Randall? No, I cannot believe that. Certainly, he seems to bear us no malice. I . . . It is only a question of his purpose, Kehler. Why did he attach himself to us, and why does he pursue Anna with such determination?"

Kehler leaned back against the rock. "Perhaps we should speak to Erasmus about this," Kehler said after a moment, which was what Hayes had hoped to hear.

"If you think we should . . ." Hayes said.

They sat in silence, watching the lightning-shattered sky, and then Kehler turned to his friend.

"I know you have tried to make me feel less responsible, Hayes, but I have not forgotten that it was my impetuosity that got us into this situation. I swayed you with hopes of wealth, even though your common sense told you not to become involved. No, what I am saying is true. You would never be here but for me promising you a way out of poverty, though in truth I had not the slightest reason to believe we would find anything of value in the cavern." He paused, faltering. "It was treacherous of me to promise you profit. It was worse than treacherous. I was lying, Hayes. Lying. And now we are involved with Eldrich. I don't know how you can bear the sight of me. Certainly no one has ever done you a worse turn. Flames, Hayes, but you should hate me. Hate me utterly."

There was the merest second of silence wherein Kehler looked down at the ground, and then he jumped up and hurried off, shaking his head. Hayes watched him go, dumbfounded by this outburst. Perhaps he *should* despise Kehler. Perhaps he should blame him for all that had happened. But Hayes could not. He really felt that what he had said was true. Samual Hayes had found himself through adversity—though it appeared the same claim could not be made for Fenwick Kehler.

They had found an overhanging rock that provided some shelter, though the wind whipped about to all points of the compass and even occasionally seemed to blow directly down so there was no escaping the elements entirely.

The storm was still dry, the dark clouds passing overhead ominously, holding back their rain as though harboring it for a final onslaught. Once they had cooked, they let the fire burn down so that they would not be subject to its smoke, which in these conditions could not be escaped for more than a moment by shifting upwind. The darkness was near total, except for the flicker of distant lightning, which lit their faces in quick, ghostly flashes.

"You are quiet this evening, Pryor," Clarendon said. "Have you nothing to tell us of this area of the hills?"

Pryor looked up, his face flickering into being. Etched with sadness, Hayes thought. "It is this place," the boy said. "I find it . . . I haven't the words."

In the next flicker of light Hayes thought he saw Rose and Erasmus look at each other solemnly.

Pryor roused himself and with some difficulty lit a lamp, heading off into the darkness to see to the horses, though Hayes thought he had really gone to be alone.

"What ails him, do you think?" Kehler asked.

A gust of wind beat down upon the trees, which creaked and complained. When the gust was done, it seemed to have carried off any answer to the question, for no one spoke.

Hayes had rolled himself in a blanket and sat with his back to the rock. If not for the wind and the branches of lightning he could have believed himself back in the cave, huddled against hard stone in the overwhelming darkness.

Suddenly Clarendon pulled aside his own sleeping rug and stood up, his movements oddly jerky in the intermittent lightning. "Someone should see to Pryor," the small man said, concern in his tone.

Kehler rose as well. "I'll come with you, Randall. It is too miserable a night to go off alone."

The two of them picked their way down the few feet of rock and disappeared among the swaying trees.

They sat for some time, and then Hayes leaned closer to Erasmus so that he might be heard above the wind. "Tell me, Erasmus, why do you think Randall involved himself in this endeavor in the first place?"

Erasmus turned toward him, drawing his head back as though wondering what had led Hayes to this question, but then he nodded. "I have wondered the same thing more than once. Something more than we have been told, I think—as do you, I collect?"

Hayes nodded. "Yes. Not that I fear his intentions . . . I think there is a story he has not told, but then we have not all taken our turn to relate our tale." He glanced at Deacon Rose, remembering how the priest had avoided telling his own story while they lay trapped in the chamber—telling of the destruction of the Tellerites by the mages instead.

Rose looked back at him. "I am gratified that others have come to have doubts about our friend Clarendon," the priest said.

"I do not doubt Randall Clarendon," Hayes heard himself say, "but only wonder if we have heard all of his story." As soon as Deacon Rose voiced suspicions of Clarendon, Hayes found himself defending the man. After all, had not Clarendon been proven right about the priest at every turn? Deacon Rose was not to be trusted.

In the next flicker of light Hayes saw the priest smiling. "If I criticized a demon, you would rush to his defense," Rose said.

"Randall's done no one harm that I'm aware of," Hayes said firmly.

"Let us not argue again amongst ourselves," Erasmus interrupted, his voice almost as deep as the drumming thunder. Hayes could see his face in the flickering light—like his neighbors in Paradise Street—flickering into being, then gone. "A man's past is not always so easily revealed to strangers, and despite any liberties with the facts, I think you will find that there was truth in Randall's story—the pain was certainly no exaggeration. Men often have good reason to keep their pasts from others. Let us judge Randall by his actions. By that standard he has earned the respect of us all. Let him paint his past in any shades he might wish, and I, for one, will bless him for it."

The lightning flashed again, and all of them started, for a figure stood at the edge of the firelight—a grimly sad Clarendon staring at them, his pain obvious.

"It is the curse of my difference," Clarendon said as the thunder rolled to silence. "I shall never be free of it."

Suddenly they heard a call above the sounds of the passing storm. Each of them became still, straining to hear, for it was not the first time that they thought they had heard a voice in the wind. Then Kehler appeared in a series of flashes, moving jerkily toward them.

"The horses! They're gone," he called out, and everyone was up, stumbling through the bowing trees.

A parted rope was all they could find of their mounts, scattered by the storm like so many leaves. Nor could they immediately find Pryor.

"He must be searching for the horses," Erasmus yelled above the thunder.

"Madness!" Hayes said. "We won't find them now until daylight."

"He will not likely come to harm this night," Erasmus said, "but someone will surely get lost if we go searching for him. Best we keep to our shelter until there is light."

"We cannot be lost between here and the cliff," Kehler said. "Let us separate just enough to comb back through the trees. The horses might not have gone far."

They split up and made their way back toward the shelter, finding their way by the flashes of lightning that drove back the darkness every few seconds.

Erasmus walked through the center of their line, and after a few moments emerged into the small clearing where the stream flowed. Here the lightning revealed two crouching figures. Erasmus hurried forward, sure that someone had fallen and been injured—easy enough to do in this alternating light and darkness.

As he came a little closer, Erasmus realized it was Deacon Rose bending down with his hand upon someone's shoulder—Hayes, he thought, but then realized it was their guide, Pryor.

Erasmus was brought up sharp. A flash revealed the face of the young man, contorted in pain, streaked with rain—yet it was not raining.

He knows, Erasmus thought. The poor boy. That is his brother's pyre.

And then the rain came, driving down upon them in thimble-sized drops. The little, burbling stream rose instantly into a torrent, swelling beyond its banks until it flooded across the fire pit, carrying the ashes and scattering them like memories.

Chapter Eighteen

M ONCRIEF received the letter from his secretary, a grimly serious man who had suffered Moncrief's employ for some twenty years. The King's Man looked disdainfully at the envelope, which was clearly not part of the day's post.

"From Sir John Dalrymple, sir. He . . . Sir John is waiting upon your reply."

"He came with a letter demanding instant reply? I should make him wait the entire day."

"He did say it was urgent, sir."

Moncrief rolled his eyes. "I'm sure he did. Send Sir John home, and accept no argument. Thank you, Horton."

Moncrief took the envelope, glancing at his name on the front written in an unfamiliar hand. It bore no title or honorific, merely Sutton Abelard, as though he were a commoner, a man of no consequence. He felt his anger well up. Sir John was proving to be more than an annoyance.

He slit the envelope quickly, and opened the letter.

Sir:
You will place all the resources in your power at the disposal of

*Sir John Dalrymple beginning immediately and until such time
as Sir John releases them. If I suspect for even a moment that
you have not complied in every way with this order, you shall
wish you had not been born into this life.*

There was no signature.

Moncrief felt such heat rise into his face that he could hardly
speak. "What kind of joke is this?" he spluttered. "Has Dalrymple
gone mad?"

He read the letter again, as though unable to believe that anyone
could send such a missive to him. As he read, his hand began to
shake with anger, and then, without warning, the paper burst into
a ball of flame, burning his hands, the light paining his eyes.

He dropped the letter, stumbling away, blinded for the moment.

"*Horton!*" he called, thinking that the papers on his desk would
catch and the whole building go.

The secretary burst into the room at the tone of his master's
summons.

"Lord Moncrief? Are you unwell?"

Moncrief waved his burned hand at the desk. "Put it out!"

"Sir?"

The bewilderment in the man's voice brought Moncrief up
short. He opened his eyes, the white flame still burned into his vision. But there was no fire. He stood mystified for a moment and
then crossed to his desk. The letter was gone, and the envelope as
well. He examined his hands.

"They are not burned?" he asked, showing them to Horton.

"No, sir."

"Did I fall asleep? Was it a dream?"

"What, sir?" His secretary looked very concerned, as though his
employer were babbling.

"Did you bring me a letter from Sir John just a moment ago?"

"You know I did, sir."

Moncrief looked at the desk, and then at the floor beneath it.

"Have you lost it?"

The truth came to him, and he put out a hand to steady himself.
The arts of the mages—of the mage. *Eldrich*. He actually felt the
blood drain from his face. Quickly he sat down.

"Sir?"

"I must have fallen asleep." He took a long breath. "Very odd dream." He tried to smile reassuringly but failed utterly. "That will be all, Horton."

"If you're sure, sir," Horton said, clearly not ready to go.

"I'm sure."

Horton nodded and backed up a pace, examining Moncrief as though he might just call a physician anyway. Then he turned to go.

"Horton?" Moncrief said as the man reached the door. "Is Sir John still waiting?"

The servant shook his head.

"Have my carriage ready, I shall be going out for a while."

"Immediately, sir."

Sir John sat at his desk, unable to concentrate to even the slightest degree. There were a dozen reports staring at him, unread all the days he had been in Castlebough. He turned and looked out the window into the common across the street. How did one carry on the normal routine after the experience he'd just had? And now Moncrief was being most difficult. What if he did not bother to read the letter at all? Eldrich would not be pleased.

"Flames," he said quietly.

A knock startled him, and his secretary's face appeared in the open door. "Lord Moncrief, Sir John."

"Here? Now?"

"This minute, sir. He says it is most urgent."

Sir John had an urge to make the man wait but had no time for such pettiness. The door was left ajar; a moment later it swung gently back, and Moncrief stepped around it rather gingerly. He still wore his cape, hat and cane clutched in his hands.

Sir John had never seen the man look so pale, as though he were very ill. The King's Man stood there for a moment saying nothing, gazing at Sir John, his look neither malevolent nor defiant. The predatory Moncrief, with his beaked nose and eyes set too close together—the pinched look of disapproval—he appeared cowed! Sir

John could hardly believe what he saw. Moncrief looked cowed! Moncrief! What was in that letter?

"I did not realize," the King's Man said at last, his voice very small. "I had no way of knowing. You need not be concerned . . . I . . . Pray, let there be peace between us, Sir John. Think of me as your friend, your ally in all things. Ask whatever you will of me. I am your servant in this matter."

Sir John nodded, not so far gone that he could not enjoy this moment. He smiled rather malevolently at the King's Man.

"We . . ." Sir John began, but then changed his mind. "*I* am looking for a young woman. A dangerous young woman. She has recently been using the name Anna Fielding. A captain of His Majesty's navy will arrive posthaste. He can identify her." Sir John held out a piece of paper upon which the woman's description had been written. He waited until Moncrief realized that he must cross the room to take it. "It is imperative that she not take ship, especially for the island of Farrow. Is that clear?"

Moncrief nodded, perhaps a little surprised by the request. He stood there like a minion, unsure if he was to be invited to sit or if he'd been released.

"I shall put the agents of the Admiralty to work this night. The pleasures of the day to you, Sir John," Moncrief said, bobbing his head and raising his cane slightly in salute. He backed out the door, closing it quietly behind him.

Sir John went to the window and watched Moncrief scurry into his carriage. Word of this unprecedented visit to Sir John would get about immediately. It was almost worth a life's servitude to the mage just to have had that experience. Moncrief currying favor—as he likely did with no one but the King. He heard himself laugh.

What had Eldrich written? Whatever it was it had frightened Moncrief like nothing else. And why did Moncrief believe it? Certainly anyone could have written the letter and signed Eldrich's name, though only a complete fool would do so, for if Eldrich learned of it the man would suffer. Sir John was not quite sure what, but one did not anger the mage. Or fail him.

Chapter Nineteen

A VAPOR wraith streamed up from the cup, fixed in the eye by a flash of lightning. Anna sipped the elixir made from king's blood, her hand trembling perceptibly.

Wind gusted down the slope and flattened her fire, spreading the tongues of flame so that they wavered but could not speak. A dry gale off the sea, and on the distant edge of the world a lightning storm the likes of which she had never seen.

The smell of king's blood was familiar to her now and the taste. Her body reacted to it with a kind of hunger, even as her mind felt growing revulsion. There were precautions she would have to take soon, for the seed had other effects—none of them desirable—and one readily became habituated.

She closed her eyes and sipped again, the lightning still thrown against her retinae. The liquid ran warm into her center, entered the blood, and flowed outward, invading the rest of her body—or so she imagined. Blessedly, the elixir blunted the sharp edge of pain that cut into her brain—the hangover from augury. She pulled her cloak close around her, sinking back into the cedar boughs she'd cut for comfort.

What did the vision mean?

Men pursued her, a group of them: Erasmus and the others from the cave, she was sure. But there had been one among them who was only a shadow. Was it Eldrich? Eldrich seeking her in the hills? Mages commonly used minions for such tasks. Or was this a measure of how desperate Eldrich was? Of how badly he wanted Landor's seed and the words written in the chamber.

The meaning was clear. Somehow they had discovered that she had not died in the cave even though Halsey had sacrificed himself and she had taken a life so that this knowledge would never surface. A life for nothing.

"They come after us," she said to her familiar which hunkered down on a branch nearby.

No response. He did not like this storm and appeared to be sulking, pulling his head back into his shoulders, fluffing his feathers. He rode his wildly swinging branch through the gusts with almost comic determination.

Her eyelids fluttered like wings and closed. Anna began to feel herself drift as though she were floating away from her body. Of course, the vision had not been so simple—such was the nature of augury. She had also seen herself in a circle of columns and at each column stood a man: Erasmus was one; Hayes and Kehler; a priest; another she could not quite see; and again the shadow figure. They performed a ritual—a rite that would make her a mage.

They will destroy me or help me, she thought. *But which? Should I run or seek them out?*

Visions never offered answers—only possibilities.

Although she kept her eyes tightly closed, shadows formed at the periphery of her vision, hissing voices whispering unintelligibly, only the loathing articulated.

Anna emptied the bitter dregs of the cup, and lay her head back, the folds of her cape fluttering about her face like the wings of bats. Lightning branched toward the world's edge, rending the fabric of night.

She felt herself rise and opened her eyes to find herself crossing to the horses, the landscape oddly illuminated, almost dully luminescent.

She slipped the hobble on her gray mare and with neither saddle nor bridle swung up onto its back and set off across the meadow, voices hissing from the shadows.

Among the trees they found a path that led up into a cleft between hills. She did not question where they went; she was in the grip of king's blood and obeyed its dictates. The shadow figures seemed to follow her, silent now, but increasing in number.

The mare stopped suddenly as though the way were blocked, and Anna heard a hiss like brittle leaves in the wind. There, rising out of the ground, was the face of Banks. He bobbed as though floating up from the sea, hair plastered to his forehead, white shells for eyes. He rolled slowly, turned by an unseen current, and his shell-eyes looked up at her, ghostly blank.

"Farrelle's oath . . . Banks?" she exclaimed, her voice barely rising above the wind. "Banks? Is that you?"

He opened his mouth, but only insects emerged, scurrying off into the night. Again he tried, but the wind carried the words away.

Anna had slumped over her horse's neck, the horror held at bay by the king's blood. "What? I cannot hear. Banks!"

"There will be a price," he hissed, and he slipped beneath the surface, one white shell left upon the ground like a tiny moon.

She slipped off her mare and plucked up the shell, turning the delicate object on her palm. Armor, she thought. The armor of some fragile creature.

"Banks," she whispered. "A price for what?"

She went on, leading the gray horse by its bridle. Tears slipped down her cheek but were flicked away by the wind. "Banks," she said again, "so many have died."

The path twisted upward among the swaying trees, over a landscape of gnarled root and shattered stone.

"An-na," someone whispered.

She looked around, searching the ground. "Banks?"

"An . . . na . . ."

The voice did not come from the ground, and she looked up to see a form hanging from a tree. Reluctantly she moved forward.

"Kells? Farrelle's blood!" she cried. "What has been done to you? Kells?" She could see him now, his neck caught in the crook of a branch, his body hanging limp.

For a moment he struggled to breathe, trying to swallow, breath gargling in this throat like a death rattle.

"I will get you down, Kells," she said.

"You cannot . . ." he managed, ". . . help me."

"Kells—" her voice choked off in a sob. "Is this what becomes of us?"

"Not . . . you . . ." She could see him blinking, and then he began to choke again, his breath cut off. Anna closed her eyes, unable to bear it. But then the choking subsided and she could hear him drawing shallow breaths.

"He watches," Kells whispered hoarsely. ". . . listens . . ." His breath caught. And for a moment there was utter silence, as he fought to draw a breath, his throat seemingly blocked. No sound, only the lifeless body and the gaping mouth, bulging eyes.

She could not bear it anymore and, almost running, pulled her mare forward.

"*Farrelle's blood,*" she heard herself say again and again. Was this a vision of death? Was this what awaited her?

"*Not you,*" Kells had said, but what had that meant? Her fate was different? Worse?

She stumbled along the path, half-blinded by tears, unsure if the shadows to right and left were trees animated by the storm or creatures of nightmare.

She burst through branches into a small clearing and there a fire burned. Was she back at her own camp?

But no, it was not the same. And someone sat on a fallen tree near the fire.

She edged closer, fearing what she might find. The branches of the fallen tree reached up, tipped in white blossoms. The woman was rocking, humming to herself. Anna could see her now. A large woman of indeterminate age, wisps of gray hair threaded among the dark.

The woman looked up, her face kind. She cradled a baby at her breast, bundled in white, and sang softly.

> "*My heart will keep the storm at bay*
> *The wraiths, the rain, the whispering night.*
> *The eye will see what's foul and fey,*

The way by darkness
Into light."

For the briefest instant Anna's familiar settled on her shoulder, but then took flight again, agitated, muttering its single syllable like a curse. The chough was battered by the wind, which then dropped to complete calm, though the shadow trees still writhed and swayed. Only here, in this small vale was it tranquil. Beyond, the world had succumbed to madness.

"Ah, child," the woman said, smiling at Anna. "You look chill. Will you not warm yourself by the fire? I've nothing more to offer, I'm afraid. Just fire."

Anna came and sat on a rock across from the dancing flames. She could see the woman more clearly, now, and was less sure of her age. Fifty? More? She shifted, great doughy rolls moving beneath her arms, visible through her blouse. The woman was thrice Anna's weight, she was sure. And she had borne a child—at this late age?

"You look sad, child," the woman said, her voice grandmotherly and filled with concern. "Sad and frightened."

Anna did not answer, although she found herself wanting to tell her troubles to this woman as though a complete stranger could put her massive arms around Anna and bring comfort, protect her.

"My friends," Anna said, then stopped.

"He watches," Kells had said, and the thought stopped her from speaking.

The woman nodded, her smile wavering. "They are among the whisperers," she said softly, nodding. She looked down at the babe at her breast, making soothing noises. "There my sweet child. There, there. It's only a wee slip of a girl. She can't harm the likes of you."

The woman looked up and gave Anna a tight smile. "It is a terrible, gathering storm. But what can we do? A gale can't be outrun. Even the birds, carried on its winds, fall exhausted at last. Sea birds swept a hundred miles inland, fall on ploughed fields, and are turned into the earth. Their sea memories weeping into the soil." She shook her head. "It is the way of the world. The way, the way."

"But why am I telling you, daughter? You journeyed through the earth's darkness. Only the darkness of the soul is more complete. There, most are lost. The one who seeks you—that is his failing . . ."

"Eldrich? Is that who you mean?"

But the woman looked down tenderly to the child again, and apparently did not hear.

"I suckled him," the woman said, not looking up. "Nourished him. Saw the light grow in his eyes. The light of the world." She shook her head. "Breaks a poor woman's heart."

"What does?" Anna said, confused. Was the woman making sense but the king's blood was muddling her brain, or was the woman raving?

Anna shook her head, pressing her eyes closed.

"What is it, child."

Anna half-expected the woman to be asking this of the baby, but when she opened her eyes, she found the woman's kind gaze upon her—filled with concern.

"I don't know where to go."

"But you must. You must. He cannot live without me," she looked down at the baby again, clucking her tongue, and smiling. "Nor you," she said. "Women are the way to life. No other. Aye, by moon and tide, we are the way."

The warm light of the fire danced across the old woman, across the folds of the skirt that covered her massive legs, like the trunks of trees.

The woman took the child from her breast which appeared like a great pendulous moon, and Anna could see crimson scars, a drop of blood forming on the nipple. Calmly the woman pulled her clothing into place, and then her smile brightened.

"See what a beauty he is," she said. "See the look in his eyes. Was there ever more promise than that?" The woman leaned forward, tugging back the swaddling folds.

But there, wrapped in white, lay a bundle of dried thistles and thorns. No child at all.

"Ah, look at how he smiles at you. You see what a pretty girl she is? Yes. Means you no harm at all."

Anna stared in frozen horror, and then the chough's wing brushed her face as it dove, screaming between them, fluttering above the flames. Anna was up, staggering away. She stumbled into the swaying wood, the grasping branches.

She fell, but as she stretched out her hands toward the ground, she seemed to tumble through and was suddenly spinning among the stars, their brittle voices echoing coolly in her ears.

The hanged man. The drowned man. The earth mother. Anna knew all the symbols, as did anyone familiar with even the lesser arts. Water, the stuff of life. There were poems that used the same imagery. Essex had made much of death by water. Death by life.

But what it all meant in her case was unclear.

Banks had drowned in the cave, so it was no surprise that he had appeared to float up out of the earth. *There is a price*, he had said. She shivered at the memory. A price for what? For her escape? A price to be paid for all the lives lost that she might go free? He might have even meant there was a price for entering Landor's chamber. Or stealing the seed. Who knew what charms the great mages had left on their chamber? They might be working their wickedness even now.

She flipped open Halsey's book again, holding it closer to the fire, trying to make out the fine hand. There had been no records set for travel that day, the day after augury and her dream vision. Anna did not think she had been more exhausted upon her escape from the cave.

Still, if she was correct in her assumptions, she was back on the trail that would lead her down into the lowlands—or at least into the right valley.

She read the carefully inscribed Darian, many of the passages followed by Halsey's explanation. The section on dream visions was not particularly enlightening. The only thing she learned was that her particular emotions during the vision could be significant, but as her emotions had seemed deadened and terribly confused, she was not sure what to make of them. Certainly, after the fact, she had been left with a feeling of dread, which might mean nothing. Or so she hoped.

Kells strangling in the tree was another enigma. Kells who had always been the most articulate of them. The hanged man was usually the innocent, falsely accused, though not always. He could be paying for his crime—relating to Banks' foreboding "there will be a price."

He watches, Kells had said. *He listens*. Eldrich, undoubtedly. She didn't doubt that it was true. The mage had somehow known their visions. He knew they watched Skye, and Erasmus, though that was easier to understand—the man who so resembled Teller.

Could he be watching yet? She had not known it had even been possible, so best to assume Eldrich still knew more than he should. But did he know she would escape the cave? Was that part of his plan? She would carry the seed out to him? But Halsey had betrayed him?

Anna shook her head. Her mind was too overcome by fatigue to muddle through these questions. If Eldrich knew something of her visions, then how would she set her course? What depth of understanding in the arts this indicated! More than she had ever thought possible.

Death by water . . .

She could not shake the dream vision out of her mind. The earth mother who spoke as though she had brought the mage into the world. Or perhaps the mages. An image only. Not reality. But still what had that part of the vision indicated? The half-mad woman suckling a bundle of thistles and thorns. The lacerations and, most significantly, the drop of blood forming on the nipple. She suckled her infant with blood.

Anna put her head in her hands, and closed her eyes. The world still seemed to be spinning. She could bear no more. Erasmus and the others were after her, Deacon Rose among them, she was sure. Now was the time for speed. If she could only stay to the path . . .

She felt sleep overcoming her, bewildering her senses. Thoughts connected oddly to emotions. She sank down on the ground in the dull glow of her fire.

A sharp pain in her chest roused her. Looking down she found a thorn embedded in her breast, a crimson tear forming at its base.

Chapter Twenty

THE storm blew itself out by night and left only ravaged clouds scudding on the trailing wind. The travelers had found their horses and pressed on, but by mid-afternoon stopped to rest their mounts and let them graze in a small meadow. Each of the travelers had slipped off on their own, apparently requiring time to themselves.

Both Kehler and Hayes fell asleep in a sheltered place warmed by sunlight. In the cold stream Deacon Rose bathed and performed his ablutions and meditations, while a much subdued Pryor saw to the horses. Erasmus went looking for Clarendon.

The little man had said almost nothing since overhearing their conversation the night before, but he would meet no one's eye and rode behind, snubbing Hayes' and Kehler's attempts to engage him in conversation.

Erasmus had chosen to leave the man alone, feeling that Clarendon would need to nurture his hurt for a while before his more rational side began to assert itself. After twenty minutes of looking, he found the dwarf settled with his back against a fallen tree, writing in the sunlight.

Clarendon looked up warily when he heard footsteps, but his face brightened when he saw it was Erasmus.

"Well, at least you, Mr. Flattery, defended me against the disparagement of that cursed priest," Clarendon said. "He will work to undermine us, to divide us, for he knows we are strong when we stand against him and his scheming."

Erasmus crouched down, feeling the ground which was still wet from rain. "Actually, Randall, I don't think it was Rose who began the conversation. I don't know how much you heard."

"Only you coming to my defense, Mr. Flattery, though it seemed you had your own doubts of me as well." He squinted at Erasmus as though expecting an explanation or perhaps an apology.

Erasmus opened his mouth but could find nothing to say. It was true; he had expressed doubts about Clarendon.

The small man nodded, staring off toward the edge of the meadow. For a moment he said nothing, the bitter look on his face slowly softening.

"The truth is, Mr. Flattery, you were not so far off the mark. I have not told you my story—not all of it anyway. Not for dishonorable reasons, I assure you, but only because . . . I have not lived the common life of a man of my time." He shook his head as though confused by his own decision. "I have experienced things that others would likely not even believe." The little man fell silent, his shoulders drooping suddenly, his face stretched as though in pain.

"Randall, it is your story. You need not share it with me if you'd rather not. Trust that I do not doubt your intentions for a moment, nor do I doubt your friendship. We survived the cave together, and that told me more of Randall Spencer Emanual Clarendon than a complete and detailed history could ever tell."

Clarendon's face softened a little. "You are a friend, Mr. Flattery. A gentleman as the term was once used." Clarendon looked down, his gaze coming to rest on the paper in his lap.

Erasmus' eyes followed this glance, and he realized that the script was Darian.

"The text on the walls in Landor's tomb," Clarendon said, shrugging. "I cannot read it, but even so my powers of recall allow me to recreate it—perfectly." He tilted the page toward Erasmus.

"I thought it should be preserved. I don't know why. Perhaps one day you will make sense of it, Mr. Flattery."

Erasmus reached out and put his hand on Clarendon's shoulder. "Even if I understood the words, it is unlikely that we would ever truly grasp the meaning. That is one of the odd things about men—we so often miss the meaning. The story you told us that night at your home, Randall . . . the meaning was clear, the emotional truth there for anyone to hear. The facts," he shrugged, "facts should not be mistaken for truth."

Chapter Twenty-one

THREE vertebrae, a dozen small willow wands, a tiny wolf head formed of gold, shells, a desiccated wasp, feathers, a butterfly wing, raven's beak, fire opal, garnet, a thimble of tin. A bit of colored string terminating in a noose, four flat stones, a crystal, the tooth of a carp. A ring of hair bound in ribbon of red, a braid of leather, a signet ring, the tail of a rat.

All these were spread at random across the table, and leaning over it, the mage, lost to the world.

The countess took a chair, keeping her silence, not expecting to be acknowledged. She looked at all the objects on the table, and except for the golden wolf, thought they looked like nothing so much as the treasures of a small boy. A child's hoard of precious nothings.

Yet this man, who had not a trace of childhood left in him, pored over them as though nothing in the world mattered as much.

After perhaps half an hour of being ignored the countess cleared her throat and said, "Augury?"

No reaction, and then slowly the head nodded, the dark curls barely shaking.

She was about to leave, though had made no motion toward rising from the chair, when Eldrich finally spoke.

"Not really augury in the truest sense. I don't know what one would properly call it. I'm sure no one in the world practices it but me. It is a useful complement to augury. It is properly called, well, *the Paths* might be a Farr equivalent." He waved a hand at the collection of odds and ends spread across the table. "Imagine that each object represents an event, a point in time or a person—perhaps even a place. All but the wands and the string—well, the string is more complex than that. The wands represent paths, though sometimes arrangements of objects indicate paths as well. These paths can be geographical, though more often they are paths through time.

"See how the wands are all different lengths and thicknesses? That is not accidental. Now imagine that time moves in one direction—different each time you cast the Paths, but discerning the direction time moves is one of the easier tricks to learn."

"All the objects on this side represent events that are already past. These in the center are due at any moment, some today perhaps. And this side of the table is the future—or the futures. More than one is indicated, unfortunately." He put his hand to his chin and resumed his contemplation.

Some moments passed and the countess began to think that was all the explanation she would receive, but then Eldrich spoke again, still not raising his head.

"Nothing is fixed except the past, and that is open to interpretation. Each time the Paths are cast, it is different. Each time an event is overtaken, decisions made, it changes." He held his finger above a jumble of objects—a smooth stone, the butterfly wing, and a wand. Here is a locus, a way-point. This is the critical juncture. From here events can unfold in different ways. This wand that touches the stone comes from the past—the path taken to get here. But look at the array of wands fanning out from here. The string is near, and this trail of objects looks like stepping stones. Five possible directions at least." He shook his head. "This juncture . . . this is the point at which the ones I sought entered the cave. When cast before, all these paths terminated here."

"But Erasmus was in that cave."

"He was."

"But you told me he was alive and unharmed."

"And that was true. But he was never meant to have escaped. Yet he did. They all did." He went on as though this lie meant nothing. "Augury is a bit like gambling, you see. The odds of rolling a die to the same number five times consecutively are very slim. Yet it can happen. Men can escape a cave believed inescapable. Now the pattern has altered radically. It continues beyond the cave; but goes where . . . ? This course," he indicated a wand leading to a white stone curled within the tail of the rat, "it leads to disaster—utter and complete. It must be avoided at all costs."

"But what is this disaster, do you know?"

"The escape of my enemy, aided by my servant, or so I believe."

"Who?"

"Erasmus, I think, though it could be Bryce."

"But your servants are so loyal. Walky."

"Ah, yes, but Bryce and Erasmus are not Walky. They despise me." Before she could form her next question he answered, "It was necessary.

"Along this path, to the white stone, she escapes with my servant—the white stone is from a river, and water is life. Along this, to the wolf, she comes to me. See this . . . it terminates at the wasp. On this path I believe she dies with another, for the wasp is a twin. But look how the white stone and the wasp are almost connected by the string. As though the path where she dies and the one where she lives are connected. . . ."

"What does it mean?"

Eldrich shook his head. "Even I do not know." He almost brushed one of the objects with a finger, though it was clear he was careful not to disturb them. "But if this path is followed, it will mean Erasmus has betrayed me."

"So he will escape. . . ."

"Escape? He can never escape." Suddenly he was still. "No. That is not true. He escaped the earth when I believed it impossible. I have watched Erasmus Flattery all of his life. I would have told you that I knew, almost without doubt, the course he would take through the years. But now . . ." The black curls shook, his focus riveted to the table and its peculiar array of deadly whatnots.

The countess could hardly credit what she was hearing. Was this not Eldrich? Was it not the mage who moved all around him while he remained still? Yet he sounded like a man filled with doubts, a bit desperate, even melancholic. A man. Not this superior being that she had come to believe in.

"And where am I on these paths?" she asked, surprised to hear her voice emerge as a whisper. "Or am I too insignificant to appear?"

Eldrich lifted an elegant hand, indicating a willow wand with a long finger. "This is your path," he said.

She bent forward to see what was indicated, and saw the wand—perhaps the longest on the table. It led directly and unmistakably to the golden wolf. The countess felt her eyes shut for a second—as though the inevitability were unbearable. As though her freedom to decide had been stolen from her long ago and she had realized it only in this instant.

"Do not look so," Eldrich said, regarding her for the first time. "It is not that you have no choice—it only indicates what your choice will likely be. Do you see? Erasmus and the others escaped the cave. A man named Halsey self-murdered to thwart me. Self-murdered, which I had not thought him capable of doing. Nothing is carved in stone. But this . . . it is what you will likely choose."

She felt herself nod, though she still stared at the wand which led to the wolf—actually touched it. "There is a second wand leading off, into the future. Your path?"

He shook his head, still regarding her with those dark, unsettling eyes. "It is yours."

"Mine," she repeated dully. "But it is not so distant from these recent events."

"No, it is not. You will complete the task I have been given."

She heard herself gasp. "But I—I am merely a . . ." She could not find a word. She was an aristocrat. A person of leisure and no particular abilities.

"You are the woman who was created to tempt me," his musical voice tinged with sadness. "But I will turn you against those who believed I could be so ensnared. You were born with a talent for the arts. Do not look so surprised—you have an intuition far beyond those around you. I'm sure you have long known this. And fortune smiles upon you. Small signs, but they have always been there. There are other things as well. But I have tested you further." He looked down at the table again. "The task I leave you to complete— nothing might be required of you at all. Everything depends on this." He gestured again at the tabletop. "On the decisions made. Things learned. Encounters between individuals. And on the choices made by Erasmus. You see, I created him in a certain mold so that the . . . so that those who came after Teller would be drawn to him. Now this might work against me." He shook his head again. "So many possibilities." He fell silent, his shoulders actually sagging. Then he sat back in his chair and looked into the fire. The storm shook the house again, and she heard a wolf howl in the forest. Already she had learned that this would always be Eldrich's familiar. No natural wolf could bear to be in its hunting grounds.

"There is a strategy at the chess board. . . . Do you play? It has been used by several great masters of the game, but it requires a depth of understanding—an ability to look into the future that is almost beyond human. It depends on you understanding the opponent's design better than he understands it himself. Then you allow him to pursue it, apparently unhindered, your own moves appearing defensive or harmlessly offensive. The game proceeds thus until, with a single move, you take the initiative—at that point your opponent can but react to your attack; there is no opportunity for him to pursue his own offense—and for good reason. . . . If you allow him a single move, the initiative will be his. You must pursue your own attack relentlessly." He closed his eyes for a second, as though exhaustion had suddenly gripped him. "I have allowed my opponent a move."

The countess paced across her room, glancing up now and then as a barb of lightning shattered the sky. Thunder seemed to tumble and roll up the valley. She always felt thus after a meeting with the mage—disturbed, confused. The heat of desire building. And tonight, something else. He had touched her in some new way.

He had seemed so sad, so disheartened. Before this meeting she had never imagined that he could be anything but arrogant—maddeningly so. But tonight that arrogance was gone.

The countess slumped down on a footstool. What went on in her poor confused heart? What of Skye? And Erasmus? What were her feelings for them? Suddenly she did not know. She worried about Erasmus, but partly that was sympathy for someone caught up in something he did not even begin to understand—caught up in it since childhood. And Skye? He had not been banished from her heart altogether. It was just that Eldrich's presence was so over-whelming that it left little room for others in either heart or mind.

And then there was Kent. Poor, noble, foolish Kent. The man had put himself in danger where no one else had, and entirely out of concern for her well-being. She had even begun to suspect that some of his affection for her was genuine, not just infatuation. Not just reaction to her unnatural appeal. And this touched her. Of the men in her life only Kent seemed to care enough what became of her.

Eldrich. Well, she did not know what Eldrich felt. He was a mage, after all. But certainly he was using her to his own end. Skye did not appear to return even a hundredth part of the affection she felt for him. Erasmus was too entangled in the web of the mage to ever have a life of his own—if he survived at all.

And that left Kent. Kent who was willing to do battle with a mage for her. It was utterly foolish of him, especially considering that she had never indicated any depth of feeling for the painter, but still he had done it. And now he, too, had become useful to the mage—had become ensnared. If she managed nothing else, she would have him set free unharmed. As soon as he finished his por-traits.

She draw a long breath and thought of the strange scene with Eldrich and his array of oddities. Had she only known what path she would find herself on—perhaps she would have run off with Kent when she had the chance. At least she would have a companion who genuinely cared for her. But what did she feel for him?

Chapter Twenty-two

HER eyes sprang open at the sound of a man clearing his throat. Anna lay still for a heartbeat, then turned to meet her captor. A few feet away crouched a priest, looking at her solemnly. He bowed his head in what seemed a deferential greeting.

"I hope you will pardon me for waking you," he said, his voice rumbling like lazy thunder.

Who in the world? Some minion of Deacon Rose, certainly.

"Have you long been lost?" he asked, his voice seeming to echo in a massive chest, though in truth he was a slight man.

Anna propped herself up on one elbow, quickly inventorying her possessions. "Am I not on the path to Wicken Vale?"

He nodded. "Not quite on it." He raised a hand and pointed roughly south. "You are one valley to the north."

A pain in her breast reminded her of the dream vision—and the thorn that was no dream. She wanted to touch the wound, which was still painful, but with the priest there—

Was he really as innocent as he sounded? Not a minion of Rose at all?

"You're traveling alone?" he said.

She nodded. "My guide was thrown from his horse and broke

his neck." She stopped, as though struggling with her loss. "I have been wandering since."

She sat up, wrapping her blanket around her. "Can you put me on the right path?"

He nodded. "But would you not care for food and a roof over your head?"

"People will be worried," she said. "I must press on. There is the family of my guide to think of, as well."

He considered this for a moment, surprised, perhaps, that someone lost would refuse hospitality.

"I have been told that curiosity will be my undoing, but I can't help wondering . . ."

"What I am doing here, traveling by such out-of-the-way paths when there is a perfectly serviceable road?"

He nodded.

"Roads lead many places, Brother, but seldom to adventure." She smiled at him. "I'm writing a book—a traveler's tale of the Caledon Hills. But what would be interesting about a journey so many have made? So here I am searching for sights others have not seen or even heard tell of, though it seems I shall have to title it 'Lost In the Caledon Hills' rather than 'A Journey Through the Hidden Hills' as I intended."

"Your guide . . . from where did he hale?"

"Somewhere near Castlebough. Garrick was his name. Garrick Lake."

"There are Lakes enough in Castlebough, and in Wicken Vale, as well. Poor man. What did you do with him?"

"I performed the rites as best I could and set him on a pyre. May Farrelle preserve him." Again she paused, then glanced up. "But I am no priest and fear what will become of his immortal soul."

"I think if your intent was good, as it surely was, then you need have no worry." He tried to smile, to reassure her. "But then I am a hermit and have come to believe many strange things, I'm afraid. I have only a poor man's hospitality to offer, but come at least and break your fast, and perhaps there will be some foodstuffs I can provide to see you down to Wicken Vale."

He stood, pointing off into the trees. "There is a path, and perhaps something for your book. Come along when you're ready."

When she was alone, Anna rolled out of her blanket and dressed quickly. Certainly she should be sleeping in her clothing now, in case her hunters surprised her. She broke camp and loaded her horses, having no intention of visiting. He had not told her his name—surely an indication of how long he had been outside society.

Anna stopped as she tightened her saddle girth, realizing that she must visit with the priest at least long enough to have him put her on the right path. There was nothing to fear from him, she was certain of that. She would have sensed it, especially now, with her king's blood-heightened senses.

Trailing her horses behind her, Anna made her way up the path the priest had followed, and in a few moments, to her great surprise, found herself before a sizable monastery. Abruptly, she pulled her train up. Had he not referred to himself as a hermit? This was not a hermit's hut.

But then she realized the buildings were in various states of ruin: roof tiles dislodged, their careful columns in disarray; climbing plants swarming over the walls. It was an ancient monastery, and had not seen use for many years.

Anna tethered her horses in the meadow and left them to the new spring grass. The gate to the monastery was left ajar in invitation. She found herself in a good-sized courtyard, shaded by trees, with water burbling in a fount. Half the area was given over to a garden, which here, in the protection of the walls, was farther along than she would have expected. It was also artfully laid out, and immaculately tended.

The buildings which surrounded the courtyard were of a locally quarried stone, weathered to the color of dark leather, but mixed with stones of natural, deep reds and occasional intrusions of quartz.

The tile roofs sprouted small meadows of grass and even shrubs, and the birds made free with window ledges and niches for the building of nests. Nature had begun to make this place of man its home.

Anna walked beneath the trees to an open door, and as she entered, heard the sound of singing, *basso profundo*, as she would have expected.

It was cooler within the massive walls, and smelled of stone and emptiness. As though the monks, in their austerity, had passed through leaving not even the scents common to the living places of humankind.

A swallow fluttered past Anna and perched on a rail of the stair high overhead, chirping at her insolently.

Let not my familiar find you speaking to me thus, she thought, and wondered where Chuff had disappeared to. He came and went on his own mysterious errands. "Familiar" seemed an odd choice of name to her, for the bird was anything but.

The singing drew her on.

To be wrecked upon the shoals? she wondered. In a great hall, once the gathering place for meals, she found the priest bent over a table which appeared to be covered in clumps of vegetation.

But this was not what drew her attention. Some climbing vine had gained entry by high windows and spread itself across the ceiling and down the walls. White flowers, like morning glories, bobbed in the small breeze that found its way in the glassless windows. It was as though she were in a vast chamber made entirely of these heart-shaped leaves and gently fluttering white blossoms.

The priest looked up and smiled, the song retreating into its own echo, and disappearing in some small corner of the room.

"Do you like my great hall?" he asked. "The Hall of the Morning Bells, I call it. Though not everyone can hear *matines* being rung with such delicacy." He smiled again, a surprisingly pleasant smile given the yellow of his teeth.

Anna realized that the clumps of sticks and grass and reeds spread over the table were the nests of birds. Some were hardly larger than thimbles, and made of soft grasses and down, while others were hat-sized.

"My collection," the priest said. "I am Brother Norbert, by the way. Do excuse my manners—I get so few visitors." He did not wait to hear her name, so Anna did not offer it.

"It is my ambition to collect a specimen of nest from every bird that breeds in this corner of the Caledon Hills," he said. "Though I have some distance yet to go."

"But they have eggs in them as well," Anna said, wondering how these had been preserved.

"So it would appear," he said, lifting an egg from its nest and dropping it in her hand. It was far heavier than she expected.

He smiled at her surprise. "I seek out stones of the correct size and form, or near enough that I can polish them into shape, and then I paint them as realistically as I can. I can't bring myself to steal the eggs the poor mothers go to such trouble to lay, although it is a common practice among naturalists, I'm told." He gestured toward a door. "I have a kettle on and can offer soup and bread as well as tea. . . ."

Anna nodded, the thought of fresh bread actually causing her to salivate. Clearly she had been too long in caves and wood.

The song of birds caught her attention, and she looked up to see more swallows in the air overhead, picking their meals off the branches of the air.

"It is really the swallows' monastery now," Brother Norbert said. "I am merely tolerated by them."

She followed him from the hall into a smaller room where a fire burned in a hearth, and the smell of bread was on the air—the scents of man reclaiming this one small room, at least briefly.

They took their meal beneath a grape arbor, Anna too hungry, she found, to speak, so Brother Norbert, contrary to the practice of monks, made conversation while he ate.

"You might wonder what I am doing here alone," he said. "As I was curious about your own journey. You might also find the history of this monastery interesting—perhaps it could even find a place in your book. There is an artesian spring here, which is the origin of the fount in the courtyard. Thus the name of the monastery; Blessed Springs, though I think originally this place was merely called the Pure Springs.

"The monastery was built, in stages, during the sixth century. A Farrellite Order, the Order of the Sacred Fire, dwelt here originally. And, no, they were not burners of heretics, but burners of books and other art they felt too 'worldly.' They even went so far as to burn some of the art commissioned and possessed by the mother church, for which they were banished to the Caledon Hills and ordered to do penance. They faded into obscurity in a few short years, and all that can be said of them after they were sent away from the larger world, is that they became master builders, for this place would hardly still be standing if not for their diligence.

"The monastery was generally inhabited after the eclipse of the Brothers of the Sacred Fire, but by different Orders with different purposes. It is so far out of the way that many of the more unconventional sects within the church found their home here. Mystics inhabited the buildings for centuries—until the Tautistian Heresy. You know to what I refer?"

"I don't remember the details but know of it generally."

"The details, as you call them; the matters of belief of doctrine are so esoteric as to make one wonder how a veritable war resulted, but suffice it to say that a struggle for power within the church itself played its part, whether Farrellites like to admit it or not. It is a blot upon the church to this day, many of us think.

The priest looked off toward the wall of the courtyard, his face drawn and a little pale. "There was a battle fought here, between the Farrellite forces and the Knights of Glamore, but the Farrellites were greater in number, and the monastery fell." He stopped to swallow. "In the meadow before the gates . . . all of the monks, and the knights who did not escape, were burned as heretics. To this day no tree will grow on that ground."

Anna noticed Brother Norbert's hand shook as he lifted his tea. "The monastery was abandoned then, and for all the intervening years—until I came. My thinking had begun to wander down paths that made my superiors decidedly uncomfortable, so it seemed the life of a hermit monk might suit me best. With the 'blessing' of my bishop, I came here." He looked over at her and raised his eyebrows, trying to smile. "The monastery has an evil reputation in the Caledon Hills, and people don't like to talk of it—likely explaining why you'd never heard tell of it. It's believed the place is haunted, and no one who visits will ever stay beyond dark." He did not smile when he said this. "So I have a strange ministry here, one which my church would never approve of, if I were fool enough to tell them. I am putting to rest the spirits of the dead monks and knights."

He watched Anna's face carefully as he said this, and for a second she thought he jested, or perhaps said this only to shock her. "It is a noble cause," she said evenly. "How goes it?"

"You . . . you do not seemed surprised?" he said.

"Spirits wander the world. I hope the spirit of my guide will stay in the glen where I made his pyre and watch over it and bear no one ill. But these monks— How terrible their end must have been!"

He nodded. "Yes. You see, I am learning their tales." His voice dropped to a rasping whisper. "The winds blowing through the windows at night carry voices, whisperings. And as I learn each tale, I speak with the tortured spirit, and I seek forgiveness for what the church has done. I try to bring them peace and let them pass through."

Anna thought it was no wonder his superiors were happy to see him off to an uninhabited corner of Farrland. She wondered if he were a bit barmy, as some spirit knockers tended to be, or if he was a man sensitive to worlds beyond their own.

"And what has this meant to you, all alone here with the spirits of tormented men?"

He raised a hand and then let it sink gently back to the table. "It has been my nightly hell, and my salvation. . . . It has given me purpose, but I wonder how my spirit will rest after I have heard of all the horror.

"And you do this for your church?"

"For the men who were wronged and foully murdered. To bring contentment to this little corner of the world, for it was once a place of peace and beauty." He paused. "And for the men who committed the atrocities against their will—believing they did the work of Farrelle, and only later realized what this meant to their immortal souls. They are more tormented than any. I sometimes think they will never find peace."

Anna felt a tear well up, quiver on the lashes, and then streak quickly down her cheek. "Yes," she whispered.

"But look what I do," he exclaimed, seeing her tears. "I try to tell you something that might be of interest for your book—a bit of Caledon Hills history—and end by sending you into melancholia." He touched her sleeve, not the flesh beneath, but where it lay on the table. "Let me tell you the good things that I have seen here. I believe that each time a bird builds a nest within the walls of the monastery it is a token—and each nestling that fledges and takes to the sky is the sign of another soul who has shaken off his burdens and gone free. And see how many they are . . . !" He waved a hand at the swallows which darted in and around the walls of the decaying buildings, lost to the joy of flight, the ecstasy of their brief life in this world.

Anna swung up into the saddle, feeling strangely renewed. She looked down at Brother Norbert, his slightly unkempt beard, his stained smile.

"You feel confident of my directions?" he said for the third time. "You don't think I should ride with you until you find the path again?"

"They could not be clearer, thank you Brother." She marveled to hear herself saying thank you to a priest of Farrelle and meaning it, too. She bent in an odd, equestrian curtsy and then turned her mount. But not thirty feet on she stopped.

"Brother Norbert? If my spirit appeared to you one day, would you forgive me and help me find peace?"

"I would, yes."

"No matter what I had done in life?"

"No matter what you had done," he said, a vertical crease appearing between his eyebrows.

The two considered each other for a moment longer, then Anna nodded and turned back to the trail. He had never asked her name.

Chapter Twenty-three

HILLS hidden in a sheen of fog and rain. A windless day, sounds seeming to originate from no discernable point but simply out of the air. Anna had stopped her horse to listen yet again. The sounds of the forest were heightened, though strangely hollow. Somewhere a raven croaked.

"Only my own horses," she told herself. Not some others following. Not yet.

Chuff appeared out of the pale air, and landed on her packhorse, muttering his signature word—a complaint, she was sure. Even the birds found such weather unsettling.

She clucked her tongue at her horse and led it on. The path was too easily lost in this fog, so she had chosen to walk, much of the time bent close to the ground. There was undoubtedly an enchantment to keep one from losing one's way, but she didn't know it, nor did it appear in Halsey's book.

She touched a hand to her breast, over her heart, feeling the tender flesh where the thorn had penetrated. No coincidence. She feared that it might even be the work of Eldrich—the child of thistle and thorn. As though he had marked her.

She forced her attention back to her path, which disappeared often, for it was only used occasionally by hunters, and perhaps a bit more regularly by game. If this was not the path Brother Norbert had drawn on his map, it was at least very close, probably even parallel. There should be a river soon.

Anna made her way through the dripping woods, rain running off the tip of her nose, seeping through her protective clothing. Her skin felt numb and softened, as though it might easily tear and she would not know.

She stumbled over rock the color of fog, finding her footing on dark, caked mud. The raven croaked again, making her feel very alone. It rattled its bill, an eerie sound in this enfolding mist.

A sound like onrushing rain came to her and she ducked her head down, prepared to be even wetter. There was no point in seeking shelter now, unless she began to shiver uncontrollably, then it would be time to make a fire—something she could do now, without flint or tinder. She might even risk it—a brief use of the arts.

The sound grew in intensity, like a downpour on flat water and broad leaves, but she could not tell from what direction it might originate. A breeze, at least, should proceed it, something to carry the squall to her.

Chuff landed on a branch, warning her bitterly of the coming rain.

She held up an arm to brush soaking fir branches aside, but they sprang back, slapping her face with wet, green hands. She spit out fir needles, and then the ground opened before her.

Anna slipped as she stopped, her horse stumbling into her, and the one behind driving it on. She was thrust toward the cliff and only saved herself by grasping a branch that mercifully did not break away. How her horse didn't go over the edge she did not know. The bank gave way under one hoof that came too close to the edge, and the horse seemed poised to pitch into the void, the others jostling behind. She hauled on the reins, and the horse desperately thrashed for footing, somehow saving the moment.

She stood looking down into the gorge, the jade-and-white river rumbling below—the sound of an approaching torrent—and she felt as skittish as her horses.

"Blood and flames," she said several times. "Blood and bloody flames." Her chough landed momentarily on her shoulder; she felt its small, blood-red feet grip her coat.

"Yes, I know. I did not listen to you, Chuff. I was tired and distracted and thought it was coming rain. But it was a gorge. Flames! Being able to swim might not have helped me here."

She stepped away from her horses as her familiar took to the air, flying out over the terrible space. Kneeling, she leaned over the edge, staring down into the green waters. A fairly calm pool lay beneath her, fed by several falls. Below this the water turned to white, flowing between rocks as it dropped from one green pool to the next—water the color of arsenic, she thought.

Two hundred feet farther along, a bend hid the river from view. Anna lifted a stone and tossed it into the pool, watching it make a star of white and then sink into the deepening green.

She looked around, rose, and stepped back from the precipice. She had almost fallen—like the night of her vision. Fallen and landed among the stars.

Chapter Twenty-four

THEY would descend into pools of mist that hung in the valleys as though they were walking down into mountain lakes. Erasmus felt each time like a forest sprite or some other creature of myth and magic. But once into the pool their pace slowed to some fraction of normal. If Anna was far enough ahead not to be caught in this same situation, she would be rapidly escaping.

Pryor assured them that they would be down in the lowlands in two days, that is if they were not in fog for most of that time.

Erasmus wondered how the lad was doing. He caught only occasional glimpses of the boy through the fog—bent inertly over his shaggy horse. Pryor was so lost to his grief that Erasmus feared he might lose the trail from lack of concentration. The poor boy was so despondent that he was not even contemplating revenge. If not for his charges chasing this woman—this woman who had murdered his brother—he would likely have lain down in the rain and never moved again. Nothing mattered to the boy—as though his future had been erased and there was no longer any reason to strive.

Grief, Erasmus thought. He was not a stranger to it himself. For several years after being sent home from the house of Eldrich he had experienced bouts of it over Percy's death.

"Mr. Flattery!" It was Clarendon calling through the mist, still insisting on using formal address for some unknown reason.

Erasmus was afraid to pull his horse up, for Pryor would likely go on, and they would lose him.

Clarendon managed to catch up with him though the path would not allow them to quite ride side by side.

"Mr. Flattery, there are signs of horses joining the trail just behind us."

"Pryor!" Erasmus shouted, shaking the boy out of his reverie. "Did you hear? Randall has seen signs of horses."

Pryor slipped off his mount, dropping the reins to the ground, effectively anchoring his horse to that place. Erasmus and Clarendon fell in behind the boy as he passed, his face so lifeless that Erasmus actually felt alarm.

They passed the others, and in a moment Pryor was crouching down, touching the marks of horses that were rapidly washing away in the rain.

"Is it Anna?" Hayes said, coming up. Pryor had an uncanny ability to tell the hoof prints of one horse from those of another, and they had seen Anna's often enough now.

Pryor moved a few feet, never looking up. Then he shook his head. "Ours," he said.

It took a moment to sink in.

"That's enough for today, I think," Erasmus said. "No point riding in circles. It's only three hours until sunset—not that one can tell on such a day, but let us rest and hope the fog lifts by morning."

Camp was struck and a rough lean-to made from cedar boughs. Fire proved even beyond the skill of their guide, so they ate a cold meal and settled down as best they could, pressed too close.

Erasmus, who had great need for privacy, was feeling the proximity of others. Couple that with the frustrating day, and he found he had to exercise great self-control to remain civil. The others were irritable as well. Erasmus could feel the strained politeness. Deacon Rose was particularly quiet, sensing the mood and knowing that it was most likely toward him that any ugliness would be aimed. Indeed, Erasmus thought Kehler and Hayes were just waiting for the priest to give them an opening.

Clarendon had not quite recovered his usual gracious manner, but he seemed to have overcome his recent bitterness and was making some effort to rebuild his bonds with the others, though awkwardly—he was a man too used to being mocked and rebuffed.

Since Clarendon had admitted to Erasmus that he had not told his whole story, he'd seemed different. Somehow he had formed an attachment strong enough with this group, and perhaps Erasmus in particular, that he could no longer live with the lie.

He feels shame, Erasmus thought.

Erasmus felt that the very air was thick with confusion and misunderstanding, emotions close to the surface, as though the worst of human frailties had been exposed by their encounter with Eldrich. Not the first the mage had done this to, Erasmus knew.

Why does he bring out the worst in men?

Hayes was being very solicitous of his friend Kehler, making a concerted effort to cheer him, though to little effect.

This is what came of meeting a force that could be neither reasoned with nor defied.

Suddenly unable to bear the company of others, as the melancholic often could not, Kehler rose, muttered some excuse, and slipped away into the falling dusk.

An unsettling silence followed Kehler's retreat.

Clarendon took a long breath and said softly;

> *"Dark, dark the night*
> *And my heart is no lighter.*
> *Bleak will tomorrow rise*
> *And each day thence no brighter."*

They all turned to stare at Clarendon, barely visible in the gloom. Pryor rose suddenly and stepped out into the fog without explanation. Erasmus almost thought he heard the boy muffle a sob.

"If that was an attempt to cheer us, Mr. Clarendon, then I must tell you it failed utterly," Hayes said.

"I—I did not mean . . ." But he didn't finish.

"You might have some consideration for the boy," Rose said. "He has suffered great loss at the hands of that . . . woman." He fell quickly silent, realizing he had meant to keep his peace that evening.

Clarendon eyed the priest with obvious disdain. "We all saw you break down our dam and drown poor Banks," he said coldly. "Do not grow suddenly solicitous of others. It is as much a lie as all the other lies you have concocted."

Erasmus could not make out the priest's face but could see his silhouette stiffen.

"And who is it who speaks of truth and lies? A man who has been so completely forthcoming with his friends that they have all come to doubt him. Lies? You have lied to us from the beginning, Mr. Clarendon, and we all know it."

Clarendon began to bluster, but this fizzled out into a protracted silence in which Erasmus could almost feel the little man's pain.

"You have all sided with the priest, is that it?" the small man managed after a moment, his tone bruised and quiet.

No one answered for a moment, and then Erasmus cleared his throat. "Perhaps, Randall, it is time that you completed your tale . . . as you suggested when we spoke."

A long silence followed. Erasmus could see Clarendon hang his head, though in the dark he could not tell if this was shame or merely contemplation.

"You do not know," Clarendon said after a moment. "You cannot." He raised his head as though contemplating the others through the dark. "You were all blessed at birth. Born neither infirm nor deformed. You can never understand what it is like for those like me. Yes, I did not tell my story in its truest form, and all I can offer in defense is that much of it is difficult to tell, or to contemplate." He paused. "I have long thought that no one would believe it, for it is hard to credit—and at times I have had trouble believing it myself. You should also remember that even Mr. Flattery did not begin by telling his true story."

Erasmus could feel the others look at him. Even if they did not, he knew why he had felt sympathy for Clarendon in his obfuscation. Not everyone's past was a tale of joy.

In the fog-bound silence Erasmus could hear the others breathing, sense them waiting for what would be said next.

"Most of what I said was true, or true in essence, if not fact. Yes, I was a performer in the traveling show I spoke of. And my father did indeed drink himself to death. His so-called wife, Lizzy, did gain custody of me. All of that is true. But beyond that . . . there begin some deviations from the strict . . . facts.

"You see, we did not leave the traveling show as soon as Lizzy gained custody. We . . . I remained for some months. During this time she did fall victim to a cad—the aforementioned Colonel Winslow Petry. But events were not quite what I claimed." Clarendon shifted where he sat, his voice now quiet and laden with sadness.

"I know that life with Lizzy was less than perfect, for she had her own peculiarities, and it became even less than ideal when Petry appeared. The man was a brute. . . ." Clarendon drew a long breath to calm himself. "And Lizzy, who was liberal with her affections, too often gave him excuse to misuse her.

"One of Lizzy's eccentricities was a belief in spiritualism and the ability of some to contact the spirits. She was a victim of every table knocker in Farrland and beyond, I sometimes think. Odd in a woman who was so shrewd in other ways."

"A new conjurer joined the traveling show not long after my father's demise and, among his many other gifts, he claimed to be able to contact the spirits. I was still quite young at the time, and though not living in surroundings that encouraged innocence, I remained, in many ways, somewhat trusting and naive." Clarendon's voice changed as he spoke, charged with sadness and loss, but with some undercurrent of pleasure as well, as though memories of Lizzy warmed him.

"This conjurer was a man of some interest, and not just because I was a child and fascinated by such things. I must have been aged about eleven at the time. He did tricks that no one in the show had seen before—and they had seen any number of such performances in the past, most of them variations on a few themes and well-worn ruses.

"Magnus was a man of some presence—tall and dark with a vast mustache that he waxed up into impressive points. He had a smile that all the ladies in the show remarked upon, and their finer qualities did not go unnoticed by him either, I suspect.

"But I digress. On a particular night Magnus offered to make contact with the spirits and perform some other feats as well. Most of the people who were paying to be part of this sham were locals,

but a few were members of the traveling show—my cherished
Lizzy among them.

'The calling,' as it was named, took place in a tent used for one
of the sideshows. As Lizzy would be inside and Petry's attentions
were taken up with a bottle and one of the other women in the
show, I contrived to conceal myself near a flap where I could watch
what occurred without being seen.

"The obligatory tapers were burning and the participants clasp-
ing hands in a circle about a table when I slipped into my place. I
had actually hesitated a while before I came, afraid that Magnus,
who seemed to have abilities that no one understood, would discover me. But curiosity won out in the end, and with a thumping
heart, I watched.

"Magnus was as good a showman as conjurer and held us all in
thrall while he worked his 'magic.' He began having the table lift—a
common enough trick for table knockers. He then performed a ritual
of sorts, calling out in what I now guess was a faux language. There
were several parts to the ritual, and I will not burden you with need-
less detail, but at the end the candles all blew out and a strange
milky light appeared to hover high above the table. To this he spoke,
and, in turn, it answered." Clarendon paused for a moment. Erasmus could feel the pain, as though he watched a man open a septic
wound.

"A distant-sounding voice came from the milky light, though it
did not speak Farr or any other language I had heard; and, as you
know, my memory for such things is unsurpassed. Magnus interpreted what was said, and soon those present were allowed to ask
questions which were then interpreted to the being in the light, or
so it seemed. No one was allowed to speak directly to the spirits
they sought, but everything went first through Magnus, and then
through his counterpart in the spirit world. Despite this device being
problematic in every way, the responses appeared to affect the people, causing them often to gasp and occasionally turn rather ashen.

"The evening proceed in this way, people breaking down in tears
as they heard from their lost loved ones, Magnus consoling them,
especially the prettier women. I hardly noticed a carriage come to a
stop near the tent, and when I did, assumed it was a lady arriving
late. Contrary to my assumption, a gentleman stepped down from

the coach, though I could not see him for shadow. A moment later he appeared behind me. As I made to cry out in surprise, he put a finger to his lips, and I was struck dumb. Nor could I animate my limbs to flee. I will tell you I have never been so frightened, though this man made not the slightest threatening gesture." Clarendon might have shrugged in the dark.

"He merely watched the proceedings, vaguely amused, or so I thought. I remained in my stricken state, too frightened to even notice what took place. And then the seance broke up, several people leaving, though two—Magnus' confederates—stayed behind to dismantle the apparatus.

"Magnus led Lizzy out into the night," Clarendon paused and drew a ragged breath, "which was warm and bathed in the light of a full moon. The dark gentleman set out in their wake, gesturing for me to follow, which I did only because I was too terrified to disobey. I could hear Lizzy's laughter and was struck by a fear that this terrible man might want something of her—for men always seemed to want something of fair Lizzy. Even then I realized he must be a mage, though I did not know his name.

"Lizzy and her conjurer went out into the meadow, and the laughter gave way to murmuring, sighs, things I had heard many times before. A round little man had appeared, following a few paces behind—the stranger's servant, I surmised. For some while we watched from shadow. I could see the conjurer unbutton the front of Lizzy's dress, two silhouettes in the moonglow. And then something unexpected—something unheard of. The heavens seemed to lose focus and shift, as though a pane of imperfect glass had passed across the sky, blurring the stars. But the world seemed to move as well. I felt it tremble beneath me and fell to my hands and knees. The meadow appeared to change, trees in different places, the faint lights of a house appearing, a copper moon over all. A rushing wind whipped about me, and then all was still, everything as it had been—except that Lizzy and Magnus were nowhere to be seen." Clarendon paused then, lifting hands to his face in horror, as though he saw it all again. But then he went on in a whisper.

" 'What did you see, Walky?' the mage asked. I did not grasp what had occurred. Certainly Lizzy and Magnus were still there, somewhere. People did not disappear into the air. 'I saw the worlds

. . . *overlap,*' the servant said, 'blend one into the other. And then with a wrench they separated again, tearing the woman and man away.'

"I could not believe what I had heard. Lizzy could not be gone. One did not walk out into a meadow and disappear! One did not! And what was this talk of overlapping worlds? 'What you saw was history being made, Walky. Never before have we been able to predict when such a phenomenon would occur. We are the witnesses to a historic event. What did you see, boy?' the mage asked, turning to me.

"At first I could not produce words, but then I realized that my safety depended on speaking and speaking true. I delved into my memory. 'The stars changed. They blurred, sir, and there were more of them, some moving, and then the meadow changed as well, trees appearing as though in fog, and the lights of a house. And then they all grew smaller, sir, as though disappearing into the distance. And Lizzy was . . . gone. All I have, sir. She is all I have. . . .' I began to weep. 'Can't you bring her back, sir? Please,' I begged. I fell to my knees. 'No one can bring her back, boy,' the mage said. 'Not even I can do that.'

" 'But where has she gone? Where can I find her?' The terrible stranger seemed to take pity on me, speaking softly. 'She cannot be found, child, for she has gone the way of Tomas and you cannot follow. But I shall make you forget this night, forget the pain you feel.' He crouched down before me, staring at me with dark, unsettling eyes. He spoke words I had never heard, but then he suddenly stopped. *He has the curse of memory,*' he said to his servant. 'Poor child, I should put him from his misery.' '*Sir,*' his servant said, as though in caution. The mage stood, staring down at me still. 'Give him some coins, Walky. There is little more we can do for such a child.'

"And they left me there, my hands filled with silver, crying like an animal wounded—wounded in spirit.''

Clarendon fell silent then, still covering his face. In the darkness he could have been the child again, weeping for his loss, for the pain he could never forget.

Chapter Twenty-five

THE world dripped with rain. The forest, the vines covering the walls of the lodge, the eaves; even the windows ran with tears.

A world overwhelmed with sadness, the countess thought, and noted her own mood was in sympathy. She realized that Kent was staring at her, and it was not with his customary curiosity (the look he donned when he was painting) or adoration (the gaze he turned toward her the rest of the time).

"Am I fidgeting? I am sorry, Kent, it's just . . ." She was not sure what she meant, and finally gestured toward the windows.

Kent turned his softly penetrating gaze there a moment, and then nodded. It was like him to understand immediately what she meant.

He returned his attention to the canvas, though he did not raise a brush. How unlike Eldrich's was his gaze, the countess thought. "Softly penetrating," she described it. Kent approached all of his subjects with a certain respect, even humility. He insinuated himself into the heart of them, whether it be nature—or human nature. She felt it herself. He made a place for himself in her, like a sparrow building a nest.

Eldrich's gaze, on the other hand, tore through all impediments until he held the heart. His approach was essentially destructive. Kent's desire was to slip in unnoticed, take an impression, and slip away—disturbing as little as possible.

Kent will pay a terrible price, she thought suddenly. *He opens himself to the world, bears his breast to the knives. The very thing that makes him great will devour him.*

He looked vulnerable, contemplating his canvas, brush in hand.

She could destroy him herself. Destroy him without meaning to.

"The light is not cooperating, is it?" she asked.

Kent did not answer for a moment, but continued to stare at the canvas. "It is worse than that," he said, turning to her and blinking oddly. "I believe I'm finished."

The countess did not move, realizing what this announcement meant, then she rose fluidly and went and stood beside the painter.

She felt it a bit unseemly, too narcissistic, to stare at her own portrait, yet she could hardly help herself. It was not like gazing into a looking glass, that was her first thought. This was the Countess of Chilton filtered through the sight and mind of one Averil Kent. This was how another saw her.

He is in love with me, she reminded herself. *But even so . . .* Certainly he had made her seem beautiful, though it was not this that stood out for the countess.

"Do you really think me so unhappy?" she asked softly.

Kent glanced at her, eyes widening a little, and then back to the canvas. "I had not thought of it. I simply try to capture what I see, what I feel. . . ."

"Is this sadness yours, then?"

Kent did not answer for a moment as he considered, and then she saw his shoulders fall a little. "It is ours, Lady Chilton," he said barely loud enough to be heard.

Yes, she thought, his sadness was there as well, mingled with her own. Sadness that she would never be his. Sadness that he would be forced to leave this terrible house.

She gestured toward the portrait. "I do not mean to criticize, Kent, but I'm sure my hands are not so long and elegant. In fact, I think those are your hands, Kent!" She teased him now, trying to lighten the mood, spoil the intimacy toward which he strived. "It is

overly generous of you to give me your hands, but it is hardly painting what you see. Let me sit again, and I will try not to fidget—
though perhaps we might wait until tomorrow? The light might be
better."

Kent's shoulders did not rise as she'd hoped, but he nodded
slowly. Outside the world continued to weep.

"It can't be changed, Kent," she said, placing a hand on his arm.

Kent took her hand, turning toward her. "But if you are here by
choice, as you say, then can you not choose to leave?"

She could not bear the compassion in his eyes, and looked away,
though she did not attempt to remove her hand from his. "No. I
cannot explain, but it is too late to change course. I . . . it is too late,
Kent. I'm sorry." She took her hand back then, glancing up once at
the terrible sadness and loss in the painter's face, and then she went
out, trying not to look as though she fled.

Back in her room, the countess threw herself down in the window seat, staring out at the weeping world through rain running
down the panes. She drew up her knees and buried her face in her
arms, but no tears came. The world might weep, but the countess
could not afford to.

Sitting up she noticed a spot of deep red upon the soft place
between her thumb and index finger: paint, from Kent taking her
hand.

"So you've left your mark upon me, after all, Averil Kent."

Kent stood looking at his painting for a long while, trying to separate his sadness from that of the countess. No, certainly that
underlying sadness was there in her. He had not simply painted his
own heart. She was deeply unhappy—or perhaps unhappy at her
center, though years of social schooling allowed her to hide it. But
not from Kent, who was trained to observe.

"*Too late,*" she had said, and Kent felt all that he desired, all that
he hoped for, slipping away. Like the words themselves, which for
a moment vibrated on the air, and then dissolved to nothing. Leaving him with what?

"Memories are but the ghosts of past events." So Beaumont had said—a man who knew something about being haunted, apparently.

"Tell me, Mr. Kent, if you will—what are you thinking as you stare at your work?" It was the musical voice of Eldrich. The mage had entered the room unheard.

Kent did not turn, though he felt a strange wariness—as one feels when perceiving a threat from behind.

" 'Memories are but the ghosts of past events,' " Kent said.

"Lapin," the mage said, his voice closer now.

"I thought it was Beaumont."

"And so it was, though Lapin said it first. Men often quote the mages and take the credit for themselves." Eldrich was standing directly behind Kent now, and the painter could feel the hair on his neck standing on end, as though it were the wolf and not the man who stood so close.

"The countess' praise was not undeserved, I see. Even I am affected. What is it, Kent, that goes beyond mere technical ability to make such a work? What is it that reaches out to others? 'Art,' I suppose you will say."

Kent shook his head. "Love," he said, speaking the truth, speaking it because it did not matter. The world of human emotions meant nothing to Eldrich.

"Ah . . ." the mage said, though Kent did not hear the mockery he expected. "And thus the talk of ghosts and memories." Eldrich was standing at Kent's shoulder, where the countess had been a moment before.

Let him do with me what he will, Kent thought. *It cannot matter.*

"The exquisite pain," the mage said.

"Sir?"

"It is what Halden called the memory of love."

Kent nodded. Perhaps the world of human emotions was not entirely foreign to him.

"Your work is finished here, Kent."

"The countess is not happy with the hands."

Eldrich laughed softly. "More than adequate for our purposes, I assure you. Tomorrow, Kent. I will speak with you before you go."

Kent remained staring at the portrait, not sure if the mage still stood at his shoulder. If so, did he see the sadness? And would it matter to him?

He began to clean the brushes mechanically, replacing each in the vessel from which they protruded like rigid tails. But then he noticed one brush he had employed only the previous day bore a tint that he had not used—a deep purple, like winter plums. He lifted the brush and held it to his nose. Certainly it was fresh paint.

"But it was not me," Kent said, and wondered how many painters Eldrich had hidden away in this strange house.

The countess looked up at Walky and then back to the text.

"I fear the countess' mind is not on her work," the small man said.

She had become "the countess" through the same process by which Eldrich had become "the mage"—or so she assumed. "Lady Chilton" was, after all, the proper form or, given that Walky was a servant, "Your Grace."

She sat back in her chair, looking at the gray old man—not quite what she imagined from the descriptions of Erasmus. Walky's mind appeared to be perfectly intact, for instance. "I confess I am worried about Kent," she said. "I know you assured me that he is in no danger, but . . . well, I find Lord Eldrich less than predictable."

Walky sat back from the table, a signal that this evening's lesson was complete. "It is not the mage who is unpredictable, it is others. Kent is in no danger, I think. Why would he be? Oh, he acted foolishly, and intruded on the mage's privacy, but even so . . . it is hardly a capital offense. No, Kent need only keep his bargain and not make a fuss. The mage will not bear interference or argument. If Kent will say nothing to anger him, he will leave no worse for the experience. My master is not vengeful in the common sense of the word—no more than the courts are vengeful to criminals. Do you see?"

"Yes, though all but the most benighted criminals know when they have transgressed upon the law. How would one know if one had violated the mage's code? It is rather different, you see."

Walky shook his head, sticking out his lower lip as he did when disagreeing. (Did he do this with Eldrich? she wondered.) "M'lady, there are a thousand tales written that describe in detail what one should and should not do to earn the disfavor of a mage. It is hardly secret. Never provoke a mage. Never. Not in the smallest thing."

"I fear I have already broken that law," she said softly.

Walky smiled. "Well, you have a special place in the mage's house."

"And what is that place?" she asked quickly.

Walky drew back into stillness as he did when questioned about certain subjects. "There are certain questions the countess must ask the mage."

She was the countess again. Not "m'lady" as she became when he was feeling less formal—less formal and more affectionate, if one could accuse Walky of affection.

"I think we must be done for the evening," he said, forcing an awkward smile. He did not like to be questioned about Eldrich. Clearly this was one of the mage's laws. The countess was aware that Walky held her in a certain affection—as though he were an old family retainer who had watched her grow from childhood to prominence with subsequent pride. Not the usual reaction she had from men—even very old ones. This meant it hurt him to not answer her questions, but he was the servant of the mage, after all.

He bade her the pleasures of the evening and made his way to the door. Halfway out the old man stopped, and stood in awkward silence for a moment. "Kent will be gone tomorrow," he said. "If you are concerned about his welfare, tell him to do nothing to provoke the mage."

It took a moment for the countess to absorb what had been said—*Kent was leaving in the morning!*—but then she nodded, and Walky slipped out.

Her reaction to the news was not what she expected. Kent was leaving. . . . She would be left here all alone, with no ally. No one who truly cared for her—cared enough to risk the mage's anger. This thought left such a hollowness at her center that she thought tears might well up. *Kent was leaving.*

She went to the window, finding only her face reflected in the night's dark mirror. What sadness had found its way into her countenance. And yet the turmoil she felt inside was revealed in no other way. No, this self-possessed woman did not appear as though she would fly apart at any moment, burst from too many contradictory emotions.

The school of Avonel society had taught her well. Only the sadness bled through, like Kent said paint sometimes would, no matter how many layers were brushed over. Only the sadness.

Even Kent had not seen the turmoil. Poor, loyal Kent. Kent who had risked everything just to prove his love. And how had she returned this loyalty? At the very least, she could carry Walky's warning to him. At the very least.

She tossed a shawl over her shoulders, swept up a candle, and went quickly out.

She knew approximately where Kent's rooms were situated, or thought she did. There were only a handful of people in the lodge, so it seemed that finding light under a door in the guest wing would answer—unless there were others there she knew nothing of. She feared that in the house of Eldrich this was not impossible.

She crossed above the great stair and waited a moment to be sure no one was below. Eldrich, of course, could walk the halls in darkness and utter silence, but there was nothing she could do about that. He would either see her and ask where she was going or not. As Walky had intimated, she was allowed to break some rules—to provoke the mage. Whatever it was he wanted of her, it gave her special status—a diplomatic impunity. Or perhaps the right to be undiplomatic.

She turned a corner into the next hall and froze in place, back against the wall. Eldrich's wolf was sniffing outside a door, and then along the baseboard. It seemed unaware of her at the moment— although that was clearly impossible. She bore a candle, after all, and had gathered in such a gasp as to be heard by the house entire.

"Farrelle preserve me," she whispered. "Farrelle preserve . . ."

The great beast, far larger than she expected, had progressed to the place where she was standing, and sniffed around her feet. She looked down at the massive back and realized that a beast so muscled would tear her to shreds before any rescue could arrive.

A mage's familiar, she thought. As she herself possessed, since taking the king's blood. A completely unnatural creature, tied to its master in ways she did not understand. Did it know her? Know her scent? Was Eldrich's mark upon her so that it would leave her in peace?

It nosed at the hem of her dress, lifting it a little so that she felt its breath as it sniffed her ankles.

She pressed herself back against the wall, and found she drew her face back and away, as though to protect it should the beast lunge.

A rough tongue rasped across her ankle.

Farrelle's blood, what if I am to its taste?

Slowly she withdrew her foot, just a few inches—and the wolf growled, hair standing up along its shoulders.

"Flames . . ." she whispered, actually feeling the teeth bare. At any second it would lunge and bury those fangs in her too soft flesh, and she did not know what to do to avoid it.

Suddenly it did lunge, but to one side, ignoring her altogether. She almost dropped the candle in her fright, starting back, hardly able to catch her breath.

The great beast had something with its paws and mouth, and then came up with it—a squirming mouse, its tiny feet running madly in the air—and then it was gone into those terrible jaws. The countess slipped away, keeping her back to the wall, a hand to her heart.

The wolf went off, sniffing along the wall again, but blessedly away from her—hunting mice, of all things! She almost laughed aloud.

The countess sank into a chair and let her racing heart come back to its normal rhythm. She shook her head. Never come between a mage's familiar and his dinner. It was not a rule that Walky had taught her. Perhaps it was in one of those old tales of which he spoke. She laughed, though largely from release. She had come face-to-face with a creature from myth, only to find this terror hunting mice! If only she could tell Marianne this story one day.

Thoughts of Marianne brought Kent to mind, for some reason, and she resumed her search.

Not three doors on she found what she sought—a glow from under a door. She stood close to it for a moment, but hearing nothing she pressed her ear to the cool wood.

Something inside. A man singing softly, and footsteps. But was it Kent?

What if this were Eldrich's room, and she knocked on his door instead. Even the thought of this quickened her pulse.

He is an uncaring creature, hardly more human than his wolf, she told herself. Briefly, she pressed her cheek against the door, trying to drive out thoughts of Eldrich and the feelings these thoughts called up.

And then she knocked, her heart in her mouth.

The singing stopped. A hand on the doorknob—she saw it tremble—and then the door opened a crack, a single eye appearing in the gap.

"Lady Chilton!" the painter said, and paused before drawing the door open. He stood there quite embarrassed, for he was in his stocking feet and wore no coat or waistcoat.

"Oh, Kent, do not worry about your dress," she said. "Only let me in. I've just encountered Eldrich's wolf and fear it might return."

Quickly he stepped aside, and she came in, shutting the door firmly behind her.

Kent was clearly taken aback to find her in his room so late, and she could see that he was torn between his hopes and not wanting to appear foolish.

"Will you invite me to sit down, at least?" she said, though not unkindly.

"Yes. Yes, of course." He took the candle from her and placed it on the mantlepiece, gesturing to a chair.

The room was dimly lit by a single lamp, and Kent had clearly been sitting close to it reading, for a book lay open on the table. There was also a bottle of wine and a half-empty glass. Clearly, Kent was on better terms with the servants than she was.

"You will be sent off tomorrow," she said, coming straight to the point. "I talked to Walky."

Kent nodded, his eyes searching hers. "I know," he said after a moment. "Eldrich came to view the portrait after you left." He stood by the mantlepiece and looked down at her, hoping for some sign, some indication of why she was here.

"Kent, I don't know if we shall ever meet again," she blurted out.

His gaze dropped to the floor for a moment, then back to her again. "And if we do, will I even remember? Is it not the practice of the mage to destroy the memories of those who have dwelt in his house? Will I remember that I painted your portrait and had the pleasure of your company for those too few days. Oh, that I had never learned to paint so swiftly! Will he tear these memories away from me?"

She could not predict what Eldrich would do, but she was afraid that Kent was right. He would remember nothing of his stay in the house of Eldrich. Remember nothing of his fool's attempt to rescue her. His noble attempt. "I don't know what Eldrich will do. I really don't. I only know that Walky gave me a warning to pass on to you."

Kent looked at her differently now, the distress pushed back a little. He listened intently. His blue eyes were soft in the low light, pupils large. His loose shirt, unbuttoned at the top, showed a glimpse of pale skin. For a moment she closed her eyes.

"Do nothing to antagonize the mage," she said. "Offer no arguments. Provoke him in no way. Do you understand, Kent?"

He looked away from her, shaking his head. "What do I care what the mage does to me?" he said.

"Kent!" She rose quickly, taking up his hands, aware of the extreme warmth of them.

He looked into her face then, so close.

"Do not speak so. Please, Kent. Do nothing foolish. I will never forgive myself if you come to harm. Promise me. . . ."

Kent resisted for a moment. "But he will take everything from me," he whispered. "Send me away from you and rob me of my memories. All that I have."

She touched a hand to his cheek. Poor Kent. He was sick with love. Desolate at the thought that he would not even remember their time together. Was it really so precious to him?

"Do you see? I will lose you in every way. Every way."

She nodded. There was no denying this. He would forget her. Forget his infatuation. Forget this night, this very moment. "But I will remember, Kent. Remember that it was you who came searching for me—unconcerned for your own safety. I will never forget."

She kissed him. Not a peck on the cheek but full on the mouth. For a second they stayed close, his wine-sweet breath warm upon her. And then he kissed her in return, and took her in his arms.

He will remember nothing, she told herself. *Not a thing.*

Chapter Twenty-six

MARIANNE Edden was more distressed than she could remember. Her carriage—actually the countess'—rolled through the Caledon Hills on a beautiful morning, birds brightening the air with both flight and song, and she hardly noticed.

She glanced over at the anonymous portrait of the countess, her only traveling companion—the countess' lady's maid had insisted on giving Marianne her privacy and was riding up with the driver, a rather transparent explanation, for there was clearly sympathy between the two. The countess stared out from her frame, beautiful and somewhat troubled.

"Too beautiful," Marianne whispered. Such unnatural radiance was bound to bring trouble, if not tragedy. Any trait in overabundance was worrisome. Too much money, significant talent, a title, great beauty, charm and wit—they were like lightning rods. The countess stood too tall among the crowd— as did Marianne herself, in her own way.

It was the reason she had always avoided the court and certain circles in Avonel, and why she was attracted to simple things and uncomplicated lives. The countess had been a rare exception, but then who could resist the attentions of the Countess of Chilton?

Even women were flattered beyond imagining just to be noticed by her. Marianne often thought that she was the countess' only true friend—or at least the closest thing the countess had to a friend. After all, Marianne was unlikely to ever suffer fits of jealousy or envy—the novelist was admired in her own right, and for entirely different reasons. They were simply never rivals.

I am doing precious little to help for the person who professes to be her only friend, Marianne thought. She could think of no other plan than to use her contacts in Avonel to gain an audience with the King, or at least with the King's Man: that despicable Moncrief. What else could be done? The King was the most powerful man in Farrland. If the King could not intercede with Eldrich, then no one could.

Certainly Erasmus Flattery had proved a disappointment. It might be true that he knew of what he spoke, but still . . . to simply accept that there was nothing to be done! It did not speak highly of him. Even poor Kent had rushed off to try to save the countess though she feared he had not come to a good end over this.

Poor Kent, foolish with love. It was not so much bravery, she knew, as hopeless desire. That point of madness where one will die to prove one's love and thereby gain the affections of the beloved. A bit pathetic, really. Better to live in disappointment than commit what amounted to self-murder to gain a love that one would not be able to enjoy from beyond the grave. After all, most lived with disappointment. It was the nature of things.

Marianne let out a long sigh. She wanted to leap from the carriage and thrash the bushes with a walking stick. She felt such frustration, such helplessness. It was an emotion she was familiar with, but only at a remove—she wrote about it but almost never experienced it. Marianne Edden was a person with too many resources to feel frustrated often.

The carriage rocked, suddenly slowing, and finally lurched to a halt.

"Ma'am?" It was the driver.

"What is it?" She pushed the window open.

"A carriage with a broken axle, I think. Shall I stop and offer assistance?"

"By all means."

Someone hailed them. She could see the carriage now, a large, old-fashioned affair. Marianne pulled her head back in and took a deep breath. Was this not the carriage Kent described coming for the countess? But certainly the mage would not suffer a broken axle, like normal men?

Steeling her nerve, she pushed the door open and climbed down before the driver could lower the step.

By the listing carriage stood two gentlemen and a driver, all with their sleeves rolled up.

"Ah, fortune has found us," a dark-haired man said.

"Miss Edden?"

"Lord Skye! What an unlooked-for pleasure. You're returning to Avonel, too, I collect?"

The empiricist nodded his silver mane quickly. "May I introduce Mr. Percy Bryce. Miss Marianne Edden."

Pleasantries were lost on Marianne. Hadn't this man been rumored to be in the employ of whoever let Baumgere's old mansion? The mansion where Kent claimed Eldrich had taken the countess?

"You do seem to have had some bad luck, Lord Skye. Can I carry you on? There must be an inn within a few hours. They can certainly send someone to repair your carriage."

A few bags were quickly shifted, and Bryce and Skye took their place in the carriage with Marianne and the portrait of the countess. An odd situation, all in all, and a bit of luck that Marianne did not intend to let slip away.

Just who was this man Bryce and what was his place in Eldrich's house? Certainly he was no servant in the common sense of the word, but one could serve in many capacities. And what was Skye doing in this man's company?

"We are a bit of a traveling art exposition," Skye said, clearly trying to make polite conversation. "I have the Peliers the countess had authenticated."

Marianne nodded. The Peliers—she had almost forgotten them. The man crossing the bridge toward the dark coach. Skye had claimed this to depict the Stranger of Compton Heath. And the other, which showed the crypt Baumgere excavated above Castle-bough. Prophetic paintings.

"Have you seen Lord Skye's Peliers, Mr. Bryce? What do you make of them?"

Bryce had been staring out the window, apparently lost in thought. Now he shrugged. "I must admit, Miss Edden, that I know little about Pelier. People say he had a gift, and far be it from me to deny it." He smiled apologetically, and as soon as it seemed even remotely polite, he returned his attention to the passing scene.

"Eldrich has an interest in Pelier. Did you know?" She wasn't quite sure what she was doing, other than falling back entirely on her novelist's intuition.

This brought Bryce back from the window, a suitably neutral look fixed on his face. Too neutral, Marianne was certain.

"Eldrich? Really?"

"Yes, Mr. Flattery told us much about the mage. I had heard that he would not speak of it, but then when he realized the countess' interest—I don't think men keep many secrets from the countess. Wouldn't you agree, Lord Skye?"

Skye barely nodded, clearly trying to warn her off with his eyes. All of a sudden he looked quite unsettled.

"Mr. Flattery could read the writing on the crypt depicted in the painting. He even made me several examples of this script. Remarkable, really. I plan to incorporate it into a book. Imagine how people will react when they discover I have the actual language of the mages in a novel! That should increase my readership, don't you think? My publisher will be pleased." She smiled at them expansively. What *was* she doing? Making this servant of Eldrich believe she knew more than she did, and that she was about to publish it in every city around the Entide Sea.

"We are actually stopping to visit friends along the way, Miss Edden," Bryce said. "I'm sure they would be delighted to meet you, and it would break up your journey."

She nodded. "Why how very kind of you. Nothing would please me more."

Marianne felt herself sag back in her seat. *Pray that I have not miscalculated and that this "friend" is Eldrich. Certainly Bryce would not do something unpleasant to me without consulting his master. Not to Marianne Edden.*

Why, then, did Skye look as he did? One would think I had entered the den of a hungry lion.

M arianne walked beneath the trees of the terrace of the inn. The buildings perched on the edge of a gorge high above a picturesque river. The terrace, walled and shaded, lay among the buildings, so that it was almost a courtyard. Emerging from under the spreading trees, she came beneath the canopy of stars. The cold clarity and sheer numbers of them stopped her momentarily, and she stared up into the depths of the heavens, as enraptured as the ancients who had organized their lives by the movements of the stars.

"Do you see the wandering star?"

Marianne started and then realized it was Skye, standing in the shadows beneath the lime trees. How long had he been there, watching?

She looked back up to the stars. "There are so many."

"Yes, but this one is unlike all the others. Look toward the Ship. Do you see there, as if hung in the rigging, like sea fire."

"That milky blur? That is a wandering star?"

"Yes. What do you think you are doing?" Skye asked suddenly. He emerged from the shadow, his mane of hair silvered by starlight. "You have guessed who my traveling companion is?"

"A servant of Eldrich, I think."

He nodded in agreement. "You think you are being clever, having him take you to the countess, but what will you have accomplished? You will have angered the mage who does not like to have his time wasted by others, no matter how talented or celebrated they are."

"You speak as though you know him," Marianne said.

"Like the countess, I have visited him in the past, though my memories of these visits were clouded. You did not tell Bryce the truth at all, did you? Flattery told you nothing, I will wager."

She did not answer, realizing he could ruin her plans, if he had not done so already.

"I will explain this to Bryce, and perhaps he will let you go on your way."

"No!"

He came a step closer so that she could make out his face, ghostly in the starlight with only shadows for eyes. "Miss Edden, you do not understand what you involve yourself in. Do you think your gift for invention will help you rescue the countess? The mage detects lies more easily than even a novelist can manufacture them. I am surprised Bryce did not see through your story. You are only letting yourself in for a trial. Mages are not patient."

"Someone must do something," she said. "At least let me speak to the countess and reassure myself that she is not there against her will. If I can do that, I will be satisfied. Why is it no one but Kent and myself are willing to take a risk for our friend?"

Skye did not answer immediately, and when he did, his voice was very tight. "Because there is nothing one can do . . . unless proving you are loyal to the point of foolishness is important to you—as it apparently is to Kent."

"And you, Lord Skye. Why do you wish to see Eldrich if his tolerance for humankind is so slight?"

He did not answer, but walked a few steps to the wall and stared down into the gorge where the dark river ran like an artery of the world. "Because he has the power to unlock memories. Unlock the past. . . ."

Marianne shook her head, moving to the wall near him. "People are in thrall to their past. Many spend all the years that remain to them trying to forget, for their pasts were terrible. Perhaps you will be one of these. You have always been a visionary of empiricism, looking to the future. Why do you take this chance?"

Skye continued to stare down into the gorge, as though listening to voices in the darkly flowing river. "Because until I know, I will always be a stranger to myself. A kind of changeling. People are in thrall to their pasts, you say. One can be equally in thrall to a mystery. Imagine if several days of your life could not be recalled—not a thing about them. Would you not wonder? Would you not imagine all manner of incidents that might have befallen you, or things that you might have done? Imagine that you had committed some terrible crime, something so revolting that your mind could not bear to look upon it? Such things happen to men who fight wars. They see such atrocities that they can no longer recall entire battles—yet they dream of little else and waste away because they cannot bear to sleep.

"Who was I before my accident? I was adopted, but from where? Do you see? I am a changeling, a man who sees things others do not: my laws of motion; the naval gun; and much else besides. I am different, marked. Appearing from nowhere as though created whole in my teen years. And you counsel me to abandon my search?" He was gripping the stone of the wall with both hands, but now he loosened his hold, his shoulders sagging. "No, if Eldrich can unlock my past, then I will live with the consequences. They cannot be worse than what I experience now."

There was nothing to be said to this, Marianne knew. No argument would convince Skye to change his course.

"But what of me?" Marianne said softly. "You may choose your course, not even knowing if Eldrich will grant your request, yet you advise me to turn away. Who are you to decide for me, as though I were a child? I will tell you in all modesty, Lord Syke, that there are few people in all the land more calculating than I. Everything I have ever done or been has been weighed upon a scale that balances with a precision most cannot imagine. You talk of being created whole as a youth, but I am my own creation, and made myself whole even later in life. The Marianne Edden, the eccentric genius that everyone knows something of is my greatest character, created with perfect attention to detail. I have a colder heart than anyone knows, and yet I am willing to risk everything to be reassured my friend is unharmed. I have only one friend, you see—a thousand admirers and passing acquaintances, but one friend only. And as you say, I am willing to take great risks, not just to prove my loyalty, but because I will be forced to live with the knowledge if I shirk. I have lived with my calculation, my flawed heroine, long enough, I do not want anything more to haunt me."

The whisper and weave of the river flowing. A breeze making small banners of locks of her hair.

"Be up before sunrise," Skye said. "Bryce likes to be on the road at first light."

He walked away without saying good night, though she felt no insult. They were alike, she and he, hidden in among the population, appearing as others did, yet as different as crows raised in a nest of doves.

Chapter Twenty-seven

K ENT was let into the room by Walky, who stood guard over his master's privacy with a dedication that no royal guard could equal. The painter stopped inside the door and waited for the mage to take notice of his presence.

Eldrich bent over a book at the table, a breakfast roll in one hand which he nibbled periodically without seeming aware of this action—as though his body had learned to seek sustenance of its own accord.

The two portraits—one on the easel, the other on a chair—were turned toward Eldrich, as though he had been viewing them, and Kent found that he suddenly craved the man's approbation. Had he no opinion? Did mages have no concern for such trivial matters as art? Any art but their own, that is.

"You are ready to travel?" the mage said. As was apparently his habit, he did not look up at Kent as he spoke.

"I am."

Eldrich seemed to nod, though perhaps it was only a random movement. Kent was not used to being treated as though he were not there—not in recent years, at least—and he did not much like it.

"Then I shall pay you your price, Kent," Eldrich said. He rose where he stood, eyes still fixed on the book. Only reluctantly did they give this up, and the mage turned his disturbing gaze upon the painter.

"You realize that you cannot go from this place knowing what you know?"

Kent felt his eyes shut for a moment. He called up a vision of the countess, her touch. Her lips. The sounds of her pleasure, her passion.

Elaural. . . .

"Kent?"

The painter nodded. "Will I remember nothing?" he asked in a small voice.

Promise me you will not provoke him, the countess had asked. And he had promised. But now. . . .

He looked up at the mage, half a head taller than Kent, even though Eldrich seemed to stoop a little.

"Nothing," the mage said.

The pain was so great that Kent shut his eyes again. "Then the price is too great. You receive your portraits, but I lose everything."

"Hardly everything," Eldrich said, his musical voice hardening. "I have let you have your life in exchange. Have you forgotten?"

"I do not value it as highly as I believed."

"Have you never heard that it is unwise to try the patience of a mage? Especially over things of little consequence."

"Matters of the heart mean more to men," Kent answered, not caring what happened. Who was this man to steal away his precious memories?

Eldrich looked at him and shook his head. A smile might have flickered across his face.

"For your insolence I should send you forth from this place." He stopped, took a long, calming breath, and let it out in a sigh. "Flames, Kent, you are young. I will leave you this," he said. "You shall not forget your rather overvalued feelings." He held up a hand. "Say a word, and I will withdraw my offer. Show some wisdom, Kent."

The painter looked into the eyes of the mage and thought that perhaps there was a trace of humanity there—not much more—but a trace.

The mage wove a pattern in the air with his hand, and began to speak words that Kent did not know. He felt himself falling . . . into a star-filled sky.

The lodge was clearly not used just for the hunt. There was every sign that the people who owned it spent significant time here as a family. Without nosing around too much, one could chart the progress of the children—and not just by portraits. The countess was sure there were two girls and a boy. She found their cast-off toys and games, as well as signs of other pursuits—the kind that parents insisted on because they were "improving." In rather mysterious ways in some cases, or so the countess thought.

One large room was set aside for a children's playroom. She had found it soon after they arrived, but had not visited it again. There was something about its atmosphere of abandonment that affected her. Childhood, not so much lost as repudiated. She remembered it, that impatience to become adult. And look where it led. . . . No, children had the best of the bargain, she was sure.

Why Eldrich had asked to meet her here, she did not know—an odd request. But then very little about the mage's household could be called ordinary, at least by the standards she was familiar with.

The countess pressed open the door to the playroom, and stood looking in for a moment. As always, she carried a candelabra, for the halls were unlit, Eldrich and his servants apparently having little need, and even less affection for light. But this room was lit, by candles and a lamp or two. Still she hesitated at the door, the feeling of loneliness growing, though she could not say why.

Kent was gone. And she was alone in this strange world, as Erasmus had been as a small boy.

Looking into the room, with its playhouse and dolls, its toy carriage drawn by a team of rocking horses, caused a terrible sadness to settle over her. A woman without child, she thought, by way of explanation, but knew it was not the truth, or only a very small part of it.

A music box began to tinkle, slightly out of tune, and too slow. She went in, and found Eldrich looking down from his great height at the music box on a miniature table. A girl in a great skirt and a dashing soldier spun on the top, dancing in the candlelight.

As was his habit, Eldrich did not look up as she entered, but continued to regard the tiny dancers—his mind elsewhere, the countess was certain. Focused on this great task that he wrestled. The task left to him by the other mages. She thought he looked more forlorn than usual, and that was saying a great deal.

While she waited to have her presence acknowledged, the countess let her eyes wander the room. On her previous visit she had not noticed the border painted high around the walls. It depicted a well-known children's tale, with its magic doors, wise wizard, and heroic children caught up in the strange events. She thought the section depicting them riding a raft down a torrential river was the best.

Shelves of poppets stared out at her from an open cabinet, their too-large eyes seeming to regard her with a certain malicious glee. Toy swords and shields stood at attention in a corner, beneath falling banners, their colors faded. Shadows, sharply defined, slanted among the blades and for some reason these seemed more solid than the objects which cast them.

The rocking-horse team, drawing a coach large enough for small children, made the countess wish she were small enough to play in it herself. It was so perfectly wrought; painted a vivid blue with wheels of yellow. Two large dolls sat inside, traveling endlessly across this children's landscape.

> *Popidon, Popidon where do you go?*
> *Down to the sea to see the men row.*
> *Popidon, Popidon why do you weep?*
> *The boats are ashore, the rowers asleep.*

"It is an odd little museum, is it not? Such effort focused on preserving childhood. Did your parents keep such a shrine to your younger years?"

The countess shook her head, looking over to find Eldrich gazing at her.

"Nor did mine. But then I had so little childhood to feel nostalgic about for I was sent off to the house of the mage when only seven."

The music box wound down so that the last few notes sounded like afterthoughts, the dancers barely twitching to this dying fall.

Eldrich had been taken away as a child, like Erasmus. It had never occurred to the countess before that this would be the case. Indeed, it was almost impossible for her to imagine the mage other than he was now.

"I have always said that having no childhood was a blessing, for it saved me from this current fashion for constantly complaining about one's younger years. No, everyone should have been sent off to serve a mage and saved us this endless prattle, that's what I think."

He fell silent, and began a slow circuit of the room, stopping here and there to contemplate one object or another.

The countess saw the room differently this time. It was not the children's abandonment that struck her, but the parents' efforts at preservation.

Eldrich paused before a wizard's cap and staff, and to the countess' surprise he actually picked up the staff. He studied it a moment, then thumped it once on the floor, speaking words of Darian as he did so. The head of the staff glowed with a soft green light, like sea-fire, and with this he etched the letter E in the air, where it hung for a moment before fading, as did the glow on the staff. Eldrich put it carefully back in its place and looked up at her. "It still works," he said, and then continued on his rounds.

The countess was too surprised to laugh. What was this? Charm from the mage? She did not think he even knew what it was. Irony, tending to sarcasm, seemed to be the closest he ever stood to humor.

Eldrich continued on his rounds. "Why have they preserved this room thus, do you think?" he asked.

The countess looked around her. "Museum" was a good description. But it was more than that. It was homage to a time, an age of life, as well as to children who had obviously been very precious to their parents.

"Despite the current vogue for complaint, there is a nostalgia in our culture for childhood. We forget all its trials and frustrations and remember only the days when the mundane world and the world of make-believe had very thin walls between them. That is what I think; we remember the magic, the stories, the hours of play—if we were lucky enough to spend our hours in play."

Eldrich nodded, seeming to consider this.

"Do you long for such a world?"

The countess had never thought of it in such terms. Did she? "We all long for simpler times," she said, wondering where this conversation was going, and why Eldrich had summoned her here. "There is very little magic in people's adult lives," she said. "Very little to surprise."

Again the mage nodded. He stepped behind a marionette theater, and one of the marionettes hanging there suddenly raised its drooping head. It looked around.

An arm lifted, as though relearning animation. It almost seemed to shrug its shoulders, as though working out the stiffness from so many years of inactivity. It took a few uncertain steps, then suddenly found its confidence. It did a little jig and threw up its hands, leaping for joy.

Eldrich looked up from his puppeteering, his eyes running sadly over the room and its contents. "I wonder if the children feel the same way about childhood as their parents? It is a critical lesson of life, knowing when to move on, when one's time is done."

The marionette slowed in its motion, like a music-box figure running down. Its head fell slowly to one side, limbs collapsing, and again the near-human figure hung lifeless.

With some care Eldrich hung the marionette back in its place, and without another word went out, leaving the countess alone.

She sat down on a tiny chair and felt her shoulders begin to shake. Why had she agreed to help this man? Was it really this promise of prolonged youth? She looked around the room at the preserved treasures of coddled childhood.

It is a critical lesson of life, knowing when one's time is done.

But youth had less to do with her decision than she realized at the time. Curiosity had taken its part, but even more than that was a sense that there would be purpose. Her life would have purpose.

For what had she been doing with her given days? What would she ever do?

She looked around the room again, seeking the feeling of child-hood, the state of it that was somehow lost within her—yet it eluded her.

And here she was, in the house of a mage, with magic all around her, and she did not feel as she did as a child. Had she moved on? How could she know that it would all be so deadly, so grave. And yet she was not entirely clear what Eldrich would do. He would erase all of the mages' arts from the world, for reasons that were not perfectly clear. And she might play some part in this. She . . . And so she stayed, while others fell away. Erasmus. Kent. Mari-anne. Even Skye. And she stayed with this man—this near-human, feeling his contained desire for her. Wondering what purpose long-dead mages had created her for, and if Eldrich made a mistake be-lieving he could turn her to his own uses.

Odd to go through life so convinced that one knew who one was and for what purpose one was intended, and then suddenly to discover that this was not true at all. Like an artist discovering that their art was larger than they; perhaps even overwhelming.

She stayed to find out who she was and prayed she would not be overwhelmed.

Chapter Twenty-eight

ANNA looked back down the long valley, thinking the situation was a great deal less than perfect. It was all a matter of distances, of timing. She would see them first—assuming they came down this path, and she had left as many signs of her passing as possible to draw them on. If there was no fog, the smoke from her fire would almost certainly alert them.

When they crested the rise, she would play at being surprised—and herein lay the problem. The distance from her camp to the river had to be gauged with precision. If they caught her before they reached the gorge . . . Well, she did not like to think about what that might mean. No, they had to pursue her, be almost upon her when they broke through the last trees at the edge of the chasm . . . and then it would be too late. She knew the cliff was there, and trusted they did not.

Anna had studied that final stretch of trail with great care. There was no margin for error.

She threw another piece of wood on the fire and walked back up the rise to resume her vigil. A swallow cut an arc through the air and disappeared into the wood, reminding her of Brother

Norbert and his promise—which brought her some small comfort.

Pryor bent low to the ground, touching the marks with a finger. He moved on, still crouched, glancing up to see where the trail led.

"They're recent," he said, standing straight for the first time since he had found his brother's pyre. "Yesterday, late, 'twould be my guess."

"But is it she?" Hayes asked, hoping, perhaps, that it was not. That he would not be forced to decide.

The guide nodded, taking up his reins and swinging quickly up onto his mount.

Erasmus looked around at the others, not all of whom were as ambivalent as he. Deacon Rose spurred his horse on and took up a position immediately behind Pryor. It was clear what these two would do; but what of the others?

Deacon Rose stood in the center of the narrow trail, holding up his hand, a finger to his lips.

"Smoke," he said, his voice low, if not an actual whisper.

Erasmus dropped down from his saddle. "Are you saying we've found her?"

The priest nodded. "Unless it is some other." Rose and Pryor had ranged ahead of the others, widening a gulf that Erasmus knew now would never be bridged. If they captured her, he would have to perform the ceremony Percy had left him.

Erasmus glanced back at Hayes and Kehler, both of whom looked a little ill.

The priest motioned them close in order that he could speak low. "The smoke appears at the head of this small hill, so it is not far. Even so, she will hear our approach if we go on horseback. Yet if we slip forward quietly on foot and she perceives us, she will mount her horse and flee, and we'll be left foolishly on foot.

"What we have decided is to go forward at the gallop, and

though she will likely take to her horse, we will ride her down. There are five of us, after all."

Rose looked at Hayes and Kehler, who did not respond with even a nod. "Let Pryor and me do your work for you," Rose said to them. "We will dirty our hands, for after what was done to his brother, Pryor has no doubt of her character." He turned back to Erasmus. "I have taken the necessary precautions, for she has some skill in the arts, and perhaps more, now. But when we run her to ground, let me approach her first. Let her not practice upon you with the skill of her tongue, for she will say anything to save herself, and she will happily slit any throat that she might go free." He looked up at the two younger men. "Will you ride with us, or will you let us sully our hands to save your necks, brave lads that you are?"

"No," Kehler said, glaring at Rose. "I will not let another commit the crime that saves my life. And as nothing short of your murder will stop you, I am bound to be part of the crime."

Rose met the eyes of the two young men who sat their horses, staring down at him with obvious dislike. "It is often that men do evil, believing that they do good," the priest said, "but it is less common that men do good believing it to be evil. Even so, this is such a case, it seems, for the woman is a threat to all that you know. In years to come, you will understand that this is so."

He looked back to Erasmus who, feeling no more confident than Kehler and Hayes, nodded his head. Pryor would have his revenge at last. A revenge of fire.

They fell in behind the priest, and in a moment found Pryor, hidden in a thick stand of pines. They each took a moment to tighten saddle girths, and then, at a nod from Deacon Rose, they set off at a gallop up the narrow path between the hills.

As they crested the rise, Erasmus heard the priest shout, spurring his horse on. Determined that Pryor and Rose would not do Anna harm before she was delivered to Eldrich, Erasmus forced his tired horse forward, clods of the forest floor flying all around him.

In a moment they swept past the fire, glimpses of a rough camp, horses dancing on tethers. And then they were into a thicker wood, jumping a fallen trunk, branches snatching at their faces and tearing clothing. Hooves pummeled the fragile earth. The scene passed more quickly than perception.

A terrible scream—*Anna*. Horses in panic; Rose bellowing to stop.

Erasmus pulled his horse up sharp, and for the first time heard the sounds of water. Then he felt the dampness. He was off his horse before Hayes and Kehler appeared, racing along the path.

Even on foot he almost went off the edge. There he could see a horse slashing the surface with its hooves, in the grip of the current, dark against the poisonous green.

Rose stood a few feet away, his face ashen. He clutched one hand to his heart and with the other he steadied himself by a ridiculously inadequate branch.

Erasmus shouted back to the others as he heard their horses coming, then slowing suddenly.

"Pryor?"

"He went over, as did my own horse after him. I still don't know how Farrelle preserved me. I don't know."

Erasmus saw a flash of dark movement in the roiling waters and without hesitation dove toward the deepest green.

It seemed like an infinite time that he was in the air. Below him he saw a horse swept, thrashing, into the torrent, engulfed in white. A kingfisher plunged into the pool, the sun catching its jeweled feathers.

And then he hit the cold water, the impact driving the breath from his lungs. For a moment he hung there, suspended in thickened green light, gliding slowly down. And then he forced himself to swim. His head broke the surface, and flicking the water from his face, Erasmus bobbed up, searching around. Someone shouted from above, but his words tumbled into the torrent and were swept away.

On the cliff above, figures pointed, but it was impossible to see where. He swam farther out and then realized that the current was sweeping him toward the pool's edge. He struck out strongly at a diagonal, aiming for an eddy which curled behind an egg of rock. But the flow was stronger than he realized, and in a moment he was at the lip, then falling again, plunged down into the depths, a weight of water on top of him. A moment later he was mysteriously on the surface, gasping for air.

Erasmus realized that he would find Pryor only by a miracle. Best not to fight the current, for it no doubt swept Pryor away, and would spin him to the surface again. And Anna. Where was she? Had they accomplished Eldrich's aim, hardly intending to? Was the last follower of Teller gone from this earth?

The current carried him forward quickly now, into foaming and confused waters. He fought to keep the surface, but was dragged under, and battered against rock. Twisting and tumbling, he struggled for air. Just a mouthful here, and then another. Just enough to live. Again he struck stone, and felt the cold river close over him, a muted roaring driving out all else. And then silence.

Hayes ran along the cliff top, trying to keep Erasmus in view, but in a hundred feet the cliff had been cut back in a deep V and by the time he had found his way past this obstacle, Erasmus was gone. There was no sign of horse or man. Pryor, gone. Anna not to be seen. And Erasmus last seen struggling to keep his head up in the world of light and air.

"Can you see them?" Kehler called, coming along behind.

"No one," Hayes hollered above the river sound.

A moment later Kehler appeared at his side, panting, and the two stood, looking down into the chasm, searching for people they knew were gone. Down the river. Alive still, perhaps, but swept away and quickly tiring.

"If Erasmus can find a rock to climb onto . . ." Kehler said at last.

"Yes," Hayes whispered, "we can hope. Could Pryor swim, do you think?"

Kehler considered for a moment, as though trying to remember if this had been mentioned. "I doubt it. So few can: only Erasmus out of all the souls I know."

Hayes nodded. "But what of Anna? She survived the cave. Perhaps she can stay afloat."

"Perhaps, but then, we survived the cave, and neither of us can swim a stroke. Or at least I can't claim to. No, it is likely that we have seen the end of the Tellerites. Deacon Rose and Eldrich will be pleased. I am sorry for poor Pryor. Both brothers gone over this woman."

"Yes, and we're alive." Hayes sat down suddenly on the bank. "Alive and done with the mage, or so I hope. All I want is life to return to normal. I would welcome a creditor or two, now. They no longer seem much of a threat."

Rose came up then, his customary vigor having returned, though he was surprisingly subdued. "Is there no sign of Mr. Flattery?"

Neither answered nor looked at the man, then Hayes relented and shook his head.

Clarendon hailed them. The small man was limping along the cliff top, and as they came up they could see that he was bleeding from a cut on his skull, and looked shaken.

"Randall, what's happened?"

"I was thrown from my horse, but never mind. Where is Mr. Flattery? Where is Pryor?"

"Pryor and his horse followed Anna into the gorge. Erasmus dove in thinking to save the boy. And all of them have been swept away out of sight. Only Erasmus was still on the surface when last we saw."

Clarendon slumped down onto the ground, looking dazed.

"Randall, you're injured."

The small man did not respond. "It is what Eldrich does. Steals away people's lives. I curse him. I curse the day he was born into this world, for surely it must have been foreseen that he would feed upon men like a wolf among lambs."

A slow, rhythmic slap of water. The sea speaking along the shore. Erasmus opened his eyes to see a rippling pattern of light sprayed over a dark surface. He felt a chill in his back.

"Erasmus?"

A face came into view, hovering over him, long tendrils of hair tumbling down to touch his cheek.

"Erasmus?"

"Anna . . . I'm cold."

She nodded. "Can you try to sit?"

He was not sure. Lying still felt so good—but for the chill.

"You're lying in an inch of river water. Come sit up. I will help."

She tugged at his arms, and with surprisingly little effort he came upright.

"It is warming a little as the sun finds its way into the gorge." She stared at him a moment, her look very pensive. "I fished you out," she said. "Plucked you from the waters though it will mean the end of my scheme. Two horses passed but no riders, until you came."

"Pryor," Erasmus said. "He plunged in behind you. Rose lost his horse but managed to save himself."

"And you dove in nobly after this man Pryor," she said. "It is so like you, Erasmus."

"Pryor's brother was your guide," Erasmus said. His wits were coming back a little.

Anna looked intently into his eyes then nodded, looking quickly away. "Yes," she whispered. "I thought I could be as terrible and pitiless as Eldrich. But I have a conscience, after all." She looked down, her hands still supporting him unnecessarily. "I hoped that no one would be hurt. That only I would go into the gorge, and all others would be spared."

"And we would think you dead?"

She nodded. "Yes, and perhaps you would not have been wrong. It is only a miracle that I survived, let alone found you."

"A desperate measure, Anna."

"Yes. But what choice had I? Eldrich would pursue me to my death, or leave others to do so. It was one thing to hide from him when he did not know where to begin searching. But to elude him now . . . now that he knows who I am— It is near to impossible. He is stronger than we realized. Stronger and more cunning."

Erasmus looked around. They were on a flat ledge of rock beneath an overhang of stone, hidden to anyone on the cliff top. "How long have we been down here?"

"A few hours now. Three, perhaps four. I have not heard your friends for some time."

The slapping of water against stone, here where the river ran quiet.

Erasmus stretched, assuring himself that he was whole, and

though he was much battered, no serious damage seemed to have been accomplished. "I will tell you true, Anna, though I owe you my life, I cannot lie to Eldrich. He will know."

She nodded, pulling her knees up into the circle of her arms, and laying the side of her head down upon her arm. Erasmus thought she did not look so drained now—as though life were being restored to her.

The king's blood, he realized.

She raised her head again, looking at him intently. "You can escape Eldrich," she said. "Escape him finally. They will soon give us up for dead, if they haven't already. I can hide us. Hide us from the arts of Eldrich." She reached out and grasped Erasmus' arm. "Even now he does not know if I live or die. But if he believes me dead—us dead—then he will pass through and leave no heir to his knowledge. We will be free of him. You will be free of him."

"I can never be free," Erasmus said.

"But you can. The others will report you dead, and I will hide you from his arts. We will slip out of Farrland and live quietly until he has passed through. It can be done, Erasmus."

Erasmus looked at her, at the hope in her eyes. "And what will we do then? It is the belief of the mages that their arts must pass away. That some cataclysm will result if this is not done."

"Even the mages did not agree on this, Erasmus, but the dissenters were overruled by the others, who were stronger if not more numerous." The light went out of her eyes suddenly, and she looked very sad. "But I will tell you true, Erasmus, I am no longer so certain that the arts should be kept alive. The cost has been so great. I only know that I am not willing to die so that Eldrich can assure this. Let us survive Eldrich, and then we will see. I have some skill at augury. If the mages' vision was true, then I, too, will find it in time."

"That is not the sworn purpose of your society," Erasmus said.

She rested her cheek back upon her arm. "There is no society. Only me." She laughed bitterly. "Is it not ironic that the moment Teller's dream is finally within reach—for I have Landor's seed and ample talent as well—his only remaining follower is no longer sure of his dream." She laughed again. "Certainly he did not foresee that. Nor did Eldrich. I have but one ambition now. Escape Eldrich and die of old age—and not a moment before." Anna fixed her sad gaze on Erasmus.

"The arts are passing, Erasmus, whether Eldrich succeeds or not. No, that is inaccurate. It is the power that is waning. Do you remember the seven touching worlds depicted in the cave? The ancients believed that the power, the power the arts draw upon, moved through the worlds like a tide, ebbing and flowing over the ages. The power is ebbing now. That is the truth of it. That is why the mages seemed less skilled from one generation to the next, whereas in truth they were likely more skilled, but the power they drew upon grew weaker."

"If this is so, then why would Eldrich care about erasing the knowledge of the mages? Why would it matter?"

She shrugged. "Their vision—of the cataclysm. Perhaps it is closer than we realize. Perhaps it is predicted before the tides have ebbed altogether. Farrelle predicted an apocalypse as well, and Pelier painted at least one canvas that is said to depict this final battle. Who knows, other than Eldrich—and the mage might not even know, for he is following a course set by others."

Erasmus stared up at the patterns of reflected light on the ceiling of stone. A breeze flooded down the gorge, causing him to shiver. "We will be cold here tonight," he said, not sure that he'd really made a decision. He needed more time to think.

To be free of Eldrich!

"We will have to stay close," Anna said, "But you are right. We daren't go out by darkness. Nor can we risk the others seeing us. How will they proceed, do you think?"

Erasmus considered a moment. Rose would want to be thorough—as certain that Anna was dead as he could be.

"They will look for us, either alive or dead. They will search along the cliff top—for not less than a day, I think, even though a few hours will really tell the tale. Certainly it will not occur to them that we are hiding here. Did you know of this place?"

"No. It was luck only, if one believes in luck. I had counted on being swept down the river. I have a map that shows the end of the gorge not far off. I hoped to crawl out there, if still alive, and hide myself until you were satisfied that I had not survived." She reached down and made a pattern on the surface of the water with one finger. "There is a ritual that we must perform this night. A rite that will hide us from Eldrich's prying eyes, for he seeks us with augury and much else besides."

"And where will we go?"

"Have you yet a house on Farrow?"

"Yes, but the island is so small. We would not be there two days before everyone would know. No, it will not answer. Into Entonne and down into Doorn. We might find a boat and live among the string of islands beyond where only the fishermen and sparmen go."

Anna nodded. A black bird fluttered down from above, landing in the inch of water, into which it dipped a blood-red bill.

"Chuff!" Anna said, brightening a little.

Erasmus looked at the bird a moment before realizing. He turned to stare at Anna. She almost looked guilty in the face of this.

"When did this happen?" he said.

Anna nodded. "He awaited me outside the cave and has followed me since."

"Then you have taken the seed?"

She nodded. "I would not have survived the cave without it. After Banks was drowned." She looked up at him oddly.

Erasmus felt his eyes close as a memory returned. "Rose got free and broke down the dam. Was Banks caught in that terrible shaft?"

"In the small tunnel at the bottom. Such a flood of water came down. Banks all but filled the passage, blocking the flow. I could not get him out until after the water had drained away. He was so close. Only a few feet more and he would have . . . lived."

Erasmus touched her arm. "Rose caught us by surprise. We would never have let him destroy the dam. No one but the priest wished you ill."

She did not shake his arm off, but looked at him somewhat coldly. "But you have hunted me from Castlebough."

Erasmus removed his hand, letting it drop into the cold water. "Yes. Though with little will. Eldrich sent a messenger. . . . We sought you under threat and with the assurance that you would cause immeasurable evil even if that was not your intent."

"Ah," she said, staring off into the gorge, where the last light of evening lit green ferns growing from the blank wall. They moved moodily in the breeze.

"Is it true, I wonder?" Anna asked. "Or is it merely another lie from the mage—who has no particular allegiance to the truth."

Erasmus could not answer. Was she really suffering such doubt, or was Rose right when he warned them not to listen to her—that she would say anything? But she had saved his life. Pulled him from the river and certain death.

"Why did you save me?" Erasmus asked in a whisper.

Anna did not answer for a moment.

"Because too many have died. I cannot live at such cost. Better to die than to become like Eldrich. Better to die."

Chapter Twenty-nine

ELDRICH paced before the many-paned glass doors, dark against the morning brightness. After several slow passes, he turned to look at his servants, Walky and Bryce, who waited with studied patience.

"I am disappointed in you, Bryce."

His servant swallowed and nodded.

Eldrich glared at Bryce. "What would lead you to do such a thing?"

"She claimed Erasmus told her many things. Showed her writing in Darian."

"Erasmus would do no such thing! Really, Bryce, Erasmus is a man of some character and intelligence, not the youth you remember. You cannot think the worst of a child because he acts as a child any more than you can judge a horse for having no sense." The mage looked at Walky. "What does she want, do you think?"

Walky tilted his head to one side, considering not so much the question as the woman he had met. "I think it is safe to say that she wants only to be reassured the countess is unharmed and here of her own choosing. I do not think she is so foolish as Kent. Miss Edden has not come here with thoughts of rescue."

"Is she attractive, this writer?" Eldrich asked suddenly.

"Well, she turns herself out very plain, sir," Walky answered, showing no surprise at the question, "but she has a great deal of charm, a dry wit, and a lucid intelligence. Attractive? In the larger sense, sir, I would say, yes."

Eldrich actually smiled. "The countess will become jealous, Walky. Careful how you go." He paced again. "Allow her to see the countess. I will speak with her this evening after I have seen Skye." He paused to look at Bryce again—as though reappraising the man in light of his recent actions. "If Erasmus and the others went into the hills after this woman, as you say, then they should emerge soon. I want you there when they appear. Bring them to me, especially this man Clarendon." He continued to look at Bryce for a few seconds and then turned away. "I trust there will be no more surprises this day."

The mage did not say more, but went back to his pacing, servants dismissed from his mind, his thoughts entirely taken up with other matters; dilemmas he pondered in his silence and essential solitude.

The countess released Marianne from their third embrace, held her back at arm's length, and shook her head. "I still can't believe it. How in this round world. . . ?"

"Well, you *will* hardly believe it," Marianne said, disentangling herself from the countess, a bit embarrassed by such a display of emotion, "but I found Skye at the side of the road. His carriage had broken down, and he was traveling in the company of this man Bryce. You remember, he was said to be the servant of whomever was staying in Baumgere's house. Well, I knew from Kent that this is where Eldrich was secluded, so clearly Bryce was a servant of the mage."

"But you did not believe Kent!"

"I did once you had been whisked away." Then her eyes narrowed, almost closing at the memory. "Yes, I know this is all my fault. If only I had listened to Kent, you would have slipped away into Entonne and all this would have been avoided."

"Yes," the countess said, "but we doubted him, and I did not want to believe that I had visited the mage and kept no memory of it."

"Then Kent was right; you are here against your will?"

The countess shook her head. "No, I am here of my own folly. Caught by curiosity and— well, suffice it to say that I entered into a bargain with Lord Eldrich—a devil's bargain, certainly. But one does not break one's word to a mage." She looked up at Marianne and tried to smile.

"Then you would leave if you could."

The countess shook her head. "No. I . . . I would not leave. It is complicated, Marianne, and much of it the mage would not want me to repeat. Trust that I am here of my own choosing, and that I am not the victim of any enchantment. It is the truth, if overly simplified."

"But, Elaural . . ." Marianne looked suddenly deeply hurt and unhappy. "What will become of you? Will you ever return to us? To your friends?"

"I have only a very few friends, and I hope I will return to you in time. I . . . I cannot say. The mage is secretive, and to be honest, I think even Eldrich is not sure of events." She slumped down suddenly on the window seat, and Marianne took the place opposite her.

"I am confused by much that goes on here, Marianne. Augury is not at all what I thought." She opened her hands and let them drop into her lap. "Imagine that you were navigating a ship through fog in changing winds and currents. Every now and then the fog opened up enough that you might see you steered toward rocks, so you change course, but the fog settles in again, and because of the changing winds and current, you can't be sure of your course. All the same, you do what you think you must to avoid the rocks.

"Outside forces, currents and winds, are operating ceaselessly. The fog might open again and show the rocks all but beneath your keel, or you might have passed them safely by, only to see some new danger. I know this hardly makes sense, but this is how augury appears to me. Nothing is fixed. A long time ago the mages had a vision of some terrible cataclysm. Clearly, this is the reason they have disappeared and taken their arts with them. The cataclysm would result from their arts. Do you see? So they have allowed themselves to become extinct, as it were, to avoid this event. But nothing is carved in stone. Events might arrange themselves so that the arts survive, despite all that they do, and the cataclysm takes place all the same. Do you see? It is not that things are fated, pre-scribed. Our actions have effects, though we might never under-stand what they will be.

"I suppose it is rather like life. We take actions that we think will be to our benefit and sometimes, despite all, they lead to tragedy. And Eldrich is caught up in this . . . trying to see deeper into the future than others. Watching the changes, trying to understand the forces at play. And I am part of it, somehow. Almost a hedge against possible events. It is not yet clear if I will have a part, or what it will be.

"It is difficult to describe, for Eldrich is convinced that others arranged events so that I would be here to tempt him in some way. Oh, I don't really understand. It is all so strange and sounds per-fectly preposterous when spoken aloud like this." The countess looked up at her friend, seeing the worry written on her face.

"But, Marianne . . . what will Eldrich do with you? Why has he allowed you to see me at all?"

"I don't know. I convinced Bryce that Erasmus had told us all manner of secrets about his time in the house of Eldrich. So he brought me here, as I hoped. I wanted to see you, to reassure myself that you were unharmed."

The countess tried not to let her concern show. "You should never have done this. The mage is not patient." She looked out the window at the line of trees that marked the boundary of her world.

"It is so very odd. I came with Eldrich thinking I would be iso-lated from my friends, and you have all come to me. Kent was here—and oddly they were almost expecting him. Oh, not him pre-cisely but a painter.

"And now you. And Skye is here, too, you say? Skye . . . I had thought I'd never see the man again. I had almost put him from my mind." She shook her head in wonder. "I've come to believe that I do not understand life at all, Marianne. Eldrich spends all of his time trying to part the veils of time, but it does him little good, for mat-ters seem to change continuously. He does not seem to believe in coincidence. In his world nothing happens by chance—as though there is a pattern, however fluid. When Kent arrived, noble foolish Kent, Walky named it a good sign, saying they had been 'awaiting the painter.' " She looked up at Marianne, a smile spreading across her face. "And then Eldrich had him paint two portraits, one of him and one of me, and sent him off. And just when I had begun to despair that I would be left alone in this strange house, you arrive and bring Lord Skye in tow. I cannot begin to imagine what will occur next. I cannot."

Marianne laughed, raising her eyebrows. "It's only recently that you've come to believe that you don't understand life? I've never understood. People praise me for my 'vision,' but I will tell you, I have none. Not as they mean it, at least. I write about people caught up in matters that mystify them, making intelligent decisions that go wrong, or drawing foolish conclusions that come out right.

"Why, I know some utterly ridiculous people—not a sensible thought in their heads—who cannot seem to do anything that does not turn out brilliantly. If they were to buy shares in a company that was bankrupt, they would discover the next day that their offices sat upon a field of gold. And they think themselves geniuses! Yet they are nothing more than lucky, for lack of a better word— repeatedly lucky! And I'm sure we both know people who are the opposite. And that is to say nothing of who is deserving and what happens to them. How can anyone make sense of it?" A silence fell between them as though neither of them could keep up this false exuberance.

Marianne fixed a very serious look upon the countess. "What are you to Eldrich, Elaural? And what is he to you? Is there . . . *sympathy* between you?"

"Sympathy. . . ?" The countess was surprised at how guarded her tone had become. "No, I would not say that. There is . . . magnetism would perhaps describe it. And there is something more. I was meant for him, Marianne. To tempt him in some way. To lead him into some fatal error that would allow the arts to be renewed. That is what I have come to believe from the few hints the mage has given and the odd thing I have managed to pry from Walky." The countess looked up at her friend wondering if she looked as forlorn as she felt at the moment. "Do you see? All along I have had some other purpose. This mad attraction that men feel toward me . . . it is not real, not me at all, but a result of the arts. And Eldrich was never meant to realize it. But they underestimated his skill, it seems, for he did realize. So I am here, partly to find out what my place is in this larger story. Can you understand, Marianne? I am like a character in one of your novels who realizes she is in a book but continues on just to see how it all comes out, what her part is."

"That made no sense at all," Marianne said, "and it frightens me a little that I understood what you meant. But if you are intended to tempt Eldrich into some terrible mistake, why does he keep you here? Why does he not send you away, or worse? Would that not be the safest thing? To not let you endanger his purpose?"

The countess shook her head. "I am not sure, exactly. Perhaps those who bespelled me knew he would not send me away—that he could not, even if he divined my purpose. It is impossible to say, Marianne. He is complicated and secretive. You have never met a man so secretive. And his pride is great. I sometimes think that he hopes to turn me to his own purpose, as though to prove his skill greater than those who sent me—as if he could prove something to the dead."

"Now that sounds more like a man. The 'great men' I have met, at least. Their pride is beyond all." Marianne raised her eyebrows. "Now, I should not pry—"

"You should not," the countess agreed quickly and firmly.

Marianne nodded resignedly.

A long silence overcame them, extending to several minutes. "Have I angered the mage, do you think?" Marianne finally asked, her voice softly harsh. "Will he exact some . . . retribution for what I've done?"

"I don't know, Marianne," the countess said, relieved that the subject had changed. "Kent was sent off unharmed, I'm sure. I think the mage will do the same with you—he does not seem to be quite so fearsome as the legends indicate. But you must realize one thing—you will not go from this place with the memory of your visit intact. Eldrich does not allow that."

Marianne's gaze flicked up, her mouth opening a little in surprise. "What are you saying? That he will do to me what was done to you? I will awake as though from a daze, and not even know if you are well or no?" She rose from the window seat, half-turning away. "Elaural . . . I transmute my memories into gold. Do you understand? They are more precious to me than fame or fortune or reputation. They are the raw materials from which I build. He cannot touch them. . . . He cannot!" She turned back to the countess, her face ashen. "You must speak with him. He must not tamper with my mind as though it were some hack's manuscript—cutting out what does not please him. You must tell him, Elaural. You must. . . ."

Skye did not remember. Bryce had said that he'd met Eldrich before, but he had not even the slightest recollection, not the vaguest image of what the mage might look like. More memories that had been stolen from him, but in this case the cause was known—as was the cure. Eldrich could restore what he had taken, of that Skye was certain. The mage might even be able to do more.

Skye had been abandoned by Bryce and put into the care of a round little man of distracted disposition who now took him to see the mage. It was odd that a man of Eldrich's forbidding reputation should have as a servant an innocuous little man easily mistaken for a retired schoolmaster. This had set Skye's overwound nerves at ease, a little.

Even so, he was not relaxed. Not so much because he was intimidated, though he would admit that he was, but because this was almost certainly his only chance. If he could not find a way to have Eldrich restore his memories now, then he would almost certainly live without them the rest of his days. It was an opportunity not to be thrown away.

And yet he knew almost nothing of the mage. Like all of his kind, he was said to be arrogant and insensible to the concerns of others. It went without saying, then, that he had no patience for men, whom he considered to be vastly his inferiors. How did one appeal to such a man?

The irony of the situation was that Skye, in his dealings with others, was usually in the position of Eldrich. Men, even accomplished men, were intimidated by him, by his vast reputation, and he had little patience for them, considering them a bother. They interrupted his important work with foolish questions and hare-brained schemes. And the truth was, he was often less than polite to them.

And now how did one proceed? How did men catch the attention of the notoriously impatient Skye? Most often, they didn't, and the truth of it was that it depended on his mood and what they had interrupted. When he did take time to listen, it was usually to men who spoke politely, but directly, and who did not presume too much. Men who obviously had common sense, and did not ask much of him. After all, Skye had been the patron of more than one promising young empiricist, the champion of a few causes. He was not as selfish and impossible as he was made out to be. Was he?

The man named Walky stopped before a door, tapped softly and then opened it a crack. "Lord Skye," he said into the room beyond, and pushed the door open, nodding Skye through.

A singular tingling seemed to run through Skye's body just below the skin. It was not a sensation he'd had before, and it left him feeling cut off from himself, like his personality had been set adrift from his body. Somehow he managed to move forward.

Was this some spell? Some enchantment that emanated from the mage? Skye felt he might lose his balance at any time.

A dark-haired man sat in a chair before the window reading what appeared to be a very ancient book. On the table, a single candle flickered, emitting a furtive light that left most of the room, which Skye sensed was large, in shadow.

Six paces distant Skye waited, and after the threshold between impolite and outrageously rude had been breached he considered clearing his throat—but didn't. Somehow he thought this would not have the desired effect.

The thought of turning around and leaving crossed his mind, but stories of mages rooting people to the spot were numerous, and though Skye was a little doubtful of these, still—

Eldrich finally looked up, the book remaining open, held by one elegantly formed hand. Eldrich regarded him for a moment, with an unsettling disinterest, and then nodded. "When you met that woman at the house of Mary Finesworth—you remember, there were some few agents of the Admiralty there in various states of stupor."

Skye nodded.

"There might have been things you observed but later did not recall. I want you to turn your mind back to that night again. Close your eyes. Imagine every tiny thing you did or thought. Tell me: You arrived by carriage. . . ."

"Yes." Skye closed his eyes as he had been bidden, forming a picture of that night. Had it rained?

"A woman answered the door?" Eldrich prompted.

"The faded woman . . ." Skye felt himself falling into a dreamlike trance. He almost believed he was there. He could smell the evening, feel the night on his skin. It had rained, though barely. The door opened, and a woman appeared.

A hand on his arm guided him through the dusk—no, he was inside in poor light.

"You're perfectly hale, Lord Skye. Just through the door now." It was the small man, returned, and he was leading Skye out of the room.

Eldrich.

Skye tried to shake his arm loose but found himself too weak. "No. . . . I—I must speak with Lord Eldrich." Unable to free himself, he planted his feet and twisted his neck to look back. A tall man stood before the window, a single candle, twinned in the dark glass, touched him there and here—as though he were composed, for the most part, of shadow.

"Let him speak, Walky," came the oddly musical voice. Why did this sound chill him?

"Sir," Skye began, trying to remember what it was that was so important. "Sir . . . I suffered the loss of my memories as a child. I don't know if I have been of any service to you, or if I can be, but I would gladly exchange anything I might have, any service, to have these memories returned to me."

Eldrich did not turn around but spoke to the glass, his words seeming to take on the night chill as they reflected back. "Exchange? But people serve me, willingly or no. What have you to exchange that I cannot have at no cost? No, Lord Skye, it would be a bad bargain—for both of us, I fear. Would you be so intent on this if I told you that you'd be a happier man not knowing?"

Skye was taken aback by this. He had been only a boy; what could a boy have done that he would be happier not knowing? Or was it what was done to him? "I would have my memories, all the same."

"Would you, indeed? I will see the woman now, Mr. Walky."

The small man tugged at his arm. "Say nothing more, sir," he whispered. "It will not profit you."

And Skye let himself be led out into the hallway, his past remaining in the darkened room with the man made of shadow.

M arianne settled herself in the chair by the single candle, drawn to the light in this strange place.

He will not harm you, she assured herself. *Whatever else he does, he will not harm you. Even Eldrich would not be so arrogant.* She counted the King among her ardent readers, for Farrelle's sake. The King! Who could say—it was possible that even the mage might read.

After all, there was a book sitting on the table, the light of the candle falling upon its leather binding. But how old and worn it was, the leather as thin as decaying leaves in some places, any title erased long ago. It was her habit to note the titles of the books people read, only partly to see if it might be one of her own, so it was natural for her to wonder what book this might be. She almost reached out to open it, but then the realization struck. This was no common book.

This was a book of the arcane, forbidden to any but a mage.

"Flames," she heard herself say. Suddenly this was an object of fascination. She could not tear her eyes from it, as though staring would reveal something. *A forbidden book:* to a woman who loved books and sought knowledge there hardly could be anything more alluring.

"Why don't you open it?"

She looked up to find a tall, stooped man standing in the garden doorway.

Marianne found that she could not open her mouth, not a word would come.

"You are fascinated, clearly. Open it."

She only stared, caught by his musical voice, the way the shadows played about him. He was more forbidding than Elaural had described. Stranger.

She reached out her hand, feeling somehow that she must not back down from this challenge. Just as her fingers were about to touch it, she stopped. "Will I be harmed?"

A smile lit his face for an instant; mocking, as she'd been warned. "Why? Do you feel knowledge is dangerous?"

"Unquestionably, when possessed by the wrong people, but I was thinking of more arcane things. A protective charm or some such."

He shook his dark hair. "No, in that way it is completely harmless."

Gingerly, she touched it, curling two fingers under the cover, but she hesitated to open it. Eldrich watched her intently, she could feel it. She took her hand away, and looked up at him, feeling a thin smile tighten her face, then dissolve.

The two gazed at each other a moment, and then Eldrich shifted on the threshold. "Wisdom as well as talent," he said, no mockery detectable in his tone. "That is not so common." He came into the room, sliding a second chair toward her.

"Eldrich," he said, bobbing his head in her direction.

"Marianne Edden."

"Let us put aside this ruse that brought you here. Erasmus told you nothing about his years in my house."

She nodded.

The mage looked a little saddened for a moment. "Bryce is always ready to believe the worst of Erasmus." He looked away from her, appearing to stare at the candle's reflection in the glass. "I trust you have been reassured that I did not abduct Lady Chilton or that I am keeping her here against her wishes?"

Marianne nodded, feeling the breath in her lungs disappear for a second. Was he angry that she thought this of him?

Eldrich sat back in his chair, almost sprawling, and interwove his long fingers before him. "How old are you?" he said, gazing at her in a manner that she thought less than polite—as though he were unaware of the etiquette of educated society.

"Twenty and nine," she said.

He pressed his lips out, as though in thought. "What would you say if I could tell you the year of your death?"

"I thought augury was less than exact," she said, hearing the wariness in her voice. Was this some jest at her expense? She did not like the sound of a mage speaking to her of death—her death!

"Oh, this is not augury. Not in the usual sense, at least."

Marianne could not remember feeling fear in a good many years—not real fear. Anxiety that she would be embarrassed or that she would not be a success, yes, but not fear for her life. "I think that I would rather not know. After all, what good would knowing do?"

"Very little, in the larger sense. You would not be able to change it. Still . . . it might allow you to complete the things that are important to you. Do the things you have always dreamed of doing. That journey to Farrow, or that book you have long planned."

"There is that, I suppose," she said. "Is this your purpose? To tempt me with some forbidden knowledge?"

Eldrich laughed. "It is a terrible vice, but you see, I am interested in knowing how long you will live for my own reasons, and I thought as I will have this information it might be of interest to you. It is freely offered."

"In all the stories I have read, I cannot once remember a mage offering something freely." As Marianne spoke, she feared that she had overstepped her bounds.

"I see that you are a friend of Lady Chilton's," he said, with a touch of humor in the irony. "But those are merely stories, almost none of them real. Fiction. And not the type that is more true than truth." He rose from his chair, suddenly, and went and stood by the door. Far off, she heard a high wail, and then realized that it must be the wolf. The famous familiar of Eldrich.

"Let me tell you a story, if I may presume to tell a tale to the teller of tales." He was about to speak when Marianne interrupted.

"Why do you bother, when I am assured I'll remember nothing that happens while I am here?"

Eldrich looked down at her, his face suddenly tight. "Do you fear you will forget your precious feelings for the countess, like Kent?"

"You misunderstand me," Marianne said, struggling to keep her tone mild. "My memories are the stone from which I build. Without them I am no different from any other unmarried woman my age. It does not matter if you have no respect for me, but if you respect my art at all, you will reconsider."

"Ah, this is about art." The mocking smile did appear, then quickly disappear. "I must tell you, Miss Edden, yours is a comparatively minor art, however elevated by your class, compared with the ancient art I practice. Excuse me if I appear vain in this, but you evoke things only in the minds of your readers. I evoke them here, in the world in which we presently dwell." He turned and gestured into the room. "There are spirits in this house. Did you know? Two children who died of influenza while still very young. The countess can almost feel them. Can you?" He began to move his hands in the air, tracing lines of glowing silver, a tracery of symbols and marks. Chanting in a language she did not know, he gestured to the candle near her elbow and its flame split into seven tongues and wavered up, so that she recoiled in fear.

A moment more, and there, in the center of the room, two children appeared, a boy and girl, staring at Eldrich, their eyes unnaturally wide and dark.

They whispered to each other, their gaze hardly leaving the mage. Once, the girl looked at Marianne, their eyes meeting, but Marianne was of little interest.

"Do you see?" Eldrich said softly. "The ghosts of the past. Can you feel the sadness? The loss? Aged three and seven, and wandering here still. Have you ever evoked a character so thoroughly? I think not." At a gesture the children disappeared, and Marianne felt an odd warmth, though in her heart she was cold.

"Now let me begin again," Eldrich said, the musical voice soft and sad, as though he could speak in a minor key—*pianissimo*. "I was taken to the house of the mage, Lucklow, when I was but seven years. Seven years. I hardly recall the time before . . . my true childhood. It is lost. Lost in a dream that slips away as you wake.

"And I awoke to find myself in the house of a mage, a ruin of a castle which was haunted by more than memories. I was a child alone in that terrible place. I would stare for hours out over the surrounding forest, dreaming of the world beyond, the world from which my parents had sacrificed me." He paused and drew a breath. "I feared Lucklow utterly. He was short tempered and prone to cruelty. His familiar was an adder. . . ."

Chapter Thirty

D EACON Rose took the warm ashes from the edge of the glowing coals and filled the cupped hands of each of the mourners—Kehler and Hayes and Clarendon. Hayes found the warmth of the ashes disturbing.

Rose strode the few paces to the water, chanting words of Old Farr in his strong voice. He released a ribbon of ashes which streamed out on the wind, and marked the sign of Farrelle on the flowing waters.

Each of them in turn did the same, and then together they released the remaining ashes into the river, into this artery of the world.

They had searched the whole day and all the afternoon before, becoming more desperate and more despondent as the hours passed. Much of the time Clarendon and his great dog had ranged ahead, wading in the margins of the current, clambering over rocks as though his years meant nothing. Often they saw him standing on some higher rock, surveying the opposite shore. Hayes had almost felt the concentration the man called forth, felt him willing Erasmus to appear on the distant bank—appear alive with their young guide in tow.

Hayes watched Rose as he knelt by the river and prayed, the Old Farr sounding regal and solemn in this place. Any triumph the priest felt at Anna's destruction was tempered by the loss of Erasmus and Pryor.

When the prayer came to an end, Clarendon spread a handful of wild roses on the water, their scent swirling in the breeze that coiled out of the gorge.

Hayes watched the roses go bobbing over the waters, lost to them in a few seconds, and then he turned away, feeling the salt of tears. He went quickly up the bank, back into the trees to be alone with his grief.

Would all this have happened if he had not involved Erasmus in the first place?

Clarendon kept assuring him that coincidence played only the smallest part in any of these events, but even so— If they had not met at the brothel, would any of this have occurred?

He found an open place three dozen feet above the river and sat himself down there, staring out over the sunlit waters. The constant flow comforted him, somehow—the steady, uncomplaining procession toward the sea. They would all go that way, or back into the earth to become part of some great tree or the ferns that grew in the underwood. So Erasmus had gone, escaping Eldrich at last, escaping the hidden scars that he bore within.

Dusk appeared out of the trees, greeting him perfunctorily, excited to be here in the wilds with his master. A moment later Clarendon came out of the wood, his small boots making barely a sound.

"Ah, here you are, Mr. Hayes. Do I interrupt you?"

Hayes shook his head. "No. No, I am ready for some company. I am just sitting here watching the river flow, and it has comforted me."

Clarendon lowered himself to the grass, a little stiffly Hayes thought. "Yes, I always find water comforting as well. I can see the lake from my home in Castlebough. And when I travel in the winter, I usually stay by the sea or some other body of water. It is not really intentional, but it just seems to come out that way. Do you know the old song? Anonymous, I think.

> "We are borne within the clouds
> Sailing landward on the winds

Falling sweetly to the grasses
Sipped by mothers, born again."

The small man smiled wanly. "So we all shall go. 'Down to the ship-proud sea.' Whole continents will go that way, if these natural philosophers are to be believed. Mr. Flattery has gone earlier than he should. Earlier than his friends would have had it, that is certain. But we will all follow. Likely, I will not be far behind, and I do not say that in self-pity, but it is merely the truth, for people born with my particular condition seldom are blessed with a natural span of years." He gazed out over the flowing river, suddenly a little sadder.

Hayes did not speak or try to offer comfort, and the two of them remained silent for some time, perhaps still hoping for a miracle. Hoping Erasmus would appear, swimming among the folds and creases of the river.

"One would think that of the lot of us, Erasmus would be the least likely to drown," Hayes said. "Yet, in the end, it was his ability to swim that brought about his ruin. None of us would have dreamed of leaping into the gorge. And so his skill betrayed him."

Clarendon nodded. "I think it is often the way. Our abilities are what lead us into danger—not our shortcomings which we learn not to test."

Hayes nodded. "What will happen now?" he asked. "Rose said something about a ritual that Erasmus was to perform if we found Anna. . . ."

"You did not speak to Mr. Flattery about this?"

Hayes shook his head.

"Well, it was not so much to alert the mage as it was a revenge upon Mr. Flattery. You see, he was to perform the ritual that had caused Percy's terrible immolation."

Hayes turned to look at Clarendon. "Do you think Eldrich was aware of this?"

The small man shrugged. "I don't know. Who can say with a mage. But certainly none of us are prepared to do it. Only the priest likely has the knowledge or talent, and certainly he is not going to risk his precious hide now that he has accomplished his purpose. No, I think we will have to find some way to contact Eldrich. Deacon Rose will likely take on this responsibility, and despite what I feel about the man, I will accompany him. I have a bargain to offer Lord Eldrich." His vivid blue eyes, which had seemed near to tears all along, glistened.

Hayes touched Clarendon's shoulder. "Randall, you will gain nothing from meeting Eldrich. Did the mage not say that Lizzy had gone where none could follow? Certainly everything we have learned would indicate this to be true."

Randall seemed almost to square his shoulders. "Eldrich knew what would happen to Lizzy. He came only to witness it—to be proven right. And there was Baumgere, who spent half a lifetime searching for a gateway to the world of the Strangers, to Faery, where Tomas had gone. A gate which I think we found, though we could not open it. And beyond must lie the world of the mages—the world Anna called Darr—and if that is where Lizzy has gone . . ." He fell silent, embarrassed, as though he had not meant to speak so openly.

"I will tell you, Randall," Hayes said softly. "I don't think Eldrich will care in the slightest that you seek a lost love. Such things mean nothing to mages."

The little man nodded, looking down and running his hand over the earth. "Perhaps," he said softly, and then picked up a small stone from the ground and hefted it, but did not seem to have the energy to toss it into the river, as Hayes expected him to do.

How many years had it been? Hayes wondered. Forty-some? Fifty? Eldrich had poisoned all of their lives—a poison that never seemed to leave the system. Would he be so in fifty years? Unable to forget what had happened? Unable to go forward in life for want of gazing always back?

"I will not feel comfortable, seeing you ride off with Rose to look for Eldrich."

Clarendon shrugged. "I am aware of the depths of his deception, to what lengths he would go to preserve his church. I do not think he can surprise me now, unless he were to display compassion or behavior one might conceive of as noble. Do not be concerned."

A dark bird soared past on the breeze billowing out of the gorge, for a moment it hung in the air before them, its blood-red bill gleaming in the sun, and then it angled away, like a ship sailing across the wind.

"Do you know," Clarendon began, "I had great respect for Mr. Flattery, even before we met—his accomplishments demand it—but this became even greater as I grew to know him. And he treated me . . . I can hardly describe it. As though my abilities and shortcomings were no different than any others. Do you understand? My small stature was no greater handicap or advantage than extreme height would have been. There were things I could do that others could not—and things I could not do. Just as a large man would never have been able to negotiate the small passages we traveled—yet he might be stronger or have a greater reach. But to Mr. Flattery, I would have been that man's equal. And as to my mental faculties . . . I think he understood the advantages and terrible failings of those, and again they were not judged, but accepted. Do you see? He did not judge me by my size alone, disregarding all else. Nor did he see only my unusual mental abilities, and not realize that I had shortcomings, as well."

"I have not noticed these shortcomings in your mental abilities, Randall."

"Ah, but they are there. I am too emotional and let my passions overcome my reason. A terrible failing in certain circumstances, I can assure you. And I have not an artistic notion in my head. Oh, yes, I learned to play the pianum, but I am no more a musician than are these devices that will hit the keys in the correct order and 'play' a tune. My mind is a calculating device, with near perfect recall, but I have little capacity for the imaginative. I could never have invented calculus, as Lord Skye did, yet even that great man has not the ability to do calculations in the mind that I have. So there you have it. Mr. Flattery saw me for what I was, and I will tell you, few have managed that." He paused. "And though I knew him only a short time, I shall miss him terribly. It is yet another tragedy we can lay at Eldrich's door." He threw the rock suddenly, far out over the moving river. Its splash attracted several wheeling gulls, crying miserably above the voice of the water.

They would not likely survive another night on this ledge awash in ice water. And even if they did, Erasmus was certain they would have no strength left to swim out, if they had the strength now.

At dusk they slipped into the water, having carefully surveyed all the river that could be seen. They planned to let the current carry them a hundred feet, then they would try to swim into the eddy behind a jumble of rocks. Erasmus was certain that it looked far easier than it was, and it did not appear easy.

Anna squeezed his hand once before lowering herself into the waters.

"When you emerge from the gorge," Erasmus reminded her, "don't become disoriented. Land on the opposite bank. We will hide another day before crossing."

The chill of the water was like a slap to a sleeping man. Erasmus could barely move for a second and then the current reached out and grasped him and be began to paddle furiously to keep his head in the air. If he had realized how weak he would be, he would have chanced the ledge for another day. Flames, but it would be a miracle if he survived this.

The rocks that were his goal swept past, and two strokes told him that making the calm of the eddy was impossible, nor could he see Anna there. They were at the mercy of the river and would survive only if their strength held and if they were not bashed to pieces upon the rocks.

The river carried him forward, the cold, green stream like a sinewy muscle stretched between the bones of the rocks. Erasmus spun about in the current, scraping along water-smoothed stones, dropping into jade pools which were emerald at their center. He surrendered himself to it, to the undeniable force of the river, and was drenched in the blood of the earth. Let it take him now, if it would. Let it grant him escape.

Let him float to the surface in some calm arm of the vast river, turning slowly beneath the sun. Wash ashore on warm stone to be picked clean by carrion crows and roving bands of insects, carrying bits of him back to feed their young. Let him return to the earth and start anew.

And then there were fist-sized boulders beneath his boots, and he danced along in the current, three yards to a step. Darkness had settled into the gorge, trees along the banks indistinguishable in their species. He found himself crawling up on a gravel bank, so exhausted that he collapsed for a moment upon the sun-warmed stones, and lay listening to the night.

Anna . . . What had happened to her?

A nightingale began to sing, its fluid notes counterpoint to the river sound. Erasmus forced himself up, climbing the few feet of embankment into the shelter of the trees. He crouched there, shivering, trying to find a place where he would be out of the cooling breeze.

He looked out over the river and saw the light of a fire reflecting off the upper ramparts of trees. His traveling companions. How he wanted to cross the river and reveal himself to them, appearing like a ghost in the warm light. He could sit by the fire and bask in the glow of friendship.

What had happened to Anna? He hadn't seen any sign of her since they slipped into the river. It was not out of the question that she had perished this time. After all, Erasmus would have drowned if not for her—after all the years he had chanced the waters.

He lay down in the shelter of a fallen log where he could see the dance of the firelight across the river, see the shadows of his companions as they moved about. He realized he could not go back to them. They would start the search for Anna again, and perhaps find her. Erasmus would have to perform Percy's ritual. The fire ritual. And if he survived, he would be in thrall to Eldrich yet again. No, better to be dead, to be a ghost, wandering in the wood. Better to have no name than to be a servant of Eldrich. To be twisted by hatred as Percy had become.

"Solve your own 'dilemma arcane,' " Erasmus whispered. To be free of Eldrich, of searching for answers in old histories, in long-forgotten letters, that was what he wanted. To think of Eldrich no more than any man who traveled the streets of Avonel. To find out who Erasmus Flattery was beyond the reach of Eldrich, beyond the obsession.

There will be no Erasmus Flattery, he reminded himself. He rolled on his back and stared up at the irregular plot of stars visible through the branches. He could not see the wandering star—his "wondering star." Perhaps it had found its place, its place among the stars, and would stay anchored there in peace.

Chapter Thirty-one

HAYES was the first to appear, rising before the sun. He made his way down the bank, stopping to survey the river before bending to drink. In the muted light, the pewter morning, he appeared small, childlike, as he crouched down by the running water, the sky above him rose and gray. Dusk appeared, and Erasmus froze in place knowing the wolfhound might sense him where the others did not.

But the dog bent down beside the young man and lapped up the water with a long tongue, raising his head to survey the world warily, as wild animals did when they came to drink.

In turn, each of his companions came down to the river. As they departed, Erasmus said a silent good-bye to each; Deacon Rose next, then the determined Kehler, and Clarendon last. Oddly, this was the hardest parting. Randall Spencer Emanual Clarendon; the small man with enormous heart. There was something about his gentleness and fits of passion, his unwavering loyalty, that Erasmus found difficult to leave. Kehler and Hayes were young and bright, they would do well; it was hardly in question. Rose, well, he was another matter. Fanatics, true fanatics, were never wrong, and this sustained them through being both persecuted and persecutor. Rose

207

would go to his death believing that Anna's murder was Farrelle's will—and Erasmus' death in quest of this, merely unfortunate.

Clarendon made his way back up the bank as the edge of the sun seared the horizon. Dusk gamboled beside him, but when his master did not respond, the dog became quiet, even pensive, if a dog could be pensive.

Two hours later Erasmus watched them ride off, leading several riderless horses. Despite being weak with hunger, and suffering the blackest of headaches, Erasmus remained hidden for some time.

What would he do if Anna did not appear? If she were dead or had abandoned him?

The sight of his companions riding away had left him feeling . . . as he had felt when delivered to the house of Eldrich, those many years ago. But now he felt ghostly as well. While his companions were camped a stone's throw away, he could still give this up—step out onto the riverbank and shout. And there would be food and warm clothing—a horse to ride. Friends.

Instead he was alone in the hills without food or the tools of survival: an ax; a knife; a bow.

Several hours passed, giving Erasmus ample time to contemplate starvation. His reserves had been so depleted by the time in the cavern that he began to wonder seriously if he could even walk out of the hills now. Certainly a grown man could not starve to death in the Caledon Hills? No, he decided, even if he wasn't born in the hills, he knew enough about the natural world to survive. There would be crayfish in the river, and fish, if he could fashion a spear. A dozen plants could be eaten. Birds' eggs would be a last resort. He would survive.

Sure that his companions were gone, Erasmus emerged onto the gravel bar, looking up and down the river. Here it flowed so tranquilly that he could hardly believe a torrent lay just upstream. Downstream the waters were shaded by overhanging trees, the shadows broken in places, sunlight turning the water iridescent green—the color of a hummingbird's throat.

As he looked, something took shape in the shadow, then stepped out into sunlight. Anna, her long legs golden in the sunlight. Erasmus moved toward her, and as he did, realized she wore only a long shirt. They met at the edge of the water, both silent and grave.

Then she smiled. "You stayed," she said.

Erasmus nodded.

Her smile broadened. "I am drying my wretched clothes. Come, swim with me, and I will show you where I've hidden the food."

She began stripping off his clothes, laughing, her smile bright and mischievous. And then, suddenly, she went bounding into the water shouting, "We're dead, we're dead! They all think we're dead." Peeling off her shirt and tossing it onto the shore, she pitched herself into the water and then emerged, throwing great arcs of water with her arms. She laughed with such abandon that she lost her balance and fell into the water, emerging in a fit of laughter and coughing.

Erasmus plunged in, feeling the shock of the cold after the warmth of the sun. He surfaced before her and she reached out and took his face between her hands.

"You realize we're dead?" she said, trying to sound serious though neither her face nor voice would comply. "Eldrich thinks we're dead. . . . Or soon will. You understand what that means?"

Erasmus said nothing, not quite caught up in the moment.

"We are free of him, Erasmus. *You* are free of him. Free of him! We may go where we please. Do what we wish. Become whom we will. Do you see?" She began to chant. "Freefreefreefree." And then she jumped up and ducked him, pushing down on his shoulders until he went under, and then she relented, slipping down, her body softly pressed to his. Their lips met as Erasmus surfaced, a long, luxurious kiss.

He could feel each of her ribs. That was his first thought as they kissed. She had come so close to starving. They both had. Flames, he was all bones himself.

When they parted, she released him, taking his hand. "Come," she said, "there is food, and then I think we can find a bed of moss. We'll have to do without starlight. I can't wait that long."

They lay close, by the light of a small fire, and gazed at a map they had spread on the ground. Anna lay half over Erasmus, propped up on an elbow, and the soft warmth of her was like a second fire, glowing against his skin. She aimed a long finger lazily at the map. "We cannot go into this village. That would be an error. No, we must go past, overland. It will be all meadows and fields and small woods. Not so hard as traveling in the hills."

"But we need to buy horses, food. Find rooms to sleep."

She nuzzled his ear. "Clearly you have not been hiding from Eldrich all your life. You can afford no mistakes. You must remember that no one can lie to him, or keep their secrets. Leave a single witness to your passing and Eldrich will hear of it." She kissed him softly. "We will travel by night, stay clear of houses and their occupants. If we must, we'll take a bit of food, and leave a coin or two— for I know you're too noble to rob the less fortunate." He could hear the grin in her tone, and she kissed his neck, wrestled the blanket around to her liking and put her finger to the map. "Here. What town is this?"

"Cobblers' Hill. Or 'Cobblers' Hell' as it is known locally."

"Why is that? Should we stay clear of it?"

"No, it is just a peculiarity of the local pronunciation, where 'hill' is 'hell,' and a 'mill' a 'mell.' "

"No one knows you there, I hope?"

"No. I've just heard the name. It is a prosperous town, by all accounts. Large enough so you can't know everyone's name or business. We'll buy horses there, I take it?"

"And a small carriage, if we can find one. Nothing that would stand out, but a lady traveling by horseback will likely be noticed."

"A dog cart," Erasmus ventured.

"Exactly. You know, when I was child, I thought such a cart would be drawn by dogs! Not carry them."

Erasmus laughed.

"I imagined all kinds of such carts. A cat cart. A goat cart . . ."

"Now there is such a thing as a goat cart."

"There is not!"

"Oh, but there is. We might even see one as we go. Usually used to draw milk to town, for some odd reason."

"You liar!"

Anna tried to tickle him, to no avail for he had not been susceptible even as a boy. After a moment she gave up. "I didn't realize you were a man of so little sensitivity."

Erasmus didn't respond, but remained still, staring at the map. "Where are we going?"

Anna sensed his mood, and grew more serious herself. This was characteristic of her, Erasmus knew—this sensitivity to others. Perhaps it was even a manifestation of her talent. It told her when to apply her abundant charm, to which Erasmus was susceptible.

She lay her head on his shoulder. "We must go to ground for a while, Erasmus. Let Eldrich become confident that we are dead. There is a place—Eldrich will not know of it—it is isolated, the house not easily found. We could live there thirty years and no one would bother us."

"And does this place have a name?"

She looked at him for a moment, as though wondering if she could trust him with such information—if she trusted him at all. "Do you know Beacon Head? There is a small island in its lee: Midsummer Isle. Very few people live there. Fisher folk, a few farmers. There was a town, but it was long ago abandoned. It is mainly known for Halden once having stayed there a year. It is said he wrote *About Ashleen* during that time. A few eccentrics have taken to living there—people who, for various reasons, no longer desire the society of men. I have a house there. High on a cliff overlooking the sea. It is dark and rainy all winter, but the summers are often fine, if not overly warm. We won't be bothered, I can assure you."

"But what will we do?" Erasmus asked.

"Well, I was hoping you might be interested in more of what we've been doing this night. . . . No, I understand what you say. We will await the death of Eldrich. That will be our primary task: to outlive the mage."

"It sounds rather a . . . slim purpose to have in life."

"Survival? It is the one common purpose of the living, though mankind often forgets that. Survive and procreate. Our lives needn't be reduced to an animal level entirely, though." She smiled. "There are other things."

Erasmus shifted around so that he could see her more easily. "Anna, why did you rescue me from the gorge? I was hunting you. I might have given you away. Tell me truthfully."

She sat up, wrapping the blanket around her, the colors of fire playing in her disheveled tresses. "Is it difficult for you to believe that I could not let you drown? Yes, yes, I know—there was Garrick. But I had a vision that he would betray me. Survival, Erasmus.

The animal desire to live." She hung her head as though ashamed. "We are alike, you and I. Eldrich used you terribly and trapped you in the cavern to die. If there is anyone who should want to escape the mage, it is you, Erasmus. If you continued to serve him, what would he do next? He cares for you not at all, Erasmus, for you or anyone else." She reached out and put her hand gently on his heart. "And I wanted an ally, a companion, for all of my fellows are dead . . . murdered. We might find something like happiness together, or at the very least, peace."

"Peace," Erasmus echoed.

They fell silent, listening to the dark sounds of the night and the river.

Anna snuggled down close to him as the fire burned to coals and in a moment she was breathing regularly, deeply asleep.

Why did she save me, Erasmus wondered. Certainly everything she said might be true, but these explanations were not the reason she had kept him alive. She was more cunning. He remembered her escape from the chamber with the seed. No, Anna had her own plans. Just how they involved Erasmus Flattery was the question.

He closed his eyes, but they sprang open again as it occurred to him that she might have murdered her guide thus—as he slept.

Chapter Thirty-two

MARIANNE woke from a restful sleep and found herself in the countess' carriage descending a long slope among the hills. And then she remembered; she was coming from Castlebough where she had left the countess to continue her foolish pursuit of Skye. Poor woman.

She shook her head and stretched in a manner that would not be deemed ladylike, but then she was alone in the carriage, and what cared she for such strictures anyway?

"Odd," she said aloud. She did not usually sleep so well in carriages; in fact, she never had before. It was something of a miracle that she had not been thrown to the floor.

She thrust open the window, feeling overly warm, as though the sun beat down on her carriage, which it did not, for the sky was nothing but cloud.

She sank back into her seat, watching a crow's erratic flight into the wind, *blown like newsprint*, she thought, and then rummaged for her notebook to jot that down.

Opening it she turned through the pages she had filled, searching for clean paper. But there, on the last written page, she found a hand not her own.

I am perfectly hale, as you will not remember—for Eldrich has blotted your memories. Such are the bargains made with a mage. Absolutely do not worry or try to contact me! I will find you when first I can.

Elaural

Marianne stared at the note for a long time, wondering if this was some strange jest. Eldrich? Marianne sifted back through her memories, verifying them against her journal entries. Yes, they had traveled to Castlebough with Skye's paintings, meeting Averil Kent there. And Erasmus . . . And then nothing was quite clear. There were shards of things she could dredge up. The anonymous portrait. A meeting with Skye. Erasmus had disappeared. It was so hard to concentrate, as though every time she tried to remember, her focus wavered and fixed on something else—as though purposely distracted. Most unsettling.

And her journal. Had she really made no entries for so many days? When was the last time that had happened? The last time she had been so infatuated, she had temporarily abandoned the practice of her craft, that was when. But there had been no one in Castlebough. The countess had enjoyed a dalliance, though, had she not? Was it Flattery? Kent? Again her mind seemed to slide off and onto some other track that caused her less distress. Certainly this note was a jest. Certainly . . .

Marianne opened the small window to the driver and had him stop. For an hour she questioned him mercilessly, until the poor man complained of a wretched headache, which she also had herself. But this questioning did not put her mind at ease. He suffered the same problem as she in that he could barely bring his mind to focus.

She closed her eyes and put her head in her hands. Had she met Eldrich? Was this true? And he had stolen her memories? Stolen her precious memories! No, she could not accept it, and the more she tried to consider it, the worse her pain became. Pain and strange distress.

"This is not right," she said aloud. "This is not natural. I have been . . . plundered. Raped. There is no word. A part of me has been stolen. And what did it contain? What secrets might I have learned? And what has become of Elaural?" She had half a mind to have the driver turn back, and might have if she had any idea where they should go. Back to Castlebough, apparently, but she was not even sure of that. It was like waking from a dream and discovering the dream was true, not the world from which one departed into sleep.

She felt tears sting her eyes. How could anyone have done this to her? And why? Did this bastard mage not realize who she was? That her mind was sacrosanct, her memories precious? Had he no regard for anyone at all?

Such are the bargains made with a mage.

The line came back to her, as though she had read it the first time but had not been able to accept it. Had she made a bargain with Eldrich? She felt her heart sinking, and a terrible stillness came over her. What had he offered her?

And what had she promised in return?

It was not an original image, but the countess had come to think of Eldrich as a spider in the center of a web. On each strand it seemed some victim struggled, many not even aware that they were caught. Whenever it suited him, he drew another in, filling them with venom or feeding off them if he hungered. And then he let them go again, out into the world where they did his bidding. Some few might have escaped—Kent and Marianne, she hoped— but then Eldrich could have use for them again one day. As he did for her.

Despite Walky's protestations that she enjoyed special status in the house of the mage, she was well aware that she was no different from anyone else. He filled her with venom whenever it suited him—in this case the king's blood.

If Eldrich treated her with a certain respect, it was because he had to, though she was not sure why. He needed her willing cooperation, it seemed, and to get it he had refrained from his usual methods—though not entirely, for he had made a bargain with her, holding out something he believed she desired in return for what he wanted. It seemed only Walky served the mage without coercion or promise of something—and that "something" usually appealed to people's baser nature.

"He is not human," she said to the rain. "He has no compassion, no heart." Her kestrel flittered across the edge of the wood, landing on a branch. Occasionally it came closer, once landing on the ledge when the window had been ajar, but she did not encourage it, for it was connected to Eldrich's schemes, and as such unsettling to her.

It was surpassingly strange to feel such physical draw to a man and be repulsed by him at the same time. Oh, yes, she knew his story now. He had rather transparently sent Marianne to repeat it to her. Poor Marianne who was led to believe her memory would return to her in some years, and she would write this tale of the last mage. Unlikely, the countess thought. Eldrich did not care if people knew of him, or understood the reasons for the things he did.

No, Marianne had been meant to tell the story in this room, and nowhere else. And it was a terrible story, and likely true. The countess found it difficult to imagine that Lucklow had been born of woman! So it seemed that Eldrich had suffered in the house of the mage far more terribly than Erasmus.

But that did not forgive Eldrich's heartlessness, his inhumanity. Not by the countess' measure of things. Eldrich was a man of vast intelligence and could make his own choices. After all, he had collected over a century of experiences to draw from.

She wondered what Marianne would make of her hastily scribbled note. It had been difficult enough to manage, for Eldrich had guessed correctly that Marianne would write a detailed description of everything that had happened since leaving for Castlebough—and this he had expunged. The countess had had only a second to jot a few words . . . and she was not even sure why she had done it.

Rebellion, she guessed. Rebellion, and because she could not bear to stand by passively while Eldrich committed this terrible crime against Marianne —or so Marianne would have seen it—if not a crime against art. But then, Marianne had agreed to this bargain, had she not?

A knock on her door roused her, and she crossed the room to open it.

The small form of Walky stood in the dark hall. Often he carried no lamp or candle, but made his way through the unlit house as easily as a mage.

Owl sight, he called it, and said she would learn it herself, by and by.

"Ah, Walky," she said, standing aside that he might enter. She could hardly think of another man in the world she would let into her bedchamber without hesitation—but Walky, though not immune to her charms, was so much a gentleman, and so loyal a servant of the mage, that he was to be trusted utterly.

"I have brought you a book," he said, proffering a small, untitled volume. This one did not seem so old as the other books she had encountered in the house of Eldrich, though it was hardly new, even so.

"Come in, sit," she said, realizing how much she missed the company of others. "And what is this? Enchantments? Hidden histories? A book of terrible secrets?"

"It is enchanting, I think, but it is poetry. Poetry and songs," he said, taking a seat. "Although it has no title on the cover the book has become known as *Owl Songs*. Very odd, for to the best of my knowledge, owls hardly sing. It is a book of lore, in its own way, but little is plainly stated. We will use it in our study of the language. Here, let me give you an example." He took the book back and found a page. He read a short poem in Darian, and then looked up at her.

"I think I gleaned about seven words."

"Allow me to offer a rough translation," Walky said.

> *"Worlds spun upon the web of time*
> *The ebb and flow and ebb again*
> *Of shoreless seas and waning light*
> *Unknown to worlds of sleeping men.*
>
> *Across the seas the seven came,*
> *With book and blossom in their flight,*
> *To land upon the island world*
> *By star and moon and fairest night."*

Walky looked up from the book, his face oddly unreadable. "What does it mean?" the countess asked.

"Mean? Well, it is poetry, m'lady, and, by its nature, means many things. It is likely only a fragment, as well, of some larger work. Upon its surface it is merely a description of the first mages' arrival in this world. 'Across the seas the seven came.' "

"They came from somewhere else? Some other land?"

"Yes, of course. The arts were not made whole in the lands around the Entide Sea. They are far older than that. Older than the Entide Sea itself, I would wager. But let us write it out in Farr, and you may study it. Nothing so ruins poetry as having it explained by another. You must find its meaning, for it is different for everyone."

She was always somewhat amused to see Walky write, for he did it with such deliberation and so slowly that she invariably thought of a child learning his letters. He finished and slid the page across to her.

They sat quietly a moment, and just as Walky was about to take his leave, she spoke.

"Why do you serve him, Walky?"

The softly benign look that he always wore altered into one of confusion—as though the question made no sense.

"He is the last great mage, m'lady. Could one need reason more than that? I have always served him. It is my purpose on this earth."

"But, Walky, certainly even you must see that he is cold and cruel. Of all those who serve him, only you do so willingly. All others, even those who might wish to serve him, are coerced, offered tawdry bargains, their weaknesses preyed upon. He has no compassion, no humanity. And yet you serve him with utter devotion. How can you?"

"But he is a mage," Walky said, wrinkling up his brow. "One does not judge a mage by the laws of men, any more than one would judge a falcon by the ways of a sparrow. A falcon is without remorse. It has no pity, no compassion, no humanity—but then it is not human. It is a lord of the skies. And so, too, is the mage, m'lady.

"He is not as you and I, if you will forgive me for saying it. He has duties and trusts that we can barely comprehend. He is the master of an ancient tradition, a discipline that few may follow. A bearer of perilous knowledge and all of its attendant responsibilities. You must understand this one truth of mages, m'lady. He cannot afford the luxury of humanity. His duties are too grave for that.

One does not pity him for this, for he would not understand it, and it would anger him, but one must at least show patience and tolerance. It is a calling that one pursues at great price. One surrenders one's heart to become a mage."

They were silent for a moment, the countess taking in what had been said, surprised that Walky was suddenly so effusive, for usually he would avoid speaking of his master.

"I thought a mage had no duties to any but himself," she said, "and perhaps 'his own kind,' as Lord Eldrich likes to phrase it."

"That is the common perception, m'lady, but the truth is more complex, as the truth always tends to be." He tapped the book. "As is poetry. We will study this and perhaps you will begin to see. *Owl Songs*, the book is called, and owls see through the darkness."

Chapter Thirty-three

THE trail became a path, the path a track, and finally a lane. A tumbledown old house appeared on its bank, smoke streaming from the chimney, but with no inhabitants in view. The way went down quite steeply now, and they encountered a few houses that had been pushed out of the too-full town. And then they were in Wicken Vale, packs of children and dogs running along beside their horses, for it was not often that gentlemen appeared out of the hills—gentlemen and a priest.

They quickly found the only inn the village possessed and handed their horses over to the livery boy. The proprietor looked them over as they came in, and jerked a thumb toward the ceiling. "There is a gentleman here asking after others who might have made their way through the hills. That would be you, I take it?"

"And who might he be?" Clarendon asked, a bit warily.

"A Mr. Bryce."

"Ah," Rose stepped to the fore, "the very man we seek. Will you please inform him of our arrival, and then we would like rooms and baths for a party of four."

* * *

Rose appeared at the door to their room as Hayes was rubbing his hair dry.

"Deacon. Dinner has not been served without us, I hope."

The priest shook his head, his gaze shifting away from Hayes' then back again. "We are to set out at first light to meet Eldrich."

Hayes dropped his arms to his side. "All of us?"

The priest nodded.

"You spoke with this man without us?"

Again the priest nodded.

"Was even Clarendon present?"

"No one but me."

Hayes felt anger boil up through his incredulity. "What would lead you to believe you had the right to speak for us?"

"There was little discussion—merely a command to attend the mage."

"He questioned you, surely. . . ."

The priest nodded, rather reluctantly.

"And what did you tell him?"

"Only that we believed Anna had perished and, sadly, Erasmus Flattery with her. He asked to see Mr. Flattery's belongings, but I knew what he was after and had brought it to him—the text of the ritual Erasmus was to perform."

Hayes tried to understand. What wasn't the priest telling him? Why had the man snuck off to speak with Bryce without them? It was more than suspicious. "Does Clarendon know you've done this?"

A shake of the head.

"Farrelle preserve you when you tell him." And without another word, Hayes closed the door.

Deacon Rose rode in the carriage with the servant of Eldrich, whom none of the others had yet spoken with. Clarendon was in a dark rage and kept entirely to himself, riding behind the others. Even the day was somber, as dark banners of cloud fluttered over in a harsh wind from the sea.

Hayes and Kehler hunched down over their saddles, as though to make themselves smaller targets for the wind. They said very little, though it was perfectly obvious what was on their minds: Eldrich and what he would do with them.

Both young men had hoped they were quit of this matter, and Hayes was even looking forward to returning to his debt-ridden life in Avonel. Not that he had a place to live or any prospects. His hopes to enter the foreign service had been abandoned, as the positions for which he had gone up were, no doubt, filled—and he had not even been in Avonel to answer a summons should one have come.

But before all of that there was Eldrich, and the anxiety of this meeting made all else seem very paltry and remote. Survive the meeting with Eldrich and anything else in life would seem child's play. Obscurity and pauperism would be almost pleasure.

"We are not traveling in the direction of Eldrich's estates," Kehler said, trying to keep his voice low.

He looked even more dispirited since their summons. Hayes was almost more worried about his friend than about their coming audience with the mage.

"What? No, we're traveling south. Apparently the mage is not in residence. Rose speculated that he was in Castlebough while we were below ground. He didn't think it likely that Eldrich could have collapsed the cave from any distance."

"Are we returning to Castlebough, do you think?"

Hayes shrugged. He felt a shiver run through him at the thought of the town, and it was not from the cold. The skeleton of a child reaching out . . . the stone constricting around him as he crawled through the dark. All to what end? He could hardly remember what had led them there to begin with.

He looked over at his friend, who slumped in his saddle, barely raising his head, trusting his horse to follow the others, lost in his own thoughts—all of them dark and filled with foreboding. Hayes knew what he felt, having lived in poverty. He knew how impossible it became to believe that anything would ever turn out right. That there would ever be light again.

He looked back over his shoulder to be sure that Clarendon was still with them, and saw the little man some way off, almost a smaller version of Kehler at that distance.

What a ragtag company we have become, he thought. *It will be a miracle if our meeting with Eldrich does not destroy us.*

Hayes longed to say something to Clarendon, something to soothe him, but he knew there was nothing that would ease the man's anger. As Clarendon had said himself, he was a victim of his passions. Even Dusk was tentative around him when he returned from his expeditions over the fields and through the woods. No, Clarendon would have to stew in the bitter juices of his anger and resentment, emotions that were too ready to rise up in the small man.

Hayes only hoped that he would not become like Clarendon in time.

Clarendon appeared so small and forlorn upon his full-sized horse—an elf prince out of song. A gray drapery of rain wafted out of the hills, then, and Clarendon was almost obscured from view in the downpour. Hayes looked back to the carriage where Deacon Rose sat in comfort, protected from the weather. Life was often thus, for certainly Clarendon had suffered and overcome enough in this life that he deserved respite. He deserved to be the one protected from the world's vagaries and injustice.

Hayes had given up guessing where events would take him next. A hunting lodge in the Caledon Hills would not have been one of his guesses anyway. They arrived in the midst of another spring storm, tired and somewhat miserable, and were left to wait in an unlit hallway beneath a stair. From a window somewhere above, occasional flashes of lightning cast angular shadows of railings and balustrades, making Hayes think, for some reason, of a jail. Thunder followed the flashes almost immediately, the lightning striking nearby. The protracted rumbling was so deeply felt and so powerful that Hayes thought it sounded like the earth splitting, breaking apart around them.

"You look rather calm and unruffled, Deacon," Kehler said. "The journey was not too arduous, I hope?"

The priest shrugged, as though to imply that sarcasm deserved no reply. Or perhaps even Deacon Rose was frightened and could think of no response.

Clarendon stood apart, still wrapped in the rage that had surrounded him since Wicken Vale. What treachery was this priest involved in? That was the question on the little man's mind. And there was more. There was this bargain that Clarendon had spoken of—something he would offer to the mage—though Hayes feared that even Eldrich could not offer what Clarendon wanted in return.

An explosion of thunder was followed by the sound of foot-falls—like very distant echoes—and a wavering candle appeared, dimly illuminating a round-faced little man. He stopped some yards from them. "Follow me," he said, and started back the way he had come. There was a moment of hesitation, and then the priest set off after the man, the others rousing themselves to follow.

Hayes could hardly make out Kehler's face in the dim light, but his friend looked terribly grim. Men went to the scaffold looking thus, Hayes was sure. And he felt it himself. A strange weakness in all his limbs—a hopelessness. Here is where their curiosity had led—to a meeting with this dreaded mage. Anger at Kehler welled up in him. Had he the strength, he might have struck his companion, such was the ferocity of it.

Clarendon caught up with the candle bearer. "Are you Mr. Walky? Mr. Flattery spoke kindly of you."

"But it is not Walky who will judge you," the small man said as he put a finger to his lips.

Too soon they came to the hall's end. The small man opened a door and motioned them through. Hayes stumbled into darkness, the room lit only by a fire that had burned to glowing coals in the hearth. A hand gently pushed him forward as he stopped. And then he realized that something moved beside the fire—a shadow darker than the rest.

With a sound of wings fluttering, flames erupted in the hearth. Hayes could make out the figure now, a large man sprawled in a chair, patting a massive beast that sat at his side.

The wolf of legend, Hayes realized.

The four of them lined up a few paces away, coming no closer than they must. Walky had disappeared somewhere behind them. The mage continued to stroke the wolf, kneading behind its ears. Suddenly he pushed it forward, making a hissing sound through his teeth, and the beast came straight for them. Hayes drew himself up, becoming utterly still.

It snuffled about his feet and knees, then passed to Kehler, leaving him almost as quickly. But Rose interested it somehow. Excited it, in some way. The hackles rose on its neck, and teeth were bared; a low growl emerged. Hayes was sure that it would have attacked the man, but a word from the mage sent it on to Clarendon. Here again, something seemed to incite it, but again the mage spoke, and it went bounding away into the dark.

A long silence followed. Hayes almost wondered if they had been forgotten, or if the mage learned all he wanted without even having them speak. Perhaps they were speaking, and he did not know.

"You . . . we've met before," the mage said, his voice surprisingly melodious. "What is your name?"

"Clarendon," the small man answered, his voice barely audible. "We met—"

"I remember," the mage said, his voice harsh despite its music. "As do you. Did I not say it was your curse?"

"Where is Lizzy? Is she yet alive?" the little man whispered, barely forcing the words out.

"Who? Oh, the woman? She is gone, gone this half-century. Not a short time, even to me. Is she alive?" The mage shrugged, unconcerned for the fate of some unknown woman.

Clarendon was trembling now, as though he struggled just to keep his feet.

"I have knowledge. Only I have it. I will offer it to you freely. . . ."

"Indeed you will," Eldrich said. "And I will pay you nothing for it. She is gone, little man. Gone where you cannot follow, unless you have the knowledge and skill of Landor."

"Not the skill, but the knowledge, I think. . . ."

Eldrich did not respond for a moment. One long hand passed over a candle which flickered to light and held, yet this light did not touch him. "She exploited you," he said coolly. "Used you terribly, though you were perhaps too young to realize. I could have let you go with her." He ran his fingers over the candle flame again. "I seldom do men favors, but you . . . your existence was hard enough. Men do not care for those born . . . unlike them."

Silence but for Clarendon's ragged breathing. In the poor light

Hayes could see the little man, bent as though he would collapse from the pain.

"Step forward, priest," the mage said, turning his attention from Clarendon and his precious bargain. The music gone from his voice. "Say nothing!" he cautioned, as the priest opened his mouth. " 'A tongue so sweet it should be cut out and fed to dogs.' I should have given you to the wolf, and I might yet. If you make any attempt to use that silver tongue here, I shall teach you the lesson that life has neglected. Do you understand? I have much to settle with you and your church for all that you think you have hidden from my kind these many years. Your precious Farrelle spoke of atonement . . . and so shall we."

The priest nodded quickly. *Afraid to speak*, Hayes thought, and he would have felt some satisfaction if he were not so frightened himself. If he were not sure his turn was coming.

"You found no bodies? Neither Erasmus nor this woman? Not even the boy?"

No one answered.

"You, Clarendon. Speak up."

"No bodies," Clarendon breathed.

Lightning lanced into the earth nearby, revealing a large room, a shadow before the fire. Windows rattled with the deep throbbing thunder, its echo impossibly long.

Eldrich rose from his chair by the fire and went and stood before one of the tall windows, staring out at the night, his silhouette flickering into being with each streak of lightning.

"Perhaps they are dead, swept away by the river. Perhaps. But I am not convinced. Not yet. Your task might not be done. There is still a ship rolling in a strange sea. But first I will have each of your stories, and I caution you to leave nothing out, and to tell only the strictest truth. You cannot lie to me, and I have no patience for those who waste my time. I have particular interest in what you saw within Landor's chamber. That which was inscribed upon the walls. Which of you is Kehler? You met with Skye: begin there."

The mage bent over Clarendon's carefully copied text, the writings from Landor's chamber. He glanced up briefly at Walky, and then turned his gaze quickly back to the page as though overcome by fascination and horror. Then he shook his head and sat back in his chair, closing his eyes. He muttered something under his breath.

"Sir?"

"Tell me I sleep, Walky, and that this is nothing more than a nightmare. The nightmare of all my kind."

"What is it, Lord Eldrich?"

"It is the cataclysm, Walky, the apocalypse. The ruin of all that I have planned."

Walky had never heard his master speak thus and found himself staring at the text with great alarm.

"We must pray that this woman is not alive, and if she is, that she has not the knowledge to understand what is written here." He took a long breath. "And she has the seed. . . ."

"If she survived, sir."

"Yes, but the Paths have not indicated her death—not yet. And they found no body. Neither she nor Erasmus."

"Nor the boy," Walky added. "It is likely they were all swept . . . away." Walky choked a little on the last word, causing the mage to look up.

"Are you all right, Walky?" Eldrich asked quietly.

The servant nodded.

"Do not be so sure that Erasmus is dead, simply because these men believe it. I told you of my vision? It wasn't until later that it occurred to me that the creature clinging to the mast could be Erasmus. His obvious hostility to me, his half-fish, half-man appearance—one caught between two worlds, two desires. And then he leaped into the waters to join a nymph and the dolphins. Sailors believe that the spirits of men lost at sea inhabit dolphins and won't harm these mammals for any reason. How neatly it all fits. Erasmus plunged into this raging river and died with this woman. But water is life, Walky. We swim in it until birth. No, I am not convinced they are dead, so do not despair."

"But if he has joined forces with this woman, sir, that is worse," Walky said.

Eldrich looked at the small man briefly, then cast his gaze down, nodding his head. "Yes, there are worse things than a clean death." The mage reached out and brushed the pages spread before him. "I am worried about the emerging faces in Landor's crypt. Almost everyone thought one to be Erasmus—though none were absolutely sure. But the other—It has barely begun to form. Could it be this girl, Anna? Or is it our countess? Do you see what I'm saying? The art that made that chamber was great. Far greater than my own, or even Lucklow's. The faces forming there are more critical than the people caught in the chamber realized. Absolutely critical, for the art that forms them is subtle and beyond our understanding. Will it be Erasmus?" He shook his head. "That seems unlikely now. And the woman? What if it is Anna? Is that possible?"

Eldrich looked down at the table, flipping over a page. "Imagine not being able to forget a thing," he mused. "A remarkable little man." Eldrich gazed at the writing for a moment.

"Everything is so unclear," the mage said, "so muddled. How I wish they had found bodies." Eldrich realized that Walky almost flinched when he heard this, and turned to examine his servant. "If he perished trying to save this young man, Walky, then it was a noble death; better than he might have found. Most die for no reason at all—and live for little more. But I'm not yet convinced of his death. Not yet." He turned back to the text, staring at it with a look Walky had never seen in his master's face before—fear.

A blind child, raggedly dressed, made his way along the wall, running his hand over the stone. Twice he stumbled and fell but stiffly raised himself and carried on with the stoicism of those who did not know they suffered injustice.

Eldrich watched, his mind too focused to even wonder who the child was or what this scene might mean. It was better to ask no questions now. Better just to watch, to let the vision unfold.

A moon floated up from behind a stone wall, casting its cool light down upon the child, who stopped, confused—as though he could sense the light somehow, almost see it. He turned about and his face was suddenly illumined.

Clarendon. . . .

The dwarf turned away from the light and continued along the ruined street, stumbling again at the foot of a long stair. Eldrich followed, keeping his distance. The small man went slowly up the stairs, using his hands on the broken treads.

The mage followed, not feeling the stairs beneath his feet, but up he went all the same, following the child-man who went, crab-like, ahead. On each stair Eldrich saw a thin smear of blood from Clarendon's hands.

Where are you leading me, he wondered, but then turned his mind away from speculation.

A massive beast appeared at the stairhead—a wolfhound—and Clarendon took hold of its shoulder and followed.

By the time Eldrich crested the stair, man and beast were gone. Slowly he turned about, surveying the place: the ruin of an ancient city or fortress made mysterious by moonlight.

"Where have you gone?" the mage wondered aloud. "Where?"

The moon slipped behind a cloud, and Eldrich woke in a chair before a tall window, lightning forking down in the world beyond, his familiar scratching frantically at the glass before him.

Chapter Thirty-four

THE dog cart rattled along the rutted track between hedges, and turned abruptly into a field. Erasmus climbed down briefly to open a gate and latch it again as the cart passed. Sheep had browsed the grasses short, leaving only the odd sentinel thistle, purple tufts weaving in the wind. Anna had abandoned her practice of traveling only by night, and had offered Erasmus no explanation.

"Why exactly are we stopping here?" Erasmus looked around. "If you have in mind what I have in mind, this is hardly the place."

Anna dropped down beside him. "It was not what I had in mind—at least not until you mentioned it—but there was something I wished to see." She walked out into the field, her skirts wafting in the breeze. Erasmus thought that she looked amazingly restored, though he was also aware that it was not just rest or passion that had accomplished this: it was the seed that she took in tiny quantities. Even her hair did not look so faded, and her face glowed with youth and vigor. She had grown remarkably more attractive, he thought.

Twenty paces out into the field she spun on her toes and pointed to the north. "Do you know that town?"

Erasmus followed her gesture and found a few rooftops showing through the trees. Looking back to Anna, he shook his head and walked toward her.

"Can you not make a guess?" She smiled, teasing. "I will give one hint. It was made famous by an incident that was immortalized in oils."

Erasmus wondered what she was on about. He looked toward the town again as he caught up with her. "Is it Compton Heath?"

"The very place. I am guessing that this is approximately the point the Pelier depicted. Do you see? There is even a brook, though it seems only to flow in one direction, unlike the one you described to me."

They continued down the slight incline to the water, looking around.

"There is no bridge," Anna said, "but then we must consider artistic license in this matter." She shaded her eyes and gazed off toward the town. "What say you, Erasmus, is it at all like the Pelier?"

Erasmus nodded, considering. "It is, and it is not. The trees are not quite right, that small wood there was larger in the painting, and this pasture seemed a natural meadow, without hedges or gates. Of course the church steeple is gone—and has been for some years. But all in all, considering that Pelier was likely never here, it is quite remarkable." He looked at Anna. "Why do I not think this visit is idle curiosity?"

"I think you are coming to know me rather better than I would like," she said, turning full circle. "I wish to employ the arts here, briefly, though I fear that we might be seen."

"It is a risk," Erasmus said. "And what would this use of the arts be in aid of?"

"Knowledge," she said, "or, at the very least, curiosity. You see, if this is really the place where the Stranger appeared, as the painting suggests, then it would mean the worlds lie closer here—or at least did briefly. Even so there might be some trace of it. Indulge me for half the hour, Erasmus, for it is a question I would have answered. Wouldn't you?"

Erasmus nodded. "How obvious would it be to anyone watching that we . . . you were practicing the arts?"

"That depends on the proximity of the watchers, and their perceptiveness. Perhaps more obvious than we would like."

"Let me take a walk along the edge of the field and see if anyone is about. Was it not you that said we should take no chances? I am becoming rather fond of being dead."

"As am I. Have a look, then, and I will begin my preparations," she said.

Erasmus struck out across the field, crossing the brook on stepping stones. From the top of a stile he looked into the next field, then walked along beside the hedgerow and the edge of the wood. It appeared they were alone, though it would not have been hard for any curious onlooker to step back out of sight while he passed.

When he returned to Anna, he saw that she had made peculiar marks in the sod with a knife and built small cairns of river stones in three places.

"You might want to go stand by the horse, Erasmus. Animals often react badly when they sense the arts in use. Lead him out of sight—onto the road, perhaps."

Erasmus did as he was told, though he wanted to see what was done. As he was trying to decide if he would leave the cart and walk back, the horse suddenly shied, and it was all he could do to stop the animal from bolting. A quarter of the hour later Anna appeared, looking exhausted and flushed.

She slumped into the cart as though stricken with the vapors. Erasmus waited patiently until she finally pushed herself upright.

"I'm recovering," she said. "Press on, but I don't think we should pass through the town. Can we get up onto that high point, do you think? I would like to look at the surrounding terrain and have my empiricist explain its formation to me."

They wound their way up the odd hill that Anna had indicated. When they got to a suitable outlook, they turned the cart off the lane under the shadow of some regal oaks. Then they climbed down and walked a few feet in order to have the best vista.

"Well? Tell me about the geology."

Erasmus looked out over the countryside and tried to dredge up what he knew from Layel. "This long flat plain was once the floor of a large lake or arm of the sea. There are places not far from here where you can see perfect beaches, twenty miles from the sea. All of Farrland was scraped by massive glaciers, or so many believe, and the few hills hereabout, such as the one upon which we stand, were formed by the glaciers, though we don't really know how."

"But what of that?" Anna asked, pointing off toward a rather broken-down hill, like the ruin of some vast fortification.

"Ah, now that is different. That is a very ancient volcano, called Kilty's Keep, like the ancient song, though which came first scholars still debate. It is a geological feature of some interest. I visited it once, and found it surpassingly strange, for it does appear to be the ruin of fortifications, but on a vast, inhuman scale. One can imagine it was built by some race of men far more powerful than our own, which is what people believed in ancient times. If we could see back to the west there is another like it, though not nearly so large. They form a line, a fault of some kind where the molten core of the earth would well up and spew forth. The fault extends back into the Caledon Hills, though farther north, as though the line curved."

"And where exactly is Tremont Abbey? Do you know?"

Erasmus turned around and looked back toward the trees which hid the view to the north and west. He swept a small arc with his hand. "In that general direction."

"But near to this flaw in the earth?"

"Yes, very near, I should say."

She nodded and, finding an area of grass to her liking, spread one of their blankets. They sat down, close to one another, kissing briefly.

"And what has all of this proven?" Erasmus asked.

"Well, clearly you see what I am getting at."

"Tremont Abbey and Compton Heath both lay along the fault that runs through Kilty's Keep. Volcanic activity took place here in very ancient times. There is some connection between this and these other worlds of which you have spoken."

"I could not have put it more clearly. Though I cannot tell you more. Perhaps this volcanic activity is caused by the proximity of the other world."

"I think Layel and his followers would find this a little difficult to accept."

She shrugged. "Many things the mages believe empiricists would find difficult to accept. These men of reason even doubt the arts existed at all. I have heard that some say it was all trickery—conjuring on a grand scale—but you and I know better." She held his eye for a moment, and then smiled. "Finally, before we give up this subject all together, does this line of vulcanism— Is that correct? Vulcanism?"

"Correct in every way."

"Does this line extend toward Beacon Head?"

Erasmus felt himself sit up, suddenly not so comfortable.

"This island upon which you have a house, is it volcanic? Is that where this is going?"

"No, that's where we are going." She smiled at her poor jest and put her hand on his cheek. "Do not look so suspicious, Erasmus. We have long thought this island to be a place of power, which is how the mages thought of such sites—Tremont Abbey, for instance. Farrow as well. But it is nothing to be concerned about. I have no nefarious plans. No Tellerite conspiracy to bring to fruition. We seldom used this house at all, keeping it as a refuge in case all our plans went awry. I hope it is still standing." She leaned forward and kissed him tenderly at the corner of his eye. "Do you think people come up here often or might we be left undisturbed for an hour?"

Erasmus covered Anna carefully with a blanket, stood for a moment watching her sleep, and then walked out under the shading trees. He sat upon a rock and looked out over the valley toward Kilty's Keep. The town of Compton Heath lay below, twisting along a road that curved into a hollow of the hillside. This was where Baumgere had first encountered a Stranger and started on his quest—a quest that led to a child dying in isolation and terror far beneath the fair surface of the world.

The surface of the world . . .

Anna seemed to believe that this was but one of several "worlds infinitely far away yet close at hand."

It did not begin here, he reminded himself, anymore than it began when I found Hayes hiding in an Avonel brothel, or when I was ordered to the house of Eldrich as a child. No, it began when the seven journeyed here from Darr—if it is not merely a myth.

"You saw the chamber," Erasmus reminded himself. And the

face forming in stone; a face that must have been him—the last Guardian of the Gate.

But he had escaped the chamber and its gate, escaped Eldrich's attempt on his life.

"But can I escape him again?" he whispered, for certainly that was why he had taken up with Anna—that and he owed her his life. She would have been far safer to let him drown, but then perhaps she knew him well enough to realize that he could not betray her now. Eldrich had attempted his murder, and Anna had saved him from certain death. . . .

But it was a desperate thing they did, attempting to elude Eldrich. Erasmus could feel the desperation in both of them. It woke them from nightmares and was present even in their lovemaking. If they were found—well, he did not like to contemplate that.

Better to think about what life would be like if they escaped Eldrich. Perhaps he would finally lay to rest his shattered childhood and live life anew. It was worth killing Erasmus Flattery to be free of Eldrich. He only hoped that isolation and secrecy would not drive him to madness.

Erasmus rose and walked a few steps, looking off toward the sea. Great, billowing, white clouds—the escaped sails of an entire fleet—lifted up above the horizon. A hawk circled effortlessly over the fields, turning its head slowly, searching for movement.

Searching.

The sea was not quite visible from this height, though he could imagine it, lying silvered beneath the great reef of cloud.

Did he trust Anna? Lovely, seductive Anna?

No, she had some purpose of her own, some reason to have rescued him. But what could it be? He thought, though, that he had a much better chance of resisting Anna than he did of resisting Eldrich. Better to throw in his lot with someone who could not so easily overpower him.

"Be thankful you are dead," he said aloud. "Even Eldrich cannot murder the dead."

It occurred to him suddenly that the countess was with Eldrich now. Had he abducted her? Unlikely that she would go willingly, but then, mages could be very persuasive. Odd that Eldrich would have an interest in this woman, at this point. Certainly in their younger years, before they passed their centenaries, many of the mages were known to have a weakness for the fairer sex. To the best of his knowledge, Eldrich had not been one of these—not that he had likely lived as a monk, but women were not his passion as they had been with some. But Eldrich had passed his hundredth year some time ago, no one knew exactly when, and here he was abducting the fairest woman in all of Farrland. There must be some other reason.

For a moment Erasmus entertained the idea that Eldrich had done it to spite him, but no, the truth was that Erasmus was probably not so important to Eldrich that he would be driven to such revenge or even to wreak a little more havoc on Erasmus' already battered life.

"Is he lost in thought and melancholia?" Anna's voice came from behind, "or is he merely contemplating the beauty of the world which stretches out before him?"

"It is the clouds," he said not looking back. "When I was a child, I imagined that there were worlds within the clouds and that magic ships existed that could visit them, sailing across the blue of the heavens, landing on islands of clouds which were all inhabited by strange races, usually with beautiful women."

She sat down and wrapped an arm about his neck, putting her head on his shoulder. "What do you mean, 'when you were a child'? Are you saying this isn't true? That we will not be able to find a good sky-ship and make our escape to the clouds?"

"Well, it is not a fancy I give up easily. But then there were some who believed that the way to Faery lay through the cave—yet we did not find it."

"No we did not, though that doesn't mean it was not there. . . ."

"You're beginning to sound like Clarendon."

"How so?"

"He . . . he was fascinated by Strangers and the idea that Faery might not be merely myth."

Anna nodded. "Myth it is, I think, but there certainly are lands beyond—Darr, from where Landor journeyed, and other worlds besides; one of them Faery, perhaps. Who can say?" She ran fingers through his hair, and shut her eyes, still in need of sleep.

"Will we escape Eldrich, do you think? Have you tried augury to see?"

"No, I have not attempted augury. Eldrich knew of our visions in the past. I . . . I am a bit afraid to use it now. Will we escape . . . ?" She shrugged.

"But you have the seed now. A familiar follows you. Do you fear him still?"

"More than I can say. There is no one who should not." She hesitated. "That is not true. Another mage need not fear him. They had strictures— No, it was more than that. There is a curse. One mage cannot murder another without bringing down this curse upon all mages."

"But there is only one remaining in all the world."

"So there is," she said. "So there is."

Chapter Thirty-five

THE soft, almost hesitant knock was becoming familiar to the countess. In fact, she had begun to look forward to Walky's visits, often remembering what Erasmus had said about the man being a good friend to him in a difficult situation.

"Mr. Walky," she said, curtsying primly.

This took him somewhat aback, it seemed.

"Do I interrupt you, m'lady?"

"No, Mr. Walky, not at all. I was simply so happy to see you that I forgot myself for a moment." She laughed and took hold of his arm, drawing him into the room and closing the door.

"I have tea," she said. "Or wine if you prefer."

"Tea would be very welcome, m'lady."

She sat him down and poured tea. "It is not entirely fresh," she said, "as I expected you earlier." She raised a hand to prevent his next response. "No, you are not coming too late. I am only sorry about the quality of your tea."

She set his steaming cup before him. "Now, tell me. What will it be tonight? More *Owl Songs*, for I will tell you I have been trying to read them, but I have not enough of the language yet to make much headway. It is tough sledging, as an instructor of mine liked to say."

Walky, she noticed, looked rather subdued this evening. It might have been her imagination, but his eyes looked a bit red and puffy.

"Is something wrong, Walky?"

He made as if to speak, and his mouth quivered slightly as though it struggled to open. "I have received some news that, though not unexpected, was still very sad, m'lady."

"Oh, Walky, I am distressed to hear. Can you tell me what this is, or is it business of the mage and therefore not for mortal ears?"

"It has to do with a . . . friend, m'lady. I do not mean to pry, but I collect you had more than a passing acquaintance with my former charge, Erasmus Flattery?"

She nodded, closing her eyes involuntarily. She felt a peculiar numbness.

"The mage is not utterly convinced this is true, but we have received news that Erasmus had an unfortunate accident." He struggled with the next word, his mouth quivering again, ". . . drowned," he managed.

"Oh, Walky." She felt tears appear upon her eyelashes, and she reached out and took the old man's hand. "Farrelle preserve us— preserve him. How did this happen? Could not Erasmus swim? Did he not tell me you had taught him?"

The old man nodded. "Yes," he whispered, "but not well enough, it seems." A tear streaked down from the corner of one eye. "The poor child," he said. "The poor, sad child. It was written in the stars. . . . What hope had he with all that was arrayed against him? What hope . . . ?" And the old man broke down and wept bitterly, the countess crying with him, for the loss of Erasmus Flattery, and the fate for which he had been born.

"It is nothing to be ashamed of," Hayes heard the priest say. "We were all afraid."

Hayes propped himself up on one elbow and looked around.

"Ah, he returns to the land of the living," Deacon Rose said.

"Hello, Hayes," Kehler said so softly he could barely be heard. "Do you feel as beastly as I?" Kehler sprawled in a chair looking like a man near death, his face positively gray.

"I have a headache for which there is no descriptor, but it is a long catalogue of ailments and probably no different from your own." Hayes closed his eyes.

"You resisted," Rose said, "which was a mistake."

Hayes noticed Clarendon collapsed against the wall, drawn into himself like a child who'd been beaten.

"Randall? Are you . . . ?"

Clarendon looked up, tried to smile, and then let his head drop again.

"Flames," Hayes said, "what did that monster do to him?"

"A favor, apparently," Rose said, looking thoughtfully at the small man. Then he shook his head. "This is about his lost love and nothing more. He was not misused any more than the rest of us—not last night, at least."

"Let him be now," Kehler said mildly, not opening his eyes.

Hayes sat up painfully. "What . . . what exactly happened? I have only the vaguest memory."

"I was just telling Mr. Kehler that Eldrich used the arts to be sure Anna had not left any form of enchantment upon us. He was also very interested in our memories of the chamber. But for the terror of it, I think we are unharmed."

Hayes nodded, closing his eyes. Yes, the fear was not easily forgotten.

"And why is it that you have so clear a memory of what happened, Deacon?"

"Because I offered no resistance, Mr. Hayes, and had I known what would be done to us, I would have cautioned you to do the same. You cannot resist a mage. But you did not do it by choice, I'm sure, but out of fear, and that is only natural. The arts are frightening and the mages even more so."

Hayes pressed his hands to the sides of his head trying to stop the throbbing. "Blood and flames, I have never felt so battered. What will become of us now?"

Rose shook his head. "I cannot say. The mage was not pleased by our efforts. The fact that we found no bodies bothered him immeasurably. Though it would likely have bothered him more had we found the others and not Anna. It is probable that the current swept them away or down into some pool with an undertow, or lodged them under overhanging rocks. But still . . ."

"Still?"

"The mage did not seem convinced. He still suspects that Anna is alive; Anna, and perhaps Erasmus as well. Only poor Pryor has been forgotten entirely." Rose made a sign to Farrelle.

Truncated paragraphs of memory were coming back to Hayes—flashes of scenes, suddenly illuminated as though by lightning. "I will say, Lord Eldrich did not seem overwhelmed with regret at the death of Erasmus," he said.

Rose nodded at this.

"An insignificant loss to be rid of his enemy, wouldn't you say, Deacon?" It was Kehler, still with them, though he appeared to be nearer the state of Clarendon.

Rose glanced over at Kehler, his look pained. "Like all of you, Mr. Kehler, I came to esteem Mr. Flattery greatly. He was a man of substance and incisive intellect. I had begun to think of him, almost, as a man from another age. A better time when men were honorable and principled in ways that many today are not. It might be true that Eldrich does not mourn the loss of his former protegé, but that is not true of me. I mourn him, far more than you will believe, I'm sure."

Hayes rose from the bed and made his way to the window, where the pale light of morning illuminated the world. He looked down into the empty garden which dripped still from the storm. "I guess an escape is not to be contemplated?"

"Only if you can outrun a wolf—and an unnatural one at that."

Hayes cringed at the thought. Kehler had come and stood beside him, and they both stared out into the dreary morning. Kehler looked like a man who had lost all desire to continue, as though his encounter with the mage had overwhelmed him entirely.

Hayes searched desperately for something to say. "What . . . what can we do for Randall?" he whispered after a moment, "for there is no one other than us to tend him." It was a clumsy attempt, he realized, but Kehler no longer cared for his own well-being so Hayes hoped to interest him in another.

Kehler turned to look at Clarendon, and this seemed to effect him somehow. He drew himself up a little. "I don't know. For the moment I think we should let him mourn, for it is a natural thing for men to do. But if this state of catatonia persists— Well, the man must eat and drink. We can't let him lay down and die. He must go on, as we did in the cave. We bore each other up then, and we will do it again."

"Yes," Hayes said, "as long as we never give in all at the same time."

Walky knew all the signs, the pale sheen on the face, the sunken eyes, the lassitude. Eldrich had gone searching in the vision world again, searching for Anna, searching to know if she lived and, if so, how she could be found.

The mage sprawled in a chair, his eyes half closed, the dawn light making him look even more ghostly and ill. "We must let Clarendon go with the others, Walky," the mage said.

Walky felt his heart sink a little.

"Is there no other course, sir?" He did not need to say that Clarendon carried the knowledge of the chamber—the ritual to open the gates.

"If she runs, Walky, we will never find her. She must try to make herself a mage, perhaps even open the gate."

"If she lives, sir, or did you see her in your dream?"

"No, but she could be hidden from me." He raised a hand, then let it fall back weakly. "Let us imagine that she is still alive. Put yourself in her place. What would you do, Walky?"

"I would find a place to live quietly, most likely in Doorn, and wait. . . ."

"Until I am dead—you can say it, Walky. It's not as if I am unaware."

"That is what I would do, sir."

Eldrich closed his eyes, and for a moment Walky thought he slept. "But you have the wisdom of your years, Walky. Anna is young and impetuous, and though, no doubt, she believes she has learned patience, she does not yet know the meaning of the word.

No, I think she will not be as wise as you. But it would help if she could be panicked. Frightened into believing she had no other course. Do you think she understands what was written in the chamber?"

"Perhaps in time she will, sir. It is not easily understood."

"Yes, that is likely so." Eldrich shifted his position, his eyes still closed, as though the faint light pained them. "Let us hope she has no record of what Landor wrote. None of the notes the others took survived their near-drowning. Only Clarendon appears to have the knowledge."

Walky stood quietly waiting for his master to speak again. The mage shifted in his chair again, as though in discomfort. "I will send out this priest and the others once more. And Bryce must make contact with his minion in the government. I will not give up this search, Walky. Perhaps it is madness searching for someone who is dead, but we cannot afford to make a mistake. Teller's people hid themselves so long—they have ways of doing this that even I don't understand. Foolish of me to not have questioned Halsey more thoroughly. The search must continue. Unless there is a sign. Bring the priest and the others to me in three hours."

Walky remained where he stood, waiting to be released. Unlike the countess, his patience was nearly infinite: he would quite literally wait all day and feel no resentment.

He is the last of his kind, Walky thought, *the final chapter of a story that is to be lost forever.* Even now, while one still lived, men were less and less inclined to believe the stories of the mages and their powers—but Walky knew the truth.

"Is she to be trusted, Walky?" Eldrich asked softly.

"This woman, sir?"

"The countess, Walky. She is from a decadent class. Has had no purpose in life but to please herself. Everything has been given to her. Everything. What will she do when I am gone?"

"It is not my place to say, but, for my money, she is a person of substance. A woman who would have the courage to take the difficult way if it were necessary, sir."

"Yes, I believe she would make her way through difficulty. But there will be some hard decisions, Walky. Decisions where some must make sacrifices. I fear she could not bear that burden."

Walky nodded. "That is not impossible, sir. She has a . . . a good heart."

"And I do not?"

Walky knew this game. Would he tell the truth or resort to a small lie, knowing the mage could detect lies. "Yours has a hardened shell, sir."

The mage nodded, the trace of a smile appearing. "That will be all, Walky," the mage said quietly, his breathing suddenly deep and regular.

The servant waited a moment, watching over his master, observing the troubled sleep. He heard him mutter in the secret tongue, yet there was nothing he could do to bring him peace.

Walky slipped out of the room. Almost as silent as a mage.

Chapter Thirty-six

Dusk upon the harvest field
Gilded stooks afire,
Aflame the shivering sky.
Clouds bubble up, burning,
And night,
The terrible night,
Is upon us.

—Ansel Bead, Harvest

THE countess gazed at the portrait, wondering what it was that so unsettled her. At a glance it was a flattering likeness, for Eldrich had a presence like no other, and all of that was there. The mystery, the brooding silence, the irony which verged on cruelty, the complete disinterest. But there was something else as well.

Sadness, certainly, though this did not begin to describe it—the right word eluded her. But even this was not what she found unsettling. She leaned a bit closer, narrowing her eyes.

Eyes.

Yes, whatever it was resided in the eyes. Dark, almost black, beneath heavy brows. A bit too sunken to be really attractive, though Eldrich's eyes had a way of unsettling her. It was likely the disinterest. The coldness. As well as the feeling that he looked through her. She might as well have been naked before that gaze, for it stripped her bare every time.

The countess shivered.

Fear.

No, it couldn't be that. He was Eldrich, the last mage; certainly the most powerful man in the known world. What could such a man fear?

She turned the question over in her mind, and came up with the not too very remarkable answer that his fear was no different from anyone else's.

"Flames," she whispered. *Is he near to death? Could that be possible? Has it come stalking even the long-lived Eldrich?*

The words from the Book of Farrelle came to her.

And the river into darkness shall carry you, away from this desperate world and the memories of men.

And there had been the Paths, the golden wolf, and from there only her path continued. In his attempts to part the mist and look into the future he had discovered his own end, and it was not distant.

"Farrelle preserve him," she whispered.

Kent had seen. Even if he had not known, he had seen it all the same.

Hayes was disobeying his very clear instructions. They had been billeted, two to a room: Hayes with Clarendon, oddly, and poor Kehler with Deacon Rose. As though the youngsters needed an older stabilizing influence.

But Hayes was worried about Clarendon, who had lain down on a bed and not moved in several hours. Neither would he answer to Hayes' entreaties, nor respond to shaking, even fairly violently done.

He was also concerned about Kehler left alone with the priest. Holding up his candle, he stared into the gloom of the hallway, searching for wolf-sized shadows. But no shadows moved. He hoped Kehler was in the next room along, and was relieved to see the faintest glow beneath the door.

Afraid of discovery, he did not knock, but only pressed the door open, looking in. "What in . . . ?"

He stared into the dim room, lit by a single candle, thinking that he looked into a land of wonder. A tiny carriage pulled by miniature horses, a castle barely taller than he . . .

"I hope, for your sake, you are not a robber," came a lovely female voice.

Hayes searched for the source, but could only tell that it came from a shadowed area by the window.

"No. No, I am a guest."

"Then you will not mind telling me the name of your host," she said quickly, though if she thought him a robber she did not seem the least frightened.

"Lord Eldrich."

"Come in then, and close the door; the beast is afoot."

Hayes did as he was told, and quickly.

"It is proper to tell a lady your name. . . ."

"Samual Hayes, ma'am."

"A pleasure, Mr. Hayes. I am the Countess of Chilton."

Hayes was sure she heard his indrawn breath. Could it really be? "The pleasure is mine, Lady Chilton."

"And what brings you to be a guest in the house of Eldrich, if I am not prying?"

His eyes were adjusting a little, and he could see her shape dimly now, sitting in the window, touched by starlight.

"Bad luck and even worse judgment, I'm afraid."

He could see her head nod. "The common reasons, I see." She turned to look out into the night as a small bird flitted before the window, nearly hovering there. She reached out her hand, and the bird darted away. "I will tell you, wandering around this house at night does not suggest that your judgment's improving."

Hayes felt a little chagrin at this slight mockery from such a woman. "I—I was looking for a friend. I thought this was his room. You see, I am worried about Clarendon."

"Randall Clarendon? A very small man?"

"The very one."

She rose, her movements full of grace. "Take me to him."

"Ma'am?"

"Take me to him." Then she paused. "He knows a friend of mine of whom I seek news, but then maybe you do yourself. Erasmus Flattery?"

Erasmus knew the Countess of Chilton? "I knew him, Lady Chilton."

He saw her reach out a hand to the window frame, and a long silence ensued, Hayes unsure what to say.

"What has befallen Mr. Clarendon?" the countess asked in a near whisper.

"Despair, I fear. It is a long story, and one which he might not wish repeated—not that his part was anything less than honorable. . . ."

"Of course. Let me see him, Mr. Hayes. Perhaps I can make myself useful in this small way at least, and then you can tell me what befell Erasmus."

Hayes opened the door, gazing out again, the countess close behind. He could feel her presence, like a source of heat. They slipped quietly out into the hallway, and through the door to Clarendon.

The little man still lay upon his bed, as though he had not moved at all.

The countess stopped and stared down at him with great solemnity. It was the first time Hayes could really see her, and he thought no description he'd heard did the woman justice. Thick, dark hair and perfect brow, her manner pensive and unbearably sad. There was nothing he would not do to comfort her, to take away the sadness—and they had barely met. The power of the attraction shocked him.

"It is not natural, Mr. Hayes," she said.

"What Eldrich has done to him?"

"No, what are you feeling. I was bespelled, or my grandmother was, I don't know which, but it works upon the men around me. What you are feeling is caused by the arts, and is an illusion. I am not really so appealing. It is good to remember." She went to the bedside. "Mr. Clarendon?" she said, but he did not stir. "Sir . . . ?"

Still there was no response. She sat down beside him and gently took his hand, and leaning forward, kissed his brow tenderly.

He stirred then. "Lizzy?"

"No, Mr. Clarendon, I am sorry to disappoint you. I am Lady Chilton, I believe we met briefly. Erasmus spoke most highly of you."

Clarendon did not open his eyes but was like a man half-roused from the deepest sleep. "Erasmus. . . . Gone, you know."

"So I have been told. May he find peace beyond this life."

Clarendon nodded, stretching a little, then settling back as though he would sleep again.

"Mr. Clarendon? That is a dream you return to. A pleasant dream, I have no doubt. A dream in which the dead live again, perhaps, but a dream nonetheless and everything that happens there is illusory. Illusion, Mr. Clarendon, no different from that which Eldrich perpetuates when it suits him." She lifted up his hand and touched it with her lips. "There are those in this world who rely upon you, who care for you. Come back, Mr. Clarendon, you will find the long sleep soon enough."

Randall opened his eyes and sighed. "Why does everyone wish to see me suffer, even you, lady?"

"No one wants to see you suffer. Certainly I have no such wish. Many, I think, would sacrifice much to see you free of pain. Mr. Hayes was willing to brave Eldrich's wolf out of concern for you, and few would risk that, I will assure you. No, your suffering brings pain to all who care for you. You have lost someone, it seems, other than Mr. Flattery?"

Clarendon nodded, looking up at this vision with wonder. "Lizzy," he breathed.

"Will you tell me about her, or would you rather not?"

"She was my guardian," he said, "my guardian angel . . . before Eldrich found us."

Hayes saw the countess shut her eyes tightly at the mention of the mage, but then she glanced up at him, and toward the door. Hayes took up his candle and went out into the fearful hallway, hoping he would find Kehler's door before the wolf found him.

Hayes returned later to find Clarendon tucked into bed and sleeping peacefully, not lying insensible, as he had been. For a moment he stood there, struggling with himself, and then went out, and into the peculiar room where he had first found the countess.

"Is that Mr. Hayes?"

"It is, Lady Chilton."

"I have been expecting you."

"Ma'am?"

"It is the enchantment, Mr. Hayes—I fear it makes men rather predictable. Most men, at least."

"Shall I leave you in peace?"

He heard her sigh. She was perched in the window where he had first seen her, the single candle burned down to a stub.

"No, come in," she said, her voice tired. "You promised to tell me a story, if it is not too . . . distressing for you."

"It is not a story to lift one's heart, that's certain," he said. "But it deserves to be known, all the same."

Hayes found a seat in the window, setting his candles atop the tiny carriage where they cast their light upon the countess. He was a little flattered that she awaited him, here, even if just to learn what had befallen Erasmus.

"I looked in on Clarendon just now," Hayes said. "I think you performed something of a miracle. He was sleeping peacefully."

"Let us hope that he wakes feeling so, though I think it will be some time before your friend finds peace." She pulled up her knees, encircling them with her arms as though she were still a young girl, not yet trained in proper ladylike deportment. "Mr. Clarendon says you found no bodies?"

Hayes shook his head.

She fixed her lovely eyes on him. "Do you think Erasmus is dead, Mr. Hayes?"

"I . . . I fear that he is, Lady Chilton." Hayes could not bear the sadness in her gaze and looked down. "Anna would, no doubt, have hidden herself had she survived, but there was no reason for Erasmus to do so, or our guide, for that matter. No, I fear they all perished and were swept away. If you had seen the waters there, you would likely think the same. I'm sure it is challenge enough to stay afloat in calm waters, let alone fast-running rivers with whirlpools and rapids and falls. I don't think anyone could have survived. Though it was the measure of Erasmus that he dove in after young Pryor without hesitation, for Pryor was no one dear to him."

The countess nodded. "I did not know Erasmus at all well, but I feel the loss all the same. I am gratified to learn that he did not falter when it came to saving another, even at great risk. I—I had wondered. . . ." She looked up at him again. "Had you known Erasmus long?"

"All my life," Hayes answered, "or nearly so."

"How was that?"

And Hayes began to tell the story of his association with Erasmus, the fall of his family's fortunes, and his "chance" meeting with Erasmus in the brothel. It took some time to tell, for Hayes held back nothing, not even his own fears and humiliations, and if he enlarged the parts played by Erasmus and Clarendon—well, it seemed to be what the countess needed to hear, and one did not wish to disappoint the Countess of Chilton.

She listened raptly, and the complete focus of her attention flattered him immeasurably.

When he finally finished his tale, the countess shook her head. "He is completely without heart, isn't he?" she said bitterly.

"Eldrich, ma'am?" Hayes lowered his voice. "I think that is being too generous."

"But it is a wondrous tale, isn't it?" she said, as though trying to pass beyond her anger toward Eldrich.

"Yes, I certainly never expected to see such things in my lifetime. It is like an old tale, from the distant past, all of it larger than life. I suppose no one will believe it in years to come."

"I don't suppose, though it is not likely anyone will ever know of it or the parts played by Erasmus and yourself, Mr. Hayes."

"My part has been small and largely accidental, I think."

"And I think you are being too modest, though it hardly matters. No one will know; Eldrich will see to that. He is secretive—strangely so, in fact." She turned and opened the window slightly, staring out at the rain and struggling storm. "Do you know, for the first time in my life I have begun to see the use of diaries. I had always thought them the most foolish vanity—the desire by the eminently unremarkable to be remembered. But now I am less sure. What else illuminates our passing through this world? We spend all our lives collecting memories, accumulating experience and some sliver of wisdom—and to what end? So that it all might be surrendered in our dotage, when memories are lost. One by one, the treasured experiences of our lives, gone. Is it not tragic, Mr. Hayes, that we lose everything in the end? I have seen great men reduced to the state of animals, unable to speak, to feed themselves. And the people who cared for them treated them with such disregard! It was shameful. As though they had not left their mark upon society—upon the world, in some cases.

"The vast majority of people born are too quickly forgotten, Mr. Hayes. And so we keep journals, hoping at least to remain in people's memories a little longer. A vain and foolish endeavor, perhaps, but completely understandable, I think. Don't you?"

Hayes nodded. "I had never thought much about it. I only know that I have never kept a diary beyond three entries, myself."

"Yes, but you suffer the illusion of youth, Mr. Hayes, if you will excuse me for saying so. You believe life is long, when it is absurdly brief—brief and shadowed by anonymity."

Hayes thought he caught a glimpse of a slim form in an upper window, but could not be sure. He smiled at his own reaction. Had not the countess said it was an enchantment that caused this response among men? She had said it so seriously that he had been half inclined to believe her. Whatever the cause, he now knew why men made complete fools of themselves over her.

An evening of conversation, and he was ready to do battle for her himself.

Steady on, now, he thought. *She certainly gave you no indication that there would even be a continued acquaintance.*

Despite that, the world did not seem such a bad place that morning. Not in the least bad. Even his continued servitude to Eldrich did not seem such a terrible burden.

Hayes glanced over at Clarendon, and this deflated him a little. Randall had not met anyone's gaze all morning, but busied himself about his horse, lifting each of its feet and cleaning the hooves with a hook.

Hayes should have looked as melancholy as poor Clarendon, for they were being sent to do the mage's bidding still. After all his hope of having escaped Eldrich . . . Apparently the mage did not believe Anna dead, for they were to seek her again, along the coast this time. It seemed Eldrich's greatest fear was that she would find a boat to take her to the island of Farrow.

Hayes glanced over at Kehler, whose mood was so downcast and black that the others were reticent to speak with him. In such a temper Kehler looked as though he had aged substantially in recent

weeks: the lines on his face cut deeper, his hair appeared more silvered in the morning sun.

Yes, Hayes thought, *this is what comes of meddling in matters that
were none of our business. We knew Eldrich might have an interest in
what the church kept hidden in their archive.*

Knowing one had acted the fool did not help. Hayes was also
vaguely worried about money, of which he had none, and now that
Erasmus was gone he did not know where it was to come from.
Certainly this expedition would cost a pretty penny. He let go a
long sigh—nothing could aggravate him for long that day, and surely
he had more important things to worry about. Someone would pay,
even if Kehler could not: Deacon Rose or Clarendon both had ample
resources.

He put a foot in the stirrup and swung up onto his horse, the
poor best hardly more recovered from their flight through the hills
than Hayes was himself. He had never fully recuperated from their
ordeal in the cave and felt constant fatigue, as though he had aged
and would never recover—and despite the cause, missing much of
a night's sleep had not helped.

Bryce stood in the door of the house watching their preparations—a darkly precise and intimidating man, and not just because
he was the mage's servant. Hayes could not wait to be out of the
man's sight, and away from this dreadful place.

Rose was on his horse, waiting. There would be no carriage for
the priest this day. Hayes felt some satisfaction at this. Eldrich had
shown so little regard for the priest and his church that even Hayes
had been taken aback. The Farrellite church was a force around the
Entide Sea, though one would not have thought so the way Eldrich
had dealt with its emissary.

They all were mounted now, Kehler and Hayes taking the leads
for their baggage horses. No one seemed ready to lead, so Hayes
spurred his horse forward, glancing back once at the window.

"Kehler!" he hissed. "Look back. At the upper window." But
when he turned again, the figure was gone.

"What was it?"

"I could have sworn it was Skye. I . . . ." Hayes shook his head.
Perhaps it had been a trick of light, silvering the head of one of the
servants. What would Skye be doing here? What in the world had

the Countess of Chilton been doing? He had neglected to ask, so delighted had he been to find himself in such company.

Riding out the lane to the road, Hayes wondered if his memories would disappear as he crossed some invisible line back into the natural world, for certainly he had been in a dream world since he arrived—nightmare and dream.

But they emerged onto the road and began, once again, the descent from the Caledon Hills, and Kehler found he could remember every word of his conversation with the countess. After the terror of Eldrich, her company had seemed like an elixir.

"Perhaps I am dreaming," he muttered.

"You look rather chipper this morning, Hayes," Kehler said, his mood lightening perceptibly. "Has the escape from the house of Eldrich caused such relief?"

"That and a night of fair dreams. Do you not feel some sense of relief that we have escaped that terrible place no more harmed than we are?"

Kehler inclined his head to one side. He was making an effort to sound his usual self. "Perhaps a little, though I would feel better if we were not still doing the will of the mage. And I, for one, have had nothing but nightmares since our meeting with Eldrich."

Hayes saw his friend shiver.

"I know; it was terrifying. For hours afterward I felt . . . as though . . . I cannot describe it. Do you know what I mean? It gave me the crawls to think that we had magic performed upon us. Eah! I can barely think of it."

Kehler nodded. "Yes, better we had never met Lord Skye and started on this whole terrible business."

"I will tell you, Kehler. It is odd, but I have begun to pine for my grotty rooms in Paradise Street, wax nostalgic for my days of poverty."

This brought a genuine smile to Kehler's anxious face. "Ah, yes. If only we could be impoverished again. . . . Wouldn't that be grand? Flames, I miss the cramps from lack of nourishment."

"And dodging creditors. Remember what fun we had!"

"Ah, yes, those splendid creditors, capital fellows. If only we could be poor again, how happy we'd be!" Kehler slapped a pocket. "Speaking of poverty, I haven't a sou, have you?"

"Not a coin of any denomination."

"Well then, our wish has been granted. HOORAY, WE'RE PAUPERS!" he shouted, causing Rose and Clarendon to look back at them, mystified.

The two friends laughed.

"I think we are a bit barmy from having escaped Eldrich," Kehler said, "though I shan't soon forget the fright of it."

"You might be wrong, there. I was told that Eldrich seldom lets those who serve him go with their memories intact."

"Who told you that?"

The countess had told him, but she had also asked him not to mention their meeting to anyone else. He did not know why but he was not prepared to break his word to the Countess of Chilton. "Well . . . Erasmus, I think."

Kehler looked at him quizzically.

"Is this another fool's errand?" Hayes asked quickly. "Is there any possibility that Anna is alive?"

Kehler looked out over the vista that had just opened up, the lowlands adrift in mist. "I would have said no, but if Eldrich has doubts—who can argue with a mage? All we can do is search, and hope this will be the last time Eldrich calls upon us." He continued to stare at the distant lands. "Hayes? I'm dreadfully sorry for dragging you into all of this."

Hayes felt a smile light his face; he couldn't help it. "Oh, don't start again. I hold no grudges." He laughed.

Kehler stared at him intently. "You are odd today. Is there something you know that I don't?"

"Only that we are away from the house of Eldrich, and, who knows, perhaps it is all a dream. Perhaps we will wake and find we never left Avonel at all."

"You mean you'll still be poor? What a pleasant thought, Hayes."

Chapter Thirty-seven

AN ancient fishing boat acted as the ferry, its owner more ancient still. A life at the sea had weathered his features until they were not unlike the distant cliffs Erasmus could see looking out over the currently passive channel.

Anna leaned against the rail beside him, gazing off toward the island, her mood thoughtful and silent.

Across the twilit deck a few islanders gathered, speaking quietly among themselves, casting the odd questioning glance at the "come-from-aways." Their interest unsettled Erasmus, but Anna seemed unconcerned—though at the moment nothing in her immediate vicinity seemed to draw her attention. Clearly, her thoughts were elsewhere.

Catspaws rippled over the slick surface of the sea, and the captain played these with skill and concentration, determined to get his passengers into harbor that night.

Anna touched Erasmus' arm softly, and nodded toward the island. "There, do you see?" she said, keeping her voice low. "Among the trees?"

"With the slate roof?" Erasmus asked.

"Yes. Our honeymoon cottage, Mr. Townsend."

They were playing at being newlyweds, thinking this would explain to the neighbors why they sought privacy—and perhaps even allow them a little of it—though Anna said the islanders kept much to themselves. She had also taken some care to turn them out in modest fashion; they might be gentlefolk but not of the wealthy variety.

Fishing wherries rounded the tip of the island, sails barely bellied in the soft airs, their motion slow as though tired from their day's labor. The sky behind was awash in the deep hues of twilight, and a crescent moon hooked itself to the heavens. The stillness was absolute, broken only by the whispers of the passengers, who, respectfully, did not speak aloud.

It was entirely dark when they finally made their landing on the island. Erasmus borrowed a fisherman's handcart and wheeled their few belongings up the starlit lane to Anna's house where they were half an hour lighting lamps and opening shutters to let the soft air of evening in and the mustiness out.

Anna gave him a tour of the house, which upon inspection was not so small. It had, Erasmus thought, a certain rustic appeal, and he felt comfortable there immediately.

"I spent a year of my girlhood here, though I was hardly allowed the luxury of a childhood. Our situation was too serious for that. But even so, this is the house I think of as my childhood home. Odd, really when there were so many, and some quite a bit more civilized, but the magic of this place—and I am speaking here of the commonplace variety—was something I never forgot."

"But where did you come from? How did they find you?"

"Halsey had his ways, I suppose, but he was a secretive man and would not say. I was an orphan, you know. I fancy my mother was a doxy, likely barely more than a girl herself. It is the common thing. But I exhibited some manifestations of talent early, and Halsey found me and brought me here. There was an old nurse who lived in the house then, a kindly woman who, though not fully a member of Halsey's little band, was an adherent in some way." Anna led him into a small room with a view out over the water toward the mainland. "She mothered me, as much as I was mothered. This was my sleeping chamber," she said, turning in a circle.

It was not particularly girlish in its adornments, Erasmus noted, just as one might expect of a girl whose guardian was an old man.

"Wait until you see the view in the morning. I loved it even as a child, for it is . . . everything a view of the sea should be, and perhaps a little more." She turned to Erasmus, putting her arms around his neck and gazing at him with very liquid eyes.

"I am only beginning to know you, Erasmus Flattery, and many of your looks are still a mystery to me. Are you anxious, Erasmus, or is it something else? Do you regret running off with me?"

"Regret, no, not in the least. But I find it difficult to believe it can be this simple to hide from Eldrich. To me, it seems we should be father away: Entonne, at least, and even more distant would be better. It isn't four days' journey from this place to Eldrich's estates. Too close. Too close by many leagues."

"Precisely. Would people not expect us to run, to get as far away as possible? Do you know there was a criminal haven in Avonel for years all but directly opposite the night watch's station? The best place to hide is where you are least expected—beneath the night watch's nose, or in the village nearest Eldrich's home. Do you realize how long followers of Teller hid within the church? Over three centuries!"

"Yes," Erasmus said, "but they were caught and burned, let us not forget."

"But Eldrich will not last the decade, Erasmus." Her arms had fallen to her sides, and she looked vulnerable standing in the center of this austere room. "Surely we can stay hidden that long. I will tell you a secret of this way of living, Erasmus: one might as well surrender to Eldrich as spend every moment in fear of apprehension. You develop the habits that keep you safe and then put it from your mind, otherwise it will drive you to madness. Believe me, our people learned much of this. You divide your life in two, very distinctly in two, and live your public life like everyone else. Otherwise you will arouse suspicion. You must acquire the proper habits and then learn to live as though nothing in your life were out of the ordinary.

"Almost no one visits this island, so to the locals you must be cordial, otherwise they will begin to talk. They will understand our desire to keep to ourselves, for we are gentlefolk and they are not, but if you begin to act though you fear discovery, in a twinkle the speculation will begin. We are criminals, we are adulterers run off from our families. It will go on and on.

"I will spread the rumor that you have been ill and have come here to recover, and work on a book of . . . natural philosophy? No, that is too much like the real you. Poetry, perhaps. You needn't worry, no one will ask to read it." She smiled at him, cajoling. "Trust me, Erasmus, and I will be your teacher in this, for I have been hiding from Eldrich all my days."

Erasmus did not want to point out that Eldrich had trapped and almost murdered her once.

"Tomorrow I will go out to purchase what we need and you can stay here—to rest and recover from your illness. I will put forth our story—or let them draw it from me, bit by bit. By tomorrow evening everyone on the island will think they know our business, and we will be quickly forgotten.

"Do not forget; Erasmus Flattery and Anna Fielding died tragically of misadventure. There is no reason for anyone to be seeking us. The notable Erasmus Flattery is dead. His family will hold services for him within a fortnight, and your many accomplishments will grow in everyone's mind until you are a genius of the rank of Skye. Already I wish I'd known you."

She gave him a gentle shake. "It was a jest. You should laugh politely."

Erasmus could not laugh. "I never believed I'd be free of him, not even if he died, for who could know what task I might be left? I still cannot quite believe it. Free of Eldrich? It is as likely as having an amputated limb grow back. You cannot know how I have been haunted by him—since I was ten years old. Haunted by my time in his house, wondering what my purpose was, why I had been taken there. Eldrich has hovered at the back of my mind all this time, like a terrible shadow. I am not quite sure how to make that shadow go away, how to banish it."

Anna pressed him down into a chair, perching on the arm.

"It will take time. Do not expect it to go away overnight. The mages haunted the followers of Teller for centuries. We learned to practice vigilance without living in constant fear. Fear of discovery will gnaw away at you, Erasmus, if you let it. Be on your guard." She went to the window and cast it open, looking out over the dark, still waters which bled into the shadowed land, the shoreline indistinguishable. "The mages hoarded their power with great care over the ages. They never numbered more than eleven at one time, and commonly there were fewer—nine, often; as few as six, occasionally—and now there is only one. One mage to hold the power, to complete the final tasks."

"And what are the final tasks?"

She glanced at him over her shoulder, then turned back to the open window. "To leave no person or text that could seed a rebirth of the arts . . . and perhaps other things as well."

"But what of me?" Erasmus said. "I have some knowledge of the arts—" But he stopped, the answer to his question obvious.

"Yes," Anna said softly. "He trapped you in the cave with the rest of us. Deacon Rose, who is the church's authority on the arts— the man who is tainted that the others may remain pure—young Hayes and Kehler. Even Clarendon, I suspect, is not without some knowledge. Banks, myself . . ." she drew a breath, "and all my brothers." She reached out and put a hand on either side of the frame. "Imagine the skill it took to manipulate events so that we should all converge in that one place. One must stand in awe. But you, Erasmus, you thwarted him and discovered the way out. Pray that he thinks we are dead. That he completes his task, leaving us behind—and that he trains no other to stand vigil."

This thought had occurred to Erasmus as well. "Would it not make sense for him to do that?"

"He will do it only out of utter necessity. It is a danger, leaving someone with knowledge of the arts. That person might be the one who maintains them so that the arts might one day be known to others. Others who have no allegiance to the original mages."

"Then I will pray that he thinks we are dead, though to what gods I would appeal I don't know, for I am a child of reason."

He could just see her jaw move—a smile. "You are a child of magic, Erasmus." She shook her head. "How can one be a man of reason when raised in the house of a mage? Our kind are capable of such contradictions. Are there not empiricists who remain within the church, though the church condemns many of the beliefs of these same men of reason?"

"Yes, though I have never thought of myself as being like them." He shrugged.

She turned to him, leaning back against the window ledge, half-sitting. "Have you ever wondered if you're dead?" she asked earnestly. "I mean really dead, not merely conveniently dead, as we are. Perhaps when we die, we slip into a dream and our life continues on with us blissfully unaware. And that is what has happened. We died in the cave or in the gorge, or a hundred other points in our lives where we might have perished. And this is a dream."

"Mine or yours?" Erasmus asked.

"Mine, of course," she smiled. "But do you know what I mean? Has this only occurred to me?"

"No, in fact I have thought similar things myself. After all, we don't know what happens after we pass through—and this is as sensible as many of the explanations that have been offered. Perhaps this is death, and life is what comes after."

"You mock me, Erasmus Flattery," she said, wagging a finger at him.

"Not really. It is not impossible that we are truly dead, and not just conveniently so, as you have said." He gestured to the room. "Then this is the house of the dead, and that makes me, madam, a necrophile."

This made her laugh, and she took two steps, landing softly in his lap. He could feel her smile as they kissed.

"And that, sir," she laughed, "was the kiss of death."

Chapter Thirty-eight

S HE found Skye in the garden in the early morning. He lounged on a bench set for privacy behind a screen of lilac trees. As she appeared, he started, then quickly rose to his feet.

"Lord Skye," she said, noting that he did not smile or look pleased to see her in any way. Why was this one man so immune to her charms? "I have wondered why we have not met."

"I have been cautioned to avoid you," he said. No greeting, nor did he make a leg.

This brought her up abruptly, but as she blocked the only exit from this small arbor, they stood there awkwardly. Certainly Skye would have fled if he could.

"The mage said this?" she asked, looking for anything to fill the silence.

"No, it was Mr. Walky."

"Oh, well, Walky. Take no notice of him. Please, sit. I'm sure a few words cannot do any harm." She tried to smile as though nothing were in the least amiss or even out of the ordinary, but all she could think about was why he had been cautioned to avoid her.

"You accompanied my friend, Marianne Edden, I collect?" she said when it became obvious that Skye would not speak. He perched on the edge of the seat and kept glancing up at the entry to the arbor as though expecting the mage to appear there out of thin air—which Eldrich actually seemed to do at times. She stole a quick glance, too, and then chastised herself for it.

"Was it the Peliers?" she asked quietly. "Is that what drew the attention of the mage?"

Skye shrugged, a little helplessly. "As astonishing as it is to me, Lady Chilton, I seem to have been an object of interest to Lord Eldrich for some time. I am not sure how long. He seems to know even of my distant past—the time lost to me. I—I cannot explain it. I have long been part of a design. . . ." Again he raised his shoulders in a gesture of complete mystification.

The countess reached out and gently touched the arm he had slung across the back of the bench. "Yes. It is shocking to discover such things. I found it a little hard to accept that I had met the mage on more than one occasion and had no memory of it. It was most disconcerting. But here we are. I had thought I might never see you again."

Skye nodded, forcing a tight smile.

"Has Eldrich told you of your past, then? It must be a relief to finally uncover—"

"He will say nothing," Skye broke in quickly. "Not a word. It would seem to take so little effort for him to relieve me of this suffering, yet he will not." He shook his head, anger and terrible disappointment appearing on his face. "What are we but the result of the lives we've lived, and if some part of a life is lost—then we are not whole. Part of us has been severed. That is what I think. But Eldrich would tell me not a thing."

The countess was not much surprised to hear this. "It is not his way to make such gestures to others, to show compassion for no reason. He is more likely to keep such information in the event that it will prove useful. Perhaps there is yet some task he wishes performed and nothing will insure your utter devotion to its success more than dangling the possibility of your memories before you. He is not compassionate as we understand the word," she said sympathetically.

She wondered how it was that his prematurely gray hair seemed to make him look younger than his actual years. Was it the contrast between the gray mane and the almost unlined face?

Skye looked down at the bench. "No, he is not compassionate, but then neither was I when in a position where it would have taken little effort on my behalf. Perhaps I am reaping the rewards of my own callousness. Perhaps the mage is teaching me this lesson."

"Oh, do not think that! No, Lord Skye, trust that Eldrich cares almost nothing for how you have conducted your own affairs. No, the concerns of men are of little consequence to him, for he considers himself above 'petty morality.' "

Skye nodded. "Yes, I suppose you're right. It just seems so odd. I was brought here by this man Bryce, spoke once with Eldrich, and then have been largely ignored. I am going a little mad with no one to speak with. One begins to have the strangest thoughts when there are no others about and one is thrown back entirely on one's own company." He looked up, apologetically. "I must sound a bit pathetic. Do excuse me, it's just . . ."

"Do not apologize. This is the most irregular household in the world, I'm sure. Left here entirely on one's own, kept in the dark as to what transpires and what the mage's intentions are: it wears on one's nerves. I have found it myself. Fortunately, I have had others to speak with, and Walky has become something of a friend."

"Yes, he seems the only spark of humanity in the entire place, present company excepted, of course. Why are you here, Lady Chilton, if I may ask?"

She glanced over at the entry, then at the lilac trees. "Well, it is difficult to explain. The truth is, I am not entirely sure myself."

"Then you are here against your will?"

"No. No, I am here . . . well, let us just say that the mage has a task for me, and that he was able to offer me something to insure my cooperation."

"Ah."

For an instant she thought he would ask what, but then he remembered his manners, even under the circumstances, which the countess thought so strange as to almost call for a rewriting of the rules of conduct.

They fell silent, the countess wondering what she should say next, acutely aware that Skye wanted nothing so much as to escape.

"The mage said absolutely nothing that would indicate what purpose he had for you?" she said when he seemed about to rise.

He shook his silver mane. "No. Well, I have mulled over the little he did say so often that the few words have taken on every possible meaning—and therefore have become meaningless. I don't know. He wanted to know about a woman I met once briefly. Beyond that, he warned me that I might not be so happy to have my memories restored, as though there were something in my past that . . ." He shrugged. "I have even wondered if this was said merely to torment me. Mages are not above tormenting cruelly, or so I understand. Is that possible, do you think?"

"Possible, though not likely. Not unless you did something to raise his ire. He does have a cruel streak that can come out at such times. I have begun to think that he is like a man who, at intervals, suffers some terrible agony, and when one of these bouts is upon him, he loses all patience and can become vicious. Knowing when he is suffering, that is the key. So far I have not been able to tell."

"But surely Eldrich cannot suffer from illness or injury. He is a mage."

"No, I said only that he was *like* a man suffering pain. Though I think the truth is even more strange. I believe he suffers fits of despair. Despair that he will fail in the task he has been left. I cannot even tell you why I think this. I have been told my intuition is good." She glanced at Skye. "Though occasionally it fails me spectacularly."

Again the awkward silence, Skye looking at the entry, perched on the edge of his seat. The countess could see that he was vastly relieved to have someone to speak with but was also terrified of discovery.

Skye suddenly sat back on the bench, slumping against the back, his face collapsing in a like manner. The look he fixed on her was one of desperate appeal. "Have you any idea why I am being kept here? Any idea at all?"

She shook her head, somewhat devastated that she could not give him an answer, still hoping to please him, she realized, to win him over, despite all. "No, I haven't, I'm sorry to say." Then she brightened. "But perhaps I could find out. I could certainly ask Walky: I am likely to get nothing from the mage, but Walky is sometimes surprisingly forthcoming. I could try."

Why was she making such an offer? Did she retain some feeling for this man that presently she could not find?

"I would appreciate it more than you could know," he said with feeling, his despair lifting a little with this small ray of hope.

"Lady Chilton," he said with great seriousness, "I really should not tarry. I do not want to do anything that would endanger my chances with Eldrich. Who knows. Perhaps he will answer my question yet."

She nodded, tilting her head toward the opening in the trees— releasing him. This time he did make a leg, even forcing a smile.

Yes, she thought, *as long as he wants something of me* . . .

Although it was really Eldrich from whom Skye wanted something this time. And as far as she could tell, the mage never granted anyone what they wanted.

Chapter Thirty-nine

THE ships in the harbor foundered in fog, the stars slipping into this same thin sea. As the carriage bumped over some rut in the cobbles, Captain James was thrown forward, and he reached a hand automatically for the window sill.

One would almost think he dwelt in carriages these days, ever since he had been assigned this duty—the search for the faded woman. The one he had met . . . his mind would not provide the name of the village and the effort to dredge it up caused a peculiar uneasiness. And here he was again, rattling along the coast, pursuing another possibility.

For a sailor, Captain James was not a superstitious man, or so he held, but this duty was changing that. There was something very odd going on in the Admiralty. Everyone who was involved in the matter spoke of it in whispers. All very dark and peculiar. They sought a mistress of the King, some said, or an illegitimate daughter. But these theories were not near the mark—not for James' money. No, it was all more macabre than that. Like his inability to remember certain things. The way his mind would shy away from them, almost slide off onto some other tack, and there he would be, thinking of something else.

His hand lifted in an unconscious warding sign.

He wished to Farrelle he were not mixed up in this matter. Better a battle at sea, a battle with the chance of a clean death. He shivered at the thought of his spirit left wandering, endlessly wandering, but he feared such could be his fate if things went awry on this duty. Though not an overly religious man, he made a sign to Farrelle.

And there had been disturbing dreams, as well. Nightmares in which he spoke to a shadow—a darkly malevolent shadow. Many of the strange events that had transpired in past weeks surfaced in dreams. The men leaping from the high window in Paradise Street, but rather than floating down as they were witnessed to do, they turned into nightjars and flew off, mewling in high, thin voices. Enough to make one's skin crawl. The woman who self-murdered in Avonel Harbor floated through the sea of his dreams, as well, muttering dark imprecations. Words that he could not remember properly when he woke.

A bell echoed through the fog-bound town, which meant sunrise drew nigh, though in the world beyond the carriage there was only darkness and mist.

The carriage slowed, almost stopped, and then rolled on another twenty yards, as though the driver searched for a house number. Suddenly the rig drew to a halt, and James felt the springs flex as the driver climbed down to open the door and pull down the small steps. The man saluted smartly despite the hour.

"I believe this is your destination, Captain."

James stepped out into the damp night, brushed out his coat, and then reached back in for hat and cane. A guard, fully armed, appeared to a knock on the door and insisted James produce his warrant, which was carefully examined. They were being cautious, which he was happy to see—though a little speed at this hour would have been appreciated.

An officer appeared in the hallway, pulling his clothing into order and trying to shake himself into wakefulness. "Captain James? Lieutenant Beal. We have her upstairs." He gestured down the hall.

"You found her where?" James said as they mounted the creaking stair.

"She had procured passage from Helford on an old coaster."

James nodded, his interest increasing. Coasters didn't commonly bear passengers. There were far more comfortable methods of travel. Ideal for someone hoping not to be noticed.

"What brought her to your attention?"

"Well, she certainly fits the description, sir, though she is not quite so refined—but that could be an act. Claims her name is Ann Fairfield, which is close enough. And she cursed a sailor who was too bold with her, and he fell from the maintop and pulled his arm from its socket catching a buntline. A wonder he survived at all."

"Well, there's proof for you," James said.

"Aye," his companion agreed, missing the irony. "What has this young wench done that we're turning half the kingdom end-over searching for her?"

"It's a complicated story, Beal."

The man looked at him expectantly.

"And I'm not at liberty to tell it."

Two more guards stood outside a door, and here Beal shook out a massive ring of keys—a man who measured his importance in keys, as some did. He turned the lock, gathered a candelabra from a shelf, and gently opened the door.

James heard his breath catch, the moment was so unreal. He had been sent here to identify the woman, and the truth was that he didn't know what she looked like, precisely. *But he had been told that when he saw her, he would know.* Who had told him that? This was always the part that was difficult to remember. A dark-haired man, exceedingly well groomed. Bryce, or Price. Something like that.

"We managed her arrest strictly as ordered," Beal said quickly as he lifted the candles to afford James a view.

A young woman lay on a cot, bound hand and foot and roughly gagged. One eye was purple and swollen closed, and the rest of her face was covered by a curtain of hair—faded red hair.

James glanced at the other officer.

"We were told to descend upon her before she was aware of our intent, and not let her utter a word, sir. It went badly for her, but that's orders, sir. Is she a spy, Captain?"

James did not answer but took the candles from the man and bent down.

"Some are saying that she is some kind of witch, sir."

James ignored the man, reaching out to tuck the woman's hair behind her ear—his hand trembling a little. She drew back from him as much as her bindings would allow.

No light of recognition lit in his mind. She was a stranger to him, of that he was sure.

"Poor child," James said. "Here take this." He thrust the candles at the man, and proceeded to remove the woman's gag.

"Sir! We were expressly warned not to do that. Captain James!"

"It is the wrong girl, Beal. There you go; Miss Fairfield, is it?"

She took a long gasp of breath.

"Here, let me get your hands."

"I didn't curse no sailor, sir. I—I swear it. You look a kind gentleman, sir. I'm no witch or whatever it is they t'ink." Tears began to run down the young girl's face. "I swear, sir. I'll swear it 'fore a priest. . . . I will."

"I know you're not a witch, Miss Fairfield, and His Majesty's government will compensate you for your inconvenience and injury. You can be sure of that. In fact this officer, Lieutenant Beal, is going to find you a room at the best inn this town can offer and send you on your way in comfort. Can you sit up, do you think? There's a girl."

A clamor sounded in the hallway and unfamiliar faces appeared in the door: two young men, a priest, and a brightly dressed dwarf.

"Who in this round world . . . ?" Beal took a step toward these strangers, his manner threatening.

"It's all right, Beal. I know them—or at least know of them." He turned to the door. "Is one of you Clarendon?"

"I am." The small man stepped forward, performing a graceful leg. "Randall Spencer Emanual Clarendon, at your service."

"This is not the Anna Fielding that I . . . know," James said. "I trust you concur?"

"Completely. But who has mistreated this woman so?" The dwarf glared at Beal as though the man weren't twice his size.

James stood up. "Send her on to the Admiralty in Avonel, Lieutenant, and they will see she's properly compensated. In a navy ship, mind you, not a coaster or a carriage. We don't want anything befalling her again."

Introductions were made, and without further farewell James followed the others out, leaving a mystified Beal bobbing in their wake.

There was some light in the fog as they emerged from the building.

"Well, gentlemen, it is my intent to find an inn and break my fast. As we seem to be assigned to the same duty, perhaps you would care to join me?"

The four glanced at each other, and then one of the young men—the cheerful-looking one—spoke. "I, for one, could use food, so it would be a pleasure, Captain James."

Forgoing carriages—it seemed they had all been cramped up in them for too long—they began to walk along the quay, certain to find an inn by the harbor. Within a hundred yards they were given the choice of three. They quickly settled on the most prosperous looking, and found a table commanding a view over the small harbor.

"Well, I think that makes an even dozen red-haired young women," Hayes said, "but not one our late, lamented Anna."

This gave James pause. *Late, lamented?* Certainly this must be a private jest. All James knew about these gentlemen was that they were searching for this same young woman and were to be given every assistance—up to and including the use of the navy's ships, personnel, and property.

"You know her?" James asked.

"Of course. Don't you? Isn't that why the Admiralty sent you down here?"

"Indeed it is," James agreed. "It's just that . . ." He waved his hand in a gesture of dismissal. "It is not worth discussing. Do forgive me. I have seen, I think, eight potential Annas, including this one whom we are both adding to our tally. I make that nineteen. How many women are there in Farrland with faded red hair and a slightly sallow cast?"

"I fear quite a number more," Hayes said, "though I hope they will not all be as misused as that poor girl."

"Yes, this entire matter is being pressed rather . . . vigorously."

"Well, you know the mage, Captain," Hayes said. "He cares little for the suffering of others. That poor girl might have been murdered, and he would not even take notice."

James wondered if his face had paled. *Eldrich. . . .* Obviously it could be no one else. Why had he never thought of that before? Whenever he considered this subject, his thoughts became so muddled that his head would soon begin to throb. *Eldrich!* This girl was being sought by the mage.

"And how is it you became involved in this matter, Captain?" the priest asked quietly. The man's question had no challenge in it, only polite curiosity, but he regarded James with a probing, intelligent eye.

"It is a difficult question to answer, Father, for I am not exactly sure. I seem to have trouble remembering. It was a man named Bryce or perhaps Price . . .?" He pressed a hand to his forehead, which pained him suddenly.

The others nodded, and Samual Hayes touched his arm.

"Don't tax yourself attempting to recall, Captain James, it will only bring you suffering. The man's name, for your comfort, was Bryce. Percival Bryce."

"*Mr. Hayes,*" cautioned Clarendon.

"Mr. Hayes has offered you good advice, Captain," Deacon Rose said. "Trying to remember will gain you nothing. Better to know as little as possible. That's my counsel. And do be careful whom you take into your confidence on this matter."

"I am an officer of His Majesty's navy," James shot back, "not a gape-mouthed fool." He had not meant to speak so forthrightly, but the pain in his head made his temper flare.

The priest gave him the thinnest smile and a nod. "Of course," he said.

"It seems a bit odd to have us all gathered in one place," Kehler opined. "Would it not be more efficient to have us spread along the coast? Why on earth does it take the four of us and Captain James as well to identify the woman? Certainly one person would do."

"I think it was merely a mistake," Captain James offered, speaking softly now, the pain subsiding. "This young woman seemed very promising—she went by the name of Ann Fairfield, did you know?—and we were all summoned with the idea that someone would get here quickly, no matter what delays the others suffered."

A midshipman came quickly into the room, glanced around once, and crossed directly to their table.

"Captain James? And your companions, sir: Clarendon, Deacon Rose, Hayes, and Kehler?"

The captain nodded. What now? Another woman he must rush off to see?

"I'm to deliver this gentleman to you so that you might hear his story." The young man turned and looked back to the door where a rather unkempt Farrelite priest stood, looking somewhat abashed. At a nod from the midshipman he approached the table, though not quickly. James was oddly struck by the softness of the man's eyes, the modesty of his demeanor, as though he were not concerned about his place in the world. A glance back at the priest named Rose revealed a great contrast. There was no question in James' mind who was the true follower of Farrelle.

"And who are you, Brother?" Deacon Rose asked.

"Brother Norbert—of the Blessed Springs Monastery," he said. "In the Caledon Hills."

James exiled the midshipman to a distant corner of the room, and a chair was provided for the monk.

"Well, Brother Norbert," Rose said, "don't keep us in suspense."

"Men came searching into the hills these few days past, and dragged me from my home and my pursuits," he said, though if this were an accusation, it was stated very mildly. "They were searching for news of a young woman—Anna Fielding by name. I told them of a visitor whom I had found wandering lost, and apparently she fit the description." He looked up. "She was a woman of singular appearance—red-haired, vivacious. One might almost describe her as vivid."

James noticed the others glance at each other, a bit surprised.

"Not pale or faded?" Hayes asked.

"Not at all, sir. She had been riding beneath the sun for some days and had the color of it, but no, she was vital, even . . . vibrant. A most unusual woman."

"And what was she doing in the Caledon Hills, and what name did she offer?"

"She did not offer her name, and I did not ask. . . ."

"You didn't ask her name!?"

The priest shrugged. "No. It's only a word and seems very un-important to me. Too much stress is placed on names, I think, which is why we brothers of the church give up our given and family names. I did not ask; she did not offer.

"She claimed to be writing a book of her journey through the hills. That is why she was visiting the out-of-the-way places. As she explained, readers would hardly be interested in localities that had been visited by half the people in the kingdom."

"And she traveled alone?"

"She did, though she had set out with a guide. A young man named Garrick Lake. He had taken a tumble off his horse and bro-ken his neck. She was most distressed at this loss—most genuinely distressed."

"And when did you meet her, precisely? The date."

The priest considered a moment. "The morning of the twelfth."

Clarendon, who for the most part seemed unhappily quiet, inter-jected, "That was before the gorge, so it means little."

The others nodded.

"Did she say anything else, Brother? Did she tell you where she was going?"

"To Wicken Vale." Brother Norbert considered a moment. "In truth she said very little, especially about herself." He thought a moment more. "Though she did pose an odd question as she left. She asked, if her spirit appeared to me one day, if I would forgive her sins and help her find peace. I said that I would, and she asked, 'No matter what I had done in life?' and I said, 'Yes, no matter what you had done.' "

"Very generous of you, Brother, but you did not know what atrocities she had committed already in this life." Deacon Rose seemed to dismiss the priest from his thoughts then, looking at the others.

"But she seemed a kind, good-hearted young woman to me," Brother Norbert said mildly. "She shed tears for her guide and wondered if the rites she performed would bring him the peace of Farrelle."

"Which of course they wouldn't as she was no priest. And likely the rites that she performed would damn him for all time. You do not know whom you are dealing with, Brother. Have you anything more to tell us?"

Brother Norbert opened his mouth to speak, reconsidered, and then shook his head.

There was a tense silence following Rose's berating of the kindly priest, and then Clarendon spoke.

"Has her spirit appeared to you, Brother?" he asked, his voice quiet and serious.

Brother Norbert looked at the small man in some surprise. "It has not."

Clarendon nodded at this news. Saying nothing more, he turned to his food.

Chapter Forty

E RASMUS walked among the overrun gardens, occasionally looking out across the sound to the mainland beyond. Fishing
wherries and coasters heeled to the breeze, stained sails among a
smattering of small, white crests.

He had left Anna poring over Halsey's writings, stepping out to
get some air. There was only so much time a man could spend
reading—or making love, for that matter. He was going a little stir
crazy. Escape from Eldrich did not seem such a bargain at that moment. In exchange, his life had been reduced in size until it seemed
bounded by the walls of the garden—an area he could encompass
in a quarter hour. Too small.

"I have exchanged all the world for this," he said aloud.

He looked out to the boats under sail, sturdy, seagoing little
ships, and all he could think was that perhaps one of these could
carry him away—over the horizon and into the great unexplored
world.

"It is being locked up in this fair prison," he said aloud.

At least he was not alone, and though Anna spent many hours
in study and contemplation, she was, the rest of the time, quite
attentive to him. He had even begun to wonder if her affections for

him were real. Whether real or feigned, they took great, if some-what desperate, pleasure from each other, and that was making his captivity bearable.

Anna's chough landed on the top of the stone wall that topped the cliff. It eyed him, jealously, Erasmus thought.

"*Chuff*," it muttered in disapproval.

"There you are," Anna's voice came to him, and he turned to find her brushing aside the branches of a laburnum. Although she carried Halsey's book and looked the part of a dutiful scholar, she favored him with a kiss that was anything but dutiful.

She held him at arm's length, gazing at him closely. "You are prowling about like an animal in a cage, Erasmus. I have begun to feel as though I have locked you up here, and against your will, too."

"It is . . . an adjustment. The world seems to have shrunk to this two acres, and I have not yet become used to it."

"You need to find some endeavor to occupy your mind. I know I have said this before, but can you not pursue your interests here? There is an old glass house that we could put into repair. Certainly horticulture can be studied as easily here as in Locfal?"

Erasmus disentangled himself from her and they both perched on the low, stone wall. "For some reason these things don't seem to draw my interest at the moment. Perhaps in time . . ."

"Well, you could assist me. I will try to propagate the king's blood. I will have need of it in the future."

This elicited an uncomfortable silence from Erasmus.

"It can't be helped, Erasmus, I am becoming habituated even now. You cannot imagine the agonies of giving it up. It is even said that it has never been done." She gazed at him intently, worried by his response.

Suddenly Anna offered him her hand. "Come with me," she said simply, and led him off through the garden and out a wooden gate set into the wall.

"Where are you leading me?" Erasmus asked.

"Astray, my dear Erasmus. You will see."

They followed a path that wound up the wooded hill behind the enclosed gardens.

"Whose lands are these?"

"Mine. Ours, now. Perhaps forty acres, or thereabouts."

They continued to climb, stopping to rest once, for it was not really so long since their ordeal in the cave and flight through the Caledon Hills, and neither of them had yet fully recovered.

Finally they came up onto a narrow, natural bench cut into the hillside. This sloped up gradually into a dense thicket of holly and gorse. They made their way slowly, leaving bits of hair and skin and clothing behind on the many thorns.

"I hope this is a vista worth the blood," Erasmus complained.

Anna laughed but said nothing, leaving Erasmus to wonder. Finally they burst through the thicket and found a stand of mature trees, evenly spaced, on a kind of natural terrace. A small spring spilled from the rocky bluff behind, and with the sun filtering through the leaves, it was a place of great charm indeed.

Erasmus turned to look out toward the mainland, but the view was almost entirely hidden by the branches of trees. He began to go forward, thinking to quench his thirst, but Anna restrained him with a hand. She seemed very solemn, suddenly.

"Before you go forward, you must first perform this short rite." And she made a motion with her hand, chanting a string of Darian.

"A *nance*," Erasmus said, realizing what he saw. It was akin to the ruin on Farrow, though made up of natural elements. Instead of columns, seven trees; two chestnuts, a pair of hawthorns, two silverleaf oaks, and a single black walnut. The trees were arranged in a half-circle radiating out from the rock wall, each tree opposite its mate, the black walnut opposite the wall.

Erasmus copied Anna's ablutions, and moved into the center of the trees, their boles standing straight, the many branches reaching up, supporting a green roof.

"You did not tell me of this," Erasmus said.

Anna shook her head. "No." She whispered as though they were in a place of worship.

"Is this a gate as well? Like Landor's Gate and the Ruin on Farrow?"

"No, it is a memorial. The gates are ancient sites, used in ages past. This is no older than the trees you see. In truth, it is more like the field outside Compton Heath. A Stranger appeared here once. My people traced it most carefully. She came into our world on this very spot, some two hundred years past." Anna put her arm out straight. "And along this line lie Compton Heath, Kilty's Keep, and the ruin of Tremont Abbey." She gestured in the opposite direction. "And far out to sea, Farrow sits, though it might not lie on this same fault—this line of power. You are standing at a place where the worlds meet, Erasmus Flattery. Or at least met in the past. On that day the earth trembled, and a great storm appeared to sweep down out of the sky. The worlds intersected here, and a Stranger appeared: an elderly woman. She did not live long—a year or two— but long enough to prove something that had been in doubt for a thousand years. The other worlds, the worlds of ancient stories, existed, and they could still be reached."

Conversation ceased, and they both remained very still, listening to the mumbling spring, and the breeze sighing through the trees.

Erasmus thought of Clarendon and his story—of seeing a man and woman disappear under moving stars—worlds intersecting. He was coming to believe it himself.

"You have never told me what you learned in the field outside Compton Heath," Erasmus said.

She crouched down with her back against a tree. "I could feel the world turning," she said. "And then I saw the heavens."

"In broad daylight?"

She nodded. "Yes. But there were no constellations I recognized."

Erasmus turned to her, surprised. "What does it mean?"

"That Eldrich has long planned to escape this world. It is why he is so desperate to complete his task. The worlds are drawing closer, aligning in some way, and there will be a chance to open the gate between—perhaps the last chance for centuries, perhaps forever."

Erasmus crouched in the center of the *nance* so that he could look directly into her eyes.

"What do you hope to do, Anna? What do you truly hope?"

She considered this a moment, biting her lip gently. "To live, Erasmus. That is the only purpose for both our lives now. To live, for surely Eldrich will destroy us if he can."

Erasmus asked the question that had weighed upon him ever since he had woken in the gorge and found Anna was his savior.

"But what of this vision of the mages? This cataclysm? If we escape Eldrich, will we bring this catastrophe upon man?"

She shook her head. "I don't know the answer to this. I do know that the mages were not of one mind regarding it, as perhaps I have said. The more powerful mages overruled their fellows. Certainly Halsey was never able to see this alleged vision of the apocalypse. But in all honesty, Erasmus, I cannot say what will happen. Perhaps even Eldrich is not sure."

"But he does not seek our death for his own amusement. . . ."

"No, he does not, but that does not mean his reasons are right. What have we done to deserve such an end?" She looked suddenly as if tears would come, but she turned and looked away, her jaw tight. "He could offer a truce. I would listen to reason. I am the only follower of Teller left in this world, and I renounce his aims. Let Eldrich convince me, and I will renounce the arts. Do you think the mage could be convinced to do that?"

Erasmus did not need to consider this. He shook his head quickly. "No. He will seek your death—and mine. Eldrich treats with no one."

Anna met his eye. "No one but another mage—"

The question must have been clear on Erasmus' face.

"There was this stricture among the mages. They could not take the life of another mage. It was more than a law, it was a curse, and a mage's curse is a deadly thing. There was one moment in the ritual which created the mage when the emerging mage could be killed, but beyond that they were immune to any threats from their fellows."

Anna met his eyes with a gaze of great intensity. "He cannot harm you, Erasmus, if you undergo the transformation—if you become a mage."

Chapter Forty-one

"IF I didn't know it was impossible, I would swear that he'd played a joke on us." Eldrich shook his head and continued to stare at the canvas. Walky stood a pace back, tilting his head to one side.

"Do I intrude?" the countess asked, for neither had acknowledged her, not that the mage made a practice of doing so. She wondered if the edge of ice was noticeable in her voice.

Eldrich glanced up at her and then at Walky. He looked annoyed, and the countess was not quite certain if it was with her unexpected arrival.

"No," Eldrich said. "Indeed; perhaps you can make something of this painting for us." His attention slid back to the canvas.

She came around the easel, taut with anger which appeared to go completely unnoticed by the mage. The story that Hayes had told her—Erasmus' story would not leave her in peace.

He used children! One of whom was set aflame to fulfill his ends. Set aflame!

Walky made a hasty bow, not nearly so insensitive as his master.

"By your leave," the little man whispered. The door closed behind his retreating form just as the countess' gaze came to rest on the painting.

She felt her balance give way oddly beneath her, and her anger toward Eldrich evaporated. "Is—is it a Pelier?"

The mage shook his head, apparently unaware of her reaction. "No. It is an Averil Kent, though painted under an enchantment that I hoped would allow him to imitate Pelier in more than just style. But what in this round world does it mean? That is the question."

Mean, indeed. The countess braced herself mentally, the same disturbing feelings that the Pelier had engendered coming over her. The painting was of a storm, or so it seemed; leaves and broken branches and detritus from the forest floor all airborne and awhirl. Rain, in streaks and torrents, spun on this same dervish wind. She could almost taste it, feel the breath taken from her, the leaves and dirt forced into her mouth and lungs. It was unbearable.

For a moment she shut her eyes, but the painting did not disappear, and in her mind's eye she could see figures in the maelstrom.

Her eyes flicked open. Yes, there they were—a woman and a man. And was that a white blossom in her hand, or merely something carried by in the torrent? The man braced himself against the wind, reaching out a hand to his companion. The countess could not tell if the woman had hold of the man's hand or not, but both of them looked as though they would be swept away at any moment.

The motion in the painting was astonishing, manic. The clothes of the figures billowed and swirled, almost seeming to move as you looked, which she could only bear to do for a few seconds at a time.

"Kent did this? A prophetic painting?"

The mage nodded, his attention on the canvas.

The countess gestured at the figures. "Who . . . ? Who are they?" she asked, her words seeming to spin away on a wind.

Eldrich shook his head. "That is what we were discussing. The woman would seem to be you." He reached out his hand, pointing a long finger. "Do you see this? The dark area? Your curls, I think. Though, if you tilt your head, they seem to be nothing but burned leaves and shadow afloat on the wind." He tilted his head experimentally. "The man is another question. Walky believes it is Kent, though I am not so sure. I think I see something of Erasmus in the

stance, the silhouette, but who can be sure? See this, however."
He gestured again. "That is the top of a column and a broken lintel.
Like the Ruin of Farrow, though Walky believes that is mere wishful
thinking. Do you see?"

"Yes. That is a column, I am sure. And it is carved with some
. . . I don't know. Shapes that I cannot identify. Yet see this corner
of sky! Kent told me that Pelier was unsurpassed in his treatment of
cloud and sky, but look at this! I think Pelier has a rival, after all."

The mage cast an odd glance at her.

"Look closely at this woman. You have gazed into a looking
glass—is it the Countess of Chilton?"

She tried to focus on the figure, but the more she tried to concentrate, the more the figure seemed to disintegrate. To see it at all
she had to look away slightly and place the figure at the edge of her
vision, as though it were not real but made up of the windborne
leaves and detritus. "I don't know. The truth is that others always
see you most clearly. What does Walky think?"

"He is not sure," the mage said, an edge of despair in his voice.
"Perhaps it is you."

"But what do the other elements mean? Is that not a king's
blood blossom in the woman's hand? And the column— These
things must have meaning."

"Must they?" Eldrich stared at the painting, his usual unreadable
countenance observably sad. He turned and walked away a few
paces, then returned his attention for a moment. He sighed and
threw himself down in a chair.

"I think Kent's price was too high, for he gave me nothing in
return."

"Then the portraits meant nothing?"

The mage glanced up at her, raising an eyebrow. "No, they
might yet have their use. We shall see."

His peevishness seemed to drain away from him as he sprawled
in the chair, and suddenly he seemed fragile and tired, his dark, unsettling eyes sunken. For a moment he laid his head back and closed
his eyes.

The countess felt her anger return as she looked at him,
sprawled rudely in a chair, concerned only with the world of Eldrich.

"Not everyone you use performs as you would like, do they? Perhaps, after all, coercion is less effective than willing participation."

His mouth turned down, as though he grimaced in pain.

"I have neither the time nor temperament to win people over," he said. "My task is more crucial than that."

"Nor do you have the respect for others that it would require."

He opened his eyes and regarded her almost coolly. She felt herself step back, but checked herself there.

"And what, pray tell, is all this? Have I offended your delicate sensibilities in some way?" He raised his eyebrows, the mockery appearing.

She felt her own anger boil up. "You would have offended the 'sensibilities' of every civilized person, if they only knew what you did."

He tilted his head slightly, the eyebrows arching up again.

She could not bear the mockery a moment more. The smugness drove her to fury. "You used children—*children!*—on this sacred quest of yours! How could you set an innocent child afire, and leave another to bear the guilt of it all his years? It is . . . *unspeakable*. It is the act of a monster. A despicable, heartless monster! And you look to me for comfort? You who feel no remorse. How could you prey upon children? How could you?" She drew a ragged breath, fingernails tearing the flesh of her palms because her fists were so tight.

Eldrich continued to stare at her, apparently unaffected by the outburst—as though he were mildly interested in the behavior of some animal.

"How could I?" he said, the mockery strong in his tone. "It was not difficult. I am a monster, after all. A man who surrendered his heart to become a mage." His gaze was suddenly not so disinterested. "How could I expect understanding from you—a spoiled child of a decadent class. You have never made a hard decision in your life. After all, what color gown you choose to wear is hardly earthshaking. Do not go on to me about what a monster I am. I would sacrifice a thousand children to accomplish my task. I would sacrifice you and every member of your inbred class, and they would be no more able to understand it than you. Now leave me in peace."

She stood appalled by his declaration, sure that it was not exaggeration. He would do it, and more. For a second she stood her ground, but then saw the futility of it and left with as much dignity as she could manage, as though she had hardly been wounded at all.

She perched on the miniature throne in the playroom surrounded by the landscape of a pampered childhood—a room outside of time. Twilight cast soft shadows across the floor and walls, imbuing the room with melancholy, though she could not say why.

It was here that Hayes had told her Erasmus' story—his time with the mage and what had happened. How Percy had been engulfed in flame—the screams Erasmus heard in his dreams even as an adult. If she closed her eyes, she could see the child burning. . . .

"I cannot be what he asks," she whispered.

Since her argument with Eldrich, she had felt a peculiar lassitude. What would she do now? Go back to her old life, all memories of this strange chapter of her days gone? Go back to worrying what color gown to wear to a ball? His words had cut her more deeply than she liked to admit.

"I have led a frivolous life," she said. Yet somehow it had brought her here.

Perhaps I cannot leave, she thought. *I am bound to fulfill my part of the bargain, though what that will entail is still far from clear.*

She looked around the room, the carriage and its rocking-horse team journeying endlessly toward make-believe. Reminders of the childhood that was stolen from Erasmus and his companion, Percy.

It was true that Eldrich had his childhood stolen as well, and had been subjected to the random cruelties of Lucklow. . . .

She shook her head. It did not matter. Generals did not send children of ten to fight their battles.

"One does not judge a mage by the laws of men, anymore than one would judge a falcon by the ways of a sparrow." Walky's words came back to her. *"He has duties and trusts that we can barely comprehend."* But did he? What, beyond this obsession to erase all knowledge of the arts, all real memory of their practice? *"You must understand this one truth of mages, m'lady. He cannot afford the luxury of humanity. His duties are too grave for that. It is a calling that one pursues at great price. One surrenders one's heart to become a mage."*

In this, at least, Eldrich had been more than successful.

Across the room a movement caught her eye.

Who has found their way in here? she wondered.

A shadow moved, and the countess froze. The wolf?

But, no, it was something else; a small phantom of starlight and darkness—a child . . . and then a second.

The countess heard her own indrawn breath.

They stood near the tiny coach, a boy and girl, difficult to discern, but certainly there. And they looked about as though lost, clinging to each other's hand, their moonlight-eyes wide and filled with sorrow.

"The children for whom this shrine was made," a musical voice said softly.

The countess started. Eldrich stood a few feet away.

"But what are they?" she asked, overwhelmed with an inexplicable desire to have peace between them, and unsettled by these spirits appearing before her.

"Ghosts, you would call them. Spirits of the dead children."

She looked around the room and realized this was what had disturbed her all along. The room was a shrine, not a museum. The children were dead.

"How old?" she whispered.

"Three and seven," he said softly.

"Why do they appear now?"

"They often appear when I am near. They are drawn to my talent for the arts. It is surprising you have not seen them yourself before now."

The countess watched the two children wander among the treasures of their childhood, forever unable to touch them. "They look so . . . *lost.*"

"They seek a way back to life," Eldrich said, "but there is no path that can take them there."

"So they will wander here always?"

"Always? No, but for many lifetimes."

The countess could not take her eyes from these apparitions. She felt a tear tremble on her lashes. "How unbearably sad."

"Yes, but I can release them," he said softly. "Would you have me do so?"

She glanced over at him, but the mage did not look her way.
"What would become of them?"

She saw his stooped figure shrug. "What becomes of anyone?"
A silence.

"They suffer," Eldrich whispered. "Can you feel it?"

She nodded. Yes, they suffered, but it was not oblivion they
sought.

"I will release them from that suffering if you will say but a
word."

"Why is this choice mine?"

"Because you believe such decisions are easily made. What will
you have me do?"

Nearer the children came, and though they were drawn to Eldrich, to his power, their eyes could not find him.

"I will leave you to consider," he said and was gone into shadow.
She heard the door latch tick.

And before her the children were distraught. They felt him go,
all their futile hopes disappearing with him. And then they sensed
her, as though she were a lesser light that they had not noticed.
They came toward her, mothlike, hands outstretched and groping.
She backed away in horror, and still they sought her. A moment
more and she fled the room, scattering a shelf of poppets as she
went.

Chapter Forty-two

THE ringing of bells sounded from all points of the compass. Samual Hayes and Fenwick Kehler stared out into the darkness where occasional sails would slip by, ghostlike in the fog.

"It is the Lochwinnie fishing fleet, or so I heard someone say."

Hayes nodded. A slight breeze moved their ship over a calm sea, and though a fog surrounded them, overhead the stars shone clear among the sails.

Kehler nodded his head toward a solitary figure who stood farther along the rail: Brother Norbert.

"Why in the world did Rose force the man to accompany us? I'm sure this will be nothing but another 'false Anna.' "

"Well, clearly, to see if Anna's spirit does appear to him."

They both laughed, and tried to cover it up.

"Do you know, Hayes, I believe the stains on his robes are from birds!"

Hayes laughed softly. "I'm quite sure they are. He told me that his monastery houses mostly swallows now, and he is merely tolerated by them. 'I am the one making my home in their eves,' is how he put it. For all his eccentricities he is a good-hearted soul. If all of

Farrelle's priests were like Brother Norbert, I think I might respect the church more."

An odd, vaguely human sound bubbled up from the water, surprising both Kehler and Hayes. Something bobbed in the fog.

"*Martyr's balls . . .*" Kehler whispered.

The object, barely visible, was long and thin with an uplifted round end. The sound of soft laughter emanated from it.

Then Hayes chuckled. "It is a gull on a log. A laughing gull, so called, or so I would guess."

They watched the apparition, so like a drowned man, float past, and then Kehler nudged his friend. "Look at our mystic."

Brother Norbert was leaning well out over the rail, his eyes wide, straining to see through the mist.

"Perhaps that was really Anna, but our unschooled senses could not perceive it," Hayes offered.

Brother Norbert turned to them then, his eyes no longer wide, face collapsed into grief. Both Kehler and Hayes went quickly down the deck to him.

"Did you see?" he rasped, barely able to find a voice.

"A log ridden by a gull," Hayes said.

The priest shook his head, half-collapsed against the rail. Kehler took the man by the arm to bear him up.

"No, 'twas a man." Brother Norbert was sobbing softly. "A drowned man, young and fair. Crying for his brother lost, swept down to the sea, to the breathing, shoreless sea."

"Pryor?" Hayes said, incredulous. It was no apparition, just a gull on a log. He had seen it clearly himself, as had Kehler.

"What a tragic end for one so young," Norbert said, "what a terrible thing—caught up in matters beyond him, with people whose concerns were far greater than his own. The concerns of the world." He fell down upon his knees, bent over like a man in agony. "May he find peace," he said, and made a sign to Farrelle. He began to pray, mumbling in Old Farr.

Hayes backed away, a bit disturbed by what went on, and realized that Kehler did the same. A few paces back he came abreast of Clarendon, who stood looking on solemnly, Dusk at his side.

"Has Anna found him?" he asked softly, his voice heavy with melancholy.

"No, he has had a vision, or so I gather. It would seem to have been Pryor." Hayes gestured out toward the sea. "Yet Kehler and I saw the same thing—a laughing gull perched upon a log, half-hidden in the mist. Hardly unnatural. It seems the man's visions spring from a fertile imagination."

"But that is the nature of visions, and visionaries. What you see will be perfectly mundane, but what they see— Do not discount the vision because you did not see it, for you are not given to visions, Mr. Hayes. Nor you, Mr. Kehler. This must be why Rose insisted the man stay with us, for there was time yet for the visions to appear. If he has not seen Anna in a few days . . ."

"Then you believe this, Randall?" Kehler said.

The small man nodded, his wolfhound nuzzling at him for more attention. "Oh, I believe many strange things—have seen many strange things. After all, when I was but a boy, I saw a mage appear and take my world away. I have crawled into the very bowels of the earth in search of impetuous friends, and found the tomb of a mythical mage, perhaps even the gate to Faery, and many other things besides." He shook his head, the fringe of hair pale in the starlight. "Perhaps Anna will appear to him yet. Perhaps even Mr. Flattery."

"But what if she doesn't? What if neither of them appear?"

Clarendon shrugged. "Then I will allow myself to hope that Mr. Flattery is yet alive, for it is terrible to lose all of one's friends at once." He looked at Hayes and Kehler, meeting their eyes for the first time since his encounter with Eldrich. "You two go carefully. I could not bear to lose everyone dear to me." Saying nothing more, he turned away and disappeared into the shadow of the sails and the mist that drifted over the rail.

It was much later, the night waning, when Hayes woke and could not entice sleep's return. Finally he rose and climbed up on deck. He heard the sound of sharp tapping on the planks, and Dusk appeared, gamboling, licked his hand, then bounded back into the shadow of a sail. It was here that Hayes found Clarendon, leaning on the rail which rose to chest height on the small man.

"Have you been awake all this night, Randall?"

Clarendon nodded.

Hayes put a hand on his shoulder. "I should not speak, Randall, for I have no experience in such matters, but even so, I cannot bear to see you waste away. It has been a very long time. Can you not give her up now?"

His words were met by silence. Hayes took his hand away, fearing that he'd caused offense.

"It is easier for you," Clarendon said softly, "you can forget. Everyone forgets—in time—even the loss of a cherished wife, a child. Memories lose their vividness, and healing begins, for part of healing is the forgetting, the softening of memories. But I forget nothing. I can see Lizzy as clearly as if she just spoke. I hear her voice—as real as yours, Mr. Hayes.

"Time wears everything away—mountains, men, and certainly the recollections of men—but my memories are the one rock that will not wear away. Time will not touch them, Mr. Hayes, I don't know why. To me, Lizzy left this morning, Mr. Flattery but ten minutes past. To heal from loss, you must forget a little, and I cannot. It is the curse Eldrich named it, and I wish it on no man.

"But do not concern yourself overly on my account, Mr. Hayes. I will not heal, but nor will I founder. No, I am made of good timber—old, gnarly oak. I shall keep myself afloat, even if Mr. Flattery could not. We owe it to him."

Dusk came up and set his chin on the rail at his master's elbow, docile, sensing the sadness. Clarendon stroked him slowly.

"Is there nothing that anyone might do, Randall?"

"Take away my memories. . . . But even Eldrich could not manage that. It is always good to have solid friends in difficult times. That is quite enough. Quite enough, Mr. Hayes. Now get some rest, if you can. I fear our road will grow more difficult before it's done."

Chapter Forty-three

H E lay upon cushions spread over a bench seat upon the terrace, his great wolf by him. The stars still circled westward across the sky, their nightly migration nearing an end. The pearl of dawn would soon overtake them, and then the infinite blue.

Walky stood in the door looking out into the soft night, watching his master rest from his labors. He needed to rest more now, and this small sign of mortality Walky found oddly disturbing. As though the mage were human, after all.

Lately, there were other indications as well. A softening of his master's demeanor, signs of regret over past actions. Small acts of compassion. It was the influence of the countess, Walky was certain. Even the mage wished to please her, though he would never admit it. But no, it was more than that. Her own compassion and heart forced even Eldrich to see himself anew.

Walky shook his head. She was a wonder.

The two, mage and countess, had been circling each other as warily as duelists for some days now, both seemingly unaware of it. She would not give herself to a man without a heart—he conscious of the folly of it all. A peculiar dance to watch.

"You should sleep, Walky," the musical voice said softly.

The mage's eyes were still closed, and he lay breathing evenly, like one asleep.

"Is there nothing I might do for you, m'lord?"

"Discover if this girl still lives. Tell me if my task is complete. Decide what I should do with this beguiling countess. Oh, and make me some coffee, as well."

"Will you not rest now, sir? It has been a long night."

"And it will be a longer day, yet. Coffee, Walky. I will break my fast later."

The mage pushed himself up, his wolf rising with him, joyful, as though his master had been absent. Eldrich put a hand on the beast's head, scratching absentmindedly.

"Time is running short, Walky." The mage rose to his feet, his slightly stooped carriage seeming even more pronounced. "There is much to do. This moon and the next, that is what the stars tell us. Landor's Gate has been rediscovered and Strangers walk among us. It is a propitious age, Walky, a time of wonder. But we cannot falter in our task. Not now, so near the end. But one cannot save the world without that unparalleled elixir."

"I shall fetch you seed, sir."

"I was speaking of coffee, Walky."

The servant did not smile. This did not seem the time for jests. But perhaps Eldrich had seen a vision in his sleep, a sign that all would come out right in the end. He could hope.

Walky was about to turn to go when his master spoke again.

"She thinks she can hide him from me," he said, perhaps to himself.

"Who, sir?" Walky asked, not sure if he was meant to be part of this conversation.

"Erasmus. She believes her art is deep enough, her skill great enough, but I am not so sure. I have had my sting in Erasmus Flattery all his life. Not long, perhaps, but long enough. We will see if her confidence is warranted. I will wager that Erasmus dreams of his days in the house of Eldrich. If he lives, he dreams of me yet."

The mage had spent all the long hours of light in his preparations, allowing no interruptions. Walky had seen this many times before, the mage lost in his labors, his meticulous arrangements for an enchantment. At such times he would forget to eat, sometimes for days. And his servants would creep about the house, never speaking above a whisper, and that only if absolutely necessary. These were always unsettling times, and Walky was not quite sure why.

Men were never comfortable with the arts. Even men who lived in the house of a mage. They acted upon a man at some level that could never be quite articulated, touched him like the cold caress of death—something one feared so completely that the rational mind held no hope of controlling the reaction to it. The arts were disturbing, and that was at best.

Walky set a plate of food on the edge of the worktable, reaching out to take the one left earlier, which remained untouched. The mage did not raise his head or acknowledge the old man in any way, but continued to bend over his work, completely absorbed.

Walky paused for a moment to see if there were any orders or requests. He seldom pried into his master's efforts, and the truth was that despite his years of service, he did not truly understand them. But tonight he could not help but notice a child's frock coat lying on the edge of the table, and this struck him as very odd. Certainly the objects Eldrich used in his toils could be very strange, even rare, but he had never before seen anything that belonged to a child.

And then it struck him. This sky-blue coat had belonged to Erasmus Flattery. If he closed his eyes, he could almost see it on the child as he raced across the lawn, going nowhere in particular in the headlong manner of boys.

The coat of Erasmus Flattery.

May Farrelle preserve him, the old man thought, and he slipped out the door.

Chapter Forty-four

WALKY woke her in the night, setting candles on a bureau near her bed. The countess thought the little man looked more distressed than she could ever imagine.

"What is it, Walky?"

"A catastrophe, m'lady. An absolute catastrophe. Erasmus is alive. Without doubt, alive!"

"What are you saying?" She sat up, sweeping her hair out of her eyes. Was she dreaming? Certainly Walky could not be distressed by that news. "Erasmus is alive! How can that be anything but good?" She felt her own heart rise at the news.

Walky shook his head, his look of distress becoming more extreme. "But he is with her, he must be. With this woman who will destroy everything my master has accomplished, and worse. You must rise with all haste. We travel within the hour. Up m'lady, please. Do not delay him this night. Do not."

And Walky was gone, almost running from the room. The countess forced herself up, the brevity of her rest causing a hollowness at her core.

"What in this round world . . . ?" She stood beside her bed in a daze. What was she to do? What would she pack? Did Eldrich still need her at all? They had not spoken since the night the mage had given her the terrible choice. Only a day, but it seemed so much longer. And she had not been able to choose. How could she?

She shook her head. Madness. There was so much that needed to be said. So much that required clarification. But what was she to do? Demand Eldrich stop and speak with her now—in the middle of crisis?

She began to pull on clothing, astonished by how often she did not seem to make clear choices but was merely swept along by currents more powerful than she. As though she were aswim in a dark river, the banks beyond sight, what lay ahead utterly unknown.

Chapter Forty-five

A lamp and several candles were spread around the perimeter of the table. The haphazard nature of their arrangement told Erasmus that they were not part of some enchantment that Anna practiced but served the more mundane purpose of providing light. She bent over a large sheet of paper, unaware that he stood in the door.

Her familiar, Chuff, hopped back and forth across the surface of the table, resentful when she shooed him off the paper. Once he took the quill she used to write with in his mouth, and she was so engrossed in her work that it took a moment for her to understand why her pen no longer obeyed her will.

"Off with you," she said, chasing the bird from the table. He landed on the window ledge and vented his resentment in a single, indignant "chuff."

She turned back to her task, then realized she had seen Erasmus standing in the door and looked up, smiling wanly, her eyes rimmed in red and glistening from her efforts.

"What has you so involved you forget to eat?"

"So that is what causes this discomfort in my stomach. Did I really forget to eat?"

Erasmus nodded. It was almost midnight, and he had not seen Anna since noon.

She put down her quill carefully and covered her eyes for a moment. "Farrelle's ghost," she exclaimed.

Erasmus came and stood behind her, softly rubbing her neck and shoulders.

"Mmm. . . . Farther to the right."

Erasmus stared down at the paper covered in strange symbols and writing, all connected with the most intricate geometry.

"What is this?" he said.

"Your horoscope," she laughed. "You shall meet a tall red-headed stranger. . . ." She uncovered her eyes, staring down at her efforts. "It is a somewhat incompetent attempt to find some pattern among the appearances of Strangers. In the past three hundred years there were about a dozen fairly certain appearances, and about an equal number of disappearances. Have we spoken of these? Cases where people have vanished in odd circumstances? Halsey was certain they became the 'Strangers' of another world. So I have charted them, trying to see if there is a pattern. Halsey did much of this work, I am really only reproducing it, and rather incompetently, I fear."

"Have you added in the disappearance Clarendon witnessed?"

This caused her to pause. Erasmus could almost feel her thoughts scattering at his interruption.

"No. When was it, do you think?"

"When he was aged ten—about fifty years past, I think—but what time of year I cannot say."

"Unfortunate, but even the year will help. More importantly, though, was Eldrich's prediction of the exact hour and place where Clarendon's Lizzy disappeared. Do you see? This exercise may not be entirely in vain. Eldrich managed it, though likely he had been engaged in this endeavor for a long time." She returned her gaze to the sheet of paper. "All I have been able to conclude with any certainty is that there seems to be an increase in frequency of the appearance of Strangers, but if there is a pattern that can be discerned . . . well, I have nothing but admiration for Eldrich if he managed to find it."

"What would be the point of the exercise, Anna? Other than the great satisfaction of solving a puzzle?"

"It would tell us if the worlds converge and if Eldrich thinks he can leave this world for another, leave it by knowing where to be at what time, as Clarendon witnessed."

Erasmus starred at the paper a moment, trying to make sense of it. Could it really be Eldrich's desire to leave this world? And if so, why? Yet, if Clarendon was to be believed, the mage was interested enough to witness Lizzy's disappearance—and there was the mage who came for the Stranger of Compton Heath, who was very likely Eldrich. Erasmus was certain the mage did little out of idle curiosity.

"I would like to question one of these Strangers," Erasmus said suddenly. "Hear firsthand of these other worlds. . . ."

Anna stared at him a moment, her look penetrating though softly pensive. "Fill a lantern," she said, rising to her feet and leaving the room.

Fifteen minutes later they were on the path that ran along the cliff top back toward the small collection of houses that passed for a town on Midsummer Isle. They made their way up the main road, unseen by the islanders, for most were asleep, and it was only the odd window from which light escaped.

It was a relatively steep road, and they were soon harboring their breath, neither speaking. In half an hour they met an empty lane that ran off between rows of chestnut trees. They set out beneath the overhanging branches, and Chuff appeared suddenly to land on Anna's outstretched wrist, his manner animated, as though there were about to be some excitement of the kind that choughs approved. After a moment he winged off down the lane, disappearing into the shadows of the trees—a chough that apparently did not fear the fabric of night or the owls that dwelt within its folds.

Anna kept their pace deliberately quick to avoid conversation, avoid telling him where they went. Erasmus was well aware that there might be no actual reason for this, other than her naturally secretive nature, and the delight she took in surprising him.

Finally they came upon the ruin of an old cottage, overrun by vines, the waving branches of an ancient willow hanging down through an opening in the roof. Anna held aloft the lantern to spread the light.

"There," she pronounced, "you have never seen such a house before."

"A tumbledown cottage?"

"No, the dwelling of a Stranger, for it was here that the old woman lived for the short time she survived. Mother Green was what the local people called her, though the reason for it has been forgotten. She appeared in the place I showed you, and the local fisherfolk took her in, unable to understand a word she said. Like the Stranger of Compton Heath, they thought she had survived a shipwreck. So provincial were they that they believed her to be from some out-of-the-way part of Doorn or even Entonne. And she came to live here, in this broken-down cottage, and had it not been for some of her writings, which were preserved, and the local legend, she would have been forgotten. One of the great wonders of the world, and she passed almost unnoticed." She shook her head.

"It was a simpler time," she said softly. "And who would have thought she could be anything more fantastic than a foreigner. Why, I'm sure that was exotic enough for the people of this island, who were never more than inshore fishermen, forgoing the deeper sea."

From a bag she carried over her shoulder, Anna removed a clay jar and pulled the stopper so that a feather of steam appeared.

"You want to see a Stranger, Erasmus," she said. "Well, here is your opportunity."

The aroma from the bottle reached him. He knew it from Anna's use, infrequent as it was. "King's blood," he said in a hushed voice though he did not know why. "Did you not warn that it was habituating?"

"I did, and for good reason, but this is diluted many times and indulging yourself once will not bring you to ruin, I think."

Erasmus hesitated, feeling the draw of it, his own curiosity. Chuff flitted out of the darkness, flapping about Anna, speaking excitedly.

"Why would I do this?"

"To see a Stranger, or the ghost of one, for she dwells here still, our good Mother Green. And who knows—the seed will produce visions for those with talent. You might see more."

Erasmus looked at the steam which coiled out of the jar like a snake, and his nostrils flared at the stark, pungent odor. He could feel the vapor curl into him, twisting down through his lungs, spreading outward . . . touching his heart.

He turned to the fallen-down house, to the shadows within.

Did the mage take you to his house only that you might lure this woman down into a cave and die? The question spoke within his mind in a voice which hardly seemed his own. *But I have defied him and lived. . . . Defied Eldrich.*

Gingerly Anna held the jar out toward him, and he took it, touching it to his lips before he could reconsider. The liquid ran warm into his mouth, the aroma filling his nostrils, almost overpowering. He swallowed it down and felt the truth of it—not the vapor which barely caressed him, but the torrent which streamed hot down his throat. Almost before he lowered the jar, the world lurched, shadows taking on dimension, pressing out of the broken doors and windows as though they had gained substance. But there was movement within them now, darker shapes within the darkness.

Anna took his hand and led him forward.

They stepped into the shadow of the door that seemed to swell outward like a bubble. He felt this darkness cool upon his face. Things moved and scuttled in the corners, just beyond vision, and he heard whispers and hissing, the sounds of branches stirred by the wind.

A stair rail came to hand and Erasmus felt himself step up. A cool light glowed faintly above—moonlight or starlight. He no longer felt Anna's hand within his own, but drifted free, as though gravity had all but released him.

Up the speaking stairs, up into the loft where the branches of trees grew from the walls and roof. And there, in the corner, made of moonlight and lamentation, an old woman hunched over her needlework, rocking back and forth and singing softly to herself.

After a moment she glanced up and blinked, a look of confusion on her face.

"Who's that?" she said in an odd whisper. This was no accent of Doorn or Entonne.

"A friend," Erasmus heard himself say, and saw her cock her head as though struggling to hear.

"Wind and mice," she said, "forest and owls." She bent back to her work, rocking again, singing a different air this time.

Erasmus moved closer. He could see her unbound hair, dull silver in the moonlight. It fell like water to her waist. Whatever it was she toiled at could not be distinguished, as though she stitched something out of the threads of night.

"Who are you, child?" she whispered, not looking up. "And why have you come to haunt me? Can you not see I am poor and of no use to any?"

"I am here to learn from where you came."

She continued to stitch, unable to hear him, apparently, and then she returned to song.

> "Upon a hill, upon a cloud,
> Upon a haystack golden.
> Within a wood, within a lake,
> Dwelt the lady Sollen."

As she sang, she rose from her stool and went to the window, moving with fluid grace, almost floating, as silent in her movements as a mage. And in the light from the moon Erasmus could see that she was young, a girl of twenty, dancing before the window.

> "Above the wood, above the world,
> Above the hidden bower.
> Along a path upon an isle
> She danced away the hours."

It struck Erasmus suddenly that she was singing Darian, not Farr at all! Darian—the mage tongue.

She spun into a shadow, and her voice changed, suddenly heavy with age, creaking like old timbers bent with the weight of years. And the song ended sadly, Mother Green humming the last lines distractedly as though the words had slipped her mind. A hand appeared out of shadow, delicate and smooth, the hand of a girl touched by moonlight. The fingers seemed to extend toward him, and after an instant of hesitation, he reached out and found the hand soft and cool.

He would not allow himself to be taken into the shadow but instead drew the hand steadily, an arm appearing, then Anna, laughing.

"But was it you all along?" Erasmus said, confused.

"Not at all, it was a spirit. The ghost of Mother Green. But let us see what more might be found, for the night is filled with whispers. Do you hear?" She unstopped the jar again, and offered it to Erasmus, who took it this time without hesitation, excited by what he'd seen, by what might be revealed to him yet. Again the liquid filled him with its warmth, and he felt that sense of lifting. Rising like a cloud.

Around him walls of stone rose up toward the stars. A ruin, Erasmus was sure. A ruin of such massive scale it seemed impossible that it had been built by men. Yet time had laid waste to it so that almost nothing was recognizable—and even so it seemed familiar. As though he had been here before.

Kilty's Keep, he thought, though it could not be, for this *was* a ruined castle. Yet Kilty's Keep it was.

A shattered stair came underfoot, and ahead he could see ghostly moonlight. Up again, and around a corner, and there, illuminated by the moon, a single tree, the only living thing in this dead city—and it bore white blossoms, gently waving in the breeze.

Erasmus stepped forward but stumbled and fell endlessly, landing upon a surface soft and level.

Lifting his head, Erasmus found himself lying atop a cliff, the moonlit land stretching out before him, windless and still—a stark geometry of fields and hedgerows, rivers and roads. And then movement. A dark line, like a flight of crows low over a road. But then they emerged from shadow into moonlight, and Erasmus could see two carriages racing as though pursued. *And they bore no lanterns.* Nor were there drivers. They raced on by moonlight, and there, upon the high after-seat, perched a small boy, staring fixedly ahead. Erasmus as a child, wearing his favorite blue frock coat.

He scrambled up and fled into darkness.

"Erasmus?"

It was Anna. He knew her voice even if the shadow he could see did not resemble her at all.

"I saw—"

"Do not try to rise yet. Lie back and rest, Erasmus."

"But we have no time to rest. He has seen me! He travels toward us even now."

"Eldrich?" Erasmus felt her stiffen. "How do you know? Did you see the mage?"

"I saw the carriage and another in flight across the countryside at night. No drivers guided them, nor were there coach lamps. Only a small boy—myself—sitting high up at the rear. But it was my—the manner of this small boy; so utterly fixated on the way ahead, so deadened of emotion. Like one given into madness and near-catatonia, or a person in a trance."

He felt Anna sit back, suddenly very still. "It might mean only that he seeks us, which is hardly news. I . . . . I must consider it. Was there anything more?"

"Yes. I was wandering in a massive ruined city. Ancient, I thought it was, and built to a scale that men could hardly imagine—massive. I saw the glow of moonlight and went toward it, and there, in what might have been a courtyard, grew a single small tree, white blossoms waving in the ghostly light. And I heard singing, though no music I knew. A dirge, it seemed, a requiem. What does it mean?"

"The city, I don't know. The singing? A death, certainly. The white blossoms were king's blood. The sign of the arts. Eldrich is near his time. That is what I think."

"But could it not be us? We have Landor's seed, after all."

She nodded, and rocked him gently, singing softly.

> *"Above the clouds, among the stars,*
> *Beyond the sacred mountain.*
> *Beneath the sun, beneath the world*
> *A gate lay ever open."*

Chapter Forty-six

THE mage traveled at a pace the countess would have thought impossible, but when drawn by horses sustained by the arts, the countryside swept past league by league. They had come down out of the hills in darkness, and followed the high road as it wound among field and wood toward the sea.

The countess slept as best she could in the swaying carriage, nearly jarred from her seat more than once, and each time she opened her eyes found Walky poised to arrest her fall, as though he never needed sleep, or could not rest while another might need his attention. The perfect servant, always.

After nearly being thrown from her seat for perhaps the tenth time, the countess tried to force herself into wakefulness. She squinted at the passing scene, sunlight and shade in rhythm as they passed down a row of evenly spaced trees.

"Have you not slept at all, Walky?"

He shook his head. "I've felt no need, m'lady," he said, though the countess thought the old man's eyes were a bit red.

He is far older than you, she chided herself, *and yet he sits awake seeing that you come to no harm.*

"Well, I've returned to the land of the living now, so you might rest if you've a mind to."

He smiled. "Perhaps, by and by."

She shrugged off the traveling blanket and rubbed knuckles into her eyes in a gesture that she thought terribly unladylike. She longed to stretch, but knew that would be going a bit too far.

"Where are we?"

"Just crossed the east branch of the Brandydrop River."

"My, but we are flying across Farrland! I don't think my kestrel could manage it more quickly."

Walky nodded. "When the mage has need . . ."

"Are Mr. Bryce and Lord Skye traveling with Lord Eldrich?" Since their meeting in the children's room, two nights past, she had not heard from nor spoken to Eldrich, and she wondered now what he did and what the state of his mind might be. He had very pointedly not requested her company in his carriage.

"Bryce and Skye have gone ahead to prepare Lord Skye's ship. He keeps a small vessel for his own pleasure. Did you know?"

She nodded. Skye's foibles were much discussed in Farr society, and none more than his ship. There was a saying in Farrland that a man who would go to sea for pleasure would fight a war for a holiday. Travel by sea was looked upon as particularly evil necessity.

"Mr. Walky?" the countess said, pitching her voice low, as though she might be heard above the rattle of the carriage. "Where is it we go? Is it Farrow? Is that why Skye prepares his ship?"

A bit of pain crossed Walky's face, as though it were terribly unfair of her to ask such questions of him. "We go in search of Erasmus. I know nothing more than that, m'lady."

She nodded, sitting back in her seat. She was having trouble believing that Erasmus was yet alive. The story she had heard from Clarendon and Hayes was so convincing. If he had survived the gorge, why had he not revealed himself to his companions? Had he been injured?

"Do you believe Erasmus is still alive, Walky?"

"The mage believes it, m'lady."

"But if it is true, why has he not revealed himself?"

Walky shrugged.

"Only the mage knows?" she asked, not really meaning to mock him.

But Walky looked very serious, as though he did not realize she was quoting his own much-used phrase. "Even the mage does not know everything," he said.

The countess smiled. "You should rest, Walky. Who knows when you shall have the opportunity again."

It was late night when the entourage of the mage entered Ports-down, a small port at the mouth of the Inglbrook, which was no brook at all but a broad river here where it met the sea.

They disembarked almost immediately for a ship, all of them in a longboat. The countess could see Eldrich wrapped in an old-fashioned cloak, his collar up against the dampness. Even sitting, he seemed stooped to her, bent under the weight of the impossible tasks he had been left.

She realized that she did feel a little sympathy for him. Perhaps a result of the choice he had given her—and that she had been un-able to make.

How crucial were the responsibilities he had been left? Impor-tant enough that one would destroy the life of a child? It was not impossible, she thought.

A memory of being sought by the ghost children surfaced and she shivered. Their terrible, unhappy eyes, as they groped toward her, toward life. Would that she had been allowed to choose life for them. . . .

But perhaps Eldrich's choice had been no less difficult. She would likely never know, for he would not tell.

They came alongside a small ship and proceeded quickly up the boarding stair. And then, after all their hours of urgency, they were told they must await the turn of the tide, for there was not enough wind in the harbor to allow them to fight the flow.

The countess watched from a few paces away as Eldrich lis-tened to Skye and his captain, a man who looked distinctly fright-ened by this apparition that had boarded his ship. Sailors, the countess knew, were superstitious by nature.

"There will be wind enough, Captain," Eldrich said, his musical voice distinctly odd here, upon the silent bay. "Indeed, there shall be all the wind you require—and more."

"But where do we travel, my lord? What course shall we set?"

Eldrich strode to the binnacle, glanced down at the compass rose, and began to chant almost beneath his breath. He drew his hand across the bronze binnacle, and the green sea fire appeared at the deck, like a glowing wreath. It spread upward slowly, until the entire binnacle was wrapped in viridescent fire.

"There," Eldrich said. "That is your course."

The captain stood back from the sea fire, frightened into silence. Eldrich spun around and went quickly below, leaving the sailors muttering among themselves, faces ashen in the fading green light.

Walky stepped forward, staring down at the glowing compass. "Due east," he said calmly, as though this were an everyday occurrence. "Captain," he said, nodding, and then followed his master below.

In the ensuing silence a small zephyr fluttered the pennant at the masthead, and then hissed across the deck like the whispering of a ghost. It began to build into a breeze. Still muttering, the sailors scrambled up the rigging, crablike against the stars, stiff with fear of who had come aboard and the ill fortune that accompanied him.

Her cabin was too small to pace, even if it had not been slanting at ten degrees and pitching slowly up and down. She hardly noticed how lovely the appointments of the cabin were, how unlike any ship she had heard tell of. Instead the closeness of the cabin reminded her of her situation, how trapped she truly was. Somehow the lodge in the hills had masked the truth, for she had the run of it and the grounds. But here, there was barely two square yards of cabin, and the little room felt claustrophobic.

She could almost feel Eldrich's presence, as though the heat of his body emanated through the thin bulkheads. She was sick of it. Sick of not knowing where they went, or why. Sick of rising in the night to be carried off to some unknown destination for some secret purpose. Sick of asking questions that no one would answer.

It was as though she had wakened from a sleep, or thrown off an enchantment, and the reality of her situation had struck her.

"Have I been bespelled the whole time?"

Never in her life had she so felt like hammering upon the walls, as it was said prisoners did—beating upon the walls until their fists were bloody, the bones of their hands shattered—but tonight she could have.

"This can't go on," she said firmly, taking herself in hand.

Sweeping up her cloak, she threw open her door and went looking for the companionway up to the main deck.

She emerged into a beautiful night, a near-full moon traveling into the west, the ship underway to a sailor's wind and only the most innocent of clouds abroad. The wind had the warmth of the south in it and ran its fingers through her dark curls in a most gentle manner.

She felt all of her pent-up frustration was suddenly illusory. The vast horizon spoke of a world without boundaries—world without end—and the magic of the night promised nothing but possibilities. She traveled with a mage, after all, the last of his kind, and magic enveloped them like the breeze. Anything might happen. Anything at all.

I am going mad, she thought. *One moment I'm ready to strike out and swim for shore—anything to escape—and then I feel I am truly blessed to be here. The most fortunate woman in Farrland.*

"Lady Chilton . . ."

"Lord Skye. I thought there would be no one awake."

Skye nodded. "I have suffered the insomnia ever since I can remember. I think it is my dreams, they are so disturbing. . . ."

In the weak light of the ship's lanterns he appeared pale, his face drawn—as a man might who had wakened from nightmare into a situation hardly less strange.

"These are dreams of your lost past?"

He nodded. "But like so many dreams, when I awake, they are just beyond my grasp. But even so they are more numerous since I have come to the house of Eldrich, more numerous and even more unsettling. As though they were more vivid and even closer to the surface, yet still I cannot reach them. I do not mean to press you, Lady Chilton, but you mentioned that you might speak to Lord Eldrich about my request."

Yes, he always wanted something of her—and almost invariably she offered it, though it was never what other men wanted. "And I must confess I have not, Lord Skye, for which I apologize. It is not that I have forgotten or been remiss in any way. The opportunity has not presented itself, and if truth be known, I think I am hardly in the mage's favor at the moment."

Skye nodded stiffly, the sadness that her words caused hardly masked.

"Well, there is little hope that the mage would grant my wish, for as he made abundantly clear, I have nothing to offer in return. One cannot make a deal with a devil unless one has a soul to offer. I, apparently, do not." He nodded off in the direction the ship traveled. "Where do we go now, do you know?"

The countess shook her head. "Farrow, I assume."

"But those are the lights of a village in the distance," Skye said. "We are sailing up the coast, not out to sea."

The countess was mildly surprised, but then why would she believe she could predict the actions of the mage?

"Then I cannot say where we go."

"Or why, I take it?"

She shook her head.

"What is it, Lady Chilton, that you do with Walky in all these hours you spend together?"

The question, and the way it was phrased, was so discourteous that she felt her face begin to flush with anger. But no sooner did the emotion rise then it seemed to have been carried away on the breeze. Like so many other things, the common politeness of Farr society was of no consequence in the house of a mage—who had little concern for such niceties himself.

"I study the arts of the mages, Lord Skye," she said, watching his face. But he was neither as surprised as she expected nor as she'd hoped.

"Then perhaps I will not need the cooperation of Eldrich."

"I can assure you," she said quickly, "that I have so little skill in these matters that I would not even know how to begin to recover what you have lost. I'm sorry, but do not look to me, Lord Skye. I have barely begun to learn even the language of the mages." She met his eye. "And I have not the slightest understanding of what use the mage will put my paltry learning to."

Skye nodded, his hope, however slight, fading.

They fell silent a moment, the breeze whispering around them, laden with the vowels of the sea and the silent language of human misunderstanding.

"Skye?"

It was the voice of Eldrich, and it startled the earl.

Skye backed away reflexively, and without even a nod to the countess, hurried below. She heard his boots scurrying down the companionway stairs.

Eldrich wore his old-fashioned cloak wrapped about him like a shadow. Unlike Skye, his boots made no sound as he came and stood beside the countess at the rail.

He said nothing for a moment, and the countess began to wonder if he had no more purpose than frightening Skye away.

"Why do you torture Lord Skye?" she said impulsively. "He will do anything to have his memories returned."

"Skye? He has brought evil enough into this world without his memories. Do not waste your compassion on Skye, Lady Chilton. He is the scourge, the outrider of destruction. I would never have let him walk abroad if I'd not needed him to find my enemies. It is a strange irony, and a tragic one. No, Skye shall not have his memories. If I were as heartless as people think, I would murder him this night." Eldrich's voice actually sounded overwhelmed by fatigue, something she had not thought possible. Where was the music now?

"He does not seem evil," she said.

He glanced at her, skeptically she thought. "No. Men seldom do. These larger-than-life, madly evil characters are generally the stuff of novels, I'm afraid."

The two remained a few moments in strained silence, mage and countess. She was about to curtsy and excuse herself, for it seemed that Eldrich had nothing to say to her, or if he had, would not say it. But then he broke the silence, his voice nearly a whisper.

"We have bargained once, Lady Chilton," Eldrich said, his voice flat and strained, "but it seems we must do so again. What will it take to have you fulfill your part?"

The countess reached out a hand to the rail, steadying herself. Eldrich was making an offer of peace. It was unheard of. Her thoughts were suddenly awhirl, and she tried to force order upon them, not wanting this moment of advantage to go to waste. "If Erasmus is alive, what will you do with him?"

Eldrich considered for a moment. "He aids my enemy," he said.

"I would have you spare him," the countess said quickly, thinking of the poor child Eldrich had so cruelly used. "Release both Erasmus and Bryce."

"Bryce can never be free," Eldrich said quickly.

"But he was harmed even more than Erasmus. Will you not spare both the children you have injured?"

"Do not concern yourself with Bryce," Eldrich said firmly. "He is another matter entirely."

"But he was a child, and the victim of terrible burning."

"Yes, but there will be no recovery for Percy Bryce. Even I cannot grant him that. The fire reached inside and burned him hollow; the fire of bitterness and recrimination. There is nothing left now but a shell. You see how fastidious he is? He is protecting the only thing he has—a husk. No, do not meddle in the world of Percy Bryce. It will not profit you, nor will it him. Erasmus is another matter. He betrayed me in my time of need."

"Betrayed you!" she interrupted, unable to contain herself. "You sent him down into that cavern to die! All he has done is survive—and try to escape you. You who would have murdered him! He cannot be faulted for that."

Eldrich rocked from foot to foot. She could feel him about to explode with frustration. He was not used to negotiating to get what he wanted, perhaps had never done it in his long life. "What do I care for the justice of men," he spat out, but caught himself, taking a long, slow breath. "I will consider what you ask. I can promise no more than that."

"And what will you have of me in return?" the countess asked, her voice a near-whisper.

Eldrich nodded. "Your part of the bargain."

"But you have never stated clearly what my part would be."

"Because I cannot know what will be asked of you." He turned to look at her. She could just make out the shape of his face, the dark shadows of his eyes.

"Walky will tutor you, guide you. Perhaps there will be no reason for you to do anything at all. But if the arts survive me—"

"But I know nothing of such matters! How can you give such a task to me?" She almost stamped her foot with frustration.

"Because there have been signs, portents. You will be the last Guardian of the Gate."

The words had almost no meaning to her, yet she found them chilling all the same. She wanted to beat upon his chest with her fists, demand that he speak in terms she could understand.

"What does this mean? Guardian? I have no idea to what gate you refer."

"The gate at Tremont Abbey, I believe, though perhaps it is Farrow."

She wanted to fall down upon the deck and weep. It was like falling into a madness, her time with Eldrich. Nothing was ever clear, or predictable. No day was like any other. Cause and effect seemed to have broken their alliance.

Eldrich reached out and touched her arm, disorienting her even more. He never touched her.

"Did Samual Hayes tell you about the sculpture in the cavern? The one with the emerging face?"

"Yes," she answered, barely able to find her breath.

He stared at her for a long, chilling moment. "It is you."

"But how can you know?" She heard herself almost pleading.

"Because I am a mage. You will stand vigil when I am gone, until all but the last vestiges of the arts have faded from the world. There will be no ember left that any can rekindle."

So there it was. Not unexpected, really, for he had all but said it before.

"But can you keep your part of the bargain?" he asked, stepping closer, and pitching his voice low. "Can you make the sacrifices? Sacrifices of others, if need be?"

"How can I answer when I do not understand what will be asked of me or even why this is being done."

"But if I preserve Erasmus?"

"And what will I do in return? Murder a thousand? Send children into the conflagration? No! I need something more. If I am to pledge myself to your holy crusade, then I must know the reason. . . ."

Eldrich nodded once and turned to the rail, looking down into the sea. From within his cloak he produced a handful of shells which he tossed onto the sea, chanting words in Darian. There was a flash of silver, as porpoises broke the surface, and there, where they sounded, the water was suddenly still and gray and of infinite depth. And here something appeared, as though through mist.

The countess could see a city of ordered streets, alive beneath a warm sun. And then from a strange, high-flying bird, a seed fell, so distant it was little more than punctuation, the full stop at the end of a line.

A shattering of light staggered her. Light like the opening of the heavens, white, mysterious, infinitely powerful. And then a roiling cloud reached up, a thunderhead of dark beauty, blossoming at its height like an opening flower.

In its wake the city was gone, only a few shattered ribs of buildings sticking up as though from a mass grave.

She reeled away from the rail, from the vision in the water, the death of the city. An entire city gone in a heartbeat! Every soul in it turned to light, carried away on that terrible cloud.

"If the gates are not shut," she heard Eldrich say. "And even then such an end might find us. Even then."

Chapter Forty-seven

THE ship lay through the evening calm in the sound between Midsummer Isle and the Farr coast. Up on the maintop, Samual Hayes sat watching the sky fade through its paling palette toward darkness.

"First star," Kehler said, heaving himself up onto the maintop. "Make a wish."

"'Tis a planet, and therefore will not answer."

"Ah, perhaps that's why my wishes are never granted." Kehler settled himself beside his friend. He seemed slightly recovered, slightly more than Hayes remembered, as though every mile they put between themselves and Eldrich expressed itself in healing.

Hayes waved a hand toward the mainland. "I take it this little fishing village is our destination?"

"So I understand. I heard the master saying they would anchor in the 'roadstead' if they ever got wind to carry them there. Anchoring in the roadstead sounds rather like running aground to me. One should leave roads to carriages and horses, I say."

"It is a term describing an open anchorage near to the shore, and quite free of coaches and all horses but the seahorse."

Kehler laughed. "And here we have another false Anna to meet.

Another innocent woman who has been set upon and gagged and is wondering if the world has gone mad?"

"Which it has. I learned something speaking with Captain James. This 'Anna,' who is not using that name, was accompanied by a gentleman, and it would appear that his description could fit Erasmus."

This silenced Kehler for a moment. "But imagine how many men would fit Erasmus' description. 'Tall, dark-haired man with rather forbidding deportment and acerbic wit.' A third of Avonel, I should think."

"Yes. That's what I thought. We'll see." He pointed. "There's a star."

They both made a silent wish, not even needing to ask what the other hoped for.

"Kehler? Could Erasmus and Anna have survived? Is it madness even to hope?"

Kehler considered for a moment. "Brother Norbert had a vision of Pryor, though unaware of the boy's existence." He paused as if to weigh what he had said, wondering if it sounded utterly foolish. "We have both seen enough strange things in the last month to make me wonder if there isn't some truth in Brother Norbert's claims. And he has yet to see a vision of Anna, or Erasmus, for that matter."

Hayes nodded. They were accepting such things as evidence now. But Kehler was right. They had both seen many peculiar things this past month. Flames, they had even met a mage!

"What if we do find Erasmus and Anna alive?"

Kehler kept his gaze fixed on the returning fishing fleet. "Anna killed Pryor's brother, at least that seems fairly sure. I would no longer be so concerned with what befell her. Let her meet Eldrich—as I have done. But Erasmus— We have received no instructions regarding Erasmus."

"I hardly think that will matter to the mage. If Erasmus betrayed him and allied himself with Anna, Eldrich will not forgive it. What do we say to the mage? 'Oh, we let Erasmus go. We were given no instructions pertaining to him.' I hardly think so. This isn't school after all. No, if we let Erasmus go, Eldrich will make us pay."

Kehler considered a moment. "Even so, I am not willing to take

Erasmus back to Eldrich, and I am as much in fear of the mage as anyone." He looked at his friend, his manner very calm and sure. Since the escape from the cave, and even more so since the encounter with Eldrich, Kehler appeared to have aged. More gray hair could be seen among the dark, the wrinkles around his eyes grew more pronounced, and his skin seemed to have lost its glow of youth. He had begun to look like a spry old man, rather than the youth he was.

But then, how did one measure age? Hayes was sure that he had aged several years in these last weeks alone, and in the year before that he had thought his maturation vastly accelerated.

At this rate I shall be ancient at thirty, he thought.

"Why would Erasmus take up with Anna?" Kehler asked suddenly.

"Don't get ahead of yourself. I'm sure this Anna will be no more real than the others, and this Erasmus, too, for that matter." He paused to contemplate the question. What if this were Anna and Erasmus? Why *would* their friend take up with Eldrich's enemy? "Hatred of Eldrich," Hayes offered. "Or perhaps a chance to escape him. There was also the ritual Percy had left Erasmus. Self-immolation would drive me into Anna's arms, I'm quite sure."

"I dare say," Kehler said. "Remember how they kept disappearing up the stair together when we were trapped in the chamber? Banks was getting quite jealous."

"What do you imagine was taking place up there?"

Kehler smiled. "I suppose one last romance before starving to death is not out of the question, but somehow I doubt that was it. That was certainly not what was on my mind. But it seemed even then that Anna was trying to win him over, earn his trust. She was capable of augury, remember, and may have had some vision in which Erasmus played a part."

"I had not thought of that."

The ship's bell rang the hour, and as if it were a signal, a small breeze came in from the sea and bellied the sails.

"Well, it is a breeze," Kehler said, "though just. It will still be some time before we are at anchor."

"It doesn't matter. There's likely nothing we can do until morning anyway." Hayes looked out at the rapidly appearing stars. "If we actually find Erasmus, what will Deacon Rose do?"

"I have wondered the same thing. And there is Captain James to consider. It would be better if we found Erasmus before they did." He looked out at the shore, not three miles distant. "A pity we can't swim."

The anchor was down within the hour, and the Admiralty agents were soon aboard. Hayes managed to squeeze himself into the captain's cabin to hear what they would report.

"They went over on the ferry some days past. Any number of people saw them. A vibrant-looking young woman with red hair and the bearing of a lady, and a somewhat older gentleman," the navy man reported. He stood abashedly before Captain James, smelling of spirits, for clearly he had been caught unawares by the ship's arrival. "Both were well spoken. They took up residence in a house which overlooks the sound on the cliff east of the landing. With a glass, one can just make it out from this shore."

"That's it?" Captain James said. "We have been rushed down here for that? The woman we seek is known to be faded, tired looking. Is that not so, Deacon Rose?"

"The woman Brother Norbert met was vibrant . . . 'vivid,' I believe he said."

"Yes, but was she the woman we seek?" He looked back at the Admiralty agent who fumbled for something to say.

"Sh-she was the right age, sir, and keeping somewhat to herself. . . . It didn't seem impossible that she had recovered from whatever had ailed her, and was looking more hale."

Captain James shook his head in disgust, his mood quite black. Hayes could see how much he detested this duty, and could sympathize. The state of this agent of the Admiralty was also an offense to the captain, who was clearly consumed by duty.

"Was there anything else at all?" Deacon Rose asked mildly. "Did anyone overhear this couple's conversation? Was there something that marked them as uncommon in any way?"

The man shook his head ruefully. "Not really, Father. Oh, someone said the woman had a pet bird. Not a caged bird, sir, but one that flies free. A chough or corn crow."

Rose looked over at Captain James, and then back to the Admiralty agent. "If this turns out to be the truth, Captain James might even overlook your present state of drunkenness."

Hayes quickly found Kehler and told him what he'd learned.

"Deacon Rose thought this pet of great significance, or so I gathered."

Kehler nodded. "Yes, I can see why. It is probably nothing more than a woman who has rescued a young bird at some point, but one can never be sure."

"A familiar? Is that what you think?"

"I will wager that it's what the priest thinks. What is the plan now?"

"They will go at first light with a party of sailors. We'll not be invited, by the way. Rose convinced Captain James that it would be unfair to ask the friends of Erasmus to arrest him, if it turns out this is Erasmus."

Neither spoke for a moment.

"Kehler? The priest seemed to become very . . . *still* when he heard about this bird. As though he were hiding his excitement. Do you think it could be Erasmus and Anna?"

"I don't know but I will say again; I'm damned if I'll let Erasmus fall victim to Deacon Rose and the ire of Eldrich."

Clarendon came upon them just then.

"Your manner hardly looks suspicious," he said. "Don't huddle so, and stop whispering. That's better. Now tell me what this is all about?"

Dusk greeted them, prancing a little so that his nails clicked on the deck.

"This woman the Admiralty have found, she has a pet bird. Not a caged bird but a chough or a crow that flies free. And she is in company with a man who fits the description of Erasmus. Deacon Rose was quite taken with the thought that this woman might have a familiar."

"No doubt!" Randall said, lowering his own voice. "Is it possible that Mr. Flattery is yet alive? That he did not perish?"

Hayes and Kehler shrugged.

"We don't know, Randall, but if there is any chance that he

survived the gorge, we want to warn him before he falls into the hands of Eldrich, though how we shall manage this I don't know."

Clarendon gestured toward the lanterns that appeared to drift slowly about the calm sea—boys out fishing.

"Rose and Captain James will not be pleased," Kehler said.

"When did we begin answering to them?" Clarendon asked as he leaned out over the rail. "*You, lad.* How's the fishing?"

"Not as bad as all that, sir. I've nearly hooked three."

"Nearly hooked? That will hardly provide breakfast. Would you like to make a sovereign for your night's work?"

"Indeed I would, sir!"

"Then keep your voice down and come over here, lad. And put that lantern out."

The boys, for there were two of them, were quickly alongside. Taking a look around the deck and finding the watch rather uninterested, Hayes and Kehler sent Mr. Clarendon down and then passed down Dusk, lest the beast bark and give them away. Hayes was about to slip over the side when Clarendon pushed the small boat free of the ship.

"Randall, what are you doing?"

"They will miss three of us more than one," he hissed, and had the boys back the oars. "If Erasmus is alive, Mr. Hayes, rest assured, I shall warn him." And with that, the boys bent to their oars, the boat carrying the small man away across the starlit waters.

Chapter Forty-eight

THEY were preparing to take flight again. Anna's plans to remain hidden on the island until the mage passed through were
to be abandoned. Erasmus could not believe he had let himself hope
that he would escape Eldrich. He found he had stopped packing
their few belongings and was staring at the wall, seeing again the
carriage racing across the night landscape, the entranced child upon
the roof.

It might mean only that Eldrich sought them—that the mage
believed Erasmus remained alive. But it might also mean that he
journeyed toward them, led somehow by his connection with Erasmus as a child.

Erasmus buckled up the case and took it down the stairs into the
entry hall, where he found Anna staring hopelessly at several cases.
They had thought it wise to procure the clothing and accoutrements
expected of educated people—so they would not stand out—and
now they were burdened with them.

"We are all packed up, but where shall we go?" Erasmus asked,
putting his case with the others.

Anna raised her hands and let them drop helplessly. "I don't
know. Farrow seems a danger if Eldrich does think you're alive."

She shook her head, staring down rather sadly at the baggage. "Entonne, and then on to Doorn." Suddenly she looked up at him, her eyes bright. "Unless you have thought more about what I said. Eldrich cannot harm another mage. . . ."

Erasmus sat down on the second stair. "But I had hoped to end my involvement with the arts forever. To escape not only Eldrich, but all vestiges of Eldrich, all memories."

"It is a lovely dream, Erasmus, but only a dream. Sometimes we can avoid the battle, but other times we must gather our resolve and wade in and fight it. There can be no other choice if we are to survive."

The truth of this, Erasmus knew, was becoming more and more difficult to deny.

"But you said yourself that Eldrich would have people watching Tremont Abbey, perhaps even Farrow by now. Do we not need a place of power to perform the ritual?"

"Yes, and I believe we have one." Anna came and crouched down before him and took his hands. "You remember your vision: the seven-branched tree with white blossoms waving in the moonlight? The ritual which makes one a mage is performed at the full moon, and the tree was certainly king's blood growing. And it was seven-branched, the mages' number of power. But even more importantly, you knew the place. Kilty's Keep, you said."

"But it was and was not. It . . ." Erasmus lost his train of thought. "I don't know. It seemed to be a ruin, but somehow I knew it was not. I can't explain."

"There is no need to explain, Erasmus. It was a vision induced by king's blood. Accept the truth of it. Kilty's Keep lies on the same fault as Tremont Abbey. The same line of power. Trust what you saw and what you felt was true."

Erasmus closed his eyes and tried to recall the vision, recall the feelings he had experienced. Somehow it was Kilty's Keep even though its appearance was not quite as it should have been.

"Erasmus?" But Anna did not finish, for there was a knock at the door.

They both stiffened for a moment, and then Anna said quietly, "I rather doubt the mage would knock, and even so, once he is at our door, there is nothing left to do."

She rose quickly and went to the door, impulsively swinging it wide. And there, in the opening, stood a brightly dressed man not four feet tall.

"Randall!"

Clarendon nodded, looking a little shaken and pale.

"Are you well?" Erasmus asked as he rose from the stair.

"It's just seeing you alive, Mr. Flattery." He glanced at Anna.

Erasmus crossed the hall and embraced the little man, the two pounding each other on the back.

"Randall, how in this round world . . . ?"

"The mage is seeking you yet, Mr. Flattery. Rose and some navy men wait upon a ship across the sound. They will be here at first light, sooner if they realize I am gone."

"Blood and flames!" Erasmus glanced over at Anna, who looked no less distressed than he.

"He is telling the truth," Anna said quickly. She tore open a bag. "Take only a change of clothes. The barest of necessities."

Clarendon held up his hands. "But there is more, Mr. Flattery. Give me a moment to tell my tale."

Anna did not stop what she was doing but shifted part of her attention to the small man, nodding for him to go on.

With the door still open so that he was framed by the night, Clarendon began. "We were met by this man Bryce as we came out of the hills, and he led us to a hunting lodge on the road to Castlebough. I will not burden you with every detail, but we were taken to the mage." The small man paused here, wiping a hand across his eyes. "Taken to see the mage, and questioned closely, me most of all. I had spent some time writing out the text from the chamber—everything that had been written upon the walls, and this interested Eldrich more than anything. The mage pored over it, speaking with his servant, Walky.

" 'It is beyond imagining, Walky,' he said. 'Beyond dreams. Look at this! The art of Landor, lost more than a thousand years!' He was beside himself with pleasure. He read parts of it aloud, shaking his head in wonder, as though it were the greatest work of literature ever created. He questioned me about Anna and Banks, having me repeat every word you had said about the text and the chamber—and as you know, I misremember nothing.

" 'She must not have understood. Is that possible?' the mage asked. 'But she will realize in time; she must,' the servant said. And then there was some debate of whether you would have the text at all, for all the notes the others had written were destroyed by water in our escape from the cave." Clarendon looked from one to the other. " 'But what will it profit her to open the way?' the servant asked. 'It will only profit her in that she can escape me,' his master said. 'But that would be to our benefit,' Walky said, but the mage only shook his head. 'If she can pass out of this world, Walky, she can return. Return after I am gone. No, the gates must be closed. Closed for all time." He pointed at the text I had so carefully preserved. 'This must die with me, Walky, as we both know." Clarendon closed his eyes for a moment. "And as it seems even the mage cannot take away my memories, I knew what that meant for me."

Erasmus looked to Anna. "Can this be true? The text was an enchantment to open the gates?"

Anna nodded. "It could be so. Banks thought it possible. It was so arcane, so complex, written in an older form of Darian, and obscure even by the standards of the mages. But if Eldrich says it is so—"

"But can it be used?" Clarendon broke in. "Used to open the way to this other world? Can you do it, Anna?"

She shrugged. "One would have to be a mage, not a near mage as I am. Could I do it, then? It would not be without risk. . . ."

"But could we not escape Eldrich thus?" Clarendon asked. He came and stood before Anna, suddenly animated.

"Randall," Erasmus said, "you have let your hopes blind you. Lizzy has been gone these fifty years. If she is alive at all, she would be very old."

"You do not understand. Eldrich will see me dead with what I know. My need to escape is as great as yours. But even if I do hold onto hope of finding Lizzy, it is not utterly foolish. Time does not run at the same pace in these other worlds—that is clear in the Tale of Tomas, and Eldrich referred to the old story himself. She might still be young, as was Tomas."

Erasmus shook his head. "It was a tale, Randall. An ancient lay."

"But based on some truth." He appealed to Anna. "Was it not?"

Anna shrugged. "We haven't time for this debate. We must fly. Find a boat and get ashore before Deacon Rose arrives."

"But fly where?" Clarendon asked. "Eldrich will catch you without doubt. Without question. And then what will we do? Throw ourselves upon his mercy?" Clarendon reached into his coat and drew out a sheaf of neatly folded papers. "But with this we might escape him. Escape him for all time."

Chapter Forty-nine

D EACON Rose walked around the razed house, glowering alternately at the ruin and than at Hayes and Kehler.

"You let him go, knowing full well that he would warn them?"

Neither Kehler nor Hayes answered. They had been seen the night before lowering Clarendon into the fishing boat—though the sailors on watch had no orders to interfere with civilians, and gentlemen at that.

Rose stepped gingerly into the ruin, testing the remains of the collapsed roof.

"Have a care, Deacon," James said.

Rose seemed not to hear, but went slowly on, perhaps relying on Farrelle to protect him.

In the center of the destruction he stopped and turned a slow circle, his lively eyes fixed and unwavering. He ran a hand over his cropped hair and made a sign to Farrelle.

"Were they . . . inside when it happened?" Hayes asked quietly.

Deacon Rose shook his head, his concentration not wavering.

"No," he muttered. "Better if they had been. Better for all concerned. But no, this house was burned deliberately. Burned so that they could not be followed by means of the arts. Clearly Clarendon warned them, may Farrelle damn him for it. But they are not far ahead now, and we shall catch them."

The Deacon looked up, his jaw set tight and his eye very clear. He picked his way carefully out onto the lawn, coming straight to Hayes and Kehler.

"What did you think you were doing, getting Clarendon off the ship?"

"Warning Erasmus," Kehler said, unintimidated. "If he were alive."

"Oh, he is alive, or likely so," Deacon Rose said. "Certainly Anna still lives, and who else would the gentleman be who fit the description of Erasmus? Eldrich will deal with the two of you."

Brother Norbert stood three paces behind his fellow priest, saying nothing, his face completely neutral.

"Captain James," Rose ordered, "you must put these two in confinement. They cannot be trusted." He shook his head, turning back to the ruin. "Well, we begin yet again. Anna and Erasmus Flattery have fled . . . somewhere. We must find their track. Find it and run them down." He turned back to the others.

"We must determine if they have fled by land or sea. That is our first task. Captain James, let us best detail your men to accomplish this." With a curt nod he set off across the lawn, taking Captain James and Brother Norbert in tow. Half a dozen sailors came forward to escort Hayes and Kehler, who glanced at each other. Rather than looking frightened, Kehler was red with suppressed rage. Hayes thought he might suddenly throw himself at their escort, then murder Deacon Rose with his bare hands. Hayes knew precisely what his friend felt. One grew sick of it. *He wanted his life back.*

They had been confined in a storeroom below decks, with only a small scuttle to allow in air, but no light.

"Who would have guessed the bowels of a ship are as dark as the bowels of the earth," Kehler said.

It had been some hours, neither knew how many, since they had heard Deacon Rose and his party depart, and they sat there miserably, imagining what Eldrich would do to them when their reckoning finally came. It was not a pleasant way to pass the hours.

"I still cannot fathom how Erasmus and Anna escaped us in the gorge. They could not have planned the entire thing."

"Leave it be, Kehler," Hayes said. "If Erasmus is still alive, then I think he will have had good reason to do what he did. Who knows what Eldrich had planned for him? Remember the ritual that Percy Bryce gave him? Self-immolation is hardly a reward for a job well done."

They fell silent, hearing only the slapping of water along the hull and their own quiet breathing.

"We seem always to be left in the dark."

"Kehler," Hayes cautioned.

Hayes could hear his friend shift in the darkness.

"It is true, Hayes. We have not understood for a moment what we're involved in. And I'm sure we don't even yet. But what is really choking me now is the thought of Rose out there tracking down Clarendon and Erasmus. He has hated Clarendon from the moment they met, I'm sure, because Randall saw what a hypocrite Rose really was. And now he will have the pleasure of handing him over to Eldrich." His anger brought him to silence.

Small waves slapped along the hull in even rhythm, followed by a jingle of metal.

Hayes sat up.

"Ah, they have not forgotten us," Kehler said, stirring to rise. "Our evening turn on the deck. I am ready for it."

"Shh, keep your peace," Hayes cautioned.

And then the lock turned, a bolt was drawn back, and lantern light spread about the tiny storeroom.

"Brother Norbert?"

"Please, Mr. Kehler, keep your voice low." The hermit held a finger to his lips. "It took three bottles to lay the bosun's mate low so that I might lighten him of his keys. Do not let my efforts go to waste." He crouched down in the door. "There is a ship's boat lying alongside to starboard. Only two men stand watch, and they have sequestered themselves with another bottle on the foredeck. It is a full two hours until the change of watch." He motioned behind him. "Let me go ahead to be sure the way is clear, and then we will be over the side and gone before anyone is the wiser."

" 'We,' Brother Norbert. Will you not suffer greatly for a betrayal of the church?"

"Perhaps, but I will suffer longer for my betrayal of the word of Farrelle. I have long known this was my choice, but hiding alone in the Caledon Hills allowed me to avoid it. Now it is no longer possible. Deacon Rose is what the church of Farrelle has become; a man who practices the very arts he has vowed to destroy, as the church is beset by all the evils they publicly condemn. Follow me to the ladder, but then wait until I give the word."

Brother Norbert slipped away, the lantern swaying as he walked. They waited at the ladder's foot, listening for the sounds of sailors. Norbert appeared, a disheveled apparition in the opening above, and motioned them on.

A moment later they were out into the night, the swimming moon caught overhead in the net of rigging. The boat was precisely where Norbert had said, and they were quickly away, silently dipping oars into the reflected sky, stars sent whirling.

Shore was their only goal—to land and slip away before the sailors missed them. Once they were ashore, the navy men likely wouldn't know what to do, and by the time the Admiralty had been contacted for orders, they would have escaped, pulled along in the wake of Deacon Rose.

"But what will we do now?" Hayes asked as the boat ran up on the beach.

"Find Erasmus and Clarendon. Take them bodily away from Anna, if we must. But Anna—she is on her own." Hayes turned to the monk. "Erasmus was convinced she murdered her guide, Brother. I am not sure why—something about the ritual performed. But this was not just some fabrication of the Deacon's to demonize her even more."

Norbert nodded. "Yes, and for this she should pay a price. But to a court of law. As to her soul: Farrelle taught that all sins could be forgiven. Whatever the case, it is not for me to judge."

They struck out into the town, wondering how far ahead Clarendon and Erasmus were, and how close behind Deacon Rose and Captain James followed.

"There must be an ostler in town somewhere. We need horses," Kehler said, suddenly energized, almost bouncing.

"Yes," Hayes said, "so that we might ride off into our uncertain future."

"Not so uncertain as all that," Kehler said, but he did not smile.

Chapter Fifty

THE moon, two days from the full, lit the roads and allowed them to ride by night. And ride they did, changing horses often, pressing the poor beasts on without regard for their well-being, or for the black looks of ostlers. Erasmus had never known the countryside to pass beneath him so quickly. Poor Clarendon looked like a man who had fought a war, and Dusk was being run to skin and bones.

Eldrich can rival the speed of a bird if he has need, Anna had said, and pressed on. They hardly spoke, for when they stopped, they fell upon their food and drink like the starving, and during their brief rests they descended into a sleep that was near to stupor.

Anna dressed in the clothing of a man, not that she was trying to pass herself off as one, but only for its convenience. And much to the scandal of ostlers and innkeeper's wives, she did not ride sidesaddle.

"Time," she said, "has become our enemy. More even than the mage."

And so they rode, stiff and sore and blistered, into the interior of the kingdom, until Anna's horse stumbled and fell, nearly landing atop her.

331

"I'm unhurt," she said when Erasmus and Clarendon reached her, but she appeared pale and shaken. They made her sit a moment at the roadside, and she became so nauseous that she was almost ill.

"It will pass in a moment," she said. "It will pass." Then she gestured at her mount. "Has it a broken leg?" she asked.

Erasmus regarded the beast as it tried for the third time to rise, obviously in agony, one limb hanging limp. "I'm afraid it does."

"You must put it from its misery, Erasmus. Look at the poor beast. . . . Have you a dagger?"

Clarendon cut the beast's throat as quickly and cleanly as he could, and with some effort they retrieved Anna's tack.

Using the other horses, they dragged the dead beast into a thicket, and then went on, Anna riding with Clarendon, though more slowly as a result.

In two hours they came to an inn and fell down upon benches to eat while new horses were readied. The patrons tried not to stare, for certainly they had never seen people of the educated classes who looked so . . . well, who looked as though they fled the law.

Clarendon took food outside to see to Dusk, leaving Erasmus and Anna alone.

Erasmus tried to smile at the innkeeper, to put him at ease, but he had not the energy to concoct a story to explain their strange flight. If they had not obviously been of good families, certainly the innkeeper would have reported them to the local authorities—and might still do so when they left.

"Tomorrow by midday," Anna said, tearing off a chunk of bread, "barring further accidents."

Erasmus nodded. "Good. I don't think I can go further. Will we have time to make our preparations?"

She shrugged. "If the mage is not upon us."

E ldrich walked around the edge of the razed building, a stooped shadow in the moonlight. Twice he stopped and performed a brief rite, drawing lines on the ground in silver fire. The countess stood well back, watching. Bryce had made his way into the middle of the ruin, his passage releasing the pungent odor of smoke and ash. Eldrich asked him a question, then sent his servant searching among the still-standing walls.

They spent an hour in that place, the countess wondering if this was the work of Eldrich, and if the enemy he sought had died here, Erasmus with her. Or if fire had been carried here by the fanatical priest of whom Walky spoke. Erasmus seemed to go from one death to the next—first in the cave, then the gorge, and now, just when Eldrich was sure that he still lived, this. *The final death,* she thought.

Walky came from his own searching, near enough that she caught his attention.

"Has . . . anyone survived?" she asked.

"Everyone, m'lady," Walky said, surprised at the question. "At least no one died here."

"What of Erasmus, then? Was he here?"

Walky shrugged. "Only the mage knows," he said, and passed on.

The mage emerged into an opening in the wall, pausing in his circuit. Where he stood, moonlight fell between the smoke-blackened stone, but seemed to pass him by.

Even moonlight shies from him, the countess thought. *If it cannot penetrate the shadow and silence, how can I?*

She watched him disappear again, behind blackened stone, his servants keeping their distance. She, too, stood back from him.

I have become like all the others who serve him, she thought, *governed by his moods.* She shook her head.

From around a corner the mage appeared, crossing the lawn, tilting his head to Walky who immediately waited upon his master. The music of Eldrich's voice reached her, but not the words. It was a sad music now, minor in key. Walky nodded and hurried ahead, leaving her to follow in her usual ignorance of what went on, of what was planned.

They followed the path along the cliff top, in a single line, no one talking, each seemingly unaware of the other. Thus it was in the house of the mage, the countess knew. Each person isolated from the others, as though Eldrich's silence and remoteness had infected them all. Everyone went before, walking through the night without lanterns, moonlight marking the cliff edge, the too-narrow path one must tread.

A nightjar roamed the sky, its buzzing call trilling through the air. She stopped and watched its flight against the stars, touched by moonlight, as it hunted. She felt as much kinship for this lone flyer as she did for those who served Eldrich. Even Walky seemed especially distant that night.

"Why do I follow?" she whispered. But she went on, along the moonlit path, the others lost from view. The vision in the water came back to her, and she shuddered.

In a few moments she came to the small wood where the path disappeared into darkness. When she had passed this way before, she had followed the others, but now—

"M'lady?"

It was Walky, standing in shadow beside the path.

"I have a gift for you," the little man said, holding out his hands like a child with a lightning bug.

When he opened them, saying a few words of Darian, she felt a strange light cast upon her eyes, and the world had changed.

"What in this . . . ?"

"It is owl sight, m'lady. From the mage."

All around her the world seemed to glow with a faint, unnatural luminescence. She held up her hand which also seemed to gleam faintly.

"Please, m'lady, we should not tarry. It will not last long."

"I'm sure it won't," she said. Gifts from the mage seldom did.

The countess did not bother to ask how they had found carriages— from some country estate nearby, no doubt. And she again found herself in flight across the countryside, desperately in need of rest, a bath, and some civil company. This time she found herself riding with Skye.

"Did you see? They have paintings, or so I assume from the bundles. Immediately I wondered if they were Peliers."

"Kent's, I think," the countess said.

"Averil Kent?"

She nodded. "Yes. He was a guest of Lord Eldrich as well."

The great empiricist shook his head in amazement and dismay. "What goes on? Why am I here? What does he want of me?"

"It is the question many of us ask, Lord Skye," the countess said.

"I think, sometimes, that he only keeps me about to torture me."

She had seldom met a man more self-absorbed. "It seems unlikely to me. Whatever small pleasure the mage might derive from that would seem insignificant in the present situation."

"Yes, but what is going on? Do you know? We are racing about the country like . . . Well, I don't know what we are like, but certainly I have never heard of such a thing. Is it all about this girl I met? The faded one?"

Despite her need for company, the countess had quickly tired of Skye. "Only the mage knows," she said.

How had she once thought she was in love with this man? Hopelessly in love?

She feared that her time with Eldrich would make everyone appear thus—rather petty and absorbed by the most trivial matters.

But there had been something else with Skye, something besides the enormous regard in which he was held throughout all the lands of the Entide Sea—he did not respond to her. She shook her head at the thought. She had not been able to bear it. He was the only one. The only man she had met who reacted to her not at all. It shamed her to admit it, but there it was.

What a child I was. A spoiled child, as Eldrich once said.

She looked out at the countryside racing by and wondered what they would do now. Where they went.

Let there be an end to this soon, she thought. *Let there be some clarity, some understanding. I will go mad otherwise.*

Chapter Fifty-one

THEY stopped only to kill and skin a snake and gather a vial of starlit water, then continued on their mad way, careening across the Farr countryside like the most hunted of highwaymen.

The final hill defeated Anna's exhausted horse, so they led their mounts slowly up through the fading light. The moon, in its silver splendor, had not yet risen, and in the warm light of the fading sun, the ruin of the ancient volcano was strangely imposing. Erasmus thought it would be easy to imagine that this was the ruin of an ancient citadel, though a citadel of giants.

None of them spoke—they had not the breath to—and Erasmus could almost sense Anna's whirling thoughts. She kept her eyes fixed on the uneven path, but when she glanced up, it was with such a haunted look that Erasmus was taken aback. He couldn't begin to guess what it meant.

The path, almost a road, wound up between steep walls of dark, coarse rock—as a road might wind up through a hilltop fortress. Here and there the rock was columnated, nature having forced the hot stone up in elongated pillars, and these were worn and broken and tumbledown.

"It is difficult to believe this is not an ancient city," Clarendon said, his voice hushed, as though afraid of disturbing ghosts.

"Yes, especially in this light," Erasmus answered, "but it is natural all the same." He looked over at Anna, who was pale even in this golden light. "Are you well?" he asked.

She shook her head, not meeting his eye. "The last time my brethren tried to make a mage they were trapped—all of them murdered. . . ."

Suddenly Erasmus felt his fatigue even more. The little energy he had left him like the dying light of day. He looked over at Clarendon, and a sudden realization penetrated the overwhelming fatigue.

Erasmus drew his horse up abruptly, but the others went several paces before they noticed he had stopped and turned to look back at him.

"What is it, Erasmus?" Anna asked, her voice terribly weary.

"Why did Eldrich let Randall leave his house with all that Randall knows?"

Neither Anna nor Clarendon answered.

"Think about it. He uses others without them knowing. Consider how he manipulated events to send us all into the Mirror Lake Cave at the same time. Randall knows things that no one but Eldrich knows: the way to open these precious gates. Yet he sends Randall looking for us, knowing full well that Randall feels no loyalty to him, that he would do anything to find the woman he lost so long ago." Erasmus looked around him, as though he might find Eldrich hiding in a shadow.

"There is no spell upon Clarendon that might be used to find us," Anna said, then dropped the reins of her horse and began to sprinkle the starlit water in a pattern on the ground.

"Come quickly, Erasmus. Pass by me up the path."

The two men took the horses, which were too exhausted to bolt even though they shied and swung their heads when they sensed the arts in use.

They forced themselves up the shadowed path, laboring for breath. A moment later Anna came up behind them.

"Eldrich is not here, nor is he nearby." She took hold of a saddle to steady herself. "We will be warned now if any come up this path.

I can do no more than that." Anna nodded and they set out again, forcing themselves to make each step.

Finally they came to the path's end. Anna stopped and slowly raised her eyes. She made an odd sign with her hand and muttered beneath her breath.

Before them lay a slope of shattered stone angling up between steep walls. Overhead, stars began to appear upon a sky in transition from darkest blue to deepest black.

"It was on a night such as this that my brethren were trapped by the mages," Anna said. "Trapped and murdered."

Erasmus found himself nodding. Trapped without the slightest warning, led on by their deepest desires.

Anna dropped the reins of her horse, pulled the bag from the saddle, and began to pick her way up the slope. Every few steps she would stop and raise her head, as though she looked upon some inescapable horror.

"They had come to make a mage," she said softly. "A mage. That miracle of all the ages. And they were murdered—murdered at their moment of joy—for it *was* a moment of joy, not triumph." She slumped down upon a rock for a moment, fighting to catch her breath.

Erasmus leaned against the rock wall. Dusk came down the path from above, where he had ranged ahead.

"But why did he let you go, Randall?"

The little man shrugged. "I had not thought of it, Mr. Flattery. He sent all of us who had been seeking Anna. I had carried this knowledge with me before, after all."

Erasmus thought this answer inadequate, but felt none of them could bring their minds to focus on the issue. Exhaustion had robbed them of their mental powers at the time when they might need them the most.

Anna turned suddenly to Erasmus. "Does this remind you of your vision? Is it the same?"

Erasmus cast his gaze around. "It resembles the place in my dream hardly at all. But it feels the same. . . ."

Anna nodded, pushed herself up, and began to climb again by sheer force of will. The others stirred themselves to follow, all the unanswered questions traveling with them.

They struggled over a massive shoulder of stone and found themselves upon a level bench. It could almost have been a terrace, with broken-down walls on three sides and open to the southeast. Against the central wall a spring bubbled up, forming a small pool.

Anna looked around and smiled for the first time in days. "Here, you see? Your vision did not fail you." She waved a hand at the spring. "Can you feel it? There is a power here. If my brethren had only known, they could have avoided Tremont Abbey and their meeting with the mages." She turned around in a graceful circle, as though the power she spoke of had invigorated her.

The moon was lighting the horizon, rising like a great, blind eye above the eastern hills. Anna greeted it in Darian, raising her hands as though she held the globe aloft. And then she collapsed upon a stone, her vitality evaporating, and stared off at the beauty of the rising moon.

"What must we do?" Clarendon asked.

"There is nothing we can do until the moon has risen higher." Anna moved down onto the ground and leaned against the rock. She closed her eyes. "I must rest an hour, and then we will begin."

"And what if Eldrich comes upon us before we are done?"

"Then, Mr. Clarendon, we will no longer suffer this misery."

Sleep eluded Erasmus, but he sat with Anna's head in his lap, his back pressed against a stone wall, and watched the moon float free of the eastern horizon. Chuff prowled the upper reaches of the rock walls, appearing in a flutter every now and then, cocking a single, dark eye toward Anna, and then springing back up into darkness.

No familiar had appeared to Erasmus, despite his use of the seed, but he kept alert watching for this miracle. The waking dreams were not so strong now, more like mild bemusement— though Anna said they could likely be induced again by a stronger elixir. Often he saw the dark carriage racing across the landscape, a small boy perched atop, alone.

"Mr. Flattery?"

He had thought Clarendon asleep, his breathing had been so even.

"I am awake, Randall."

"Will you become a mage, sir? Will you go through with it?"

The very question he was avoiding. He smoothed Anna's hair, assuring himself that she still slept. "I don't know, Randall. Anna is convinced there is nothing else that will protect me from Eldrich, but I am not so sure. He has spent all his later years dedicated to eradicating the arts from this world, I cannot see him allowing another mage to live, whether there is a curse or no."

"Exactly my thinking, Mr. Flattery, which is why I think we should try to open this gate, sir. It might be our only chance."

Erasmus felt his shoulders lift. "I don't know, Randall. She said herself it could not be done without risk. . . . But perhaps you are right. There will be no other escape for her in this world."

"I did not hear you include yourself, Mr. Flattery."

Erasmus looked up at the pure ball of the moon. "Did I not. . . ?"

There was a sudden pealing of a bell, a sound not entirely incongruous in this place that so resembled a city.

"What in Farrelle's name—"

Confused, Anna roused and sat up, rubbing her eyes. "Someone comes," she said, rising stiffly. She called out in Darian, and her chough appeared. She sent it winging off down the path. A moment later it was back, fluttering before them and speaking its single word excitedly.

"It is not Eldrich," she said and sat back on the rock to wait.

"I hear horses, I think," Clarendon said.

Then Erasmus heard it, too, the hollow sound of hooves coming slowly up. And then it stopped.

Finally the sound of voices, and boots on stone, then, in the near darkness, a man appeared. He stepped out of shadow into moonlight and stopped as though confused by the pale light.

"Mr. Hayes? Is that you?"

"Randall? Erasmus?" He turned and called out. "I've found them!"

Hayes swayed on his feet, tried very hard to smile, then collapsed on the ground. He held up a hand as Erasmus and Clarendon crossed to him. "I will be all right in a moment." He looked up at his two friends and shook his head as though unable to believe he had found them.

"Deacon Rose and the agents of the Admiralty can't be far behind. We managed to outdistance them by riding unnumbered horses into the ground. Your trail has not been so hard to follow, I will tell you."

"But what of Eldrich?" Anna asked. "Where is the mage?"

Hayes fixed her with an odd look, as though assuring himself that she was not a ghost, and then he shrugged.

Fenwick Kehler appeared upon the terrace, and then, most oddly, a Farrellite priest.

Anna shook her head. "Brother Norbert? What in this round world has brought you here?"

"Ill fortune, I fear," the priest said. "Men came looking for you in the hills. When they heard my tale, I was taken away from my home and my work and embroiled in this . . . madness."

"Brother Norbert helped us escape," Hayes said. "We would not have been able to reach you otherwise. But there is little time for stories, Erasmus. Although we managed to pass Deacon Rose, for his party was larger and consisted of too many sailors, we cannot have left them more than a few hours behind. Perhaps not even that."

Fenwick Kehler hobbled painfully into the patch of moonlight. "Yes, Erasmus, you must flee," he said. "Deacon Rose is near, and I worry that Eldrich is not far behind."

"No," Anna said softly. "We cannot escape them—not now. Not in this world."

They collapsed at the foot of a wall, protected from a rising wind which moved among them almost silently.

Hayes and Kehler kept looking to Clarendon, and then at each other, both so exhausted that they could hardly bring their minds to bear.

"There is no choice, nor time for soul searching," Anna said suddenly, then covered her eyes for a moment as though her vision swam. "I will attempt the ritual of Landor, and if we open the gate, you may pass through or not. It is your decision, but the ritual will be easier the more people who are involved."

"I will come with you," Clarendon said quickly, rising to his feet. He swallowed once, hard, and looked at the others for support, though his stance evidenced a desperate resolve.

"As will I," Kehler said, shaking his head as though he could not believe what he was saying or perhaps what a pass his life had come to. "I saw what was done to Doctor Ripke. Better to become a Stranger than suffer that." He turned to his friend. "Hayes . . . ?"

Hayes got slowly to his feet. "I—I will but no more help," Hayes said, fighting a sudden panic. *To pass beyond the world.* It was too frightening, too inconceivable.

"There will be no mercy from Eldrich, Mr. Hayes," Clarendon said, "and you will never escape him. You have no choice, whether you realize it or not."

"But I do not want to pass into the land of the Strangers," Hayes said plaintively, "even were it possible. Despite all my ill fortune, this is my world, here; Farrland and the Entide Sea."

"But, Mr. Hayes," Anna said, her fatigue filling her voice with emotion, "Eldrich is likely on his way to this place as we speak. He will make you pay the price for your betrayal."

Hayes nodded. He felt near tears from exhaustion and from the decision being pressed on him. "Yes, well, it will be my price."

Anna rose almost noiselessly. "There is no more time. If you will not help us, then I suggest you go now. Better not to be here when Eldrich arrives. Even Deacon Rose and his followers are to be feared."

"The time for discussion has passed," Clarendon said. "Come, those who will, let us begin. And any who will not—I wish you all speed." The little man turned away, though not before Hayes saw a tear in the small man's eye.

The despair in Clarendon's voice could not be missed.

Let him go with Anna, Hayes thought. *Let him pass from this world that has so injured him.*

Hayes looked at the forlorn figure of Randall Spencer Emanual Clarendon, his fine clothes torn and dirty. There was no thought of the future with the small man now, but only of escape. Memories had overtaken him like a storm at sea; it would be a wonder if he did not founder.

"I will help if I may," Brother Norbert said, his deep voice very solemn. He had risen with the others but stood apart. "Despite the teachings of the church, Farrelle never spoke against the practice of the arts. I will help in whatever way I can. Let Eldrich do with me as he will, I follow my own conscience now."

"I think you have little reason to fear Eldrich," Erasmus said. "It was not chance that brought you here. Just as it was not chance that took a priest to Tremont Abbey the night the mages trapped the followers of Teller. You will be the witness for the Holy See. And you may pray for us as well."

They all turned silently to the spring and the open area before it.

At Anna's instruction they placed seven rocks in a semicircle around the spring. Taking out a dagger, she began to etch lines onto the stone that recreated the intricate geometry Erasmus remembered from the nance in Landor's chamber. The same pattern that was etched on the floor of the Ruin of Farrow.

"We must perform the ceremony without mistake," Anna cautioned. "Let no one set foot on the nance without the proper ablutions, for it will endanger us all."

Hayes found his heart had begun to palpitate oddly, and he had not a drop of moisture in his mouth.

Each in turn did as Anna instructed: speaking words of Darian in dry mouths; gesturing as she demonstrated; then going to the spring to drink a cupped-palm of water. And then she began to teach them their parts, fear focusing their minds completely.

Chapter Fifty-two

E VEN horses driven by a mage must stop for water, and the countess found herself on a riverbank at the bottom of a deep, narrow valley, waiting while the horses were tended. The trees on the hillsides bent to a rising breeze, and the river seemed to clatter past, as though it tumbled stones through the shallows. Dusk was gathering in the east, even as storm clouds climbed the southern sky.

The countess had taken the opportunity to escape from the confines of the carriage. They were following Eldrich's familiar which was apparently tracking a wolfhound that belonged to Clarendon. The odd thing was that this did not seem the slightest bit strange to her. So they were careening across the countryside led by a wolf that anyone would describe as magical; what of it? Such absurdity now made up the fabric of her life. After all, who was she but a woman under an enchantment which made men foolish with infatuation?

She shook her head.

Sweeping aside a branch she found Skye and Eldrich standing on the riverbank, and though the conversation had lulled, their bearing spoke clearly in the silence. Eldrich was half turned away, his shoulders hunched, looking down at the empiricist with undisguised disdain. Sky stood back, his arms slightly open, palms out as though in appeal.

"From where?" Skye said, sounding as though he had been punched in the chest.

"A world where your great discoveries are common knowledge, *Lord Skye*. Where children know the laws of motion. So all of this puffed-up vanity over your great genius is nothing but so much empty posturing. That is what I have kept from you. Are you not overcome with joy and gratitude that I have revealed the truth at last? Now pester me no more." Eldrich swept off along the embankment, leaving Skye stricken, wavering on his feet. The empiricist took two steps and then seemed almost to collapse, sitting down in a heap on the grass.

The countess came and stood by him, tempted to reach out a hand to console him, but somehow she could not. "It isn't true," she said, not sounding terribly convincing. "It was said only in a fit of anger and cruelty. They were always thus, the mages."

But Skye shook his head, staring down at the ground. "No, it is true. I am a Stranger. I have always known it. Have always known my discoveries were but memories—nothing more." He put a hand to his brow, shaking his head almost desperately.

"What can I do for you, Lord Skye?" the countess said, almost a whisper.

"Lord Skye . . . ? That is not me. I am . . ." He shook his head again and, rolling awkwardly to his feet, pushed aside the branches and disappeared.

For a moment the countess stared after him, but then she turned to look for Eldrich. She knew he was caught in a fit of anger, and at such times would say whatever would hurt most—truth or lie. In this case she hoped it was a lie, and that she would be able to tell Skye so. Poor man. He might be a genius, but provoking Eldrich would hardly prove it. Of course what was she about to do?

This brought her headlong flight to a sudden stop. Perhaps this was not the moment to confront the mage over this matter. There was so much afoot, so many things she did not understand. Eldrich's mood was dark. Dark and fearful, she was sure. He had been left such terrible responsibilities. She remembered the vision he had shown her—the vision in the water.

Beneath a willow leaning out over the river, she found Eldrich plucking leaves from the branches, muttering to himself. Darian, she realized, and kept silent.

She remained a few paces off, afraid to intrude, wondering suddenly what he had decided. Would he release Erasmus unharmed? He had never clearly answered yea or nay.

For an instant he glanced her way, but went immediately back to his task, stopping only when he had a handful of the new leaves.

"It is not in my nature to gamble," he said, his voice and manner mild, and she sensed that he regretted the scene with Skye. The mage stared off over the river. "I allowed Skye out into this world against my better judgment only because I could trap the renegades of Teller no other way. I knew it was likely that some of his knowledge would surface in time. And now I have been forced to do the same with Clarendon—and he bears knowledge of even greater danger." He shook his head. "Is it not ironic?"

He shook his head, then crouched down by the river, his oddly bowed posture making him look like a penitent—something the countess suspected he had never been.

He began to chant, moving his free hand in intricate patterns. Across the bank before him, he drew his fingers, and a pattern glowed upon the grasses. Dusk seemed to flow up the valley, like flood waters, overtaking them. The mage continued his chant.

The countess was familiar enough with Darian now to glean a few words, and knowledgeable enough to guess that this was augury that Eldrich performed—something Walky said his master resorted to too often.

Caught by the wind, the willow branches writhed around him, like tendrils, she thought, as though animated by the arts.

With a final powerful syllable, Eldrich threw the leaves upon the water, staring fixedly where they fell, and then he toppled forward almost into the river, struggling to balance himself as though the riverbank tried to throw him off.

The countess fought through the grasping branches and took hold of his shoulder, pulling him back from the water. He flailed awkwardly with his arms, as though blind or stupefied.

He still mumbled, half in Darian and half in Farr. *"The nance . . ."* he kept saying. *"They are upon the nance . . . !"*

At that moment Walky appeared.

"I will tend to Lord Eldrich," he said, making it very clear that her presence was neither required nor wanted.

"Walky?" the mage said, staring blankly as though his sight had left him. *"They are upon the nance. . . . Do you hear? Upon the nance!"*

A moment later the countess found herself bundled into Eldrich's carriage, the mage slumped against the side, wrapped in his enormous old cloak; shivering, she thought, though in the failing light it was difficult to be sure.

He looked suddenly frail—frail and old—and this she found quite disturbing. So much so that she turned her attention to the dark window, the passing scene barely distinguishable now. Far off she thought she perceived something—something on the edge of hearing, on the edge of the world. *Thunder.*

Eldrich was staring at her. She realized it before she turned her head to look. His eyes seemed as dark and cold as ever—no sign of age or frailty there. In fact, he looked to be quickly recovering.

"What is the nance?" she asked.

Eldrich continued to regard her, and then finally spoke, the music still there, but brittle. "It is a place of ritual and power, and it is a gate. In the past, a gate that led to other lands . . . infinitely far away yet near at hand."

"And this woman is there? This woman you seek?"

"And Erasmus, yes."

"What will you do with him?" she asked quickly.

"It will depend upon the degree of his betrayal."

"What does that mean?"

He stared at her, eyes darker than the dark corner he inhabited.

Yes, he does not like to be questioned, she thought. She steeled herself for what she would say next. "We spoke of a bargain," she said, forcing out the words. "How else will you assure yourself of my cooperation?"

"You saw the vision of the mages," he said evenly.

Yes, she had seen it. The end of the world, or so it appeared.

What would she not do to avert that? Her bargaining position was not strong, and he knew it. Her chance of saving Erasmus was slipping away.

"Is it true, then, that one can trust a devil more than a mage?"

"I have never met a devil," he said, the old mockery returning to his voice.

"If Erasmus is harmed, I cannot guarantee that I will be able to keep my part of the bargain."

"You would allow a cataclysm to spite me?"

She forced herself to meet his gaze. "Can you be sure I won't?"

He continued to stare. "Do you really care so much for him?" he asked after a moment.

The question caught her off guard. Did she, indeed? Why was she making such a fuss over Erasmus Flattery? Certainly the mage treated any number of people callously—Lord Skye, for instance—and she was doing nothing on their behalf. A memory of her evening with Erasmus—the way she had used him to gather information for Skye, and how he had reacted.

Perhaps that was it; the feeling that Erasmus, despite all that had befallen him, was a man of essential goodness, and considering how few such men there were, he had been terribly misused.

"Yes," she said, knowing it was said partly to wound. "Yes, I do."

But he is a mage, the countess reminded herself, *and can sense a lie. Can sense a lie and its purpose.*

Eldrich turned away, staring out at the passing night.

"Do you remember the Paths?" he asked, his voice mild and matter-of-fact.

"Yes."

"I have cast them recently, and something has changed. There are two paths now: one on which I live and another on which I die, or perhaps merely leave this world."

"Which will you take?"

"I am not certain I shall have the choice."

"Why are you telling me this?" *Sympathy,* she thought. *He wants my pity.*

"Why? So that you might prepare yourself. . . ." And he would say no more.

Chapter Fifty-three

THERE was a mage at large in Farrland for the first time in per- haps five decades, and Captain James wondered what in this round world could have roused Eldrich from his slumber.

A faded woman whom Captain James would know only when he saw her.

James glanced over at Deacon Rose riding beside him. The truth was he did not like the priest. He much preferred Hayes and Kehler and their diminutive friend, but Clarendon had slipped away to warn those the mage sought, and the others had aided him. Captain James had been left no choice but to throw in his lot with Deacon Rose. He had been ordered to offer all assistance to these people, never guessing that they were not all of one mind.

By default the captain ended up supporting Deacon Rose, a priest of the church of Farrelle who was far too much of an author- ity on the mages and their secret knowledge. The arts were pro- scribed, after all, and certainly it was a mortal sin to pursue them. Yet here was this priest, only a deacon in rank, who knew more than any priest should about matters arcane and had an air of au- thority that belied his modest station. And he sought the faded woman, apparently knowing a great deal about her—more than James could say.

When you meet her, you will know.

Moonlight lay upon the road, shimmering the gravel and casting ruts and potholes into shadow. The river chortled along its course, and wind raced them down the valley floor. From all his years at sea, James knew this to be a storm wind, yet there was not a cloud to be seen. Instead, the sky remained unnaturally clear, the stars bright and large for such a moonlit night.

The man who led them, a local huntsman, halted his horse suddenly, pointing at a path winding into the trees.

"They were seen going this way; a redheaded woman and a dark gentleman, and not long ago three horses were found wandering on the roadside, all of them spooked and lathered."

"Then that will be all we require of you," Deacon Rose said. "May Farrelle smile upon you and your endeavors." He turned away, dismissing the man. "I will go first, Captain James."

As they went into the shadow of the trees, whispering broke out among the Jacks, like flames among grass. Their uneasiness with this priest and his involvement with things arcane had festered to the point where open mutiny was no longer just a remote possibility. For his part, the priest didn't seem to care what the jacks thought, perhaps believing that the navy was like the church, where those lower in the hierarchy did as they were bid, and kept their peace. Captain James, however, knew better. He hadn't enough armed officers here to ensure the Jacks would follow orders, especially if these orders required they face the arts. It was a volatile situation, and the priest's utter insensitivity to it made it much worse.

What appeared to be a ruined city endured upon the rise, alchemic moonlight turning stone to muted silver. Out of shadow, two horses appeared, like limping ghost mares.

"They are here before us," Rose said, and spurred his exhausted mount on.

After half an hour's climb they came to a place where the horses could not pass, and Deacon Rose jumped quickly down, pulling a bag from his saddle.

Fanaticism makes a man strong, James thought.

The priest dropped the bag upon the uneven ground and pulled open its fastenings. Not paying any attention to James or the gathering Jacks, he began to spread out articles in the moonlight. Softly he began to chant, and a small brand caught fire.

The Jacks reacted by backing away, making warding signs, and uttering oaths. The Deacon began to sprinkle gray dust, like fine ash, upon the ground, drawing careful lines and curves. Touching these with the flaming brand, the design caught fire, revealing a finely drawn geometry. The Jacks fled in dismay, Captain James making no effort to stop them, but only watching the priest in terrible fascination.

Deacon Rose continued to chant, and flames, the green of sea fire, rose to envelop him.

And then, at a word, they died away, leaving only a flickering pattern traced upon the ground.

Deacon Rose looked at James, and then his eyes widened. "Where is your crew?"

"Gone. Threats of death would not have held them, for they fear death less than this." He waved a hand at the dying flames.

Deacon Rose picked up the still-burning brand and turned in a circle. "Then there is only thee and me," he said, "but if we are in time, that will be enough. Draw your sword, Captain. We might have need of it." He took up his bag and began to climb, holding his flaming brand aloft.

Up they went, among fallen boulders, then along a narrow ledge that looked down over the valley below from a great height. Twice the priest stopped to perform rites, flame from the brand forming strange patterns in the air.

"They try to thwart us, Captain," Rose said. "Do you see? But they shall not, for I am more skilled than they know. With this flame I can protect us from arcane assault, but you must not hesitate to use your blade—against man, woman, or child, no matter wealth or station. You must be utterly ruthless, Captain, for everything depends upon it. Everything."

They continued up until Rose stopped. From above voices echoed. The priest beckoned him, and not for the first time Captain James found himself reluctant to continue. Place him in an action at sea and he would face death unwaveringly—nothing less was expected—but this . . . ! It was more than the unknown. It was the darkness, the secret arts.

Despite his fears he crouched down beside Rose, feeling the cool rock press against him, reassuringly substantial. From above, a strange light wavered and a single voice spoke: a woman's voice.

"Thank Farrelle; we are in time," the priest said, his voice almost breaking. "You must stay close and be prepared to defend me at all costs, from that woman most of all. She is the true danger."

They toiled up the last thirty feet, and there, in the center of a level area, a woman was bent over in concentration, red tresses falling about her in a torrent. *And he knew her!* Without realizing why or from where, James knew her! Like a dream long forgotten, suddenly surfacing. He felt some strange triumph in this.

Rose began to draw in the air with his flaming brand, speaking low in another tongue. Without stopping, he nodded to James and went nimbly forward.

They were in moonlight, and high up among ruined walls, as though in a tower taller than any known. He hardly had time to notice more than that. Somewhere before them water fell: he could hear it slapping stone.

The woman had moved to the edge of the clear area now, and bent to her labors again, so focused that she did not see them, but someone called out in warning and she rose, tossing back her hair.

"Ah, Deacon," she said, "we have awaited you. Do not step on the floor, Captain James, or you will be consumed by fire. Only those within the ritual may set foot upon the nance."

"But you are too late," the priest said. He cast his eye around the others, measuring the situation. "I cannot imagine Eldrich's rage when you meet him next—and he approaches even now."

"Do not listen to his ravings," Anna said, her voice mocking; more than a little triumphant. "We will be gone before Eldrich comes, and Deacon Rose can be our witness, for all who follow me will escape."

"So that is what she has told you," Rose called out, his voice strong and reasonable, "that you will escape to this other world? But I am here to tell you that you will not. No mage in a thousand years has opened a gate to elsewhere, though many of the greatest spent a lifetime in this pursuit. No, she will make herself a mage.

That is what she intends—just as Teller always planned. A mage to stand against the last master of the arts.

"You know something of these matters, Mr. Flattery. Think on it. . . . Only a mage can open a gate. Even if she were planning this escape, still, she must first become a mage. And as such she will bring calamity upon the world. An emerging mage at this point in time—it is a curse that even the mages feared." He waved his brand in the air as though to emphasize his words. "Mr. Kehler. You have read of the fears of the mages. Here they are, manifest in this woman. It does not matter that her intentions are not evil, evil will result—the worst evil ever brought upon mankind. Here is the moment the mages feared above all others. *Do not do this,* I implore you."

"We have heard your speeches before," Clarendon called out, unable to contain himself. The little man stood in his appointed place upon the makeshift nance, and shook his fist at the priest. "Even Eldrich warned that your tongue was charmed. We shall not fall victim to your 'reason' again. No, priest, you are the last person we shall believe, for you have uttered nothing but lies since the ill-fated day we met. Stand and watch if you will—your church dearly loves to have witnesses—but we will not heed you again."

Anna had gone back to her preparations, ignoring the conversation around her and the threat of the intruders.

Captain James noted a shadow move beside the spring.

"Is that Brother Norbert?" he asked.

Rose took a step forward, holding his flame aloft.

"Brother Norbert! What madness is this? You will be damned for all time for what you do."

"And you, Deacon. How is it you practice the forbidden arts and escape this same fate?"

"Perhaps I will not, Brother Norbert, but I do it for my church. I will die the true death so that all of you might live. Come away from this now; I order it. In the name of the mother church and all that we hold sacred. Come away while we might still save your mortal soul."

"No, Brother, I no longer believe such threats. I have seen the evil that priests have done in the name of mother church. I will no longer condone it, nor will I be allied with it. I will make my own decisions about what will endanger my soul, for certainly a murderous church cannot."

"Leave him be," Erasmus called out. "Nothing you say will change our course now. Eldrich created our fear and hatred, let him pay the price. In an hour we will have done what no man . . . no mage has done in a thousand years. You saw it, Rose, written upon the walls in Landor's crypt: the enchantment to open the way. And we have Landor's seed. It is enough. May the devils take you and your world of lies."

Anna had gone to the spring and, whispering a few words, cupped her hands and drunk. To each of those upon the nance she carried water, whispering as she let a few drops fall upon their tongues.

Taking up a jar of palely luminescent liquid, she unstopped it and began to sprinkle it over the pattern upon the floor where it glowed like the substance of the moon. Rose's brand went out as though snuffed by a sudden wind. In the pale light James could see the priest put his hands over his eyes, then quickly reach to his tunic, patting his side. And then in the silence, Rose began to pray.

When her pattern was complete, Anna poured seed from a bag into a mortar, crushing it with a small pestle. From a second bottle she poured an inky liquid, mixing it with the seed. A pungent odor reached Captain James, igniting a strange hunger. Anna lifted the mortar with great care, raising it in both hands, and stepped to the center of her pattern. After speaking a few words she drank the mortar dry and cast it into the small pool of water at the wall's foot. She stood and hung her head, wavering as though she would fall.

But then she drew herself up, staring at the wall before her as though steeling her nerve. She opened the cuff of her right sleeve, and reaching down, wrapped something about her exposed wrist—the skin of a snake, James realized. Her other hand she raised aloft, and a crow—a crow with a blood-red bill—lit upon her wrist. Rearing back, the bird struck, tearing open her skin so that drops of crimson appeared, some few falling to the floor. She stamped her foot hard on the stone.

"Curre d' Efeu!" she called out, the words echoing in the chamber. *"Curre d' Emone!"*

* * *

Erasmus felt the words resonate inside him.

"Heart of flame! Heart of the world."

And behind it all, Brother Norbert chanting; . . . *naisannais-anna . . .*

He struggled to keep his wits about him, to keep his focus, for it was either history being made, or his last moments of life. Either way he wanted to be conscious and aware.

Erasmus had no illusions. Anna was very likely not capable of opening the gate and having them pass safely through. Lucklow had not managed it, nor any who came before him, and they had spent their lifetimes studying the arts. But what other course was there? Only the retribution of Eldrich, and that would be a hell as terrible as any he might find. No, better to risk this than face Eldrich again. Better death than that.

"Your servant calls out in darkness."

Out of the corner of his eye, Erasmus saw Deacon Rose fall to his knees in prayer.

Anna was making herself a mage. . . . Rose was right in this. Only a mage could open a gate. But once a mage, what would she do?

"Vau d' Efeu. Ivanté!" Anna called, her voice gaining strength and resonance.

Voice of flame. Come forth!

Again she called out in Darian.

Speak from the mouth of your child.

Erasmus found that he trembled, his knees weak, heart pounding like a stone upon the wall of his chest. He fought to breathe, and then called out in Darian, words he did not know.

A sound like water and wind funneling down a narrow gorge, and then flame erupted from the pool and Brother Norbert disappeared in a blossom of fire.

Captain James staggered back as the flame erupted, raising his hands to ward off the heat and light—but only a warm breath touched him, though the fire boiled and curled barely yards away.

Beside him, Deacon Rose continued his prayer, hands clasped before him, eyes tightly closed, as though even a glimpse of such blasphemy would endanger his soul.

The navy man found himself sinking down beside the priest, for there, where Anna had stood, a great serpent struggled with a massive bird, locked in a deadly battle. He shook his head to clear it, but still the vision persisted, though not quite clear or focused. The bird and serpent seemed to have climbed into the towering clouds, thrown hard against the dome of stars.

And then they fell, writhing, to the earth where they burst into flame as they struck, lying still, locked together in death.

But when he thought there would be peace and an end, they rose again, like martyrs from the pyre, and battle was renewed.

Seven times he saw the serpent arise and seven times the bird struck, and each time they fell in flame, flame that consumed them both.

Captain James felt as though he floated within a dream, where things made some terrible sense that could not readily be explained, as though another logic held sway here.

Finally, a woman lay broken upon the floor in a pattern of cold fire, her face hidden in a blaze of red hair.

Anna lay like one who had fallen from a great height—still, as only the dead could be still. A breeze wafted a few strands of hair. Erasmus wanted to go to her, to cradle her, push back the hair from her face, say some final words, for surely she had failed.

But then a hand moved, searching, as though it had a will of its own. Then a quivering arm. Her chest heaved as though life had slipped back into empty clothing, and with a moan she rolled and began to force herself up on trembling limbs. But she could not rise past her knees. There she stayed, head bent, shoulders shaking with silent sobs. And then she straightened, pushing back the mane of hair.

"*Tandre vere viteur . . .*" she whispered.

Hear me, Erasmus translated.

"*C'is m'curre.*"

Here is my heart.

From somewhere she produced a sprig of green—*king's blood*— and tossed it toward the flame. From above, her chough swooped down, taking the offering in the air, winging straight into the fire where it vanished with barely a swirl of flame, the sound of a wave dying on the shore.

And then darkness. Erasmus felt his knees strike stone, and struggled to keep his balance.

They were in a high place, or so it seemed, among the stars. A cool breeze tugged at his clothing, and a high keening, almost beyond hearing, blended in strange harmony.

Anna rose from the floor beside him, bent like one in prayer.

"Where are you?" Hayes whispered in a voice not his own.

"Alone," Anna said, her voice small and flat, "among the alone. Among the stars."

"What do you hear?" Clarendon asked in that same terrible voice.

"The songs of stars."

"Tell me your true name."

"Annais."

"Then you may scribe it here, among the stars."

And they were returned to the keep, a high note still ringing in Erasmus' ears.

Anna knelt in the center of the nance, weaving intricate patterns with her hands, speaking words of power. Erasmus felt the cool wind blow through him, stripping him bare, as though he were exposed to the world in some way he had never known before.

Captain James still knelt upon hard stone, his sword lying before him, forgotten. What had he seen? A mage being born? Born among the stars? Had anyone alive witnessed such a thing?

Movement caught his eye, and he realized Deacon Rose had risen from his place, and was moving deliberately forward toward the nance. The priest chanted, tossing something before him— white down, James realized—and in his hand he grasped a blade. But then a shadow coalesced to rise in the priest's path, moonlight turning it into a great dog. It stood before Deacon Rose, fangs bared, barring his way—the wolfhound of Clarendon.

The priest stopped. Then, as he went to step forward, the dog lunged, faster than moonlight could trace, and Deacon Rose stood, pressing a hand to his wrist, the dagger lying on the stone.

"Do not move, Deacon, or he will savage you again," the seaman said.

"Take up your sword, Captain, and slay this beast for me."

"I will not, Deacon, for it is not a natural beast and is not to be trifled with."

Deacon Rose began to protest, but as he turned toward James in anger, the dog growled, and the priest froze in his place.

Around Anna the pattern came to life again, and Anna rose, speaking the words of Landor's enchantment—the ritual for opening the gates.

It was long and complex, and even if Erasmus' Darian had been up to it, he likely would not have understood what went on. He felt the power of it, though, felt it grow within him, felt the majesty of it, like some glorious music rising inside him, reaching toward a crescendo.

And then, when he was sure the time had come and some glorious opening would appear, the flame rose up again, trembled against the heavens, and then fell upon them like a great wave.

Chapter Fifty-four

THE countess came over the shoulder of rock behind Eldrich and Walky to find a priest and an officer of His Majesty's navy kneeling upon the rock like stricken men. And there, before them, a great, towering flame trembled, split in two, and in its center a cavern seemed to have been opened into the solid rock.

"They have opened the first gate," Eldrich said. "Flames, but we have no time to waste. Bryce!" he called.

Bryce appeared, assisting Skye who was clearly not used to such exertions.

"Come, all of you. We must go in, but once inside, we will be separated, lost in a colorless land. I have no time to explain. You will see things that are not possible, but you must not falter. You must always go forward. If you falter, you will be lost. Make your way up, always up. We seek a long stair to the highest point, and if you find each other, stay together. Make all haste. All haste. You, priest, come with me. We must stop them by whatever means we can. Bring this sailor—even he might have a part."

Not waiting for any discussion, Eldrich plunged into the opening in the flame, speaking words of Darian as he went. The countess hurried after, fearing to be lost in this colorless land.

E rasmus stood upon a rock awash in a sea of fog—a gray ocean whirling slowly in the complete and unsettling silence. Across the colorless expanse, reefs of barren stone broke the surface, solitary and oddly substantial in the vaporous landscape.

The mist lapped about Erasmus' knees, a languid wave, and then drew back, revealing more of the island upon which he had been cast away.

It was the top of a wall, Erasmus realized. A ruined wall. And there, far off, a shattered tower thrust up out of the fog, mist breaking around it.

A ruined castle, Erasmus thought, *or an ancient city,* and somehow that did not surprise him, though he did not know why. He began to feel his way along the narrow isthmus of stone, his boots making no sound.

A moon shone down through a high, thin overcast which diffused the light of the few visible stars. Featureless, pearl-gray clouds hung almost motionless in the heavens, like daubs of plaster on the dome of the sky.

"Where am I?" Erasmus said aloud, the words seeming to come from far away, as though they were echoes.

The mists parted some distance off, and for a moment a figure was revealed—the silhouette of a man. Erasmus waved, but the figure looked elsewhere, and then the mists closed again, seeming to sweep the figure off its perch.

For a long moment Erasmus remained in place, turning slowly, surveying the strangely illuminated world. There, three stone arches surfaced, and he thought he saw movement. But after a long moment no one appeared. He considered shouting but found the place so unsettling that he feared drawing attention to himself.

It is a king's blood dream. But how had it begun? When had he taken the seed?

A silent wave of mist combed over the wall, submerging it in gray. Erasmus dropped to a crouch and felt his way forward.

Abruptly the wall turned to the left, and it was only by luck that he did not pitch off . . . into what?

It is a dream, he told himself, not sure if he could suffer injury in such a place.

Suddenly he was on a stair, and as he descended, the mist settled with him so that he seemed to be wading in fog to his waist. Level stone came underfoot, and in a moment the mist had streamed away like an ebbing tide. Movement caused him to whirl, but he caught only a glimpse of something disappearing into shadow among the ruin. *An animal,* Erasmus thought.

He went on, through the ancient city of dark stone. Down another stair, past a pool of mist, across a bridge arcing over a finger of the gray sea.

Up again, and then, over a parapet, he saw movement below.

"Randall . . . ? Is that you?"

"Who is that?" came the small voice, distorted by mist and stone.

"Erasmus."

"Do I know you, sir?"

"It's me, Randall. Erasmus Flattery."

He could see the small man shake his head. "But who is Randall?" he said, and was swept by a sea of fog.

"Randall . . . ?" But there was no answer.

Erasmus went forward, wandering aimlessly, now driven up by inflowing mist, or turning this way or that to stay in the clear air. Twice he was submerged in fog so thick that he crept forward, groping like a sightless man.

And then he heard a sound, a high, thin keening like some small animal in pain or terror. It echoed among the stone, seeming to originate from nowhere. Erasmus searched for what seemed a very long time before he found the source—a small child curled up in the high window of broken wall.

"What is it, child?" he asked. "Have you lost your way?"

The boy raised a darkly twisted hand, and pointed with a finger blackened and charred.

"Percy . . . ?"

But a snuffling caused him to whirl about, and there was Eldrich's wolf, regarding him coldly. Erasmus felt himself back away and ordered himself to stand his ground—show it no fear.

The wolf had its ears pressed back, fangs partly bared, hackles raised like scales. For some reason Erasmus noted that its shadow, cast by the moon, was not canine at all but long and stooped.

"Take me, then, and leave this child in peace," Erasmus whispered. "He has suffered enough. We have all suffered enough."

The wolf bared its fangs and growled, raising one paw as though about to spring. Erasmus bent and swept up a heavy fragment of stone, but as he did so, the wolf leaped past him, snatched the child from its perch, and disappeared into a tongue of mist. Erasmus threw himself into the fog, but in a few steps he was lost and could find no trace of the wolf.

He tripped and sprawled on the ground, and felt tears form, like ice upon his cheeks.

It was a city like the one in her vision, where she had seen Kent and heard the lament for a lost king. She walked on, mist appearing now and then to blind her, and in this unnatural mist she thought she saw the scenes of her life drift by. Lovers, her late husband, the half-formed spirit of a miscarried child. All of these things wafted into view, dreamlike, then faded into the mist, the crying child-that-was-not most disturbing of all.

The countess didn't know where she was or how she had come to be here. Even the idea that it might all be a dream did not occur to her. She was merely here, in this colorless world, this ancient, abandoned city—here without reason or meaning.

And she wandered among the ghosts of her past, which seemed to haunt her but never came close enough to touch or even to be clearly seen. Kent appeared, his lips forming soundless words—but this was an aged Kent, wrinkled and bent, yet with the light still in his eye: vivid blue in this world bled of all color.

Marianne chasing leaves carried up on a breeze—leaves like escaped words. Erasmus standing on a stair, alone. He would not look at her, nor did he seem to hear when she spoke, but looked always away—abashed. Ashamed.

"Why did you not come after me?"

But he ascended the stair and dissolved in moonlight without answering.

Through an arch she found a fountain filled with mist, as though a cloud had settled into this small bowl. Reaching down, she swirled the mist and her own reflection appeared, the stars behind.

But it was not quite her, for she seemed as gray as the world around her, as though drained of . . . what?

"Glamour," she whispered. "The countess without her enchantment." She stared for a long moment, then closed her eyes. "How plain I am," she whispered.

She looked again and reached out tentatively, but her hands found only ash, cold and fine between her fingers.

She fled that place, wandering aimlessly, and came upon a balcony which looked out over the ruined city swept by a sea of moonlit mist.

What a cold, inhuman landscape, she thought. *But who had built this place? Had men not dwelt here once?*

It seemed to her they had not. That the race that built this place was not quite a race of men.

And then she heard the song, a swelling of voices in a strange tongue. A dirge, it seemed. A song of great power and sadness. A lament for some fallen hero or king, and oddly familiar to her. Where had she heard this?

"Death stalks someone here," she said, and turned away, the music fading as she went.

She came into a sculpture garden, the statues broken and eroded upon their pedestals, and there she saw movement—two small children hiding among the statuary.

"You still have not chosen." It was the musical voice of Eldrich, oddly insubstantial here. She could not see him, for the voice emerged from shadow.

"What choice was I given? To let them die. But I would choose life for them, for that is what they desire."

"Look around you. Regard this endless, lifeless night. This world without warmth, or compassion. Would you choose this for them? This for many lifetimes of men?"

"You must give the choice to them," the countess said, and fled.

They pursued him, the cacophony of voices, the thousands and tens of thousands, and he ran; stumbling among the fallen walls, plunging into the pools of mist, scrambling up stairs and over balustrades. Closer they would come, and the noise of their voices would almost overwhelm him. Stopping up his ears was little help, but running, keeping ahead of them, that was his only hope.

"*Randall. . . ?*" someone called, someone who was not of the hordes that pursued him, but he did not know the voice and ran on.

Cold stone at her back: a pillar around which her arms were bound. About her feet a green flame flickering out of a rubble of stone—the tongues of a malevolent earth, but cold beyond enduring. Through the flame, her accusers silently watched, their shadowed faces ghostly grim.

Garrick. Pryor. Banks. Kells.

"*I am not a witch,*" she said, but her words came out as silence.

"You, Banks, Kells. I did what you asked of me. I became a mage. A mage. . . ."

But they remained as still and uncaring as the ruined walls. The flame flickered around her knees, catching at the hem of her robe.

Someone appeared among her tormenters, someone touched by moonlight which shimmered in his gray robe.

"Brother Norbert!" she called out, her hope suddenly rising. "You gave your word that you would bring me peace."

"Yes," he said, and led her tormenters silently away, leaving her to the flames.

"Kehler? Thank Farrelle! Kehler, it's me; Hayes. Samual Hayes."

Kehler lay in a huddled heap at the foot of a stone wall, his back near a small opening.

"I cannot go through with it, Hayes. I cannot. I don't care if I die, but I will not go back in there."

Hayes put his hand gently on his friend's shoulder, dismayed by his state. "You don't have to go into the passage, Kehler. It's all right. We will stay out in the open. In the moonlight. Come on—up with you now. Out of this, lad. We must go on."

"But there is never an end," Kehler sobbed. "There is only this dark world forever. Cold stone. Passages choked with water."

Hayes began to gently lift his friend, bringing him to his feet. Flames, but he felt light! He had not realized how badly their ordeal had depleted them.

"He is in there, Hayes," Kehler said, pointing to the opening, and backing away. "Inside, waiting. Reaching out. Don't go near!"

"Come away from this place," Hayes said, turning his friend away.

"But he spoke to me—the buried child. Asked why we meddled in the affairs of the dead." Kehler shook his head, leaning heavily on Hayes. "Asked why we would come to join him when we could be buried in the living earth. Oh, Hayes, Hayes. We are dead, and wandering. Wandering where memory and dream can never be pried apart."

Erasmus climbed the tower stairs and then up the stone to perch upon the wall. The gray and endless sea spread beneath him, made substantial by moonlight. High up like this, he almost felt more than heard a cold and brittle music. It drifted down to him as though falling from the heavens—falling like snow.

The choral stars, he thought, not sure from where that knowledge had come.

On a section of shattered wall, like a jagged peak, a robed figure appeared, and a flight of swallows swept down from the sky to weave an intricate pattern about him, like a spell. All the while he turned slowly within it, hands half-raised, as though in awe.

"Brother Norbert," Erasmus whispered. *"Look what honor they give him. The very birds of the air."*

And then the mist washed over the scene, and it was lost.

He found Anna huddled in a corner, shivering, muttering to herself.

"Leave me," she whispered, though it was almost a hiss. "Have you not haunted me enough? Will I not pay all the rest of my days, and beyond?"

"Anna? It is Erasmus."

She raised her head slightly but not enough that he could see her face. "Erasmus . . . help me," she whispered desperately. "I am a ghost. A shadow. I will dwell here always for what I have done, for the crimes I have committed."

He crouched down and put a hand on her shoulder. She flinched away. Through the flimsy robe he could feel her flesh was cold—ghostly cold.

"Anna, come with me."

"Where could we go that would be different? You don't understand, Erasmus. We are ghosts. Spirits. We will wander here for a thousand years."

He shook his head. "No. I remember. We are lost in the ritual. Like a king's blood dream. You were attempting to open the gate, perhaps did open it."

"Then we failed, and we are lost in the limbo between the worlds."

"No, it is something you once spoke of: the way by darkness. It is an ordeal of sorts, and we must go on."

Erasmus wrapped his frock coat around her, then took her in his arms, trying to give her warmth. She leaned against him, shivering so badly that her teeth actually clicked.

"Why are you so kind to me?"

"Because you have been haunted by Eldrich all of your days, as have I. We have common cause in our fear and hatred."

He felt her head nod. She began to sob bitterly. "But it led here, to this toneless world, this world without desire or sustenance or human warmth."

"Can you not feel warmth from me?"

She hesitated. "Yes. . . . Yes, I can."

"Then perhaps we are not quite ghosts yet. The others are here. I have seen some of them. Perhaps even Eldrich, for I saw his familiar. Rest a moment, and when you are ready, we will seek them. Perhaps there is a way out of this limbo."

Anna shook her head. "No, I shall never escape what I have done. Three times they have burned me this night, and I fear they shall burn me a thousand times more before the end. Whether I escape or no."

The moon crept endlessly across the sky as though the celestial clock had run down. The night lingered beyond enduring, and Erasmus wondered if a sun ever rose here.

Are we between the worlds as Anna said?

The mist had begun to rise again, as though the tide flowed instead of ebbed, and this drove them up through the bones of the city. Up to the crest of a hill.

Once, they heard a piercing howl of despair. It froze them, and then they forced themselves to go on warily.

At last they came to a great stair down which a cloud seemed to pour like liquid, lapping over each tread, spreading eerily about their feet, then dissipating as it flowed from the open square. They went up without discussion, as though both knew there was no choice. Up the cloud-stair, toward the moon and stars.

At the top they found an officer of the King's navy, huddled on the stair, mist breaking about him.

"What brought you here?" Erasmus asked.

"Eldrich," the man said, not stirring.

"Eldrich. . . . Is he here?" Erasmus asked. "Does the mage know the way out?"

The man looked up, eyes wide with fear. "Better seek a sea devil or the eye of a storm than seek the mage. This is what comes of meddling in the arts. You lose your soul and wander here. Wander until the world ends."

"You're not a ghost yet, Captain. Come along with us. We seek a way out of this limbo, for surely there is a way. A way to the world beyond."

The officer followed in their wake as the cloud swirled around them, leaving a curling furrow behind. They went down a columned avenue, and finally arrived at the foot of a flight of seven stairs.

"Here is the way out, if such exists," Erasmus said.

"But where are we?" the navy man asked.

"At the nance, Captain," Anna said, suddenly straightening. "The nexus of this world. The gate to the worlds beyond."

At the stair's head they found seven palely tinted columns; two of rose, a pair in white, two of green, and one of shining black.

Anna no longer seemed lost and overcome with despair. She drew herself up and looked around with a clear eye.

"We might manage it yet, Erasmus. Do you remember? We opened the first gate, but there is a second. Where are the others? Where is my charm? I hope nothing has befallen Brother Norbert."

"I saw him," Erasmus said. "The swallows paid homage to him. It was surpassingly strange. Men have been made saints for less significant occurrences."

"Not in this world," Anna said.

Chapter Fifty-five

KEHLER and Hayes appeared first, helping each other up the final stairs. Anna bade them perform the proper rites before they set foot on the nance, and then they collapsed with their backs to a pillar.

"There, we have found our way out, Kehler," Hayes said. "We are not ghosts after all."

"I am recovered now, Hayes," Kehler said, the edge of desperation gone from his voice, which now sounded only profoundly fatigued. "I . . . I was lost in my own fears, the horror of the crawl into the chamber and our escape. You see, I remember it all now."

Anna stood looking down on them. "You saw no others?"

"None that I knew," Kehler said. "Only Hayes, who rescued me from my demons, it seems." He looked over at Erasmus. "I hope your own journey here was less harrowing than mine."

Erasmus shrugged. He remembered it with something less than clarity. He had seen Clarendon and Brother Norbert. And the countess . . . or had that been a dream?

The naval officer whom they had found—the man who had accompanied Deacon Rose—stood looking up at the figures carved above the fount. He seemed like a man lost—far more so than sailors normally did on land. The captain was out of his depth and knew it. His only hope now was to return to the world he knew; other than that, he no longer seemed to care what this struggle was all about.

Erasmus closed his eyes and felt himself begin to drift. He snapped his eyes open, but found himself still upon the nance—the others there as well.

He shut them again and drifted into a dream of a fair green place, where sunlight played upon the forest floor and a sweet breeze spoke among the trees. He could almost understand what it said. Almost.

A hand rocked him gently, then again, and Erasmus opened his eyes.

"Ah, Mr. Flattery," Clarendon said, for the small man was there, as was Brother Norbert. "We must all awake from our dreams now. Dreams or nightmares. Anna says it is time." The small man smiled at him in open affection, looking more than a little adrift.

Erasmus scrambled up, shaking his head to clear it.

"What must we do now?" he asked.

"The second gate must be opened," Anna answered. "Take your places as before. We must not tarry. Erasmus saw the wolf among the ruins, and I do not think it was illusory. Captain James? You must remove yourself from the nance. It will be dangerous for you otherwise."

The man stepped quickly down onto the top step, not needing to be asked twice, but then turned and addressed Anna. "Is there any hope that I will see my own land again?"

Anna gazed at him a moment. "There is hope, yes. You must return to the gate from which you came, Captain, and not tarry, for it will close soon after this gate is opened."

"But I don't remember how I arrived here. I only recollect being engulfed in a wave of fire and then found myself wandering, bewitched and lost."

"You must go down, Captain." Anna pointed. "Down to the edge of the sea of mist. The gate is there. I can tell you no more."

The sailor's gaze dropped to the ground, and he shook his head, more than sorry he had ever become involved in the affairs of mages.

Anna bent to begin her preparations when Clarendon called out.

Deacon Rose approached the stairs to the nance, his manner as determined and malevolent as ever. Without thought, Erasmus pulled Captain James' sword from its scabbard and pushed the surprised seaman so that he stumbled down the stair.

"Ah, Deacon," Anna said in mock solicitation, "you have arrived too late once again. In a moment we shall take our leave of you—unless you have it in mind to pursue me into the other world. . . . Don't look so disappointed, at least you are rid of me—though not in the manner you would have preferred no doubt."

"Eldrich is here," Rose said, barely containing his fury. "I have seen his familiar."

"But even he has not arrived in time, Deacon."

"Do not let him up the stair," Anna said, and turned back to her preparations, leaving Rose fuming below. A fair voice was suddenly lifted, chilling everyone who knew it.

"But it seems you are wrong, Anna. I have arrived in time."

Erasmus looked up to find the stooped figure of Eldrich approaching at the head of a small band, all masked in shadow.

Anna quickly drew a line of green fire across the stair head, and stood beside Erasmus, who held up his sword, certain that it would seem little threat to Eldrich. The others gathered around Anna, as though determined to make a stand, however futile. Deacon Rose backed away deferentially, quickly retreating from the field between Anna and the mage.

"Come no further," Anna said, her voice trembling. "I am more skilled than you know. Stronger than you guess."

"Are you, indeed?" Eldrich seemed amused, but stopped all the same. "One hundred thirty-three years I have lived, one hundred twenty-six of them steeped in the arts. Give me some credit, child. You are but four and twenty, after all. It takes seventy years to make a mage—a true mage—which you are not."

"I have undergone the transformation," Anna said, her voice no more steady, though more defiant, "and won my struggle with the snake."

"Won? You never win. It is but an uneasy peace, though perhaps you will manage that. More than I would have expected for one so poorly prepared. I was sixty-five when I stood upon the nance, and that only because Lucklow was near his death, and there was a task to be completed. And even so, *I* was not ready."

Erasmus could see the countess, now, lurking behind the mage in the dim light, and this sight somehow made his plight seem even more hopeless. Walky and sad Percy Bryce were there as well—all the lives that Eldrich had ruined. He looked again at the countess, who was coldly beautiful in the moonlight. Did she hold a memory of their evening together that was near as sweet as his? Did she keep a memory of it at all?

And then another appeared, silver-maned—Skye, of all people. Erasmus had no time to wonder what Skye's part was in this. Eldrich was here, and all their hope of escape was gone. They had been so close! So close to being free of him.

"You cannot touch me," Anna said, her voice very quiet and unsure. She seemed exceedingly young, suddenly, not even four and twenty, but a mere girl confronting an angry parent. "I have knowledge of the curse. . . ."

"But not enough, it seems . . ." Eldrich said.

A spray of white down fell over Anna and Erasmus, catching fire where it touched the nance, and then suddenly Anna was tumbling down the stairs, in the embrace of some other—a whirl of red hair and priestly robes. At the bottom the priest rose over her prostrate figure, speaking words of Darian, crimson hands clutching a dagger.

At his feet Anna shuddered once, tried to rise, but fell back trembling, her mouth agape as though searching for air. And then she was still, a coil of hair moving in the breeze, blood pooling around her ghostly pale face.

What Erasmus noticed was the horror of the countess, and then Clarendon snatched the sword from his hand and leaped down the stairs before any could move. With all the force of his charge, the dwarf plunged the blade into the chest of Deacon Rose, and then in a fury, pulled it free and struck again. The priest was driven to his knees, the dagger clattering to the stone. Again Clarendon struck him, cursing him with each blow, and even when the priest toppled forward over the fallen Anna, Clarendon still cut him.

Then the little man dropped the blade and fell to his knees, sobbing.

Erasmus descended the stair and put his arm around the small shoulders, edging Clarendon back from the bodies. Poor Anna, lying there, her fugitive life at an end. Erasmus felt such cold in his heart at that moment—such utter cold.

"I have done murder," Clarendon wept. *"Farrelle help me, Mr. Flattery. . . . Murder."*

Eldrich stepped forward, chanting solemnly over the bodies, his hand moving quickly in the air. Then he looked up at those standing before him. "That is enough killing," he said, all the mockery gone. "Life is short enough." He looked down again at Anna and the priest. "The last follower of Teller has fallen. My task is done."

"You let him do it," Erasmus said, eyeing the mage, feeling his own anger rise. "You saw the priest with his blade and let him murder her."

Eldrich stared at Erasmus until he realized his former charge would not look away. "She could not live, Erasmus. She had the knowledge and the power to open the gates, and that could not be allowed. She is dead, and so is her murderer. Let it end there. Let it all end."

"And what of me?" Clarendon asked, suddenly very still. "I have the knowledge as well. . . ."

Eldrich stared down at the dwarf, and Erasmus could hardly credit what he saw. Compassion softened the mage's face.

"You shall not outlive me, little man. But you will have to come along. There is no other choice."

"Where?" Clarendon asked, Erasmus hearing the hope in the small man's voice.

"We shall make the journey of Tomas. But there is no time for talk. Even this tardy moon sails toward the west." He turned to Bryce. "Bind up her wound and carry her up onto the nance."

"But she is dead, sir."

"Yes," Eldrich answered, "but she is a mage, for all that she has done, and I cannot leave her to wander here. Bear her up." He strode past Erasmus and Clarendon up the stairs, speaking Darian as he went.

Quickly everyone was arranged; Bryce next to Erasmus, then

Skye. Anna was laid before the central pillar, then Hayes, the countess, and Clarendon, still shaken and white. Brother Norbert stood by the small stair that led to the perch above the fount.

Eldrich approached the hermit, the only one there who did not draw back when the mage came near. For a moment Eldrich stared into his eye, and then nodded. "A priest who is pure of heart. . . . Live long enough and even one's most cherished prejudices are shattered," the mage said. He beckoned Kehler, who came near reticently. For a moment the mage spoke quietly to Norbert and Kehler, who nodded frequently, then bowed as the mage finished.

Walky then delivered a long roll to his master and the two stood whispering softly. Erasmus heard nothing but the murmur of Eldrich's musical voice, the sound of water on stone. Walky did not look at his master, but kept his gaze cast down, nodding often. For a moment nothing was said and then Eldrich reached out and placed a hand on the small man's shoulder. Walky looked up as Eldrich turned away, and even in the poor light Erasmus could see the servant's eyes rimmed in red.

And then Walky hurried off the nance.

Finally Eldrich spoke to the countess, the mage glancing once at Erasmus, the two nodding, and then he saw them take each other's hands before Eldrich returned to the center of the nance.

The rite began with Eldrich bringing the pattern to life, so that it glowed as though made of the substance of the moon. Brother Norbert chanted a word Erasmus did not know—the mage's true name: *Adorian*. In the mage tongue it meant *last*.

And then Eldrich called fire from the fount. From there it was all a blur to Erasmus' mind. The clarity of the scene dissolved, and Erasmus felt himself slipping into dream—like a king's blood-induced vision.

Erasmus as a child, balanced atop the driverless carriage, gazing fixedly ahead. And then an uncurling rose; Percy blossoming into flame, crawling toward Erasmus, screaming. His howl of pain cut into Erasmus' consciousness so that it rang always in the ear.

Eldrich walking in the garden below, a child perched in the window overcome by a fear that he felt in his heart, in the center of his being.

And then an old woman before a fire, suckling a baby and singing softly to herself.

> *"Upon a hill, upon a cloud,*
> *Upon a haystack golden.*
> *Within a wood, within a lake,*
> *Dwelt the lady Sollen."*

A warm wind crossing a bay, far off the sound of surf and strange birds. Night. A procession winding up a mountainside through lush vegetation, bearing an old man wearing the mask of a bird and a cloak of feathers. Overwhelming sadness and loss.

A woman before him, dancing among tongues of flame, many armed, blonde hair streaming, and Erasmus felt himself chanting in Darian, felt a presence within.

He did not know if minutes or hours passed, but finally the flame trembled open—a gate into the world beyond. A place lit by the soft light of stars and moon. Erasmus inhaled the scent of flowers, of spring and woods and meadows.

The roll Walky had carried had been spread upon the nance and now fire burned about it like a frame, the portrait of Eldrich appearing to float, wavering upon some invisible surface.

Eldrich spoke and sent the flaming likeness floating through the gate, and then he turned to Clarendon and then Skye. "Follow close behind me," he said.

The mage bore Anna up as though she were no burden at all, her hair falling in an arc like the skirt of a gown. He laid her in the center of the pattern, brushing the hair from her face and laying her hands upon her breast. Quickly he bent and kissed her on the brow.

He stepped back from her, then, and intoned words of Darian. Green flame began to burn around her, and then it spread across the still form, hiding her from sight. For a moment it persisted, and then flickered and died. Anna was gone. Gone utterly.

Eldrich bowed to the dying flames, speaking Anna's name three times, and then he straightened and looked around.

"Mr. Bryce," he said quietly, and then straightened his stooped form and walked slowly through the gate, growing immediately distant, as though he'd crossed a field in three strides.

A dark shape shot through the opening—Eldrich's familiar.

Clarendon hurried behind, barely hesitated at the flaming gate, then quickly stepped through, glancing back once. Skye went forward, faltered, gathered his resolve, then walked on, his shoulders squared—a Stranger in search of his past.

"Erasmus . . . ?" It was Percy Bryce, his voice low and harsh. He moved toward Erasmus, trembling, a sheen on his brow.

"I cannot," he whispered. *"The fire . . ."*

"He calls you, Percy," Erasmus said. "You must go."

"Not into the fire. Not . . . fire."

"Bryce . . . !" It was the voice of Eldrich, strangely distorted, stripped of its music.

Erasmus reached out and took hold of Bryce's shoulder. "Close your eyes, Percy. I will guide you."

Erasmus steered him toward the gate, which seemed to have grown smaller and pulsated strangely.

"Hurry, Percy," Erasmus said. "I see the mage coming back for you."

Bryce dug his fingers into Erasmus' arm, moving forward stiffly, each step so small.

"Erasmus. . . ."

"A few steps more, Percy. You're almost through."

The portal was weakening now, Erasmus was sure. It wavered before him as though about to collapse. He pressed Percy on, hardly able to continue himself. Eldrich seemed to be running now, waving an arm, but Erasmus could hear nothing over the sound of the blazing gate.

And then Percy spun toward him, striking Erasmus hard on the temple with an elbow. Erasmus stumbled, and felt Percy shove him, fear making the man strong.

Erasmus sprawled on the floor and Percy fell upon him.

"Now you shall know my pain," he whispered, dragging Erasmus up.

The world spun beneath Erasmus. He tried to take hold of Percy, but his fingers would not grip.

He felt himself thrust forward, falling.

And then he collided with something solid. The world went red, then dark, spinning madly. And then pain, like fire running along the strings of his nerves.

Fire.

Chapter Fifty-six

STARS wavered overhead, spinning slowly. Erasmus closed his eyes again. He lay upon a surface that seemed to be moving, like the deck of a boat. More than that he could not say. Searching with a hand he found his throbbing brow.

"Mr. Flattery?"

He knew that voice. . . .

"Walky?"

"Yes. Are you well, sir? Are you . . . whole?"

It seemed a strange question and even more strangely phrased.

"My head is throbbing terribly."

"Yes. Mr. Bryce struck you savagely, sir. And we have all been . . . sleeping."

"I must get up, Walky. We must make our way back."

"We are back, sir. Back to this odd ruin of a mountain, and it is night, sir, though whether the same night I cannot say."

Erasmus opened his eyes again. The world spun, then caught and seemed to hold, like a boat suddenly aground.

Walky crouched over him, his face drawn and profoundly sad.

"How can we be back?"

"I don't know, sir." The little man shrugged. "The arts are mysterious, or perhaps it was the work of the mage. I cannot say, for no one has opened a gate in more than a thousand years." He paused. "Only the mage knows."

Erasmus struggled to prop himself up on his elbows. "But I have a memory of pain, of going into the flame. Was that not true?"

Walky nodded. "The mage managed to save you, sir. Do you remember? Mr. Bryce forced you into the fire, but you are untouched by it."

Yes, he remembered. Percy had duped him into venturing near the flame. And he had felt it. The memory was strong. It had touched him, burning along the paths of his nerves. He felt himself cringe involuntarily.

"Are you hurt, Mr. Flattery? There is no sign of it."

"No. No, I will recover." Erasmus took a long breath. "What happened to Bryce?"

"I do not know, sir. He went into the gate as it closed. Whether he is in the other world or not, I cannot say." A strange hesitation. "Nor can I say what happened to the mage."

Erasmus heard Walky's breath catch, and the little man sat back a little.

"Walky?"

"Perhaps he is safely on the other side, sir. That is my hope."

Erasmus shut his eyes, trying to remember. The entire night was a blur. Nothing but vague images that he could not connect into any logical sequence, as though the narrative had been lost.

Could the mage have actually died? Died saving Erasmus? He could not conceive of Eldrich dead. It seemed impossible.

But even if it were true, Erasmus could feel no remorse. No guilt. He was more than surprised that Eldrich would make the slightest gesture to save him—the mage, after all, had tried to kill him once. But somehow Erasmus felt the mage owed him as much. After what he had done to Erasmus, Eldrich owed him a life.

"Who else?"

"Do you remember, sir; Rose murdered Anna."

"Yes, and Clarendon avenged her." He searched inside himself for some reaction to Anna's death—they had been lovers, after all—but there was nothing but a terrible numbness. As though the flame had burned away all feeling.

"Clarendon passed through, as did Lord Skye," Walky said. "Though Skye will not find what he sought. He did not come from Darr, but from the worlds to the east. The worlds of reason, not magic. All others are unharmed."

"And Anna— He set her upon a pyre. Is that right?"

"She was a mage, Mr. Flattery. He would not leave her to wander in the dark."

"But what of Rose, then?"

"The priest was a different matter," Walky said darkly.

Erasmus felt a small shiver pass through him. He was ordering his memories of the gray world. Was Rose condemned to that place? Erasmus was not even sure he would wish such a thing on the treacherous priest.

"And what of you, Walky? Are you whole?"

"Untouched, sir. Which is lucky, for I have much to do."

Erasmus looked closely at his old teacher. Walky drew in a long breath, and his face fell a little.

"It was his time, Mr. Flattery. The mage knew. And he passed into the other world—the fabled world, sir. And though few will ever hear of it, he took his place among the great mages of history. And at the very last he saved you, sir. An act of compassion. I am not a religious man, Mr. Flattery, but it seems an act of redemption to me. Somehow, an act of redemption. May he find peace now. Certainly he did not find it in this life."

Erasmus nodded. But poor Percy had been bitter and treacherous and murderous in the end. If he was lost between the worlds, what a horrifying ghost he would be. Erasmus shuddered at the thought.

"The countess is well?"

"Yes. Perfectly, sir. And the others are unharmed, in body, at least." The little man hung his head, his gestures small, voice suddenly very old and frail.

He grieves, Erasmus thought. *In mourning for his master.*

"Mr. Flattery?" It was another voice. Deep and solid.

"Brother Norbert?"

"Are you well, sir?"

"I appear to be unharmed—at least to the eye."

The hermit came into Erasmus' view. He looked very solemn. Very still.

"We are ready to make our way down. Will you need help yourself? Or can you manage?"

"I will manage, I think."

Brother Norbert nodded. "Will you take up your sea fire, Mr. Walky, and light our way?"

The little man rose stiffly, and he and Brother Norbert helped Erasmus to his feet. For a moment he wavered, but then he seemed to gain strength. Walky's doing, he suspected. The old man knew more of the arts than he ever let on.

The others were there. Kehler and Hayes. The countess, strangely distant. The captain sitting alone, staring off at the horizon. Kehler and Hayes came over to greet him, though they were hardly exuberant. They looked like men who had not yet assessed the cost of their adventure, but feared the result. Still, Hayes patted his shoulder, and spoke warmly.

They began the climb down from the Keep, single file, their way lit by the moon and Walky's flaming brand.

Brother Norbert began to sing, his strong voice echoing like water running over stone, swelling in a song of sadness and great beauty.

They struggled down, all of them exhausted and near to collapse. It seemed they'd crossed a kingdom when they finally found the road where carriages were drawn up, and horses were being tended by the drivers.

Brother Norbert turned back toward the looming mountain and made a sign to Farrelle and spoke a prayer. No one objected, perhaps feeling, as Erasmus did, that there should be some ritual or rite to mark such a solemn occasion. The last mages had passed from this world.

The last mages.

Chapter Fifty-seven

THEY sat in a circle around a small fire, watching the eastern sky turn pale, the moon still riding into the west. Dusk had found them, going anxiously from one to the other, as though seeking news of his master.

They all seemed reluctant to leave. Kehler and Hayes sat upon the ground, their backs to a stone. The others perched upon stones or logs that had been set about the fire pit.

All of them seemed lost in their own thoughts, emerging occasionally to make a statement that almost invariably did not lead to conversation.

Erasmus could not describe what he felt—hollow, empty. None of these words did justice to the void he felt inside. He could hear his own thoughts echo.

It was fire, he thought, *the unnatural fire. It burned me away inside, and like Percy, there is no sign of it on my skin.*

But perhaps it was merely exhaustion and the trauma of what they had been through these last weeks, beginning with their exploration of the cave, and if so, it would pass. Certainly it would.

"I wonder if poor Clarendon will find his lost Lizzy?" Hayes ventured.

"He had no choice but to go," the countess said softly. "His memories were ravaging him. He could not escape them. Going through the gate was desperation. Perhaps he hoped Eldrich would help him, would take away some of the pain of it. He was a singular little man, bearing a terrible burden of memory, wrongs he could never forget, betrayals, all manner of cruelty because of his difference. And yet he had created a persona for the world that belied the truth. He did not seem haunted when one first met him. Indeed, he seemed to be a man at peace." She shook her head.

"He was an individual of great complexity, Randall Spencer Emanual Clarendon," Erasmus said. "We knew him only briefly, and though we saw him under the most revealing circumstances, even so . . . I think it would have taken many a year to know him well. He had been so injured by the world of men that he seldom ventured forth into the light. I felt honored that he trusted us enough to reveal what he did. But the countess is right; he hid his scars well."

Unlike Percy, Erasmus thought.

Silence settled itself among them again.

Occasionally the countess would raise her eyes from the fire and contemplate Erasmus, but each time he met her gaze, she looked away, a great sadness etched on her beautiful face.

"What will we do now?" Hayes asked.

"You, Mr. Hayes," the countess said, "we shall certainly find you a position in the foreign office, if that is what you still desire. I think Sir John Dalrymple will be particularly sensitive to your application."

"And I will go with Brother Norbert to root out all the records of the arts from the archives of the Church of Farrelle," Kehler said, with some satisfaction. He looked over at Norbert. "I expect it will take some little while."

"And when that is done," Brother Norbert said, "I will return to my monastery in the hills. There is a task there I left unfinished. So many spirits that wander still. . . ."

This caused the countess to look up, her gaze thoughtful.

Erasmus felt himself shrug. "Perhaps I will go to Farrow for a while. I don't know. Where does one go after such an experience? Where does one go that memories cannot follow?"

"Forward," the countess answered. "Westward, Halden would have said, traveling with the light. That is what you should do, Erasmus. That is what we all should do—if we can."

Walky took up the reins of the team and looked down once more at his former charge and the countess who stood by to send him off.

"Will I see you again, Walky?" Erasmus asked.

"Perhaps, sir. The world is full of surprises. But I have duties yet and must complete them before my time comes."

Erasmus saw the way the old man glanced at the countess, and with a small bow to his former teacher, he left them alone.

He saw the old man reach down and take her hand. She put a foot on a step and rose up to kiss him tenderly, touching a hand to his cheek. Erasmus was certain there were tears in the old man's eyes as he shook the reins and rolled the carriage forward.

The countess came and stood by Erasmus, watching the carriage disappear down the hill. Dusk appeared beside them, watching as well. He seemed almost to quiver, as though it were Clarendon who left. Then, suddenly, he raced off after the carriage, having apparently made his decision. Who among all of them was most like Randall, after all?

"What will he do now that he does not have Eldrich to serve?" Erasmus said.

"I don't know. It was his life, and when the duties he was left are done, I am afraid poor Walky will be done as well. Try to imagine never having a will of one's own. Having no life that was not in service to some other. It is beyond imagining."

"Yes," Erasmus said softly.

The countess turned to look at him, drawing herself up. Even tired and travel-sore as she was, the countess still seemed almost unnaturally beautiful to him.

They regarded each other a moment, Erasmus searching for something to say.

But then she reached out and touched his arm. "I forgive you,

Erasmus. Eldrich put a fear into you in childhood that you could never overcome. I . . . I forgive you."

Erasmus nodded, but before he could speak, she turned and walked away, answering the question he struggled to form.

She went then to Brother Norbert, speaking quietly to him, the hermit nodding solemnly, acquiescing to her request as men invariably did.

The countess took the second carriage and Eldrich's driver and set off at first light, leaving the rest of them wondering if it had all been a dream.

"At least Eldrich is not here to steal our memories away," Kehler said. "Or perhaps unfortunately he is not. I do not know which."

"No," Erasmus said. "We shall have to learn to accommodate them or make peace with them, whatever it is that one does with memories." He looked over at Brother Norbert. "What was it the countess asked of you before she left, Brother? Or can you say?"

Brother Norbert nodded. "When I am done with searching the archives of the church there are two ghosts—the spirits of small children—to whom I might bring peace. We shall see."

"Yes," Erasmus whispered so that none might hear, "but who will bring peace to the living?"

I do not know why Eldrich chose me to tell his story, or why he chose anyone at all. It was, after all, the practice of the mages to maintain a wall of secrecy around all that they did. But then, Eldrich was the last, and in the end I think he succumbed to the very human desire to be understood, to forge a place in human memory. The common anonymity of death frightened even him.

Marianne Edden: The Last Mage.

Epilogue

ON midsummer's eve the carriage came to Hyloft manor, making barely a sound as it rolled up the uneven lane. In the circle before the old house it rocked to a stop, and there disembarked a man so small that his weight did not even jiggle the carriage. He straightened his breeches and frock coat carefully and then, from the carriage, retrieved a flat package wrapped in plain paper.

For a moment he stood in the starlight, as though unsure of his intent, but went forward, pausing with a hand raised to knock on the door. He remained thus for some time, then slowly let his hand fall to the package, caressing it.

Bending with the slow motion of an old man, he leaned the package gently beside the door. Again he hesitated, staring down at the package in the faint light, his face in shadow, then made a quick bow, pausing at the bottom of the motion, and rising slowly. Looking back only once he turned and retreated to his carriage, reaching up to grasp the high handle.

"Would you not rather keep it yourself, Walky?" Erasmus said.

Walky turned to find his former charge emerging from the shadow of a hedge.

"Does it not mean more to you? Did she not?"

Walky stared at the silhouette, the emotions on his face hidden, but his posture a riddle of contradictions. "I shall not have the pleasure of it long, Mr. Flattery. Best the portrait go to you, who will treasure it as I have."

Erasmus nodded. "Are you unwell, Walky?"

"Not as any could tell, Mr. Flattery, but I lived to serve the mage. . . . He is gone and so shall I be soon. No, do not express regrets, it was the life I chose. A life few others have lived, I dare say. Do not pity Walky, for it would be wasted sentiment."

Neither man said anything for some moments.

"You are the last magical thing in this world, Mr. Walky," Erasmus said, surprised at the emotion in his voice. "What kind of world will it be without you?"

"The mage was the last magical thing, Mr. Flattery. Not me."

"That is where you are wrong. The mage was hollow in his center. A creature of certain appetites and desires, perhaps of duty. But you— You are good and kind and compassionate. Better you had been the mage, Mr. Walky, then magic would have been of a different character. You would have cast your enchantments on the fields of peasants, and eased the aching of the old, even their aching hearts. No, Walky, you are the last magical thing. I am sure of that."

"Well, sir, I think you're talking a lot of nonsense to please an old man, but I bless you for it all the same." He opened the door, a little embarrassed, Erasmus thought. Placing a foot upon the step, Walky looked back at Erasmus.

"Good-bye to you, sir," he said, his voice coming out as a whisper. "Be at peace, Mr. Flattery. Do you hear? Be at peace."

"And you, Walky."

The old man nodded and climbed up into the high carriage, pulling the door to behind him. His face appeared at the open window, and Erasmus crossed to stand below him.

"Call me your young lion," Erasmus said quickly.

"Sir?"

"Call me your young lion. I want to hear you say it once."

Walky stared down at his former student, his mouth working

silently, and then in a whisper. *"Fare thee well, my young lion. Fare thee well. . . ."* This last word swallowed whole.

He reached out the window. Erasmus took the small, tough hand in his own for a moment and then the carriage rolled forward. For a few steps Erasmus clasped the hand, and then he let it go, like a bird into the air.

Walky looked back at him, raising his hand once in the starlight, and then the lightless carriage made its silent way down the lane. A shadow among the shadows. A dream of magic. Gone